Y0-CAA-446

Praise for the Stratford Man Duology

Hell and Earth
Ink and Steel

"Tremendously deep and potent: Bear goes right to the core of love, its costs, and its rewards.... The richness here is something that has been hovering over Bear's work for a while, and now it's full-blown ... immediately engaging and remain[s] engaging, of the 'can't put it down' kind of engaging that one generally associates with action thrillers. Bear builds an almost unbearable tension in the narrative out of ambiguity, both of events and motivations, and out of the characters, each drawn in subtle detail.... And the books are full of touches, some small, some more central, that provide great resonance ... and the sure ear for the rhythms and patterns of English during the time of Elizabeth, not only the words of the great poets, but the everyday cadences of the commons.

"Where others are writing mythic fiction, Bear has written mythic history: It may not be history as it happened, but it is history that rings true in a much deeper way than a mere relation of events could ever accomplish. What's left to say? Brava!"
—The Green Man Review

Hell and Earth

"Exciting ... the story line is fast-paced from the onset yet also contains intriguing references to the real Marlowe and Shakespeare, which in turn makes the magic of their words seem even more genuine as well as their relationship. Elizabeth Bear's terrific two-book entry is the Promethean Age at its seditious best." —Alternative Worlds

"Bear's research and attention to detail make her fantastic approximation of the Tudor-Stuart transition shine."
—*Booklist* (starred review)

"Campbell winner Bear proves again that she can fill a stage as well as any Elizabethan playwright, entwining tragedies of betrayal and blood-soaked revenge with country pastoral and domestic comedy ... a complex and character-driven tale."
—*Publishers Weekly*

continued ...

Whiskey and Water

"Bear mixes classic and modern supernatural archetypes to craft a beautiful tale." —*Publishers Weekly*

"The many varied plots skillfully and subtly interweave into a finale with serious punch. Elizabeth Bear's writing style is as dense, complex, and subtle as her plots and characters. The style reminds me a little of Tolkien. This is definitely not a book to sit down to for a light fluffy read. But, if you immerse yourself in this rich, dark world, you will be rewarded with characters with layers of motivation and relationships that weave through the world's destiny like an intricate spider's web."
—SFRevu

"[*Whiskey and Water*] reaffirms [Bear's] skill at creating memorable—and memorably flawed—characters as well as her sure hand at blending together the modern world with the world of the Fae. Her elegant storytelling should appeal to fans of Charles de Lint, Jim Butcher, and other cross-world and urban fantasy authors." —*Library Journal*

"Bear brings a new level of detail to the subject and her magical creatures are an interesting mix of familiar and unfamiliar traits." —Don D'Ammasa, Critical Mass

"Bear succeeds in crafting a rich world.... It's a book that I couldn't put down, with a world in which I found myself easily enthralled and enchanted, not necessarily by Faerie, but by Bear's poetic expression and knife-sharp narrative."
—Rambles

"Enthralling.... Intrigued and delighted sums up my reaction to *Whiskey and Water* as a whole. Don't think of it as a sequel, because it's not: It's the next part of the story.... I'm hoping for another one." —The Green Man Review

"The wonderful Promethean Age series just keeps getting better. Bear has a knack for writing beautifully damaged characters, who manage to be both alien and sympathetic at the same time, and then putting them in situations where they have no choice but to go through the fire. The result is glorious."
—*Romantic Times* (top pick)

"Terrific urban fantasy ... cleverly designed and well written ... a delightful tale filled with all sorts of otherworldly species." —Alternative Worlds

Novels of the
Promethean Age

Blood and Iron

Whiskey and Water

Ink and Steel

Hell and Earth

Hell and Earth
The Stratford Man, Volume II

A Novel of the Promethean Age

Elizabeth Bear

A ROC BOOK

ROC
Published by New American Library, a division of
Penguin Group (USA) Inc., 375 Hudson Street,
New York, New York 10014, USA
Penguin Group (Canada), 90 Eglinton Avenue East, Suite 700, Toronto,
Ontario M4P 2Y3, Canada (a division of Pearson Penguin Canada Inc.)
Penguin Books Ltd., 80 Strand, London WC2R 0RL, England
Penguin Ireland, 25 St. Stephen's Green, Dublin 2,
Ireland (a division of Penguin Books Ltd.)
Penguin Group (Australia), 250 Camberwell Road, Camberwell, Victoria 3124,
Australia (a division of Pearson Australia Group Pty. Ltd.)
Penguin Books India Pvt. Ltd., 11 Community Centre, Panchsheel Park,
New Delhi – 110 017, India
Penguin Group (NZ), 67 Apollo Drive, Rosedale, North Shore 0632,
New Zealand (a division of Pearson New Zealand Ltd.)
Penguin Books (South Africa) (Pty.) Ltd., 24 Sturdee Avenue,
Rosebank, Johannesburg 2196, South Africa

Penguin Books Ltd., Registered Offices:
80 Strand, London WC2R 0RL, England

Published by Roc, an imprint of New American Library, a division of Penguin
Group (USA) Inc. Previously published in a Roc trade paperback edition.

First Roc Mass Market Printing, December 2009
10 9 8 7 6 5 4 3 2 1

PUBLISHER'S NOTE
This is a work of fiction. Names, characters, places, and incidents either are the
product of the author's imagination or are used fictitiously, and any resemblance
to actual persons, living or dead, business establishments, events, or locales is
entirely coincidental.

The publisher does not have any control over and does not assume any re-
sponsibility for author or third-party Web sites or their content.

This book is dedicated to William Shakespeare, Christofer Marley, and Benjamin Jonson—a glover's boy, a cobbler's son, and a bricklayer's redheaded stepchild—for building the narrative foundations upon which we poor moderns now twist our own stories, as Ovid and others laid flagstones for them.

May this humble effort honor their memories, and what they have left us.

Touchstone: If thou beest not damn'd for this,
the devil himself will have no shepherds; I cannot see else
how thou shouldst scape.

—WILLIAM SHAKESPEARE,
As You Like It, Act III, scene ii

Hell and Earth

Act IV, scene i

It is too late: the life of all his blood
Is touch'd corruptibly; and his pure brain,
Which some suppose the soul's frail dwelling-house,
Doth, by the idle comments that it makes,
Foretell the ending of mortality.

—WILLIAM SHAKESPEARE, *King John,*
Act V, scene vii

L ondon had never seemed so gray and chill, but Will
was warm enough in the corner by the fire, at the
Mermaid Tavern. He leaned back against a timber,
a cup of warm wine in his hands, and sighed. *A man
taken by the Faeries can never truly be content again.*
And then he remembered Kit's voice. *You must not say
such things—*

*Nay, nor even think them, Christofer? I hope you've
found us that Bible, my friend.*

The wine was sweet with sugar and cinnamon, concealing the pungency of Morgan's herbs. Will sipped a
little, and held it in his mouth for the strength and the
sting before allowing it to trickle down his throat. He

stretched his feet toward the fire, dreaming, and almost spilled the steaming wine across his stockings when a heavy hand landed on his shoulder.

It was the playmaker Ben Jonson, his ugly countenance writhing into a grin. "An old man sleeping by the fire," Ben said. He was gaining weight, and no longer resembled an overtall hat-tree with a coat slung around it.

"A young cur snapping at his heels," Will answered irritably. He sat up and set his wine on the table, beside an untouched portion of beef-and-turnip pie.

Ben shrugged shamelessly and pulled the bench opposite out. "You've not been in London of late—"

"Home with Annie," Will said. It wasn't at all a lie; he had been to Stratford. And before that, months in Faerie with Kit Marlowe, who had dwelled there since his murder. There he had met the Queen of Faerie, and another Queen, the redoubtable Morgan le Fey. Will cleared his throat, and continued. "But back now. Richard said he'd meet me. How went the construction of the new Theatre?"

"Dick's calling it the Globe," Ben said. He raised his chin inquiringly, searching for a servant. " 'Tis up. Have you seen the landlord, gentle Will? I'm famished—"

Will craned his neck but couldn't spot the Mermaid's landlord, who was also named Will. They heaped thick on the ground, Wills, as leaves on the streambank in autumn. "Here"—he pushed his pie to Ben—"I've no appetite tonight."

"Pining for your lovely wife already? Will, you don't eat enough to sustain a lady's brachet." But Ben took the food up and chewed it with relish; he was renowned a trencherman. "I hear you've a new comedy—"

"You hear many things for a Saturday morning in January. Aye, 'tis true. Not much like thine *Every Man,* though." Will's hands grew cold, and he retrieved his cup for the warmth of it. The worn blue door swung open, and a cluster of five or six hurried through it, unwinding their cloaks and mufflers just inside and shaking off the snow. "There's the famous Richard Burbage now, with all his admirers." Will waved to his friends, half rising from his bench. Morgan's herbs made a world of difference; better than any cure the doctor Simon Forman could offer. "And there's the landlord gone to take his wrap. Richard's arrived in the world, Ben—what? Why'rt regarding me so?"

"Richard's not the only one arrived," Ben said. "And resting on his laurels, mayhap."

Will deflected both flattery and chiding with his left hand. "Not after me to write a humors comedy again?"

"They fill seats—"

"Aye," Will said as if that ended it. "And so do I. Look, there's Mary Poley. Can that great blond lout beside her be Robin?"

Ben turned to look over his shoulder. "In the apprentice blues? Aye, 'tis. He's the image of his bastard of a father, more's the pity."

Aye, he is. The lad—Will's dead son Hamnet's age, near enough, and Will pushed that thought firmly away—was growing from round-faced boyishness into Poley's sharp chin, his high forehead, and straight yellow hair that showed no signs of fading to honey-brown with maturity. *And should I tell Kit thus-and-such?*

Mary's eyes met his over Robin's shoulder, and she smiled and tugged Burbage toward the corner.

—no.

Ben had turned on the bench and watched as Mary, Burbage, Robin, the poet George Chapman, the landlord, and the golden-haired cavalier Robert Catesby made their way into the corner already occupied by Ben and Will. "Master Jonson," Will the landlord said. "Ale, perhaps? Something else to eat?"

"Ale"—Ben coughed pastry crumbs and wiped his lips with the back of a hamlike hand—"would go nicely. Good morrow, Mistress Poley, Master Robin. George, Dick, Robert."

"Good morrow," Burbage said as the landlord departed, and slid onto the bench beside Will, who gestured Mary and Robin to sit as well.

"Good morrow, all."

Robin Poley blushed his shy smile, too proud to step behind his mother the way he might have, a few years earlier. He bit his lip and rubbed calloused, burn-marked hands on the wax-stained blue broadcloth of his apprentice's gown. "Master Shakespeare. Master Jonson."

His voice cracked halfway through each name, and Will laughed. "Sit, lad. Master Catesby, I have news of your family from Stratford—"

Robert Catesby, encumbered by his rapier, did not sit, but leaned against the wall on the far side of the fire. It popped and flared, spreading warmth, and he peeled off his meltwater-jeweled gloves and tucked them into his belt. "You were home for Christmas, Master Shakespeare? Did you celebrate with my cousins, then?"

Will met the handsome man's eyes, understanding the question. The Catesbys, like the Ardens and the Hathaways and the Shakespeares themselves, were among the Stratford families who clung to the old religion, and Robert Catesby was asking—obliquely—if his family had been to an outlawed Catholic Mass. "All the families gathered," Will said. "I understand your cousin Richard is betrothed."

"Excellent news—" Catesby grinned, showing good teeth, and Will looked down. "And all your family well?"

"My parents are growing old," Will said. It galled him to admit it, and he hid the emotion behind a sip of wine. *Time, lay thy whip down—* "But my brothers and Joan are well, and mine own girls. My youngest brother

Edmund is here in London, playing for Henslowe, poor fool—George, you look uneasy, sir."

Chapman shrugged, taking a steaming cup from the tray of the landlord's daughter-in-law as she fulfilled their orders. "Speaking of Edmunds. Hast seen Edmund Spenser recently, Will?"

"I've been in Stratford," Will answered, reaching out to tousle Robin's hair. "And I barely know Spenser. He moves more in thy circles, George." With his eyes, Will directed the question to Ben. Ben shrugged and pushed the ruins of the beef pie away, taking his ale from the young woman's hands.

"Nay, not in a week or more . . ." Jonson shrugged. "He's not the common tavern sort. No matter how stirring the company."

"Methinks I'll pay his house a visit when my wine is done," Chapman said.

"He may be with his patron, the Earl of Essex. Perhaps a letter?" Burbage leaned forward and pinched his nose between his fingers to stifle a sneeze. "Although they say Essex is back in Gloriana's good graces, and Spenser never left them. They could easily be with the after-Christmas progress."

Burbage's eyes were level on Will's, and there was a warning there. Burbage, like Will, was a Queen's Man— an intelligencer in service of Elizabeth. And more: both of them were members of the Prometheus Club, using story and sorcery to sustain England against her many enemies. And the Prometheus Club was divided. Essex was not their ally, and Elizabeth had never hesitated to play one faction against another if she thought it would lend strength to her own position.

Will had, as he had said, been away. If Essex—with *his* Promethean links—was in the Queen's graces, did that mean the Lord Chamberlain's men were out of them? Or was there equilibrium again?

Will raised his eyebrows in silent question, but Richard had no chance to suggest an answer in such a crowd.

"Nay," Catesby said. "I'm well known to the Earl, and came from his household but yestermorn. Spenser is not among Essex's servants at this time."

Mary patted Burbage on the back. "He might be ill," she said slowly. "It took my brother Tom so quickly, I had not time even to visit before he died."

Her quiet statement left the table silent. Tom Watson, the poet—and a Promethean as well—had died of plague with a young wife and a baby left behind. Plague was one of the weapons that Will's faction spurned.

Essex's group was not so fastidious.

Will glanced up at Chapman, who pursed his lips. "We'll go when we finish our wine," Chapman said. Ben nodded and inverted his tankard over his mouth. Will gulped what he could of his own wine through a narrowed throat, casting the herb-tainted dregs among the rushes with a would-be casual gesture and upending the cup on the table to drain the last droplets, lest he poison some unsuspecting friend on the wolfsbane Morgan had prescribed for his ague.

"I'm ready," Will said as Ben stood. "Keep the bench warm for me, Robin." He stepped over the boy with a smile.

Mary half stood, her hands wrapped white around the base of her cup. Catesby and Richard too would have quit their places, but Ben shook his head. "You're cold: stay and get warm. Will and I will walk out—"

"And George will walk out with you," Chapman said, raising his hand to summon the landlord from his place near the taps.

Despite snow, the streets bustled; after the idleness and revelry of the Twelve Days of Christmas, London had business. Will, halt with his illness, minced carefully on the icy stones, Chapman holding his elbow. "How much farther, Ben?"

Ahead, Ben checked his sweeping stride to allow Will and Chapman to catch him. He turned back over his shoulder. "Just down the street—"

Edmund Spenser's lodgings in King's Street were on the ground level, a narrow door opening on a narrower alley, leaning buildings close enough that Ben's shoulders brushed one wall and then the other, by turns. Only a thin curtain of snow fell here, for the roofs all but kissed overhead.

The big man drew up by that doorway, waiting for Will and Chapman to come up behind him before he raised his fist to knock. His breath streamed out in the shadows under the storm clouds, reminding Will uncomfortably of other things. Will looked at the black outline of his boots against the sugared cobblestones.

Ben's fist made a flat, hollow sound like a hammer. Will held his breath: no answer. Something about the door and the dark light in the narrow alley and the *chill* breathing through the planks and the old, whitewashed stucco of the wall made it harder to release that breath again.

"He's not here," Chapman said, twisting his cloak between his hands.

Ben grunted, raised that maul of a fist, and hammered on the door again. *I hope his glover charges him extra for the cheveril.*

"Edmund! *Spenser!* Open the door." Nothing. He rattled it on its hinges. Latched. "Shall I fetch his landlord, then?"

Will edged into the narrow crack between Ben and the house; he peeled off his glove, put his hand out, and laid the palm against the wood. That dank chill that was more than the January and the falling snow swept through his veins and gnawed at his heart, like a ferret through a rabbithole. Will gasped and cradled the hand to his chest, tugging it under his cloak to dispel the frost. He stepped away, leaned against the far wall of the alley. Not far enough.

"Ben," he said, rubbing cold fingers to warm them enough so they'd uncurl and he could wedge them back inside his glove. "Break the door down."

Ben hesitated only a moment, and glanced only at Will: never at Chapman. Will looked down at his hand and finished settling his glove.

"The door."

"On your head be it," Ben said. He swept off his cap, handed it to Will, and hurled himself at the warped pine panels.

They never stood a chance. Will thought the door would burst its latch; instead, the panels splintered before Ben's hunched shoulder with a sound like split firewood. The big man went through, kept his balance, and staggered three steps further, one hand on the broken wood to keep the door from bouncing closed. He covered his mouth with his free hand, doubling as if kicked in the bollocks. Will stepped forward after Ben as the cold within the room flowed forth. It clung to Will like icy water, saturating his body and dragging him down.

The cold.

And the smell.

Ben, to his credit, held his ground—gagging, but unflinching. Will paused with his hand on the splintered door frame, wishing blindly for a moment that Kit were there—for his witchlight, for his blade, for his witty rejoinders—and then kicked himself into movement. *'Tis better than Sir Francis Walsingham's deathbed,* he thought, and then wondered if that were only because the room was so very, very cold. Colder than the cold outdoors, but well appointed, with two chairs, a stool, and a bench beside a table near the shuttered window on the front wall, for whatever light might edge through the gap between houses.

Will's fingers wrapped something in his pocket: a sharp iron thorn. A bootnail, the one that Kit had asked back of Will before his departure from Faerie. Which Kit had passed through flame and fed strange words to, and dropped a droplet of his own blood upon. A talisman from a lover to a loved, and black witchcraft, and the sort of thing that damned one to Hell. And Will, clutching it so tight his signet cut his flesh, would have spat in the face of the man who said so.

The floor creaked under his feet, creaked again as Chapman stepped over the threshold and hesitated, his blocky body damping what little light entered. "George, step in or step out," Ben said. Chapman lurched left, leaning against the wall inside the door, a kerchief clapped over his mouth and nose.

"Contagion," Chapman said, voice shaking. "You know what we'll find."

Despite Will's earlier thought, he realized now that the smell was precisely the reek of Sir Francis' sickroom. Will came within, noticing the door to a second room slightly ajar. What had killed Sir Francis—*aye, and probably what carried off Lord Strange as well, and poor Tom Watson*—was neither plague nor poison, but blackest sorcery. He knew because he felt its prickle on his neck, identical to the sensation of Kit waving his hand, bringing every candle in a room to light. Identical to the sensation he felt when an audience was rapt in his power—

—that prickle, of observance, as if something roused itself and watched. There were parchments on the table, beside a stub of candle. Will drew out flint and his dagger and kindled a light; the ashes in the grate had long gone cold. Ben lifted the pages toward the door. *"The*

Faerie Queene," he said. "Just one stanza. Over and over and over—

> *"When I awoke, and found her place devoid,*
> *And naught but pressed grass, where she had lain,*
> *I sorrowed all so much, as earst I joyed,*
> *And washed all her place with watery eyes.*
> *From that day forth I lov'd that face divine;*
> *From that day forth I cast in careful mind,*
> *To seek her out with labor, and long tyne,*
> *And never vow to rest, till her I find*
> *Nine months I seek in vain yet ni'll that vow unbind."*

Damme. Will understood almost without understanding, found himself chanting lines of poetry, anything that came to mind. A history play, *Richard II,* and Ben gave him an odd look and then nodded, understood, picked it up, murmuring lines of his own—clever epigraphs and riddles, damn his eyes, but Will was in no position to complain. "Poetry, George," Will said, between verses. It was the only magic he had, and the only protection he had any hope for.

"What?"

"Poetry. Anything. Recite it—"

George blinked like a frog, but obeyed—

> *"And t'was the Earl of Oxford: and being offer'd*
> *At that time, by Duke Cassimere, the view*
> *Of his right royal Army then in field;*
> *Refus'd it, and no foot was moved, to stir*
> *Out of his own free fore-determin'd course;*
> *I wondering at it, asked for it his reason,*
> *It being an offer so much for his honor."*

Infelicitous, Will thought, but held his peace to murmur his own talismanic words.

"I am a stranger here in Gloucestershire:
These high wild hills and rough uneven ways
Draws out our miles, and makes them wearisome,
And yet your fair discourse hath been as sugar,
Making the hard way sweet and delectable."

Will's voice and Chapman's combined with Ben's—

"At court I met it, in clothes brave enough,
To be a courtier; and looks grave enough,
To seem a statesman: as I near it came,
It made me a great face; I asked the name.
A Lord, it cried, buried in flesh, and blood,
And such from whom let no man hope least good,
For I will do none; and as little ill,
For I will dare none: Good Lord, walk dead still."

—a strange and uneven sort of round between the three of them, but Will felt the pressure ease reluctantly. Raising his voice, he lifted the candle and steeled himself to pull the handle of the half-open interior door.

He thought himself prepared for what might confront him, he who had been to Hell and back again, who had stood watch over a wife's near demise in childbed and the second death of Sir Francis Walsingham. He was prepared for the peeling cold, like a wind off the ice-clotted moor, and he was prepared for the horrific stench.

He wasn't prepared for the huddled shape under the blankets, Spenser's form curled thin and frail into an agonized ball. Chapman stayed in the front room. The creak of Ben's footsteps stopped at the bedroom door.

Will raised the candle and went forward, just in case, but Spenser's open eyes and the hard-frozen outline of his form—*I am a stranger here in Gloucestershire*—told him already what he would feel when he laid his left hand over Spenser's right: cold stiff flesh like claws of ice, and the candle showed him Spenser's pale eye rimed with frost and sunken like a day-old herring's.

"Contagion," Ben said softly.

Will shuddered and crossed himself before he quite knew what his hand was about. Something cracked and yellow lay frozen at the corners of Spenser's mouth; Will remembered Sir Francis and did not think the stuff was mustard. He stepped back, scrubbing his glove on his breeches, tilting the candle aside. "*I am a stranger here in*—God in Heaven, Ben. Let us quit this place and summon a constable of the watch."

"Aye," Ben said, and he and Will trotted from the rancid little room.

They leaned against the wall outside, breathing the cold, sweet air like runners, having dragged the rabbit-frozen Chapman between them. Ben caught Will's eye over Chapman's head, and coughed into his palm. "Edmund Spenser, starved to death for lack of bread."

"Essex would never—" Chapman began, and Will knew from Ben's level, warning regard that the big man's mind was already churning through some subterfuge.

"Go look at the body yourself," Ben said, lowering his hand again. "Essex obviously hasn't been keeping him very well, if it has come to this."

"I don't understand," Chapman said, so softly Will barely heard him over the whisper of snowflakes through the air, over the squeak of their compression underfoot.

Will lagged back as Ben paused under the swinging sign for a cobbler, snow thick on his uncovered hair, and turned to look Chapman in the eye. " 'Twas no plague carried Spenser off," he said. "But mere starvation. And I mean to see the whole world knows it—"

Will bit his lip in the long silence that followed. It wasn't starvation either, but sorcery—but Will thought he understood the broad rationale of Ben's untruth, and was content to let the younger man's plot play itself out. They turned down the alleyway near the Mermaid before Chapman gathered his thoughts enough to speak again.

"You're not doing yourself any favors provoking Essex." Chapman pressed the worn door open on its hinges. The Mermaid had filled in their absence, and a commotion of warmth and noise and smells tumbled past Will as they entered. "If that's what you mean to do with this accusation that he cares for his servants inadequately."

"I care not for Essex," Ben answered, making sure the door shut tight against the snow. "Especially when England's greatest poet starves to death under his care."

Act IV, scene ii

And to be short, when all the world dissolves
And every creature shall be purified,
All places shall be hell that is not heaven.

—CHRISTOPHER MARLOWE,
Faustus, Act II, scene i

K it turned, gritty stones under his feet: the broad
rooftop pediment of a gray stone tower. The limitless sky lofted overhead. Ravens and swans circled
in confusion, a tumult of cawing and jet and alabaster
wings. Then a glitter of black pinions, white weskit, a
shiny bauble in a smaller bird's sharp beak as it settled
on the battlements before Kit and cocked a bawdy eye.

The magpie spat something ringing on the stone.
A silver shilling, spent until the face of the King upon
it was smooth as a water-worn stone. Kit crouched to
pick it up and found himself eye to eye with the magpie, something—his cloak?—tugging at his wrist as he
reached. The magpie chuckled softly and settled its
feathers. *Ware the Church. Ware the Queen. Ware the*
raven with the wounded wing.

"Doggerel?" Kit asked. It made perfect sense as he said it. "Can't you, of all birds, do better than that?"

The magpie chuckled again and hopped off the battlement, climbing to dart between circling ravens and swans. Kit pulled against the cloak, but it seemed to bind his wrists tighter. He stood and spread his arms, stretching against the fabric. The wind caught and luffed under the patches, ruffled his feathers, stroked his pinions. Lifted him, and he fell into flight as naturally as breathing. His dark wings rowed the sky; he arrowed in pursuit of the magpie—faster, more agile, more deft, his barred tail flicking side to side like a living rudder as he avoided the broad wings of the regal swans and ravens. One of the ravens limped through the air; Kit saw a spot of bright crimson on its wing, vivid as a tuft of rags and feathers, as it spiraled down to rest within the Tower's walls.

Hawk Hawk Hawk, the ravens cried in alarm, which was foolishness. Kit's sharp triangular wings showed him a falcon, no hawk. And no threat to anything as big as a raven. Or a swan. *A merlin,* he realized, amused, as the magpie led him flitting over the rooftops and marketplaces of London. St. Paul's Churchyard, where the booksellers were. King's Street, and the merlin caught a glimpse of a balding human who seemed familiar, somehow, leaning against a stucco wall between a big man and a stout man, all three of them shaking, slumped, breaths smoking in the cold.

Blackfriars, Whitefriars. Charing Cross and then somehow it was sunset, it was nightfall, and through the gray twilight five men were unloading a barge on a bank near Westminster. One a cavalier with shining golden hair—hair that *glowed,* even in the gathering dark—and to look at him, the little falcon's wings skipped a beat in fear and distant—or perhaps forward?—memory. He dropped several feet before he caught himself, and went back for another look. A big man stood in the barge, handing barrels up the bank to the other four: a broad-shouldered soldier with a luxuriant red mustache and a kind, hooded eye.

The merlin circled over their heads. The magpie flew out over the river, dipping and diving, chattering still. The air sustained other sounds and odors, as if there were a wood across the water and not the stews and bear-pits of Southwark: dry leaves and tannin, a hollow knocking like the rattle of a stag's autumn-velveted tines among the low branches of oaks.

And then a cry, a lamentation or a sugared moan of delight, a voice too sweet, chromatic, resonant to reveal the difference.

The belling of a stag, the entreaty of a falcon, the toll of a carillon. Wingbeats. A name that seemed to resonate over his taut-drawn skin like shivers through a tapped drumhead.

Mehiel.
Mehiel.
Mehiel.

Kit woke curled tight in the layers of his cloak, the French seams he'd stitched flat still prickling his skin, a name on his lips. *Mehiel.* Sweat soaked his brown-blond hair and his face itched with dried salt, eyes burning, scars burning. The fists pressed to his face smelled of tears, so very like blood.

So very like blood indeed. "Not a night terror, at least," he said, sitting up, at sea in a giant bed. "There was a prophecy in that one, I wot." His bedroom was empty; he spoke only to the walls and to the sunrise beyond his window. *Mehiel.* He knew the name. An angel's name, by the sound of it.

He was sure he had heard it before.

He stood and washed, cleaned his teeth, relieved himself, combed his hair. Once he had dressed, he gritted his teeth, tugged down his doublet, and made his way to the hall to break his fast. The patchwork bard's cloak he swung around his shoulders smelled of smoke and sweet resin and strong whiskey, so every time he inhaled it was as though the Devil's hand traced his spine.

He had anticipated the silence in the hall when he entered, still mincing on feet worn sore by—barefoot—climbing the steps from Hell. He'd known heads would turn and voices would still, that the clink of silver on Orient porcelain would halt. And he'd called himself ready for it.

His steps didn't slow. He was Christofer Marley, brazen as they came, and he would walk down the center row between the long tables and find his breakfast of porridge and honey and sheep's milk—such homely stuff, for Faerie, but man did not live by thistledown and morning dew alone—and take a seat, and he would dine. And let them mutter what they would. He was Christofer Marley—

Except he wasn't. The name had no power over him, for good or ill. It was no longer his.

He had sold it.

His stride did lag when he recollected that, and he nearly stumbled on the rushes. But he recovered himself and squared his shoulders, thinking *Needs must replace my rapier* when his hand went to his belt to steady the blade, and found it absent. That, too, was left in Hell.

He carried on, limping more heavily now that he'd hurt his foot again. But chin up, eyes front, not because he was Christofer Marley but because he was not willing to bow his head today.

When he was halfway to the board, the silence broke. At first, when but a single pair of hands struck together, he thought the clapping ironic. But then another joined, and a third, and by the time he stood ladling porridge into a bowl, he did so at the center of a standing ovation.

Two days previous, he would have set the bowl aside and turned and given them a mocking bow. But he was not the man he had been, two days previous. He had passed through that man, passed beyond him, been transformed on his quest to retrieve his beloved Will from the devil's grasp. And as with Orfeo, there was no looking back to see where he had been.

Now, he was a man who had been to Hell and back again, and whose feet still hurt with the journey. He turned, and nodded blindly to the room, and found his seat with as little ceremony as possible.

When he sat, and hunched over his bowl, the rest sat too, and that was the last that was said of it.

It's time wert about thy duties, Kit, he thought, half hearing the rattle of antlers on wood. *Thou hast charges from the Queen and thy Prince that thou hast much neglected, in pursuit of love and poetry.*

He would to the library, and see what he could find there. And perhaps start researching Will's crackpot scheme to retranslate the Bible.

For once, Amaranth was not in the library. Kit sought through old texts until near the dinner hour, and found nothing on the names and ranks of angels, and little after the fashion of Bibles. Which should not have surprised him, he knew: there was little of Christian myth in the Queen of Faerie's archive. *Hast never heard to know thine enemy, and keep him close?* And then Kit laughed. *Why, no. Of course not—*

—I wonder if the Book itself could do them injury.

He wiped dusty hands on his doublet and then cursed the mouse-brown streaks across its front. A wave of his hand spelled them away again. It seemed frivolous to use hard-won power for such petty purposes, but there was no reason not to. *No one told me witchcraft was so useful. If word gets out, 'twill be all the rage indeed.*

He cast one more lingering glance around the room before he left, but lunch—truthfully—held a greater allure. *And mayhap I can find Puck or Geoffrey there.* It suddenly occurred to him to find it odd that a being with a stag's head would eat beef and bread like a man, but he shrugged as he stepped through the open double doors of the hall and walked silently across the fresh-strewn rushes.

The Mebd, Queen of the Daoine Sidhe, sat at the high table, although she did not usually take her dinner in public, and the Prince, her husband, sat beside her. Kit might have slipped aside and taken a seat just above the salt—there was one near Amaranth, on the bench she had pushed aside to make room for the bulk of her coils—except Prince Murchaud raised his head and smiled, and beckoned with one refined oval hand.

Kit turned his head to get a glimpse of Amaranth through the *otherwise* vision Lucifer had awakened in his right eye. She seemed to him a long spill of dark water, a black surface shattered with ephemeral reflections of light. Murchaud and the Mebd—all the Fae—shimmered like dust motes in dawnlight as Kit walked down the center aisle of the hall between the long trestles. He didn't need the second sight to show him every eye guardedly upon him. It was there again, the way they had stared in the morning, before the applause. Climbing the steps to the dais, Kit realized belatedly what it was. *You're among the legends now, Marley.*

Or not-Marley, as it were.

The Fae were in awe of him, mortal man in a journeyman bard's cloak who had gone to Hell in pursuit of his mortal lover—and brought them both back out again, alive and to all appearances whole, no matter how much a lie that might be. "Your Highness." Kit bowed low before the Mebd, scraping his boot on the floor. The only sound it made was the rustle of rushes: damned elf-boots.

The Queen of Faeries smiled and inclined her head. She seemed drawn, her rose-petal skin pinched beside her eyes, and as if she—always willow-slender—grew thin.

"Prince Murchaud," Kit said, with a bow almost as low. Murchaud favored him with a sideways glance, and nodded to the empty chair at his left hand. Kit circled the table with some trepidation to take it, not allayed when Murchaud laid a buttered roll on his trencher and served Kit with his own hands.

Kit picked idly at the roast laid before him, trying to find his appetite again. "Thank you, my Prince—"

Murchaud laid a hand half over Kit's. A carefully casual gesture, and Kit would not shame him in public by flinching away as if struck. "Kit," he said, tilting his head to hide his lips against Kit's hair. "I am not sorry I tried to prevent thee going, love. But nor am I sorry thou art home and safe; I did not lie when I said I cared for thee. Can we not be friends at least, if thou canst abide not my closer company?"

"Aye," Kit found himself answering, and then halted. " 'Tis not thee," he said, as something in Murchaud's tone ripped him to honesty. "I would fain—"

"Aye?" Murchaud's voice, and close and tight.

Kit bowed his head over his hands, and stifled a chuckle at the image of saying grace over fey victuals. He stole a sideways glance at Murchaud's pale, intense blue eyes, the midnight coils of his hair, the elegant line of his nose, the faint sequined glitter of magic behind it. "Thou didst seek to protect me," Kit said.

"I did wonder when thou wouldst notice—"

"And," Kit continued, unperturbed, "I might ... call thee friend. An thou wouldst permit it."

Murchaud drew a breath. "Is't so bad, Kit?"

" 'Tis worse," Kit said, and busied himself with his bread and beef. A little later he looked up, and waited for the quiet conversation between the Mebd and Murchaud to flag. He spoke when it did, knowing the Mebd could hear him as well as the Prince. "I have not been about my duties—"

"Thou'rt absolved," the Prince answered, absently.

"Nay," Kit said, still wondering at the words that seemed so inevitable as they passed his lips. " 'Tis time I accepted my place, here in Faerie. 'Tis time I chose a side."

Kit missed Amaranth leaving the hall by a few moments, and hurried his step as he followed the flicker of her tail through cool, sunlit corridors. Her progression was stately enough; he caught her up by the doors to a balcony overlooking the rose garden. "Lady Amaranth."

"Sir Poet? How may I be of service?" She turned from the waist, her long body twisting like a ribbon, and extended a cold hand in welcome.

He bowed over it and mimed a kiss. Her chuckle sounded as if it rose the length of her in bubbles. "I had hoped you might assist me in finding a book. Some information on an angel—I think an angel, by his name. And perhaps a very old Bible."

"In Faerie?" She drew her hand back as he straightened, and gestured him to accompany her. Not to the gardens after all, but down the corridor and back toward the library where he had spent the morning. "A Bible? New Testament and Old? Apocrypha? I might have one of those. How old?"

"Whatever you have. And as old as possible," Kit answered.

Amaranth laughed. "Read you Aramaic?"

"A little Hebrew," he admitted. "Greek would be better."

She shrugged fluidly, dropping her body to a merely human height to grasp the handle of the library door and twist it open. "I can teach you a spell 'twill render tongues—human and otherwise—comprehensible to thee. It can be done with music also, now thou art both bard and warlock, but the bardic spell lasts only as long as the song."

"Rumors fly, I see," Kit said. He followed Amaranth's train into the room and turned to shut the door behind them. She draped a coil of herself over a massive dark wood table with legs as thick as Kit's thigh; Kit hopped up on the table opposite, hugging a knee.

"Some of us see more than others," Amaranth said. "And you came back from Hell and an interview with Satan with mismatched eyes. Tell me, Christofer—how look I to thee, now?"

"A bottomless sea in moonlight. Are mine eyes mismatched?"

She smiled, her hair writhing about her head. "You have not looked in a mirror since you came back from Hell, I see—"

"How could I? There are no mirrors in Faerie."

"That is a difficulty." She slid from the table edge like a fall of silk and crawled off among the rows of bookshelves. "I shall return," she said. "Take your ease."

Kit obeyed her, listening to the rustle of her scales over stone and carpet as she searched the shelves. "And so you will teach me more magic, Lady Amaranth? To what end?"

The room smelled of serpent's musk and dried autumn leaves. Kit breathed deeply. Her voice drifted back, muffled as if the paper and leather absorbed its tones. "Fondness for thee and thy mortal poet are not answer enough?"

"And I should trust a Fae's fondness?" He lay back on the weighty table and looked up at the gilt plaster relief netting the ceiling, letting his feet dangle over the edge.

"I'm not a Faerie," Amaranth reminded him, over the sound of sliding books and rustling pages. "And just as happy not to be. William told me before he left that he thought the Fae might be responsible for the murder of his son."

"More than thought. Had on good authority—"

"Aye." The lamia sneezed, a sharp and diminishing hiss. "Did he tell you the culprits, then?"

Kit shook his head. "He did not say he knew them. I had assumed whomever it is who supports Baines and Essex's faction of Prometheus, if they are still allies."

"You know," she said, emerging from behind a monumental bookcase with a black, leathery tome resting on the flat palms of her hands, "the spell I shall teach you can also be used to talk to trees. If the trees are forthcoming."

"And if they're not?"

"Many a wood hates man for wrongs wronged in centuries past." Noncommittally. "Men generally win, when they go forearmed to deal with trees. Will you talk to Geoffrey, then?"

Why should I care to talk to trees? "I had meant to ask you if you knew where he was to be found," Kit said, sitting up. "Why this sudden interest in politics, Lady?"

"Oh," she answered, tipping the dust-stippled Bible into his hands with an amused hiss. Her hair darted forward, every black eye bright with curiosity. "I care not for politics."

"Then what is your interest?"

She shrugged. "Snakes are always interested in mysteries," she said. "And Mehiel is well-enough known. You can no doubt find him easily when you do return to London to speak with your friends. Now—about that spell—"

Forty-five minutes later, Kit was halfway up the stairs, holding the fragile old Greek Bible reverently in both hands, when he realized that wherever Amaranth had gotten the name *Mehiel*, it wasn't from Kit's lips at all.

Act IV, scene iii

*If thou dost marry, I'll give thee this plague for thy
dowry: be thou as chaste as ice, as pure as snow, thou
shalt not escape calumny.*

—WILLIAM SHAKESPEARE, *Hamlet,* Act III, scene i

In January of 1599, Edmund Spenser was buried under
the towering pale vaults of Westminster Abbey alongside England's greatest poets—*save Marley,* Will
thought uncharitably, blowing on his reddened fingers.
As if stung by the whispers of his criminal neglect of
Spenser in the hour of his need, the Earl of Essex paid
for an elaborate funeral, which the Queen herself attended. And eight of the poet's most renowned fellows
carried the body down the memorial-cluttered aisle and
laid it into a cold hole in the stones beside the grave of
Geoffrey Chaucer.

Elizabeth slumped heavily in a cushioned chair as if
she could not stand through the burial, and her courtiers clustered about her. She turned as the prayers
ended and the mourners moved forward, a still-regal
gesture, and caught the eye of Shakespeare upon her.

And Will, standing a little apart from Chapman, Jonson, Fletcher, and the rest of the small band of poets and playmakers hurling flowers and pens into Spenser's open grave—*and how our number is lessened from what it was ten years ago . . . and why did I never stop to wonder at that before?*—saw her lift one elegiac hand and beckon him.

He came forward, stepping past the crowded graveside, and shakily genuflected before the Queen. Longfaced Essex stood behind her, all in white with his wooly beard oiled into ringlets, and the ascetic Sir Robert Cecil stood at her right hand. The Queen acknowledged Will and gestured him to rise; Sir Robert's eyes asked a question over her shoulder, and Will met them, inclining his chin in a nod. *We'll speak later, my lord.*

Before his sojourn in Faerie, and then Hell, Will and Thomas Walsingham had arranged to plant counterfeit coins in the home of Richard Baines, Promethean and mortal enemy of Will's faction. Will wondered what Tom had told Sir Robert about their ill-fated attempt at reverse burglary. *Add Tom to the list of people I must make time to speak with, and sooner than tomorrow.* "Highness," Will said, and inclined his head again.

"Master Shakespeare." Elizabeth, swaddled in furs against the cold, leaned back in her chair rather than sitting stiffly upright under the weight of her massive tire. Her cheeks were hollow under the fine high line of her bones, and her wrists seemed fragile as twigs and wire below the heavy jeweled points of her sleeves. She tilted her head to Sir Robert and then to Essex; both men moved back, withdrawing without seeming to. "We missed your presence in our revels this winter."

"I missed as well the privilege of performing for Your Highness," he said. "I was—"

A small pursing of her painted lips might have been a smile. "In attendance upon our sister Queen. Aye, and we know it. We trust we may rely upon your presence in our court for Lady's Day—"

"The New Year? Madam, I would be honored beyond words."

"Wilt have a new play for us, then?" Her eyes flickered past Will's shoulder, and her mouth twisted to one side. It could have been distaste or amusement for whatever she saw; her eyes would not give him enough to say, and he could not in politeness turn to see what she had deigned to acknowledge.

"It will be as Your Highness wishes." He looked into her sharp, averted eyes, and pushed back a memory of Morgan. Nipping kisses and temerity, and he was shocked to suddenly see Elizabeth—*Gloriana*—as a woman, a lover, and haunted by love. *Has she ever been kissed like that?* And then another thought, of Edward de Vere and his trust in his immunity.

She probably beheaded de Vere's father, Will realized, half his mind on history. *Has she ever loved where she has not had to kill?* "A comedy or a tragedy? Or a history, my Queen?"

Her eyes came to his face again, and she opened her fan with a rustle of lace, but did not stir the air with it. "We are weary of history, poet. Give us a comedy."

As you like it, he thought, and inclined his head with its treacherous tendency to nod, and folded his shaking hands. "Your Highness, I would beg a favor of you—"

His voice trailed off at her expression. She chuckled, and it sounded as if it hurt her. "A favor, Master Shakespeare?"

"Aye—" He swallowed, bowed again. "I have it in my heart to make a poetical translation, a new edition of the Bible, with great and glorious words to uphold the great and glorious Church of England—"

"And there is something amiss with the Bible as we use it?"

She turned her head and caught Sir Robert's eye; he limped closer. Will caught the sparkle of her humor in the gesture, and decided to risk a joke. "It could be better poetry."

He caught his breath when she looked back at him, gray eyes hard over the narrow, imperious arch of her nose. And then the corners of those eyes crinkled under her white-lead mask, and she looked up at Sir Robert. "Robin, my Elf, how are we predisposed to new translations of the Bible?"

Sir Robert rose from his bow to regard the Queen, and then glanced at Will. "Surely we have all we need, Your Highness—"

"Aye," she said. " 'Tis as we believed. We'd rather have plays of thee, Master Shakespeare."

Will bowed very low, aware of Sir Robert's eyes measuring him. "You forbid it, Your Majesty?"

"We do," she agreed, her voice low and sweet. She extended her hand to Sir Robert, who helped her from her chair. Will did not miss how white her knuckles seemed on the arm as she pushed herself to her feet. "We trust we will have the pleasure of thy company for Lady Day, then, and that of thy Company." She smiled, pleased at her pun.

"An it please Your Majesty—" He held his genuflection until the Queen moved away, her ermine trailing her like the wings of some vast white bird, Sir Robert in his austere black attending like a gaunt-cheeked raven and Essex following a few steps behind.

Well, that could have gone better. Will stood, trembling more than he liked, and turned over his shoulder to see if he could make out what had caught his Queen's attention. The poets had withdrawn from the graveside, and most of them dispersed, although Will saw Ben's tall shape bent down to spindly crook-toothed little Tom Nashe further down the eastern aisle. And then a flicker of movement by the graveside drew his gaze, and Will focused his attention more plainly on the shadows between the statues there.

A whirl of color, patches like autumn leaves tossed in a wind, and when Will squinted just right, knowing what he was looking for, he could make out a slender man huddled under a black velvet hood, his shoulders aswirl with a cloak that caught the light through the leaded windows in all colors and none. When Will looked at him directly, he seemed to fade into transparency and shadows.

"Kit," he said softly, coming up behind the sorcerer. "I should have known you'd come."

The black hood lifted and tilted to encompass Will, and he caught the glitter of Kit's dark eyes. "Pity about this," he said, and with ritual solemnity he held out his right hand and let something fall into Spenser's grave. It caught the light, shining, and spun like a thistle seed as it fell; a white, white feather, the tip stained with ink and cut as a quill.

A feather from the Devil's wing.

"I know what that is," Will said softly. "Edmund might not appreciate the symbolism, though."

Kit shrugged, stepping away from the grave. "I've all the gifts I need of that one, I think. He's got no claim on my poetry, and I shall offer him none."

"Wise Kit," Will said, falling into step beside him. "Didst come to London only for the funeral?"

"Nay . . ." A sigh. "To see thee, and ask of thee a question. And ask one of a priest as well."

"A priest?" Will swallowed worry.

"Oh, 'tis nothing. A name I heard, the name of an angel. I wondered who in God's creation he might be. No, I wanted to speak to thee of thy son Hamnet—"

"Ah, Kit." Unexpected. Will glanced over his shoulder at Spenser's grave, and swallowed. Sharp tears suddenly stung his eyes. "That pain is—"

"Aye." Kit clapped Will on the shoulder, and Will looked up, surprised by the contact, and then sighed as Kit abruptly dropped his hand, his fingers writhing as if he'd touched something foul. Since the Devil, human contact hurt him.

He's trying. Will forced his tongue to stillness until he could say, "Lucifer tried to cast blame on the Faeries."

"Which Faeries?"

Will stopped walking and turned to meet Kit's gentle, measuring gaze. "Those that love not the Mebd, he said. Nor Gloriana. Didst think to root them out for me, Kit?"

"I am tasked to root them out for the Prince," Kit answered, fussing with his well-cleaned fingernails. "We have sought them in Faerie a half decade now, and I could hope they revealed themselves somehow here. Were less cautious, or—"

Will shrugged, and saw Kit watching the trembling of his hands, the nodding of his head out of the corner of his eye. "All I know—" Will swallowed and tried again. "All I know, 'twas Lucifer told me the oaks murdered my boy. Faerie oaks."

Kit looked up, startled, something yellow as topaz gleaming in the smoky quartz of his right eye. He quoted a rhyme Will would as soon not hear again. "Oak, he hate— Damme, Will. What thou toldst me now, hast told any other? Annie? Amaranth? Anyone?"

The quick answer was easy, but Kit's intensity caused him to pause and think through the past months. "No," Will said, after several seconds dripped by. "Not a one, but for thee."

Kit reached up as if to run a hand through his curls and laughed when he touched the black velvet of his hood instead. "Amaranth told me to talk to the trees. She knows more than she ever speaks, that one."

"Aye," Will said, worry blossoming dark in his heart.

"And I'll lose no other piece of my soul to a witch-hearted tree—"

"Peace, Will." He saw the twitch of Kit's hand toward his arm, saw it fall back among the folds of Kit's bright, shifting cloak. "I'll come to no harm. Must do this thing in any case: wilt trust thy vengeance to thine Elf-knight, love?"

It hurt, the fear. But Will saw the promise on Kit's face, and nodded nonetheless, and remembered something that Kit should know, that might link one group of enemies to another. "Robert Poley. Kit, Poley was in Stratford when Hamnet died. I thought he'd come to threaten me—"

"Will? What are you doing, standing muttering in corners to yourself—" Ben Jonson's big hand clutched Will's shoulder, turned him half around. Will put up a hand to cover Ben's and saw his pupils widen. "I beg your pardon, sir," Ben said to Kit, pulling the hand back to rub his eyes. "I did not see you there in the shadows."

"By all means," Kit said, his voice dangerously soft as he drew his cloak about him.

Ben glanced at Will and at the door. Will shook his head. "The Queen said no."

"Damn," Kit said, in unison with Ben. "How could she ... ?"

"Who is this fellow, Will?" Ben's hand on Will's shoulder again, possessive, and Kit's eyes almost glowed in the shadows of his hood. *Who is this fellow to know so much of our affairs?*

Oh, this is not how I would have chosen to handle this. "Kit Marley," Will said. "Meet Ben Jonson. Ben, this is Christofer." *And God ha'mercy on my soul.*

"Please. Call me Merlin," Kit said, his face very still, and Will knew at once that he had made a mistake. A very bad mistake indeed. Both in introducing Kit first to Ben, and more, in letting Ben lay that companionable hand on his shoulder in Kit's view.

"Marlowe?" Ben blinked. "The poet."

"The dead one," Kit said irritably. "Aye." And moved along before Ben could react. "And your fellow conspirator, though I see Will has informed you not. So. No dispensation for our Bible. Damme. Again."

"That's fine," Ben answered, after a moment of slow consideration in which he apparently decided to deal with supernatural manifestations some other day. "We'll write it anyway."

"Against the Queen's word?" Will shook his head.

Ben dismissed it with a gesture, and spoke without much lowering his voice. "She won't be Queen forever, Will."

Act IV, scene iv

Marriage is but a ceremonial toy
If thou lovest me, think no more on it.

—CHRISTOPHER MARLOWE,
Faustus, Act II, scene i

Such a small grave, neatly tended, evergreen branches laid atop the snow and the marker swept carefully clean. Two or three sets of footsteps; Kit couldn't be sure. He crouched in the snow beside it and tugged his glove off, touched the frozen needles of a pine branch, the soft bow of a red velvet ribbon not yet faded by the wet and the sun. "Merry Christmas, little man."

He sat back on his heels, the leathern bag over his shoulder almost overbalancing him, and glanced around the churchyard. The horizon already glowed orange with winter's early sunset. Unobserved, he decided, and quickly freed the bit of ribbon from the greenery. He folded it inside the palm of his glove; the edges of the wet cloth itched and made a splotch on gray kidskin.

I'm sorry, lad. If anything, 'twas my fault, what befell thee, and not thy sire's. And a measure of Will's kindness that for all he could have blamed me for every ill that's touched his life since Sir Francis dragged him into this unholy mess, he never held me responsible for a bit of it.

Well, I did nearly put his eye out with a hot poker trying to reason with him—Kit shook his head as he stood, shaking his cloak to snap the snow from the hem. "Bloody hell." *So it's Robert Poley and the Fae, is't? Well. One more blood debt for Robert Poley. One more shouldn't bother him a little.*

Kit's hand clenched around the bit of ribbon. *Pity I can only cut his heart out once.*

It wasn't much work to find the New Place, as Will's grand house was called. "The playmaker's done well for himself," Kit said, pausing on the roadway and looking up at the five peaked gables, the smoke drifting lazily from several of the chimneys. He paused, scuffing his feet on the frozen earth. *Come, Kit. Put a bold face on it*—

He squared his shoulders and stepped up to the door, tapping squarely. It opened a moment later, so promptly that someone must have seen him standing on the road. He hoped he'd looked like a man considering if he had the right house, only.

The dark-haired girl within might have seen fourteen winters, or fifteen. Kit bowed as low as he would to any lady of the Mebd's shining court, and swept his hat off too, making a flourish with his patchworked cloak. "You must be Mistress Judith," he said. "And as lovely as your father described—"

"He said no such thing!" she said, and stepped forward to block the door. "And who are you, you fabulous tatterdemalion, to pretend to such a gallant tongue?"

Kit straightened and let his cloak drop in natural folds. The girl's eyes sparkled: she knew her advantage, and Kit rather thought the tart-tongued wench would have him twisted around her finger in a moment. "I am expected, I hope," he said. "My friend Master Shakespeare said he would send word ahead of my visit, and that I might be assured of my welcome here. I see he underreported the sweetness of his daughter's speech—"

"Did he say so?"

"That he underreported your sweetness? Nay—"

"Nay, that you could be assured of your welcome here." She cocked her head back, her black hair spilling over her shoulders, and stared up at him. Kit bit his lip: her eyes were the same dark blue as her father's, and made him shiver.

"Judith? Judith, if thou wishest to warm the outdoors, build a fire behind the stable—" Annie Shakespeare paused in the doorway, her faded eyes narrowing at the corners when she caught sight of Kit standing on the path. He waited while she examined him from boots to hair. A thoughtful moment, until she nodded and tugged Judith out of the doorway. The braided ribbon around Mistress Shakespeare's neck caught Kit's eye; he smiled in spite of himself, bitter and sweet. *And joy you in it, Will.*

"Welcome, Master Marlin." After the country fashion, she kissed him in greeting when he came through the door.

Kit forced himself to stillness, to returning the quick peck she offered, but he knew from the lift of her brow that she noticed his discomfort. She reached out, deft as a bird, and brushed his hair behind his ear, her fingers quick on the rounded tip. He shied like a startled horse, and she nodded satisfaction as he shifted from foot to foot.

"Some Elf-knight," she said, when Judith was out of earshot, scampering into the house to let Cook and the maid know the company had come. "You look like an overdressed university lad, if you ask me, which you haven't. Will you eat beef and bread and apples like a mortal man?"

"Madam," Kit said, stamping the snow from his boots. "And glad of it. Mistress Shakespeare, you keep a fine house."

"I do when I can," she answered, and hung his cloak on a peg once he handed it to her. "Will wrote to say you were here on his business—"

A note of suspicion in her voice, and not unwarranted. Kit let his gaze wander as she led him to the hearthside, concealing a swelling blister of sorrow. *Will's an idiot not to come home more often. Had I a family such as this—* "And he told you I was an Elf-knight?"

"Nay, he told me my rival was an Elf-knight under a curse, who could not endure a mortal touch. 'Twas not too difficult a study to know of whom he spoke, once presented yourself at my door in your hobgoblin cloak and your boots of green chamois."

"Ah." Kit kept the little bubble of—not homesickness, exactly—behind his smile as she led him to a chair by the fire and pressed a mug of warmed wine into his hands. "Your rival, madam?"

"Not his words," she admitted. "But you're no elf, Master Marlin, or I am very much mistaken."

"Changeling," Kit said with a shrug he meant to be casual. He closed his eyes, afraid of what Mistress Shakespeare might glimpse in them, and then opened them again, uneasy when he could not see. "It makes little difference in the end; I was born mortal, but it seems I am mortal no more."

Mistress Shakespeare glanced over her shoulder, assuring their privacy, before she sat across the hearth from Kit. She lowered her voice so it would not ring through the house. "What is my husband to you?"

Kit's breath stopped half in and half out of his chest. "My"—he swallowed wine to cover his hesitation, and managed only poorly, by the look in her eyes—"oh, there is no one easy word, madam. What did he say to you of me, to put that savagery in your gaze?"

Silence, and the dent of her teeth in her lip. Her skirts, twisted between her fingers, showed him a flash of red flannel petticoats. "He said he loved you."

"Ah." *There is no answer that can make that better.* "Mistress, and I him."

She shrugged. Her skirts fell smooth. Her small foot twisted on the hearthstone, clad in a shoe of good blue leather, the stitching stretched over the rise of her great toe.

"I could mend that for you," Kit said, pointing with his chin.

She started, expression darkening as if he indicted her housewifery, and then saw the angle of his gaze and looked down, extending a hearty ankle to inspect her shoe in the firelight. "A seamstress, are you?"

"I can darn a stocking, too," Kit said. "Such it is with students." The wine was sugared, sweet and thick. It heated his cold feet at least as much as the fire did. "Especially the overdressed ones."

A laugh, but not a warm one. *Aye, and she's a reason to love thee, Kit?* She tucked her shoe away under her skirts and dusted her hands together, as if about to rise. "Your supper will be a little while longer—"

" 'Tis no matter," he said, sipping his wine, trying to puzzle out what the even tone of her comment meant. *Is she inviting some sort of a battlefield alliance, I wonder? Or running her banner up over Will's castle?* "The company is good."

She blushed dark; Kit rather enjoyed imagining Will's reaction to his flattery. He smiled wider when she absently brushed fingers across the pouch resting against her bosom. "I wanted to hate you," she said.

"You would not be the first. Or likely the last."

"He came home— Master Marlin, why did you send him home again? And healed. Half healed, at least. . . ."

"Aye, and I wish I could claim his health my doing," Kit said. They matched gazes a little while, and Kit finished the wine. "Madam, I thank you. That was very pleasant."

"And unpoisoned," she said, with a little shrug and half a chuckle. She leaned to lift the cup from his fingers, turning it with her own. "This time, at least. You did not tell me why."

Her answer was so dry he had to laugh before he hoisted himself to his feet and swept a bow. "Mistress Shakespeare. I beg your sympathy, madam, and I pray you understand that there is nothing in me so base as would take a man from his wife and children. Even could I."

Mistress Shakespeare lowered her voice. The firelight fell across her face; Kit liked the way it outlined the high, arrogant arch of her brow. "If he knew them better, that might be more of a promise, Master Marlin."

Ah. Touché. And the heart of the matter. "Madam," Kit said, as kindly as he could through an ache and a coldness that ran from his throat all the way down to his fingertips, "Will's heart is yours. No matter what else transpires—"

"Words are easy," she answered, but she didn't rise.

"They are. And they are yet all I have, and all I have ever had." Kit sighed, and stared down at his boots. *Hanged for the lamb is hanged for the ewe.* "Did Will tell you why he sent me?"

She swallowed, a little bobble behind the worn silk of her throat, and whispered, "Hamnet."

With his witch's sight, Kit wouldn't have had any problems walking through the woods after sunset, as long as there was some little starlight. But he was not eager to go among Faerie oaks in the darkness and the dark of the moon, and less eager even to drag Annie Shakespeare out into the snow and the night. "Tomorrow. When it's light. Can you show me where he died? That is all I need of you; I can stay the night at the inn."

"Aye," Mistress Shakespeare answered, and gathered her skirts to rise, his cup still dangling from her fingers. "Your supper will be ready. Come join us at board, Master Marlin. And then Peter, our lad in service, will show you up to bed. There is no need for any lover of my Will's to share a buggy inn bed."

She turned then, and Kit stopped her with the quick brush of fingers across her sleeve. "Madam . . ."

"Master Marlin?"

He coughed, a prickling throat. It was all inadequate, anything he could say, any flowery line he could quote, in the face of her grace and her strength and her composure. "If I had someone such as you at home, I would not leave her a moment."

She regarded him evenly, only the corners of her eyes giving a trace of a smile. "As well-favored as you are," she said, "how can it be that you do not?"

Snow creaked over crunching leaves as Kit left Mistress Shakespeare at the edge of the Arden wood and tromped forward, feeling her gaze on his back. His rucksack swayed against his shoulder. There was no path under the trees. Their black branches shone wet and rough against a dawning sky of pale porcelain blue; the white powder underneath was trellised with fallen laceworks of snow, but only Kit's footprints marred it.

Not even a crow or a fox. And canst blame them? He glanced around, tugging the velvet collar of his cloak higher as if to ward the gaze of chilly eyes from his neck. The trees leaned over, their wind-stirred fingers interlaced like bones. Kit found himself ducking as if through low doorways whenever he looked up, and drawing shallow breaths that tasted of moss and musk and mildew.

His right eye showed a smoky power moving within the coarse-barked trunks. The trees were young, saplings scattered among a few old giants; the wood had been cut in living memory, and Kit wondered if that were the reason for the appalling stench of hate and old blood clotting his senses.

The bit of ribbon had bunched in the palm of his glove. He tugged his digits free and wiggled his hand out, checking over his shoulder to make sure Will's wife was out of sight behind the barren oaks. Her silhouette had vanished. He stretched the band of scarlet velvet between his fingers—one hand gloved, the other bare—and blew a cloud of steam into the still morning.

His cherry-varnished viola was in his pack. Kit crouched and slid it out, the ribbon dangling from his fingers as he balanced the case on his knee and opened it reverently. He tied the ribbon around the viola's waist, under the strings, with a tidy bow at the back, returning the case to his pack to keep it dry before he stood. He would have hung the whole affair on a low branch, but given the wood and his purpose here, he thought perhaps that would be unwise.

That smoky pall of force began to shift as soon as he plucked the strings to tune, mentally apologizing both to the fae bard Cairbre and to the fine old instrument for bringing it out in such chill and unwholesome air. The smoke was not the only vitality in that wood: there was a power in the viola's pregnant belly and graceful neck as well, a strength as red and resonant as its stain.

Kit felt the oak wood tremble, expectant, *loathing* him and his music, and every mortal touch and scent on his soul and on his skin. He shrugged his cloak back from his shoulders and raised the viola and the rosined bow.

The trees screamed when he scraped the first note

from the strings. Branches wore on branches like chalk on slate, a sharp grinding that sent Kit's shoulders up around his ears and all but drowned the hollow lucidity of the viola's tone. He persevered, found the upswing into a reel, planted his feet wide in the snow, and leaned into the music as best he could.

He would have closed his eyes and found the rhythm, submerged himself in the song, but a witch's *otherwise* sight showed him that smoky puissance rising in the trunks of the oaks and the coiled crimson, potent as lifeblood, in the music streaming from his fingertips, and he didn't dare let his attention waver.

Gauzy tendrils reached out and brushed his hair, his face, his moving hands. Kit felt a slight resistance, a child's plucking fingers, and fiddled through it. The tendrils struck his cloak, the oaks' gnarled branches grasping after; both slid back like oiled hands clutching ice and Kit played faster, fingers sailing over the viola's neck, bow flying back and forth like the shuttle on a loom. He stumbled a note, almost hesitated as the crimson light quailed before an onslaught of dark —*smoke and firelight*—staggered, found his theme again, twisted his reel around it, and made it his own, gliding the tune over the discord of branch on branch that sought to drown him out.

The music soared. The chafe of wet bark became— not words, but something like enough words that Kit understood them, though the voices raised the hair along his spine. *Witch. Witch. Witchery.*

"Aye," Kit said, lowering the viola a moment, and holding the red light no other's eyes would see steady about himself. "Witchery. And I command you in the names of my dread master Lucifer and of the Queen of the Daoine Sidhe to answer my questions, and answer them true."

Like a saw on bone. Terrible, those voices. *Thy master. Witch. Thy queen.*

Not ours.

Not ours.

Not ouurzzz.

The black hands grasped as the first golden fingers of dawn filtered through branches. Kit stood fast, telling himself his shiver was cold and the morning mists, nothing else. The black hands touched his cloak and pressed it against his body, but could not push past. "Be that as it may. I am here, and I command you."

A rattle of branch on branch, a stag knocking velvet from new tines. *No. Witch. Witch. Not ours.*

A white pain flared over his breastbone, and he flinched. *Hell.* No, not Hell; what burned was the mark over his heart, the final brand left on his skin when Richard Baines and his Prometheans had raped and tortured him in Rheims, when he had been a mortal man and innocent. Then, like a lightning caress down Kit's belly and thighs, wherever the irons had touched, the same pain, brighter, so sharp it was almost sweet. He tasted blood but did not scream.

Kit spoke through grinding teeth, forcing his spine straight. *I've felt worse.* "Who ordered the death of Hamnet Shakespeare?"

Not ours.

Witchery.

He touched the red ribbon on the red viola with the tip of his bow. "Who ordered the death of Hamnet Shakespeare?"

No answer this time, just the clawing and sawing of the branches, the leaning threat of the sapling trees bent over him, their limbs poised like daggers. Smoky fingers coiled and drifted, wavering thick as banners now, redolent of hate. Somewhere, not too distant, a dead branch crashed to earth. A sort of croaking moan followed, the splintering resonance of splitting wood. Kit turned, following the path of the smoke of power against the wind, and yelped. He dove aside, a deadfall landing close enough to heave snow and splinters on him. He kept his grip on the viola, clutched it close when he rolled, guarded it with his body when he rose with a swordsman's grace.

"Dammit," he swore, and took a deep breath. Snowmelt trickled from his hair, down his neck. "Third time I command you then—as I am a man and the master and shepherd of trees since the wild God of the World gave Adam their naming—answer me not, and I shall return with *fire*."

Silence, shivering silence. Kit spoke into it, each word measured and plain. "Who ordered the death of Hamnet Shakespeare?"

A breath held. A silence like the silence of any mortal wood in the golden sunrise, in the January snow. The smell of rotten wood, of loam under snow. No whispers. No mutters. No ghosts.

But a name.

Robin Goodfellow, the wood said.

Puck.

Act IV, scene v

Will glanced around the candlelit confines of a smoky little room in the chapel of Westminster Palace—almost more of a hallway with a narrow table and six tall chairs in the center—and sat himself down with a sigh. At the head of the table, near the flickering candelabra. He plucked a beeswax taper from one arm of the fixture and toyed with it while he waited, letting the wax drip along its sides in layered arabesques, making the shadows dance.

No matter how he tilted the taper between his fingers, the flame rose upright through the biting chill, shivering slightly in response to his palsy. He shook free beads of liquid wax and rising bubbles of smoke, amused by their transformation from transparency to a milky crystallized splash when they struck the cold wood of the table.

Beyond the windowless walls, a clock struck seven. And Sir Robert did not come. *Am I forgotten? Or is this meant to teach me humility?* He tilted the taper further, and this time the wax that fell dripped down the wick and flamed as it scattered through the air. *A good effect,* Will thought. *'Tis pity there's not a safe way to adapt it for the stage. 'Twould be too fine a detail to read well, anyway.*

The door opened, admitting the spare black-robed shape of Robert Cecil; Will twisted the candle upright and stood, hot wax splattering his fingers as his trembling knocked it loose. He bowed, careful not to set himself on fire, and tucked the candle back into the candelabra. "Mr. Secretary."

"Master Shakespeare," Sir Robert said, and shut the door firmly. "Sir Thomas passed along your note regarding the disposition of your ... investigation ... of Masters Baines and Poley. I would have preferred a personal report."

"I am afraid that was impossible," Will said, coming forward. "If I had been in London, I believe I would be dead."

Cecil limped to the end of the table. "We've had the house under observation." He pulled a chair out but did not sit. "The Inquisitor's body has not turned up."

"Then it's still in the house," Will said, as if the situation could not be more plain. He picked wax from the crease of his thumb with his left hand, steadying his right when it would have trembled. It didn't help, and he dug in his purse for a shilling, hoping the gesture looked absent. "He's most certainly dead, Mr. Secretary."

"I did *not* receive a satisfactory explanation from Sir Thomas of how you yourself managed to escape, although I'll not complain of any man who brings me the demise of a Papist pawn."

Will looked down, watching the silver coin cartwheel

across his knuckles in the candlelight. "You've not had Baines arrested yet?"

Threadlike lips writhed as Sir Robert tried and failed to repress a smile. "We are arranging a suitable frame for your painting of Baines as counterfeiter. And an excuse to search the house. If he's buried a body in his cellar, so much the better; at the very least, we can force Essex to act to protect him, and perhaps the Earl will show a soft underbelly." Cecil sighed. "You know he supports James as the heir."

"I know the Queen thinks it treason to speak of it, Sir Robert," Will said.

Cecil coughed into his hand. "And yet speak of it we must."

"Nay, Mr. Secretary." Will shook his head. "Baines, Oxford, and Essex, and their Prometheans, are my concern, and the safety of the Queen we have. When that changes, I'll address it, but I leave finer matters of politics to those who are equipped to understand the implications."

Cecil watched Will silently, running his hands over the back of the chair, his brow furrowed as if he added sums in his head. "Marlowe would have argued the succession for an hour."

"Marlowe cared about such things," Will answered, feeling disloyal. *Well. He does.*

"And what do you care for, Master Shakespeare?"

Marley, Will almost said, and stopped himself just in time. It wouldn't have been worth Cecil's bewildered look. "The realm," he said, which at least was true. Cecil stayed silent, and Will couldn't resist. "The coins are hidden in the straw tick of a bed on the second floor. You'll want to have the house searched before spring."

"Before the housemaid turns them out with the straw, to dry in the sun of the garden?" It drew a smile, at least. "Very well, Master Shakespeare. One thing more—"

"Aye?"

Sir Robert pushed the chair he had not sat in back against the table. "Your play for Her Majesty?"

"Aye."

"Make it a potent one. An you value the realm of which you speak."

Will nodded, running his thumb across the raised profile of Queen Elizabeth on the coin in his hand. And decided not to tell Robert Cecil just yet that he wasn't entirely certain that the magic the Queen's poets put into their words was still effective, given the fate of Edmund Spenser, and the way Elizabeth herself seemed to crumble before his very eyes.

Will wasn't surprised to find Kit waiting in his rooms when he returned to Silver Street, shaking the cold rain and the night out of his hair. Half a dozen candles gleamed on table and mantel, and Will didn't like the dark circles under Kit's eyes, like the smear of an ink-marked thumb, or the snarls drying in Kit's uncombed hair. Or the hollow expression he turned on Will when Will opened the door and came in, already unlacing his jerkin, his cloak bunched over his arm.

Will paused just inside, making sure the door latched behind him. "Ill news."

"Aye." Kit stood and stretched, crossing to the fire he'd built up either to warm himself or in anticipation of Will's return. He was dressed in a plain linen shirt and black wool breeches; another, waterlogged, shirt and a jerkin were laid across the back of a chair not far from the fire. "Where hast thou been?"

"Sir Robert," Will answered. He stepped out of soggy boots and found a flannel for his hair. "The entrapment of Baines and Poley proceeds apace. We hope. Art planning to impart thy news?"

"Bulldog." Kit rose and came to Will, close enough

that he could feel the warmth and moisture rising through Kit's shirt, steaming from curls sprung tight in the humidity. Kit reached out and took the flannel from Will's hands to dry his hair. Will ducked to permit the intimacy, smiling. "Dost think thine entanglement of Baines will succeed?"

"He's close to Essex," Will answered. He reached to touch Kit's arm, and Kit stepped away with a smile that was half apology. "And he and Poley both useful to the Queen—"

"Aye, I think it unlikely too. Still, perhaps we can give him a bad moment. I went to Stratford, Will."

"And?"

"Thou toldst me not that Annie knew something of us."

"Ah." Will nodded, half to himself, and crossed the room, intending to pour wine for both of them. "I should have known she'd read through the riddle of thy presence. What didst thou tell her?"

A low chuckle, honeyed with that pleased smugness that always put Will in mind of a satisfied tomcat. "That, dear William, is her business and mine. An thou wishest to know such things, shouldst arrange to be present when they are discussed. Thou'rt still wet through, love: take off thy shirt and dress thyself dry. I brought thee that Bible, but Ben or I shall have to read it thee."

"Greek?"

"Aye."

Will turned in time to catch the clean woolen shirt Kit tossed. He tugged soft, scratchy cloth past his face while Kit cleared his throat once or twice, fussing with the wine cups; by the time Will had the shirt comfortably settled, Kit pressed a goblet into his hands. Kit's hesitance—the way he turned his eyes aside when Will tried to catch his gaze—burrowed into Will's composure as if with hook-tipped nails. "Kit." Will disciplined himself, leaning back against painted plaster, long fingers curved around the bowl of his cup. "Is thy news so dire?"

"Dire enough. I interviewed the oak wood—"

"Interviewed the oak wood." Will said it more to taste the sound of the words than because it needed saying. "What didst thou discern?"

Kit shrugged, staring at Will as if he expected Will to look down. The fireglow and the candlelight snagged in his right eye and flickered golden, the left side of his face cast into shadow. "I've questions to ask in Faerie before I come to thee with final answers."

"Dammit, Kit—"

"Nay." A clipped, flat gesture with Kit's right hand. Will swallowed his protest with a hasty mouthful of wine, and waited for Kit's explanation. "I won't lead thee to a hasty conclusion on a matter so dear. Don't ask it of me."

There was more darkness in Kit's eyes than the angle of the light, Will decided. "What thou'rt doing— It takes a toll of thee, this witchery. Does it not?"

Kit turned down, away. He brushed a bit of lint off the shoulder of his shirt. "It leaves me stronger than before," Kit answered. "Full of strange echoes of power, and knowing things no mortal man should know. I know not who I am, Will."

That hollowness—the only word Will could think of—echoed in Kit's voice, and Will itched to go to him. "Thou'rt Christopher Marlowe," he said. "Poet, playmaker, Queen's Man, and the friend and lover of a lucky few who cannot hope to deserve thee—"

He didn't understand why Kit flinched at his name, or the watery grin which he offered Will when Will's voice trailed off. "Aye, thou dost deserve better," Kit muttered, and set his cup aside and turned to open a shutter. " 'Tis raining still."

" 'Tis." Will straightened away from the wall, turning

his cup in his fingers to steady his hand, and scuffed a foot through the winter-rank rushes on the floor. "We must put paid to Baines and Poley, Kit. Sir Robert didn't say as much, but from him I have the impression that Gloriana is—unwell."

"When she passes—" Kit chewed his lower lip. He glanced down at his hands, and latched the shutters again. "It will have repercussions in Faerie. We'll deal with it when we must. Needs must move faster than we have, in any case—"

"Sir Robert won't like it."

Kit grinned. "Sir Thomas will. And your side of beef, Jonson, or I miss my guess."

Will snorted. "Jonson is ever eager. Now that he knows you live, I may as well tell Burbage too. Wilt meet with us at Tom's house, and we can start our Bible? If you have the book—"

"Aye, I have the book." Kit's fingers drummed on the window ledge.

The pattern was erratic, a touch too quick, and ragged. It made Will's heart feel as if it beat irregularly, in counterpoint. He kicked his heel against the wall, waiting for Kit to continue.

"Did Sir Robert say the Queen was dying? Dying now?"

"He insinuated she had not a year left in her."

"Damme," Kit said. "We need more strength, Will. If things go the way I think they will in Faerie, I may very well provoke a war. What that means for England I am not sure, but Morgan and Murchaud and others all have told me that there will be battle when Elizabeth dies. And I suspect Elizabeth's passing may not go easy on the Queen of Faerie, either: the two are story-linked. We're weak, our faction. Damned weak—"

Will exhaled. "There's the witchcraft you got in Hell."

"Aye, and if I'm clever I may make Baines regret his alliances. I mean to go there from here, and try my hand at the evil work of an evil eye. But there's Oxford and Essex and our old friend Southampton—" He shook his head.

"We can't trust Sir Robert either," Will said, at last putting a name to the conviction the evening's meeting had left in him. "He's already searching for the place he'll put his feet when the Queen is gone. He's not his father's vision—"

"Nor his father's shortcomings, I hope," Kit answered bitterly. "So it's thee and me and Tom and Jonson and Dick Burbage against half the peerage and two of England's greatest intelligencers." His lips pursed as if it pained him to admit as much of Baines and Poley. "We need to take control back: we've lost the initiative utterly. Thy Lady Day play. Whatever Jonson's working on. Has anyone talked to George?"

"Can we trust George?"

"Can we fail to?" Kit slumped, forehead to the shutters, taking his weight on locked elbows, his hair parting in ringlets at the nape of his neck. "He may already know more than we suspect. Tom was George's patron before he was mine."

"I'll tell Richard," Will said. He turned his cup over on the window ledge by Kit's hand, and fumbled in his pocket for the silver coin so he wouldn't reach out to tidy Kit's hair. "I'll ask Tom about George—"

"Feel George out." Kit pushed himself upright and turned to the chair by the fire, sliding his jerkin off the back and testing the dampness of the leather with curious fingertips.

"I will."

"Who else have we?"

Will stopped and closed his eyes. "Edmund." He pressed his fingertips to his eyelids and bowed his head.

"Edmund? Spenser? Will—"

"No," Will said. "Edmund my brother. He's playing at the Curtain now, Kit."

"And thou wouldst risk him?"

Will laughed, slicking both hands back over his ever-rising brow, and met Kit's gaze more squarely than he felt the need to. "He'd be furious with me if I kept him from participating in any justice meted to Hamnet's murderers. He had more to do with my son's raising than I did myself—"

He let the sentence hang, and Kit left it there long enough that Will filled the silence. "And thee?"

Kit shrugged the jerkin on, and found a bit of raw-hide in a pocket to twist his unruly curls into a tail. "I'm going to try to kill Richard Baines."

Act IV, scene vi

Behold and venge this Traitor's perjury.
Thou Christ that art esteem'd omnipotent,
If thou wilt prove thy self a perfect God,
Worthy the worship of all faithful hearts,
Be now reveng'd upon this Traitor's soule,
And make the power I have left behind
(Too little to defend our guiltless lives)
Sufficient to discomfort and confound
The trustless force of those false Christians.

—CHRISTOPHER MARLOWE,
Tamburlaine the Great, Part II, Act II,
scene ii

The January rain drew cold fingers through Kit's hair and down the back of his neck. *The only lover's touch you're like to feel again.* He shivered and tugged his cloak higher, settling the weight of his rapier at his hip as he made the turn from Muggle Street onto Silver. His fingers brushed the red velvet of Hamnet's ribbon, tied to the hilt, and he laughed to himself at the irony. *So Will raises Poley's son—who might be Kit's son, rather—and Edmund raises Will's son.*

And what dost thou contribute to the equation?
Blood. Blood and more blood.
That is all.

Kit left his hood down. The streets were deserted with the early winter curfew, leaving him without company except the odd stray dog and the odder feral pig, and the shadows he called would conceal his passage from most casual eyes. He pursed his lips and whistled an air, summoning a swarm of greeny-gold glowing midges out from darkened alleys. They swirled like a minuscule waterspout over his open palm; he blew his breath and his music across it and they flocked like swallows and schooled like fish.

There was one useful thing in the marks Baines had branded into his flesh. They were a palpable trace of the man, and Kit could use their resonance to find him. "Richardum Baines mei invenite," he commanded. The motes rose and sparkled, darted and flitted, arrowed in a general easterly direction and then jigged back and forth like a dog leading its master to the gate, impatient for supper. As Kit followed the guiding will-o'-the-wisp through London's slick, dark streets, the night grew colder. Water froze in his hair.

White flakes superceded the icy rain, turning the footing slushy and treacherous. Snow whispered on the reddish roofs as Kit's guides led him to the theatre inns near Bishopsgate, each one closed for the night, narrow doors barred for curfew, and then through the twelve-foot archway into the innyard of the Green Dragon.

Some candlelight still glowed through shutters on the second and third floors. Kit leaned back, shading the snow from his eyes with a hand held flat, and contemplated the diamond-patterned railings on the galleries. Despite his better intentions he found himself glancing about the innyard; he'd lodged here when he first came to London, and seen several of his own plays performed to audiences that crowded those very galleries and the pavement upon which he now stood.

His witchlights twinkled along the railing by one shuttered window, a handful of emeralds set out in the sun. The second gallery, of course, and he wondered why it was that he never needed to scale a trellis in dry sunshine and gentle warmth.

I wish I'd brought a pistol.

"Aye, 'Marlowe,' " he muttered. "If a sword and black magic won't suffice, perhaps thou shouldst ensure thou hast a firearm so thou canst blow thine own clumsy fingers off when the damned thing misfires. How am I going to get up that gallery with the front door closed and no doubt barred?"

Add burglar to thine accomplishments.

He huddled under shadows in the innyard, watching the soft green jewels of his will-o'-the-wisps shifting like sleepy doves on the railing, glowing dimly through the downy fall of snow. The chill on his skin, the numbness of his hands and tongue, *could* have been the cold. *Aye, and thou hast lied to thyself so many times before.*

Kit looked down at his hands, knotted in front of his belly. "Courage, puss." His own words, meant for irony, startled him; he'd captured Baines' calming tone—the voice a man might use on a skittish animal—better than he'd expected. He drew a breath and kept on: intentionally now. "Come, kitten. It'll soon be over. Be a little brave—" He tasted blood, and couldn't decide if it was real, or a ghost of memory. But his cheek stung; he'd bitten it hard enough to break the flesh. He turned and spat into the snow. *Blood and more blood.*

He looked up, untangling his fingers from their knot and then tangling them again when they wanted to creep up and press his jerkin and his shirt against the scar in the center of his breast. Fist doubled in fist, Kit punched himself in the thigh and snarled, "Baines was right. Here standeth as God-damned a white-livered coward as needeth a keeper to wipe his arse. Now get thee up there, Marley, and do thou what thou camest for." *If thou'rt going to whore thyself for the power to do, it ill befits thee to stand shaking in terror when couldst be doing.*

He shuffled forward, eyeing the lower gallery. White flakes dusted it, caught in the ripples on toothy icicles, but it wasn't more than ten feet above the pavement, and Kit rather thought he could get his fingers over the lip. If he didn't slip and dash his brains all over the pavement.

Here standeth a fine gallant figure of a hero.

Kit scrubbed his hands on his doublet one more time, made sure his sword was settled, and tucked his cloak tight. Then he took a breath and crouched, and leapt into the air.

I should have thought to sand my hands. But he grabbed and held, right hand burning on the ice, something gouging the softer flesh between ring and middle fingers. He wedged his left hand through the trellising, fingers around a rail post and jammed by the narrow gap, and he hung there, kicking.

And didn't fall.

He wasn't sure he could have managed what he did next when he was a student or a poet, and soft. But he had relentless Murchaud and their fencing sessions to thank for the easy strength across his shoulders and in his forearms that let him drag his leaden body higher. He levered himself up to the gallery and twisted to get an elf-booted foot over the lip, then pushed himself upright amid a rattle of dislodged ice. He froze against the timber, calling his shadows about him, and listened for any sign that the landlord or his custom might have heard.

The whisper of snow softened everything. In the stable, a courier's or a courtier's steed snorted, stamped. Somewhere a church bell tolled, and that was all.

Kit leaned his forehead against the timber and gasped, holding the beam as close as a lover. *I should have begged Lucifer for wings, while I was begging.* And then he found himself pressing his free fist against the hollow of his chest like a man in panic, a pain like a cramp flexing his ribs.

Christ wept.

Aye. And is weeping still.

The witchlights gleamed under their icing of snow. A gentle glow: it put Kit in mind of sunlight through fine worked jade, or the new leaves of spring. *Infinite riches.*

And not a man would give a penny for them.

Lord, what fools these mortals be.

A grin to himself and one for Will, and no look down at the knotty cobbles behind and below his boots. *Infinite riches.* Aye, and they showed him precisely where to place his reaching hands.

The second gallery was harder, as it matched the overhang of the first. Kit hoisted himself, still clinging to his post, and balanced himself on the ice with trepidation. Still, his boots never slipped and the witchlights gave more guidance now that he pressed his hands into the snow between.

He lifted himself over the railing on the second gallery; his guidelights vanished as if snuffed. Kit stood in the heady darkness, sweat freezing with the rain under his hasty ponytail, and drew ragged breaths of the dank night air. A crack of brightness gleamed under the shutters of the nearest window, and he smiled and pressed his ear against the wall.

There were spells for listening, too, and for hearing more plainly. Easy enough: he mouthed one and cupped a hand.

No words, but Baines' voice and then another, cultured and cultivated, and the rattle of bottle neck on cup. *And if thou hadst not been as paralyzed with fear as a maid on her wedding night, thou wouldst have paused to wonder why Baines was sleeping in a coaching inn instead of his own good well-warmed house. Arrant fool. Arrant. Bloody. Fool.*

Damme.

Ah well, he thought, and resigned himself to more murders than one. *It profits us not to damn fate nor ourselves, but rather we must trust in Providence.* Which almost made him giggle. *Not Poley with so cultivated a tone. Nor de Vere. Even now, I would know Edward—*

Still. 'Tis a familiar voice—

The snow fell harder, but, under the gallery roof, Kit was dry. He shook his cloak free of his belt and drew his rapier into his hand, frowning as he leveled himself at the door, which would be barred, without a doubt.

And can I not charm a bar from its pegs?

The tune he whistled under his breath. It didn't matter: magic had no need to be *loud*. And then Kit leaned back and kicked with all his might at the door latch.

He felt the wood deflect under the ball of his foot, the door springing back an instant before the wood splintered under the impact and the bar jumped free of its slots. The door had rebounded against the frame by the time Kit's foot touched the floor; as he started forward it swung open again and he blocked it with his left hand, brandishing the silver rapier in his right as he came into the presence of Richard Baines.

Richard Baines, who stood by the hearth in the bare little room, leaning against the warm stones, handsome and only a little wide-eyed as he reached for the rapier at his hip. "Kit!" he said, smiling as the cold steel extended his reach. "What a pleasant surprise. What's happened to thine eye?"

Beside him, rising from the stool he'd been straddling,

another man Kit recognized—blond and well-favored, a broad-shouldered Adonis with eyes as heavenly as Lucifer's. Robert Catesby, and Kit made sure his flinch didn't show on his face. *Just a dream.*

Catesby's sword was not at hand; the stool clattered and rolled as he scrambled after it, getting his back into the corner by the bed that was the only other bit of furniture in the room. *Neither as cool as Richard Baines, nor as deadly smooth.*

Kit stepped through the door and closed it with his heel, sealing plank to frame with a sandpaper-surfaced word. Baines' sword-tip never wavered but Kit saw his head tilt, his brow wrinkle in a genteel manner that had never presaged aught but ill. "Interesting," he drawled, examining Kit from his dripping hair to the slush-stained boots and then slowly back up again. "Did he heal *all* thy scars, my darling?"

The word had left Kit's throat as raw as a coughing fit. He managed to get his teeth apart enough to speak clearly, but it took courage. "Where's Robin, Dick?"

Catesby lifted his chin, and his blade did waver, but Baines knew which Robert Kit meant. "Poley's on errantry," he said. "Some matter, no doubt, of direst import for the Queen. Thou knowest how valuable she finds him."

"Indispensable. Of course. Master Catesby, my apologies"—Kit didn't turn his head, but he could see from the blond cavalier's stance that Catesby knew what end of a sword was which, and it did not comfort him— "I'm afraid your presence here does not bode well for your continued well-being. I've come to kill this man."

"Arrogant puppy." There wasn't any harshness in Baines' voice; only that controlled, chilling amusement. Catesby moved to put himself between Baines and Kit. Baines stepped forward, blocking him. "Don't worry, Robin. I can handle this." Baines drew himself up, smiling rather than sneering down at Kit. "Becoming Lucifer's leman has made thee bold, I wot. Although whoring should be nothing new to thee—"

The words were like a wall. The dismissal in them, the amusement, Baines' quiet confidence and mastery. As if he could not even be bothered to despise Kit. Kit leaned into them, forced himself a step forward. Catesby would break first, he thought, would not permit Baines to shuffle him aside so easily, not to judge by the stallion set of his neck.

"At least I've never held down a boy half my size while five grown men forced themselves on him," Kit answered, trying for something of Baines' bantering tone. What got out between his teeth was bitterness.

"No, thou hast an easy time finding lords and libertines to make of thee their Ganymede. Thou didst think not thy patrons kept thee for thy *poetry*."

"Bastard—" Kit moved forward, a firm step where his feet wanted to shuffle, and called on the rage and the roiling power stewing in the hollow of his gut.

Baines only laughed. "Going to scratch mine eyes out, puss? Come on, then—" and came forward to meet him. Catesby moved at the same moment, supporting Baines, two swords pressing as Kit sidled sideways to get his back into the corner by the door.

Kit freed his main gauche before the bigger men got within sword reach, hoping the cramped quarters would cause them to foul each other. Catesby had to come around the bed, at least, and hop over that tumbled stool. Baines advanced straight in; Kit's right eye showed him something dark and potent twist itself around Baines' left hand, as if he swung a cape of some black force to supplement the bright blade of his rapier.

Baines never took his eyes off Kit's face when he spoke, and that unconscious caution made Kit feel suddenly lighter. "Don't kill him, Robin," Baines said. "Not until I get a look at him with his shirt off—"

"As if you could manage my death," Kit scoffed, and whispered a few words in a pidgin of bastard Greek and the sleek, fluid language that Satan had taught him. He looked Baines in the eye when he said them, but Baines' left hand moved, that cloak of darkness flickering around his fingers, and it was Robert Catesby who slumped to his knees and fell back upon the floor, his sword blade ringing when it dropped from his fingers, a wide snore drifting from his parted lips.

Kit never looked away from Baines, but Baines looked down at Catesby and then back at Kit with a nod that might have been edged with respect. "Nicely done."

Kit drew a ragged breath and formed his sleeping spell again. Baines shifted onto the balls of his feet, and for half a drawn breath neither man moved. Then . . .

Fuck this for a lark—

It wasn't the sleeping spell that Kit spat hastily—as Baines lunged—but an older, wilder magic; something Lucifer had shown him but had not bothered to explain. A curse, very simply, simple and uncontrolled, related to the old weird magic the black Prometheans used to call down God's wrath in plagues and famines and the strange wild storms of winters such as no living man remembered—winters that froze the Thames, and plagues that killed men like Edmund Spenser and Ferdinando Stanley.

Die like Sir Francis, Kit thought, and hoped a subtler magic wouldn't slip off Baines' black spell-cloak like water off oiled silk. The words didn't slow him: Kit hastened to parry Baines' gliding serpent of a blade. He stepped to the right, hopped over Catesby's sprawl, and found himself with his back to the spell-locked door.

Baines had the reach and the weight and the heavier

blade; he came in hard, let Kit parry, and took the stop-
thrust of Kit's main gauche through the meat of his own
left forearm with little more than a grunt and a curse.
"Blast—"

Steel ground on silver; Kit's head spun with the
clean, sharp reek of Baines' sweat, the cedar from his
doublet. Baines shoved Kit's sword and his right hand
hard against the wainscoting with all his oxlike shoulder
behind it. A close bind: Kit released his main gauche,
still fast in Baines' arm, and dropped to his knees between Baines and the wall, dragging his rapier free with
a sound that should have showered sparks on both their
heads. *I should have twisted the damned knife. I should
have run him through the neck and not the arm.*

Dammit, Kit, fight better than this.

You know how to fight better than this—

Too close in to use the rapier. Baines brought his
knee up before Kit could dive aside—*a great reckoning
in a little room,* Kit thought, as the blow under his chin
slammed his teeth together, his head knocking a dent
in the plaster of the wall. His mouth was full of blood:
Baines' blood, dribbling from the wound in his arm, and
Kit's own blood streaking his teeth and roping down his
throat. He gagged on it, rolled aside, and almost got his
rapier up in time.

Baines kicked him in the belly, hard, and Kit went
down with his head between his knees and the acid burn
of vomit chasing the stringy sweetness of blood from his
mouth. "Christ," he whimpered, and Baines kicked the
sword out of his hand. It rang like a dropped coin when
it struck the wall and fell, blade angled like a broken
wing, into the corner. Another kick, one more, center of
his chest and Kit felt something flex and twist over his
heart, a green buckling noise like a twisted stick.

Christ.

And then, ridiculously, as he doubled up, gagging

again: *I'm sorry, Will.* Something else rang on the floor. Kit's main gauche, Baines swearing heartily as he yanked it free and cast it aside. "That's two scars I owe thee, puss."

Don't touch me. Don't touch me. But Baines' hands were gentle, lifting Kit against the wall, smoothing the wet curls that had escaped his ponytail out of his eyes. Kit spat blood and bile in Baines' face, slamming the side of his hand down on the dagger wound still weeping blood from the left forearm. Baines grunted, grimaced, and let go of Kit. Kit folded like a corpse, trying to push the sharp words of a witchcraft into his mouth. But whatever he had done—the twist and rill of the curse he'd spat out earlier—seemed to have stripped the power out of Kit, and the words were nothing more than doggerel.

"Christ, puss," Baines said, half irritated and half pleased. "Stay where I put thee for once. There's a pet—"

Kit slumped, wheezing. Almost got a leg under himself, but Baines' command held him to the floor like the clink of chains. Something rattled. Something splashed. Tearing cloth and cursing: Baines must have been binding his arm. Kit forced himself to one knee again and again fell, defeated. Surely if he could stand he could reach his sword, a few short feet away, just in the corner by the hearth.

Every breath hurt enough to dizzy him. Baines crouched in front of Kit and washed the blood and vomit from his face with a wine-soaked rag. "Hush for a moment," he said, and slapped Kit's cheek backhanded when Kit—weakly—fought him. "Hush, puss. This wouldn't happen if you didn't fight me so." His fingers probed.

Kit winced and swore, squirming back against the wall, not liking the strange, concerned gleam in Baines' eye.

"Oh, thou'rt not bad hurt. A cracked rib is all." And then he doubled both hands in the lawn of Kit's collar and shredded the shirt as if ripping up rags, tearing it down to the lacings of the jerkin that Kit wore on top.

"Come, puss. Give us a kiss."

He leaned forward. Kit slammed himself against the wall, harder than Baines had managed, feeling the strain in his neck as he twisted his face aside. *Kill me and get it over with,* Kit thought, shivering.

Instead Baines grunted in satisfaction, mock-loving fingers outlining the scar on Kit's breast, and let him go. "Good. That saves us time. Now get out, Marlowe. Before Catesby wakes."

Kit blinked, focus eluding him. He got a hand and a knee on the floor; the effort made the walls spin. "Get out?"

Baines had turned his back on Kit and was wiping the blood from his hands. "I can't keep thee in a bird cage until I have use for thee. And thou'rt no good to me dead: surely even a poet could have deduced that by now. I'll be back for thee when I need thee, never fear."

Back for thee when I need thee. Kit made it to a crouch, steadying himself on the wall. Stood, and staggered to the corner to retrieve his sword. Bending over was a trick; he managed it with one hand braced on the wainscoting, trying not to hear Baines whistling merrily as he washed and rebandaged his wound. Kit staggered for the door.

Baines' voice arrested him. "Don't try this trick again, or I'll see thy friend Shakespeare on the rack. Dost hear me?"

"Aye," Kit said, and somehow released his own spell on the door and tumbled through it onto the gallery and into the cold. *At least,* he told himself—trying not to giggle—*at least from here thou canst leave by the interior stairs, and out through the front door. Because thou* wouldst *dash thy brains out if thou hadst to climb down now by the way thou camest.*

Past the house-cleaning landlord, it turned out, who raised a questioning eyebrow as Kit came across the common room to the barred front door. "Master Catesby's guest," he said, tugging his cloak tight and hoping the shadows would conceal the ruin of his clothes.

" 'Tis past curfew." Friendly enough. "Stay the night."

"My mistress expects me. I'll mind the watch—"

"See that you do," the man said, and came around the bar to lock the door after him.

The cold cleared his head. He staggered into an alleyway and leaned against the wall, under the overhang. *Damme. I won't make that mistake again. Next time, it's a shadowy alley and a bullet in the back of the head, you son of a whore.*

He wants me alive. He's wanted me alive all along, except when I made it too difficult to keep me that way. Kit pressed his back against the timber and plaster, tasting acid and bitterness, remembering Rheims, remembering the taste of blood and gentle hands holding his hair back while he vomited, again and again. As if that, as if anything, could clear the poison and the filth from his body. Remembered pleading for his life, and braced his hands on his knees and vomited again, into a rain-pocked slushpile this time. In Rheims, Baines had argued for his life. Had told the others that if they spared him, they could *use the same vessel.*

He never meant to kill me.

No. Kit forced himself to stand, to ignore the ragged ache in his chest. He rinsed his mouth with dirty snow, scrubbed more on his face for the chill and abrasion of the icy granules. His brands ached like blisters. His hands stung with the cold. *No. He just means to keep me alive for however long it takes and then what? Rape me again? Something else?*

God in heaven.
I don't want to know.

Kit used the frozen surface of a public basin for his
mirror—more Promethean witchery, that, that London
grew cold enough to freeze her fountains of a winter—
and slipped through it and into Faerie with a sigh that
was very much relief, even though the court's fey night
shadows twisted around him and small things scurried in
the dark. *All it would have taken to make my night complete would be to be caught short out of Faerie, and die in
some alleyway.*

Still staggering, steadying himself with one hand on
the wall, Kit moved at first automatically to Morgan's
room and then stopped himself. *Not welcome at court.*
Hell. But Murchaud's room was closer anyway, and only
one flight of stairs away.

The flagstones whirled under Kit's boots. He pressed
his shoulder to the wall, as if the palace needed his assistance to stand as much as he needed its. They leaned
together, shoulder to shoulder, flying buttress and
cathedral—

A better image than most, for once. He ran his right
hand up the banister, cool stone against his ice-abraded
palm, and pulled his torn shirt collar closed at the hollow of his throat, and forbade himself to weep. A command he managed to obey until Murchaud opened his
door in a nightshirt Kit had given him, blinking sleepily.
"Kit. Thou'rt hurt—"

"Not so sorely," Kit answered, and fell through the
door.

Murchaud bound his ribs in linen, tight enough to
squeeze like a giant's fist whenever Kit drew a breath,
and ignored Kit's feeble remonstrations over the un-
dressing and the necessary handling. Murchaud warmed

water for him—with his own hands, when Kit wouldn't permit him to call for servants—and combed Kit's hair, and dressed him in a nightgown twice as large as it needed to be, and carried him—as he had carried Kit that first night in Faerie—to the big chair by the fire. Murchaud settled him there with his feet up and a cup of warmed wine in his hands. It was a blur of action, with Kit trembling like a trapped fox under the Prince's care and reminding himself not to bite.

Kit drank half the wine without tasting anything but the alcohol's sting in his lacerated cheek, and then he raised his chin to look Murchaud in the eye. "Thou'rt alone," he said, wondering.

Murchaud turned away and squatted to poke the fire higher, turning a smoldering log so the bark would catch alight. "I'd be in the Mebd's rooms if I weren't, love. She does not come to visit my chambers."

"No," Kit said. He covered his discomfort with a sip of wine. "I'd have thought—"

Murchaud shrugged and looked up from his angle-kneed crouch, shapely limbs protruding from his night-shirt this way and that. "I've all the lovers I want," he said, and stood, limber as a cat, and went to pull the bed-curtains back. The covers were as disordered as Murchaud's hair; the prince had struggled out of a sound sleep to answer Kit's knock, and Kit felt a rush of sudden, hopeless gratitude.

And then a moment of wry self-exasperation. "Damme—" Kit set his cup down with a click.

"What?"

"I left Cairbre's viola in Will's lodging." He made to stand; his knees failed him, and he slumped back in the chair. "Thou didst drug the wine," he accused, as tiredness pressed the center of his chest like a broad, flat palm. His fingers curled on the textured brocade of the chair cushion, but failed to shift his body.

"I'll save that trick for when I need it," Murchaud said. "I rather thought the wine would be enough. Come, let me take thee to bed."

"Murchaud, I—"

"Hush. I'll carry thee to thine own rooms if thou likest. Or thou canst sleep in that chair. But I don't believe thee when thou sayest thou dost wish to be left alone, this night."

Kit subsided, his eyelids too rough and heavy to hold up. *Liar. He did drug the wine.*

It didn't matter. He hadn't even the strength to protest the discomfort of the Prince's touch when Murchaud lifted him and laid him in the bed and drew the feather comforter up to his neck. "Puck," he said, remembering.

"What about him?" A dry kiss on Kit's forehead. Lights and candles, the dimming of the room. The pressure of a body in bed beside him, and then an arm across his waist. Over the covers. Almost tolerable so, and Kit hadn't the strength to roll away.

Puck is the villain, Kit meant to say. But then he remembered, he owed Puck a chance to answer the charges to his own face. Before he, Kit, named another friend for treason. As he had named so many before.

He'd seen too many friends hang.

"Nothing," he said, but he wasn't sure the word took breath before the darkness folded him deep.

Act IV, scene vii

Thou hast years upon thee; and thou art too full
Of the wars' surfeits to go rove with one
That's yet unbruised: bring me but out at gate.

—WILLIAM SHAKESPEARE, *Coriolanus,*
Act IV, scene i

Will crouched in the chair by Tom Walsingham's fire, his damp boots draining onto a rush mat, turning Kit's glorious old Greek Bible in his hands. Will's Greek had never been good, worse even than his grammar-school Latin, but he could tell from the handscript, the margins, and the way the sections abutted in the glove-soft, gold-embossed red leather of the binding that he held three or four books stitched together. Their pages had been carefully trimmed to match in size; now scallop-shell flakes roughened the fragile gold edge. He held the book close to his face, open, cupped in the palm of his hands, inhaling the oak-leaf scent of the pages. "George, have you ever *seen* anything like this?"

Chapman set his wineglass on the mantel before he

came closer, crouching before Will to get a better look at the text. "Seen? Aye. Never with such a freedom to read as I pleased, however . . ." Chapman reached forward, hands like wings on either side of Will's, but didn't *touch*.

Teasing, Will pulled the book closer to his chest and hunched over it like a mantling hawk. "Ah—"

"Can you read it, Will?" asked Ben, who leaned against the window frame, his dark eyes hooded as if with weariness.

"A word here and there," Will said. He looked up as Tom returned to the study, two bottles of wine in his hands. "It's missing some rather large bits, Kit says. We'll have to resort to Tom's Erasmus, too. Tom—"

The bottles clattered on the sideboard as Tom dug in his purse for a penknife to draw the corks. Ben cleared his throat and tossed one, pearl-handled, which glittered in the afternoon sunlight as it tumbled across the room. Tom's hand came up; he plucked it from flight. "Thank thee, Ben—"

"Not at all, Sir Thomas."

"Will? Thou wert about to speak?"

Will looked from Tom to Chapman, to the book in his own hands, and shrugged. Ben concealed a smirk behind his sleeve, his regard steady on Will. Chapman stood, puzzled, looking from one man to the other, until Tom smiled. "Why not?"

"Gentlemen?"

"We've a plan to translate the Bible into English," Will said. "Wouldst care to engage in it?"

Chapman looked down at the book open on Will's palms again. "From the Greek, Will? May I—"

"Aye." Will held the book up.

Chapman lifted it reverently, in broad fingers knobbed from hours of holding the pen. "There are translations—"

"None like ours shall be," Ben put in from his place

by the window. He set his cup down and went to relieve Tom of the wine bottles. Ben poured first for their host, who watched, amused, and then filled a cup for Will now that the precious book was out of his hands.

"Will." Chapman's voice was barely a breath. He looked up, across the pages, awe on his broad-cheeked, broken-nosed face. "*Where* didst come by this book?"

"Kit gave it me—" Will said distractedly. He covered his slip with a coughing fit and rinsed his mouth with wine, but Chapman paused, bald forehead wrinkling over bushy brows.

Tom stepped in. "It was Marlowe's. It went to Will after his death."

"He thought highly of thee." Chapman touched the book the way a man might stroke flower petals. "How he ever afforded such a thing—"

"It must have been a gift," Will said.

Chapman shook his head sadly. "Rare skill, had he. And a foolish manner of spending them—you've heard his *Ovid*'s to be burned?"

"*Burned?*" Tom, unbuttoning the neck of his doublet, looked up.

"Aye." Chapman shrugged sadly and set the precious Bible down on a high table, away from the fire, the wine, and the window. "The Archbishop of Canterbury's men seized copies from St. Paul's on Monday. Along with everything of Nashe's, and Gabriel Harvey's. If you've your own copies, you'll want to keep them quiet. Perhaps even out of the city—"

"Burned?" Will heard his own voice as the echo of Tom's, and thought *a chorus. Yes.* "Well, Harvey's no loss to posterity. But Nashe?"

"It's the *Isle of Dogs* back to haunt him," Ben said. "That and his wrangling with Harvey: the Puritans are growing stronger, Will, and it's foolish to deny it. There's something to be said for masques."

"Aye, nobody ever finds a bit of meaning in one, to want to burn it. Gods, poor Tom. I suppose that means they'll be burning *Dido,* too, with Kit's and with Tom's hand all over it. How can there be any sedition in a translation of *Ovid,* of all things, to draw Archbishop Whitgift's ire? It's *love poems*—"

"It's the Puritans," Ben said, pouring himself another cup of wine. The big man moved like a cat, for all his weight bent the floorboards under their rush mats. "It's the Puritans, as I said. They think the translation lewd, and Whitgift bends his neck to the bastards. An Archbishop." Ben looked as if he wished to spit.

Baines, Will thought. *And Essex behind him. Another attack on the poets—*

"The Queen's ministers grant them more power, aye. I suppose they think, better Puritans than Catholics." Chapman leaned against the mantel, but he didn't lift his cup again. Instead, he edged closer to the popping grate, as if the fire could warm him. "I wonder who would give Kit a book like that," he mused.

Will saw Tom's glance, and didn't need it. "I'm sure I don't know. So what think you, George, of our Bible in poetry?"

Chapman shrugged. "It could never be published. And a man must eat—"

"Drudge," Ben said. "Toiling only for coin—"

Tom laughed with him, and Chapman dismissed both with an airy wave of his hand. Will might have joined them, but the cough that followed bent him over with his hands on his knees, and only Ben thumping his shoulders gently with those massive bricklayer's hands put an end to it before he choked.

Only two days later, Will scratched another line out and crumpled the scribbled palimpsest that had been meant to become act II, scene i of a tragedy into a fist-sized ball, which he pitched into the grate. He glanced up again at the steel mirror over the mantel and the single candle burning before it—despite the daylight through the open shutters—with a sealed letter propped against it, and swore under his breath. "Dammit, Kit. A week is too long to make a man wait for news." *He could have returned to Faerie, and an hour or less gone by in his world. Thou wouldst have heard something if aught had gone wrong.*

And if thou hadst not, Tom Walsingham would have. That Tom also said that Richard Baines was, to all reports, alive and well and fulfilling his obligations told Will only that Kit might be biding his time. Kit was certainly crafty enough—

—crafty as Tom himself, or Sir Robert.

I am not like these men, Will thought, not for the first time. *I cannot see as they see, in shades of advantage and degrees of subtlety.* He sighed, and glanced at the light on the wall: the noon bell would toll any moment. He couldn't leave the candle burning in an empty room, and he couldn't put off meeting the rest of the Globe's shareholders for another instant. He pushed his stool back from the table and stood, scuffing the rushes aside as he limped to the hearth. *Dick's had me playing old men for ten years now. A shuffle and a quaver in my voice won't limit my roles.*

Perhaps there is prophecy in the stage after all.

Will blew out the candle, banked the fire back, and picked up his jerkin and cloak, fumbling the door latch a moment before managing to twist it open. He chose to walk through the garden rather than the house, using the side gate onto Silver Street as the bells finally tolled.

London bustled on a sunny Tuesday in February. *Kit's birthday,* Will realized, and cursed himself for thinking about Kit. *He's hard to kill.*

He's also terrified to the soles of his shoes when it comes to Baines, he thought, turning sideways to edge between a goodwife arguing with a carter and the wall. At least the overhang kept the heavily laden carts and the tall draught horses to the middle of the road, although it seemed the crush of hireling carriages grew thicker each year. *And frightened men make mistakes*—

"Master Shakespeare!"

The hailing voice of Edward de Vere broke Will's musings open like an egg on cobblestones. He turned and strove to hide his limp. His hand found a coin in his pocket and he tugged it back again, resisting the temptation to fuss it forth and spin it across his knuckles, over and over again.

"My lord," Will said, bowing as best he could. Oxford swept his tall hat off as he ducked the overhang and came up before Will. "I am surprised to see you afoot, my lord, and so far from your usual—lairs."

Oxford paused, his hat in his hand—a dramatic gesture ruined by the revolted wrinkle of his narrow nose. "Master Shakespeare," he said. "I had thought you might prove more amenable to a personal visitation, as you have returned my notes unopened. You"—careful choice of the formal pronoun, and a careful stress against it, to be certain Will noticed the respect—"have done me good service in the past, and I am inclined today to remember it. You are too fair a poet to fall with Cecil and Raleigh and Walsingham. And fall they will, make no mistake."

Will blinked. Oxford stepped closer and let his voice drop. "Essex's star is rising, Will, and it's said Scottish James is fonder of masques and entertainments even than the Queen." He coughed. "There's no guarantee the Lord Chamberlain your patron will remain in favor after the succession. It would be a pity to see the Globe go empty, her players all jailed as sturdy vagrants and masterless men."

"If I wrote masques I should be more interested." Wondering where he got the courage to brush past a peer on the street, he nodded curtly to Oxford and turned his back on the man.

"Master Shakespeare. Halt your step."

"My step is halt enough," Will said, but he paused, although he did not turn. *What could be dire enough that the Earl of Oxford would call after a common playmaker on a busy street?* "As you have no doubt observed, my lord."

Oxford laughed and strode up beside Will, seating his towering cap once more on his head. His ruff was starched fashionably pale pink, maiden's blush, stiff enough that it rustled against his beard. Will smiled, glad of his own plain murrey doublet. *Puritan,* he thought, and then pushed the memory of Kit's teasing away. "There's more," Oxford said. "What you offered Her Majesty at Spenser's funeral did not go unremarked by all, Master Shakespeare. Nor did the disgrace with which she refused your gift. I have friends—"

"More than one?" *Oh, Will. You shouldn't have said that.* No, but he couldn't close his ear to de Vere's simpering tone, and hearing it he recalled some measure of Kit Marlowe's close and thready rage. And wonder of wonders, de Vere laughed and forced a smile, although he dragged his fine kid gloves between his hands hard enough to stretch the cheveril.

"If it's a Bible you want to write, Master Shakespeare, there's those would pay you to get it. Our side"—he cleared his throat, as if it were distasteful to him—"has an interest in the nature of god as well."

Will swallowed. *Politics. And yet—* He turned slowly, feet shuffling, cursing the slow, nodding oscillation of his chin, and looked Oxford in the eye. *And yet he's a bad enough poet I rewrote mine own plays under his eye, and he never saw the power I put in them. I could manage. Work for* their *Prometheans and undermine their very agenda from within. Ben and Kit and I could manage very well—*

"What would you wish of me, my lord? In return for such patronage?" Although he already knew what Oxford would demand.

The Earl smiled, reaching up to tilt his hat at the proper angle as he stepped back into the hurly-burly of Silver Street. "Don't answer today," he said. "But the Lord Chamberlain's Men perform before Her Majesty on the Feast of the Assumption."

"We do," Will said, struggling with feet that wanted to step back into the shadows, get his back to the wall of the tack shop he stood before.

"Consider," Oxford said, smiling, "whether your play will be a success, and the Queen's reign will be sustained. That is all. Consider it. And consider whether your Bible means more to you, William Shakespeare. These friends of mine. Friends of ours, I should say. Mutual friends. They're impressed with your work. They could give you everything you need. And you know"—a lowered tone—"her Majesty *is* unwell. And what's one old woman, past her three score already, in the face of the future of all Christianity?"

Will fixed a smile on his lips, thin as stage paint. His throat tightened. Just the palsy, doubtless. *Everything you need. Freedom to work.*

Yes, and all it cost is a brave old woman's life.

He hesitated, watching Oxford grin ironically, touch his hat—as if to an equal, or a rival—nod, and turn away. *One old woman's life.*

That's all.

Sweet Christ. This could be trouble for the whole company. I need to talk to Dick Burbage about this right away.

Act IV, scene viii

What virtue is it that is born with us?
Much less can honour be ascribed thereto;
Honour is purchased by the deeds we do.

—Christopher Marlowe,
Hero and Leander

Kit's heart weighed like a dreadful lodestone inside the linen that still bound his aching chest, but he pressed fingertips to the carved frame of the Darkling Glass and bent his will on Robin Goodfellow. He grasped the Puck's image without difficulty, surprised at his own confidence, and brought it close. The bandy little elf sat cross-legged in the embrace of a shaggy great willow, a triple pipe held in his hands and his head bowed over it. He blew breath through the reeds, but his fingers poised unmoving and the sound that whispered forth was more the wind through withies than any tune that Kit could call.

Kit clapped a hand on the pommel of his sword to steady it and grasped the rim of the mirror more firmly, pulling himself up as he stepped over the frame—the threshold—and *through.*

And down into crunching twigs and crisp leaves
under a crown of swaying yellow boughs like enchanted
snakes. Kit landed lightly, with flexed knee, sudden
movement still sharp as a dagger in his breast. The silver
sword flickered out like a tasting tongue as he advanced.
He didn't level it—quite—but he let it sway lightly in his
hand. "Robin—"

The Puck looked up, ears rising to attention, but the
flute didn't drift an inch lower. "Sir Poet. So fierce."

So many words, and so few of them useful. Kit made
himself steel and closed his heart to remembered kind-
nesses, pushing on. "—tell me thou had naught to do
with the murder of Will Shakespeare's little child?"

Puck drew his knees up and draped gawky arms
about them, letting his pipes dangle from his fingertips.
"Interesting you should phrase the question thus-and-
such, Sir Poet."

"Intentional. But should you lie to me, Robin, I'd
know."

The Puck stood, somehow graceless and fluid all at
once, gangling as a colt. He hung the pipes on his belt
and stretched up along a bough. "Poets are too precious
to sacrifice carelessly," he said, his long mouth down-
turned at the corners. "It had to be something other than
Shakespeare himself."

The blade of Kit's sword grew heavy, as if a hand
pressed down the flat. He let it sag until it touched the
gnarled root of the enormous tree, and came a step
forward. "Robin." Whatever the next word might have
been, it hung unvoiced on the air between them, leaden
with betrayal. Kit shook his head, slowly, and forced his
heavy arm to raise his sword as he tried again. "Will
Shakespeare was my friend. Even when thou didst this
thing, he was my friend—as thou knewest then. And I
thought I was thine."

Which was the heart of it, Kit knew. Of all the folk

he'd met in Faerie, there were only three he might have called that, *friend*. And Puck foremost among them.

Robin shrugged and leapt down from the tree branch, passing over Kit's sword like a tumbler. He leaned back against the trunk in a deceptively insouciant slouch. "There were reasons," he said.

"Reasons." Kit's hand shook on his blade. The wire grip cut his palm, and every breath hurt him. "What *reason* could possibly suffice for the murder of a boy barely old enough to prentice?"

"What's one mortal boy, more or less? They die soon enough, and one can always get another. Breed like rabbits, mortals do. And I needed thee, Kit, and needed thee fighting and thinking, not drowning in the dark. I thought if thy Shakespeare stepped back from his Queen, and thou didst go to comfort him, that there was a chance thou wouldst see the Mebd and dark Morgan for what they were, and win thy soul free. And it worked, it worked. How canst condemn me for that, when I had thee at heart, my dear?"

Oh, it was no use. He couldn't hold the sword up, and he couldn't have run little Robin through like a game hen on a spit even if he managed to lift the point. "It worked," Kit said. "Aye. And so Morgan sent me to Hell."

"And thy Shakespeare won thee back, and thou him free. And the tithe paid, and thou what thou art." Robin grinned. *See me? How clever?*

"Familiar demon," Kit said, unbearably weary. He dropped the sword on the leaves and stones, and sat down beside it on a willow root. Puck came closer, sat down beside him, companionate but not touching. "Robin, what hast thou done? Mortal boys are not for slaughtering like cattle. And why dost thou undertake that which harms thy mistress?"

The little Fae turned his head and spat. "That for my

mistress, Kit. Slave I am, bound in her hair, and so I may not defy her. We are all her slaves, all but Morgan, who is too strong for binding, and besides, I think me that Morgan knows the Mebd's name, and the Mebd knows not Morgan's."

"So how is it that you do oppose her? If she holds thee in thrall?"

"She never thought to forbid me of the deaths of mortals not taken in her service," Puck said, and shrugged. "If you tell her what I've done, she'll punish me."

"And if I kill you myself?" Kit made no effort to pick up his sword, and Puck made no effort to move away from him on their impromptu bench. Kit buried his head in his hands, fingers knotting in the dirty tangles of his curls.

The Fae leaned back, kicking his toadlike feet. "She might be displeased. Of course, you could prove I conspired against her." He laid a hand on the crease of Kit's elbow and squeezed; Kit shied away, twisting from the waist and leaning back. "And yet I imagine you of all people, Kit Marlin, would understand."

Kit nodded, savagely. "Aye. I know her glamourie. And Morgan's too, and would not feel the touch again."

"Imagine thou couldst not fight it," Puck replied. "What then wouldst do to be free?"

Kit had no answer. He shook his head. He bent down between his knees and picked the hilt of his sword off the earth. "What if I told Will?"

"What of it? Would he ask thee to take his vengeance, in his name?"

"I know not," Kit answered. He turned the blade over and over in his hands, watching dappled light ripple on the temper marks. "Thou hast done what thou hast done in accordance with thy nature and understanding. And thou hast preserved my life and freedom. Aye. And I do understand the freedom which thou dost seek. What, thee and Geoffrey too? Who else?"

"I cannot disclose to thee—"

"Never matter. I understand. And yet *thou* wilt understand that I cannot be thy friend, Master Goodfellow."

"'Twas thee thyself that saidst thou wouldst liefer lose thy life than thy liberty of speech, Sir Poet."

"Aye," Kit said, standing. *These are not people. Lest you ever forget. The Fae are not people. And who am I to judge someone who has done what he has done because he did it?* "I do recall saying it. And I do recall dying for it too, Master Puck. Good day to you."

"Wilt speak to thy Shakespeare?"

"Probably . . ." Kit answered, sheathing his sword and walking away. "Not," he finished, halting for a moment where the willow's ring of branches touched his hair. "Nor am I like to tell my Prince of thy machinations. And thus I am a traitor again to every soul I name friend."

"A traitor? Or a man?"

"Is there a difference?" Kit asked, and turned toward the palace again, and the mirror, and the pain of old injuries. And a conversation and a lie that he did not want to have, to tell.

Act IV, scene ix

Edgar: *The foul fiend haunts poor Tom in the voice of a nightingale. Hoppedance cries in Tom's belly for two white herring. Croak not, black angel; I have no food for thee.*

—WILLIAM SHAKESPEARE, *King Lear,*
Act III, scene vi

On the last day of 1599, in a receiving room at Greenwich Palace, Will leaned into the glow of an inconveniently placed lamp and frowned over his own atrocious penmanship, one of several players camped singly or in clumps in the puddles of light around the great dark hall. The windows were shuttered against a March storm, but the Queen was said to be in renewed spirits with the turning of the year, and the show must go on. He bent over his lines again, cursing the tremor in his hand that made the words shiver on the page, and trying not to think of his last, strange conversation with Kit and the long silence since, broken only by hasty letters.

A cultured voice interrupted his concentration. "Hast thought upon our offer, Master Shakespeare?"

Will glanced up from his part-script and frowned before he remembered to bow. He'd thought the contact would come from Oxford, perhaps in a form as simple as a note. He wasn't prepared to meet the ferrety countenance of Henry Wriothesly, the Earl of Southampton. The Earl was clad in snowy velvet, trimmed in white lace at the wrists. Whatever beauty the man had had in youth had dissipated, though he still wore his hair long enough to drape his shoulders and oiled in lovelocks like a girl's under his hat. His one visible hand was silk-soft, long, and white; he idly tapped its back with the cuff of the embroidered glove he held in the other. Will frowned to see the ring on Southampton's smallest finger: black steel, edged in a band of gold.

"You're wearing iron, my lord."

"And thou art not." A tilt of the head and a carefully elevated eyebrow.

Will did not press his fingers to his doublet to feel the iron nail in its soft leather pouch against his breast. Southampton drew his glove between his fingers. He switched it, Will thought, like a cat switching her tail.

"Master Shakespeare. Thy play today, what is it called?"

"*As You Like It,* my lord." And Will had thought hard about performing that one before the Queen, it was true, and deemed it not unmeet to prick Her Majesty's conscience a little. And if Essex were offended, or Oxford, so mote it be.

Even Southampton's smile was greasy. "And if I like it not?"

"Then may it please the Queen." *Bandy words not with me, cockerel. I may be a nodding invalid and a common player, and you an Earl. But I fence with the likes of Kit Marlowe and Ben Jonson, and you limit yourself to sycophants and tyros.*

Honesty forced him to, *And Queens,* but Will couldn't

imagine Southampton had ever won a round with Her Majesty.

An oily ferret, perhaps, but as dogged as a weasel. The Earl stepped back, a little further into the light, so it gleamed on his careful curls. "Dost expect it might?"

"Lies it within my power." Will found his shaking hand tightening on the sheaf of playscript; he raised the pages against his breast like a buckler, like a talisman. He glanced over Southampton's shoulder, across the room to where Burbage and two of the Wills bent Titian curls and dark over their part-scripts. Burbage posed between the taller, browner players so that they leaned over him like framing trees. He must have felt Will's gaze, because he glanced up; for a moment their gaze bridged the darkness from one puddle of light to the next.

"I rather hoped thou mightst have missed my patronage, Master Shakespeare—"

Will's eyes asked a question. Burbage's lips pursed, a gesture meant to be read. He glanced at the back of Southampton's head and shrugged once, softly, as if to say *do what thou must, I trust thee.* And then Burbage lowered his head again, and Will loosed a breath he hadn't realized he'd trapped, and fixed Southampton on an arch look that would have done Ned Alleyn proud.

"I am content," Will said, covering his cough with the back of his hand. He was aware that those three words were as bold a declaration of war as any he had penned into the mouth of an upstart lord. He bowed, but would not look down until Southampton nodded, slowly, and withdrew in a cloud of civet and rosewater.

The show must go on.

And go on it did, disrupted only slightly by the storm whining against the shutters and by Her Majesty's rattling cough, which diminished—Will thought—as the acts proceeded. She laughed at Touchstone the clown, and at Will's own appearance as a countrified version of himself, speaking direct to the audience for a moment's wit. He thought that boded well, and hoped perhaps he had been mistaken that the enemy had overcome the power of his words, although he wished her lead paint gone so he could see if her cheeks were flushed with fever or with delight.

It would in any case have been hard to tell by candlelight.

Spring wound into summer and high heat brought a resurgence of the plague and a cessation of the cough that had haunted Will all through the cold months. The winter's rain presaged a breaking of the long drought, and though the theatres were not closed for the inevitable plague, Will circulated sonnets and Ben staged poetical dinners. Under their influence the famine eased with the early crops and the fat spring lambs.

It was well it did, for in June Will heard the first rumors that the Spanish had landed at the Isle of Wight. Rumors he might have discounted if Elizabeth hadn't sent Essex and his men to Ireland to suppress rebellion abetted by Spanish Catholic troops. Will himself stood and watched as rattling chains with links a man could wear as bracelets were draped from shore to shore across the Thames, the inconvenience to shipping judged slight against the threat of the Spanish. There was talk in the nervous streets that the city might be defended by a bridge of boats, if the Spanish sailed up the mighty river; the city gates were locked and curfew enforced as it had not been in Will's memory, and all London breathed shallowly under threat of invasion. The Lord Chamberlain's Men performed *A Larum for London,* transparent fearmongering—but if Baines, Oxford, Southampton, and Essex's faction had hoped to use the threat of Catholic conquest to raise emotions against the Queen, Will was satisfied that he and Burbage had done what they could to thwart the plot.

My darling friend—

I send with great news, and some of it ill. Much of it, to tell you true, for oh, how I regret our old masters. Though Sir Francis labored under many a failure, and though he was as much a prince of lies as any Lucifer, still I did not doubt his loyalty. Now, I know not which spymaster nor weasel-keep to turn to in any extremity.

Sir Robert Cecil finally came forth with the order to raid the London home of a certain Richard Baines, my dear Mercutio. And I find my eyes big with wonder at the timing, for who did Cecil's men find a-slumbering in the deadly bed but Nicholas Skeres? And so it was Skeres arrested for counterfeiting, though he swore he knew not from whence the pewter coinings arose.

The house was searched on this evidence, but— worse luck—no bodies were discovered, buried in the earthen cellar or otherwise. Ben was beside himself with wrath, and had strong words with Tom Walsingham, as you might imagine. Tom, of course, had naught to do with the delay; so he says and so I believe him. Cecil, I fear, plays one of his double games.

Will rested the quill on the stand and frowned, rubbing his aching hand. He could tell Kit about young Robin Poley's golden hair—and why hint to the man that the boy he'd cared for as his own was the scion of the knave who helped to murder him?—or he could tell him about seeing Richard Baines in the crowd watching poetry, broadsides, and playscripts all burned in the bookseller's yard at St. Paul's, under the supervision of none other than that selfsame Sir Robert Cecil, the Queen's Secretary of State.

That last, yes. Kit should know.

Will leveraged his pen once more.

There is some small joy. Essex has returned from Ireland disgraced and defeated: the Queen would not see him. Ben is writing for the boys' companies. He grows stout and quarrels with everyone. It would include me, if he could raise my ire. Since I will not take the bait, he turns his venom on Chapman and Dekker and Marston—and especially Dick Burbage.

But Cecil's duplicity is manifest in what he burns, dear Mercutio. He is the very consuming flame, leaving only charred scraps of knowledge for those who come after. We attended his book-burning, Dick Burbage and I, and it was Dick who whispered in my ear, and now we are on our own in troth, gentle William.

I fear me he is only right. We cannot rely on princes and their agents any longer, gentle Mercutio. We must act by the strength of our own hands, if we are to preserve what we have won.

Come to London. Meet us at Tom Walsingham's study. We will craft our Bible no matter who says us nay.

And at the end of the long, fat, flyblown summer, Burbage and I and the others will open the Globe.

May it be our final weapon.

With love, my friend.
Your Romeo

Act IV, scene x

Kit leaned against the wall beside a bright window in Tom Walsingham's salon and watched Tom pace, and Will nod, and Ben trim the nib of a pen and smooth its shaft with a knife Kit thought was likely sharp enough to shave with. Which reminded him of his own need for a barbering, and he brushed his hand across rasping cheeks. *Unlikely as you are to be kissing anyone that cares. Or anyone at all, for that matter.* He sipped his wine and swirled it in the goblet, wishing bitterly that he could close the distance to the little coven by the fire and be one of them again. Wishing he could remember the touch of Will's hand, the press of Tom's mouth, without tasting the enormous soft emptiness that threatened to open like black wings and enfold him.

"Master Marlowe, if you are sufficiently refreshed, we could resume?" An *otherwise* light swirled from the tip of Ben's pen as he dipped it and bent over the papers spread on the table before him, never looking at Kit.

Kit set his wine well aside and came back to the musty-smelling book, gently sliding the ribbon aside to resume his place on the page. "Matthew?"

"Thereabouts," Ben answered.

Kit bristled at the big man's tone, backing down chiefly because Will turned enough to catch his eyes. Kit angled the Bible for better light and began to read aloud, in Greek, with, he thought, fair facility. Ben scribbled a literal and far from poetic translation, and Will read over his shoulder. Kit tried not to watch the casual camaraderie between the two, or the way Tom lounged by the fireplace, smiling his pleasure at the poets hard at work in his salon.

Kit's shoulder itched under his doublet. He reached up and over without pausing in his reading—nearly a recitation by heart, to be truthful—and absently rubbed at the tenderness of the witch's mark before he realized what he was about and forced himself to stop. As if in response, the scars on his torso and thighs flared white pain. He jumped and yelped, almost dropping the book. "Edakrusen o iesous!" *Damme, while Lucifer was healing things, he could have healed those too.*

"Christ," Ben growled. "Is there a cinder in your eye, now?"

"An old injury," Kit said, straightening the hang of his rapier. "Shall we continue?"

"Can we do it without interruptions?"

"Gentlemen—" Will, standing and moving between them. Kit cringed at the way his steps seemed hobbled, and set the Bible down, careful of its pages and spine.

"Your pardon, Will," Kit said, as Ben dropped his quill into the inkpot and turned over the chair back to face Kit.

"Tell me, Master Marlowe," he said. "Is it true a witch kisses the Devil's bunghole to pay for his powers?"

"Master Jonson," Kit replied, letting his left hand fall

from the hilt of his sword as he moved away from the wall. "Come, kiss mine and find out."

"If I were to play the sodomite, I should choose, I trust, a less slant-heeled paramour."

"Gentlemen." Tom Walsingham, this time, stepping away from the fireplace to lend the support of his stature to Will's plea for peace.

"As a point of fact," Kit said, through that same imperturbable smile, "that's only part of the process. An enjoyable one, if performed faithfully"—ignoring Will's livid blush, and Tom's sudden coughing fit—"and I might offer to demonstrate, but I prefer my bedfellows agreeable in—"

"Christofer, so help me God—"

"—body *and* temperament, and you, dear Ben, are neither, and have neither—"

"Kit!"

"Yes, Sir Thomas?" Sweetly, with his best and gentlest smile.

"Enough. Just enough, both of you."

"Yes, Sir Thomas—" Kit gasped and doubled over as another ripple of fire caressed his body. He went to one knee, pushed both hands before him to keep from collapsing to the floor, and bit down on a scream. "Will, my cloak. . . ."

Will was already moving; not fast enough, as Jonson levered his bulk from the chair and swept Kit's cloak from the pile in the corner. He threw it about Kit's shoulders and tugged it tight. Kit leaned back on his heels, breathing again, gripping the collar in his left hand.

They crowded him, and he waved them back, wobbling to his feet with assistance and a warning glance from Tom. Kit looked from Tom to Will, and Will to Tom. "What, sweet Thomas, not devilish enough for thee?" But he gave himself over to the half a smile that bubbled up, despite his frustration, and offered it to Tom as an indicator of peace before turning back to Ben. "A kindness, Master Jonson," he said. "I will not forget it."

"What was that?" asked Tom, concerned.

Kit shrugged and reached for his wine. "The Prometheans seeking me through old scars, perhaps—"

Jonson's mouth twisted as he nodded. "Then shall we continue?"

But Kit felt a hot wind ruffle his cloak, and saw Ben's eyes suddenly widen. :Come:

The light that streamed past Kit was brighter than that from the window. White, and not the pale gold of winter afternoons. Kit set down his cup and turned into it, facing a jeweled, starlit darkness that seemed to unscroll within the room. He tugged his cloak close.

"Kit." Will and Tom, as one, and Ben a moment behind: "Master Marlowe—"

:Come, my love:

"I have to go," Kit said, turning over his patchworked shoulder to regard the other three. "He's calling me." He looked away with effort and squared his shoulders, and stepped into the light.

Angels singing, and cries—those cries that might be ecstasy or might be grief: he could not say. Broad arms, white wings, enfolded him in comfort; the last lingering burning of his scars faded into cool and calm as Lucifer held him close and stroked his hair.

"What have you done to me?" Kit asked, recovering himself enough to step away, for all the brush of those wings fanned the longing in him to a sharp, pale flame. He stood beside the Devil as if on nothingness, surrounded by stars. Despite himself, he threw back his head, his hair brushing his collar, and stared up into the vaulted, sparking void above.

:Not I: Lucifer regarded him, smiling, a vision in black breeches and a billowing shirt of ivory silk, which seemed dark against the milk and roses of his skin. He cupped a wing forward, extended a hand: fingers and feathers swept down Kit's arm as one. :Those scars and what they contain came into thee before I did:

"Why did you not heal them when you did mine eye?"

:They suit me:

"Can the enemy find me through them?"

:Perhaps. But what touched thee just now was the reaction of that which lies within thee to the Word: Again the caress, a drawing close, the encirclement of those sheltering angel wings.

Ah. Kit pulled back. "I do not wish your touch, Father of Lies."

:Who knows a lie when he hears one. What other touch dost crave, who was Christofer Marley?:

There was no answer, and Lucifer knew it. Kit turned to track a blazing comet tumbling across the heavens. "What do my scars contain?"

Silence. He turned and looked Lucifer in the eyes. The Devil's soft smile never altered.

"Will said Morgan said something similar—" Something shifted in Kit's breast, an emotion seemingly just beyond the brush of his fingers. "I do not understand what you wish of me, Morningstar, or why you have come to me now."

:I came for that within thee calleth me in his suffering, at his grief to hear the Word:

"That within me?"

Silence, and a smile.

Kit shook his head like a horse reined too tight. "Surely you have poets aplenty, and one more damned soul cannot mean much to such as you—"

:How many damned souls: the Devil said, his words no more than the susurrus of wings, :dost suppose have ever gazed on me with pity?:

"Oh." *Damn me,* Kit thought. *And here I thought Edward was my masterpiece.* "A companion heart."

:Neither am I permitted such: Even in darkness, Lucifer's wings shed light—a deep and subtle glow like moonbeams, that seemed to turn every detail of Kit's clothing and form into a thin sketch in charcoal, echoing his heart. :And only the damned believe in me:

"Is that what you need them for? The damned? To believe?"

:Canst feel God here?:

"No."

:Nor can I: Lucifer's eyes were dark, and bright. :Ask again what thou containest, and I will tell thee—:

"Morgan said to Will that I could not bear to know it."

:Neither canst bear what thou hast locked in thy breast, my love:

"Lucifer." Kit put his hand to his mouth, shocked at the name that escaped his lips, the exasperation in it.

:Thou hast not said that name in my hearing before:

"I wrote it—"

:Aye. *His waxen wings did mount above his reach / And melting, heavens conspir'd his overthrow*—I have paid thee for the poetry, in mine own coin, and thou hast bought what else thou hadst from me. Wilt treat with me now as a friend?:

"If such as I could be friend to such as . . . thee."

:We are alike—damned and not-damned, abjured by God for that which he created us. An he be all he claims, who was Christofer Marley, has he not failed in creating us irredeemable?:

"The Catholics would redeem us," Kit said, crouching to warm his hands before a star that grew and flowered close beside his feet. They stood on one of the crystal vaults of heaven: far below, he could discern the shifting blue-white orb of the Earth. "If we forswore all for the love of God." He paused, pressing his fingers to the crystal, so pure it was invisible. "An we were closer, I might amend some maps."

A laugh, and the brush of feathers along his spine, affectionately disarraying his hair. :I keep the damned because the damned believe in me, my love, and belief is my power. Ask me thy question again, an thou wouldst hear mine answer:

"Lucifer." Fear darted on bright wings in his breast as he stood. *He's right. I do not wish to know the answer. And yet I must*—"What sorcery did Richard Baines work upon and through me?"

:A binding and a sealing within. A rape to abrogate the barriers of thyself, and a star burned into thy flesh to lock within that which thy prayers lured into thee, when thou didst raise thy voice to God for aid, and aid was sent:

Kit turned to look the Devil in the eye. "Thou"—an effort to say it, and Satan's amusement made it worse—"sayest I have a cage for an *angel* burned on my skin?"

:Aye:

"Why?" Kit staggered. His scars flared so hot he thought they might burn through his doublet, and he drew his cloak tight as Lucifer cupped his shoulders with one bright wing. Kit hunched into the Devil's arms. "And moreover, how?"

:Tell me who the angel Mehiel is:

Kit closed his eyes, thinking. *Mehiel.* Amaranth had been right: he'd found the name easily in London. "Protector of poets, authors, and lecturers. He's also the angel under whose wardenship my birthday falls, if thou dost believe such things. But those are papist superstitions—"

:Are they?: The golden brows rose, rumpling the ivory

forehead. :Tell me, then, which of my brothers would come to thee in thy hour of need, Sir Poet?:

Oh, God.

:Nay. But a bit of His creation, more kindly disposed to thee than most, to help thee bear thy pain. And now he hears the name of God and seeks to burst his prison, but his prison is thy mortal flesh:

"No," Kit said. He pressed his fist against his chest, heart thundering against the backs of his fingers. "No. It is not so."

:If devils may be bound: Lucifer murmured, pitiless, :why, so may God's angels, for we are brothers, all:

"But *why*?" Such a small voice, Kit could hardly believe it came from his own throat. He would have fallen if Lucifer's white wings and arms hadn't borne him up; the pain in his breast was incapacitating, his eyes burning so hot he could not think anything but fire flowed down his cheeks.

Lucifer lifted the folds of Kit's patchwork cloak with a wing tip, violent colors draped over the whiteness of his feathers, and held it before Kit's eyes. It caught the light of all the vaults of heaven, the planets spinning below and the stationary stars all around. :The magic of sympathy: he said. :To bind the angel within thee, and then to bind thine own magic and thy voice, and then to take thee in servitude, and cripple thy power with fear and loathing and the hatred of thine own weakness they put in thee. 'Tis half the reason their opposition of thy plays, and Shakespeare's, has been so successful. That thou hadst any success at all is a testament to the power of thy will—and thy Will, also:

God, Kit thought, understanding finally why it was that Richard Baines had let him live, until he'd proven once and for all that he would *not* let them control him. Why everyone—Prometheans, Faerie, Hell—seemed bent on owning him, no matter the cost. "But why would God send an angel to—*me? Why would He care?"*

:God will not save thee: A knowing voice, and one burning with pain like embers banked and buried in the ash. :But He will of a time give thee the strength to endure what horrors His servants do visit upon thee:

Kit swallowed, hearing the voice, feeling that filthy caress on his filthy hair—*If we have a chance to complete the wreaking in London, it would help to use the same vessel. Even more if he were willing, of course. Although mayhap our little catamite liked it, considering his tastes.*

Did you like it, puss?

They raped an angel. Through me. They raped an angel in my body. My angel. It wasn't rage he felt, but a great disbelief and weariness; the rousing of an exhausted, possessive jealousy.

Consummatum est. Lucifer's gentleness made Kit want to retch. "He wasn't only talking to me, was he?" *Did you like it, puss?* "It was a promise to—what they put in me. Something to think about."

:Aye:

"I thought the dark Prometheans thought they were—God's chosen."

:They are: Lucifer answered calmly. :The God they intend to create. And what is bound in thee is part of that creation, a chink in the armor of the Divine. As thy cloak offers thee a symbol of the scrap of protection and grace offered thee by each one who contributes to it—so what is done to thee is done to Mehiel, and that which is done unto Mehiel is done unto God:

The spaces underfoot and overhead made him dizzy. *This is Hell too,* he thought. *For it is not Heaven.* "If this works," Kit asked, a spark of doubt flaring in his soul as he thought of Will and Ben hard at work over verses and translation, "why have you not taken it on yourself to make a God of your own?"

:Sweet Poet: Mockery, and a warm wing across his shoulders. :Have I not? Why didst think I chose thee, my love? What dost thou think thy *Faustus* will create, given history and the acclaim it deserves?:

"I have an angel burned on my skin," Kit said, wondering. "What happens if I set him free?"

:If thou canst discover how. I do not know that he can be freed without the destruction of the prison that contains him:

Me. Kit sagged, and turned his face to the silk of Satan's shirt when the angel embraced him once more. The tears were dry on his face, if they had been water and not flames, and he leaned into the embrace and the scent of smoke and forgetfulness that surrounded Lucifer, and the warmth of those wings, and the cold starlight gleaming between his boots and on his hair. *God sent an angel to bear my pain. And I have hated God all these years for failing to answer my prayers.*

As they said in Faerie, all stories were true. But some stories were more true than others.

Did you like it, puss?

:Well?: Lucifer asked, some eternity later. :Was Morgan correct, again? Has't broken thee, this knowing?:

"Yes," Kit said, and somewhere found a last black scrap of humor, and managed not to shiver as he spoke. "At least for today."

:Brave Poet: the Devil said, and held him among the darkness and the stars for a little while longer, until Kit raised his face from the soft white curve of Satan's wing.

"There's a shining sort of irony in Lucifer giving God back to a man God doesn't want."

:Poetry grows through the broken places, brother: The wings opened around him; Kit stood under their arch, but they no longer restrained or warmed him.

Within and yet without, and boldly he laid his hand

on the feathers again and ruffled them up, stroked them smooth. Whatever moved in Kit was vast and slow, a symphony of emotion that swelled from discord into something complex and bittersweet and whole. "Brother . . . an we are friends, then. And thou dost value my friendship—" It wouldn't come into words, exactly, but he knew perfectly well that Lucifer could read his tangle of emotions and half-formed thoughts as plainly as a poem. The Devil might claim he could not see in human hearts. But Lucifer was, after all, the Prince of Lies.

And when those lies went cloaked in truth, so much the better.

Lucifer tilted his head, considering, watching Kit's hand linger among his feathers. :The pain and sickness thou feelst at thy lovers' touch. And yet not at mine—:

"If we are to be friends—"

:Sir Poet: When Satan ducked his head and smiled crookedly at Kit, it folded sharp creases from the corners of his long, slightly crooked nose to the corners of his mouth. The blue eyes crinkled in an interested sort of mockery, and Kit felt suddenly as if some bright fluid buoyed him. :'Tis thine own soul's wreaking, and a sensible one; 'tis but that the wall Mehiel and thyself didst build about thy garden of suffering—and his—after Rheims has fallen:

". . . fallen?"

:The angel Mehiel has seen the truth, that hiding thy pain from thee has not made thee strong, but concealed the flaw within. He hath lifted his wings, and thou must needs now tend the blasted heath within. Friend Poet, heal thyself, and thou wilt be whole:

"The blasted heath? Or the blasted *heart*?" Kit asked wryly, but he found himself stepping back from the angel and the devastating truth in his words. Something within Kit's breast stirred with a pain like trapped and beating wings. "How many men does the Devil call friend?"

The broad wings folded with a breeze that savored of lavender. Lucifer too stepped back. "As many as offer him understanding."

Barely on a breath, a murmur, a whisper—and the sound of Lucifer's spoken *voice* staggered Kit nonetheless. It resonated through the crystal under Kit's feet, through the chamber of his lungs and heart, striking sparks from his hair and his fingertips. That tolling bell, that falcon's cry, that shriek of joy and agony that Kit recognized from his dreams hung inside his mind, and he knew it now for the voice of the angel within.

"Oh, my," Kit whispered, as the Devil reached out and took his forearms in white fingers, and smiled again, and met his gaze. Lucifer's eyes shone transparent, blue as the sunlit vault of Heaven, and Kit held his breath. *Thou art—*

:I always suspected that thou didst thy Mephostophilis love, a little:

Kit laughed and would have broken the eye contact, but the Devil's smile held him. He shivered and swallowed, and with an act of raw will managed to look down. "Rather I fancied myself a sort of Mephostophilis—"

:And not Faustus?:

"Who would wish to be Faustus?" Kit said, and stepped forward, and boldly, chastely, kissed Lucifer on the mouth. The Devil permitted the caress, returned it— a gentle, considering tasting as unlike the blinding passion of another time as kiss from kiss could be. Kit did not step back after, but spoke against Lucifer's smooth-skinned jaw, feeling the prickles of his beard rasp the angel's cheek. "Poor damned fool, reaching beyond any sane measure of wisdom for something he could see, but scarcely understand. I would not wish to be him, but aye—I understood and pitied him."

:And hast thou who wert Christofer Marley not reached all thy life for that which eluded thy grasp?:

"Thou must find somewhat less unwieldy by which to address me," Kit said, but the Devil would not be diverted.

:If thou art Mephostophilis:—Lucifer spread wide his bright, beckoning wings—:then I am Faustus. Come and teach me thy pity again:

Act IV, scene xi .

***Antonio:** A witchcraft drew me hither:*
That most ingrateful boy there by your side,
From the rude sea's enraged and foamy mouth
Did I redeem; a wreck past hope he was:
His life I gave him and did thereto add
My love, without retention or restraint,

—WILLIAM SHAKESPEARE, *Twelfth Night,*
Act V, scene i

Curfew and the failing light forced Will home before
sunset that night; he walked through London's
crowded streets, his breath streaming before him
like a cart horse's in the cold. He turned his ankle on an
icy stone, but a passerby caught his elbow and saved him
from a nasty fall, and he made it to the double-gabled
house on Silver Street intact. And wasn't sure if he was
startled or passionately unsurprised to find Kit waiting
for him, curled on the narrow bed with his back to the
corner, his cloak pulled up to his chin like a child's favorite blanket. Will saw with gratitude that Kit had built
the fire up and set wine to warm beside it.

"Back from Hell in one piece, love?" Will tossed his gloves on the table and crouched at the hearth, pressing his palms to rough, ashy stone for the warmth.

"Never out of it," Kit replied. "It turns out Mephostophilis was right. Who would have imagined it?"

"Thee."

"Aye—" He sighed, and didn't stand. "If thou'rt pouring the wine, bring me some."

"Of course." Will did, and stood, and leaned on the edge of the bed facing Kit. "Ben rather didn't handle thy vanishment well. But thank thee for coming to prove thy health to me—"

"I imagined he might not." Kit sipped the wine Will pressed into his hands, and made a face. "I let it sit too long."

" 'Tis better than a chill in the belly," Will answered complacently. "No, Ben's troubled on many fronts. He's started a little war of wits with the redheads, and Chapman has it he's angry with me because Her Majesty— much improved in health, I mention in passing—" Kit grinned, showing wine-stained teeth. "—has commissioned a play for Twelfth Night. Another comedy."

"I saw the pages on the table."

"Thou'rt incorrigible."

"I am. I liked the tragedy you've half done better, and the history was quite good."

"Kit, how long have you been here?"

"An hour or six." Kit hid his face behind his wine. "Her Majesty was never much for blood when she could be made to laugh. Pray, continue."

"A masque of Ben's was passed over." Will shrugged and drank his wine, redolent of the spices Kit had stewed in it. "He's fussing."

"Over a *masque*?"

"Times have changed," Will said, and set his cup aside. "Masques and satires are all the rage. I have to finish the

Henry quickly: there's a rumor that history plays will be forbidden. Books have burned, and not just Catholic treatises—" He stopped himself. Kit raised his chin and blinked long, dark gold lashes.

"Books?"

"Nashe," Will said unwillingly. "Harvey too. And new printings forbidden. I think our enemies have some hold over the Archbishop now. Whitgift. Or perhaps he simply fears the Puritans and their rising strength. And Elizabeth doth love him."

"Oh, poor Tom." Kit fell silent for a long moment, and leaned back against the wall. "Masques and satires the fashion. And comedies."

"Aye, and comedies—"

Kit smiled. "But the great William Shakespeare is immune to fashion. I'll wager what you like that your *Hamlet* will outdraw whatever Ben puts on."

"Kit—" Ah, what do you say, and how do you say it? "Oxford and Southampton have been making . . . grappling runs. They want me to poison the queen."

"With arsenic? A pretty trick, when she will not dine in company."

Will shook his head, and said, "With poetry." And then he turned and twisted his hand around his wrist, and said, " 'Twere treason even to hear them, Kit."

Kit licked his lips. "Wilt testify to what they asked?"

Will snorted. "Would Elizabeth hear me?"

Something in what he said had started Kit thinking. His fingers moved idly on the base of his cup; a line drew itself between his brows. "Mayhap," he said, and then finished his wine at a draught and gave the cup over to Will for disposal. He hitched himself forward and let the cloak fall open over his habitual black doublet, this one sewn with garnets and tourmalines.

"You're a sumptuary fine waiting for a magistrate," Will said cheerfully, abandoning other concerns.

Kit laughed. "They may leave the writ with my land-lord. Will—" He reached out, and to Will's startled pleasure, laid hands on his shoulders where the neck ran into them, pressing slightly. "I've looked into Hamnet's death." *Murder.* Kit didn't say the word, but it shone in his eyes.

"And?"

He sighed, squeezed once more, and drew back. "I'm—investigating."

"You know something."

Kit's supple lips pressed thin, twisting at the corner. "I know who gave the order and why."

"Kit." A forlorn pain he'd almost managed to forget drained the blood and breath and warmth from Will's body, left his fingers wringing white and shaking. Kit laid a hand over Will's, and almost managed to make it look as if the gesture did not pain him.

"Will—" Kit sighed. "It's a fey thing. I don't know if human justice . . . Dammit. Yes. I could kill someone. And I know whom to kill. And I could bring thee his head on a pole, and call it thy son's murderer brought to justice, love."

"But . . . ?"

Kit waved his other hand hopelessly in the direction of the table and its neat stacks of foul copy. "I would do it for thee. Will do it an thou but ask. And it will turn into *Titus*."

"A revenge tragedy. Oh." Will squeezed Kit's hand tight enough that the palsy deserted him. Kit flinched; Will saw it in the tightness at the corners of his eyes, and let the contact ease. Slowly he drew his hands back and folded them on his knee. He swallowed pain-fully and met Kit's eyes very carefully as he changed the subject. "Nick Skeres hasn't been executed yet. Or even convicted."

Act IV, scene xii

'Twere a far easier thing to obtain an audience with the Queen in Faerie than with the Queen in London, and Kit was grateful for it. At the appointed hour, he presented himself—not in her Presence Chamber, but in the red study she used for privy conversation. Kit had never seen her private chamber, and expected he never would.

Robin Goodfellow showed him within and drew shut the door, and Kit stood blinking in the dimness, bowing before a shadow he thought might be the queen.

"Stand up," the shadow said, a rustle of stiff embroidery punctuating her words. "Come, Sir Christopher. Kindle a light; there are candles all abound."

"I have no flame, nor spill," he answered.

"Need you such?" And oh, the stark mockery in her voice. She knew he did not.

Silent, he touched every wick in the room into dazzling light.

"How prettily you answer," she said, while he frowned to see her. The Mebd looked gray and drawn, her golden hair dry in its braids and rough as hay. She curled in a great chair, knees drawn up under her robes so the skirts draped empty down the front.

"Your Majesty," he said, stepping forward. "You seem—"

She smiled, and the smile silenced him. "Your audience, Poet," she said. "Use it fitly."

He swallowed, and nodded. "Your Majesty. I have evidence of a plot against your sister Queen, and thus by extension, against your own person. And I have witnesses willing to give that information."

"And you come to me, Sir Christopher, and not your Elizabeth?"

He closed his eyes, and hoped she would not see it for the depth of his genuflection. "You are my Queen," he said. "And Elizabeth may hear you, my lady, where she will not hear another."

Act IV, scene xiii

Words before blows: is it so, countrymen?

—WILLIAM SHAKESPEARE,
Julius Caesar, Act V, scene i

The winter saw their translation of the New Testament creeping forward between other commitments, and the Christmas season passed without incident. On January sixth Will found himself again in Greenwich, helping Burbage with his paint and wondering at the boys who, only a handspan of years before, had shivered in their boots at the thought of a court performance. The play was *Twelfth Night,* which Will thought was a bad title, but it suited the day. "Thou drinkst too much, Richard," he said, smearing the broken veins on Burbage's nose with ceruse. " 'Twill be thy death—"

"—if playing isn't," Burbage said, indifferent. "Thy lips are pale."

"We've fucus and vermilion enough to paint a court." Will suited action to words, dabbing a brush into a pot, and then bending over Burbage's face. The hand that bore the pot trembled. The one holding the brush did not.

"We should drop that vile old history of John from the repertory."

"Vile?" Will jabbed Burbage lightly on the lip. "What wouldst replace it with?"

Burbage leaned back to give Will more light and a better angle. He arched a calculated brow. "Thou'lt write me somewhat. And if not thee, Dekker—"

"Dekker will pen thee somewhat that will stand ten playings, half to half a house. Hardly worth the learning of the lines." Will grinned wickedly. "Mayhap I'll to Henslowe—"

"You wouldn't."

Will shrugged, and Burbage laughed. "Aye, he'll pay thee eight pound for five acts, and get Tom to mend it bloodier—"

Will set down his brush, a warmth like a good hearth lightening his limbs. "Here, look thou in the mirror—" Will glanced up, feeling someone's regard on his neck. He turned, caught a glimpse of patchworked cloak in the sunlight through the windows, and patted Richard on the shoulder. "Remember thy kohl."

"Will—"

"I must see a man," Will said, and retrieved his cane from where it leaned against the makeup table. He trailed the swing of the patchwork cloak into the shadows, caught a glimpse of dark hair and the heavy sway of layers upon layers of cloth, and knew it was not Kit he followed.

Cairbre waited for Will in a niche between a massive pillar and the painted, embossed leather upon the walls. Light reflected from the spotty snow beyond the window and brightened the little space; the Faerie Queen's bard turned and laid a gloved hand against the glass. "So cold," he said.

Faerie had no cold like England; rather it had the

dream of cold, and the memory of frost. "Master Tattercoats."

"Master Poet." Cairbre turned and smiled. "You must visit us again. Your plays are missed, and you keep our own Sir Kit so busy on your errands he scarce has time to sing for us—"

Will blinked—*my errands? I do not think so*—and remembered to smile before he gave the Fae anything for free. He came to stand beside Cairbre, who stepped aside to offer him half the view. The Thames stretched long and ice-rimed between her banks, the tide brimming. The snowbanks along the palace's walkways slumped. No new snow had fallen to make them fresh and crisp again. "You've come on Twelfth Night to castigate me for o'erborrowing your poet?" he asked, dryly ironical.

Cairbre glanced over, warmth rounding his cheeks. "No, I've come to tell you that the Queen of the Daoine Sidhe will be in your audience tonight, by special invitation of the Queen of England. Under glamourie of course—"

"Morgan?" Will coughed, put his player's game face on and corrected the stammer. "I mean, will Morgan le Fey be here as well?"

Cairbre chuckled, raising his eyes to the horizon. "That," he said, shrugging his cloak off one shoulder, "is for Fata Morgana to decide. If anyone has informed her of the expedition. Or if she has discovered it through means of her own." He glanced sidelong at Will and winked. "She's not invited, if that's what you mean."

Will sighed and nodded, unsure if the lightness in his belly was relief or disappointment. "If I am invited, Master Bard, I would love to return to Faerie some day."

A long gloved hand touched Will's earring, and the black-haired bard smiled. "You would be welcome," he said, white teeth flashing behind his beard. "And now you must see to your painting, player. Your audience awaits."

The play was plainly unopposed, although Oxford and Southampton lingered uncomfortably close throughout. Will attributed that as much to Essex's absence as the power of his own words. Sir Walter Raleigh was in attendance, his star evidently on the ascendant given his post close beside the Queen—as Oxford's seemed to be waning. Raleigh's black doublet glistened with pearls, reminding Will painfully of Kit whenever he turned his eyes to the audience. Raleigh was masked as a fox, and Will thought it went very well with his expression; Sir Robert Cecil was a natural as a wolf on the Queen's other hand.

Elizabeth herself wore a red little smile, painted lips twitching with restrained mirth above the fabulous abundance of her red-and-white feathered fan, her face unmasked but her hair twined with pearls and swan's feathers, and her gown all white and worked to look like snowy plumage. More interesting to Will was the chair of estate set close beside Elizabeth's and only a little lower, against whose cushioned surface reclined a lady whose pale golden hair was dressed in a jeweled tire tall enough for a Queen. Her face was concealed behind a black velvet mask strewn with diamonds, and diamonds gleamed in the candlelight among the gauzy black silk of her veils. *The Queen of Air and Darkness,* Will thought, meeting the eyes of the black-clad and velvet-masked man who was the smallest of three identically clad standing at *her* left shoulder.

Kit blew Will a kiss across the gathered courtiers as Will made his final exit, and Will tripped on the smooth boards of the stage. Burbage caught his elbow, and—with playerly flamboyance—made it look like a bit of business as they exited left. Not what Kemp would have managed before he left them, but the Queen threw back her head to laugh.

"Hast heard who the mysterious beauty by the Queen might be, Richard?" Will wondered what the court gossip said. He knew very well who the lady was, with Prince Murchaud of the Daoine Sidhe, Cairbre the bard, and Sir Christopher Marlowe standing like a bishop, a rook, and a knight at her back.

Burbage glanced over his shoulder as they stepped off the boards. "There's a rumor 'tis Anne of Denmark."

"Anne of Scotland, thou meanst? James' Queen?" It *was* a delicious rumor. Will resolved to spread it at every opportunity.

"One and the same," Burbage allowed, shrugging his doublet off. "By any name a Queen."

It had been Will's last exit; he helped Burbage hastily with the change. "Why should such a woman come to England?"

Will buttoned from the bottom; Burbage buttoned from the top. " 'Tis said Gloriana favors Scottish James. 'Tis not impossible she would send for his Queen, to be taught the ways of the court."

"Essex favored James—"

"Aye, and Essex is out of favor, with Oxford. I wonder that Gloriana has not noticed how her health improves when they are sent from her side. But see how close Cecil stays by his Queen? Like a hound on a lead."

"What of it?"

"Cecil favors the Archduchess Isabella, they say."

"A Spanish Queen," Will said. "After all his father's wars on the Catholics?" Only a player's practice kept the bitterness out of his voice. *These wars are meaningless—*

—aye, Will, and thou art a soldier in them nonetheless.

"Anne's Catholic too." Burbage finished his buttons

and lifted his chin for Will to pin his ruff. "I hear it put about that Arabella Stewart has a stronger claim than either."

"Shall England be ruled by Queens forevermore?" But Will glanced around the screen at the slender, gracious blonde upon the dais, her fair head turned in appreciation of one of the many misguided seductions in his play. Disloyalty stabbed him as he regarded the fair head and the auburn one, one face masked in velvet and the other in swan-white ceruse. *And would Queens do a worse job of it than kings?*

The Mebd was never Anne of Denmark. And the earring in Will's ear weighed heavily as he opened his mouth to amend his speech—and Will Sly bumped him from behind. Will swore, and Sly flinched and steadied him with a hasty grip. "Zounds, Will, I'm not made of glass—"

Sly looked him hard in the eye and frowned. "Nay, Will. Nor so steady on thy feet as thou might be. Forgive it for a courtesy—"

"Nay, Will. 'Tis an apology I owe thee. I am tired and in pain. . . . Dicky-bird, thou'rt done—"

"Dicky," Burbage snorted, and flashed Will his legended grin before he stepped away, in place for his entrance. Will's eye followed him as Sly followed. He made sure neither man saw him cling to the edge of the tiring table.

The Mebd would have liked it if Orsinio got the rack. Elizabeth preferred the conventional ending. *Alas.* But both Queens praised the performance, and Will smiled in a childlike delight in being the only player there who knew how rare a thing that was. He didn't smile at all when Sir Walter—with his fox-mask pushed up over his carefully coifed hair and his beard dyed an unnatural, foxy red—cut him out of the crowd of players and drew him into the shadow of an arras. "The Queen should like to see thee in private, Master Playmaker."

Will looked in Raleigh's glittering eyes. His mouth was dry; he licked his lips before he answered. "What do you know about poets and poetry, Sir Walter?"

"Enough to pay Edmund Spenser a pension," Raleigh answered. "And I did my bit to keep Kit Marlowe overdressed as well. Oh, you didn't know that? No, I see you didn't. I know it was foolishness what Jonson put out about Spenser's death." He grinned, showing blackened teeth. "And I parroted it to all those that liked Essex least. Pity about poor Ned, however."

Will laughed. "Essex's enemy is any poet's friend?"

"When that poet is for England and her Queen, aye. Be careful tonight, Master Shakespeare. We can ill afford to lose you, too." Raleigh laid a gloved hand on Will's doublet sleeve just below the lacings and turned him away from the bustle of the room. "Come, I'll show you where."

Both Queens were in the retiring room when Raleigh ushered Will inside. He crossed—not rushes, but a thick carpet he almost recognized, doubtless a gift to Elizabeth from the Faerie Queen—and knelt before the gilded chairs in which the two monarchs sat, giggling behind their fans like girls. The image was shattered when he saw their faces, though: Elizabeth was no girl, and the Mebd seemed thin behind her mask.

The Mebd's three knights flanked her chair; Will caught a glimpse of Kit's pouting lower lip below the black velvet of his mask and bit his own lip hard at an utterly inappropriate flaring of desire. Behind Elizabeth's chair stood Sir Robert Cecil and George Carey, the Secretary of State and the Lord Chamberlain. Carey carried the conceit of the fox and the wolf to completion: he was masked as a hunting mastiff, his ruff arranged in fantastic spikes like a bear-baiting collar. His long jowls under the mask completed the picture. Sir Walter Raleigh went to join them. *The Queen's fox, her wolf, her hound.* In contrast, the Mebd's men wore black simply, and their masks were soft black velvet sculpted into stern vacancy.

Will, watching through his lashes, might have smiled at the perfect staging of it: a woman in sable scattered with diamonds, and a woman in white wrought with pearls, and behind each one three masked gentlemen all richly garbed in black.

And before them, slightly off center so his burgundy slashed doublet and round hose would be displayed at advantage against the fiery white of the Swan-Queen's gown, one supplicant poet with his hat upside down in his hand.

"Master Shakespeare," said Queen Elizabeth, after a suitable time had elapsed. Her fan moved gracefully. "We wish to thank you for all that you have done for us. Please rise."

"Your Highness' thanks are unnecessary," Will said, when he had collected himself and pushed himself up with his cane. "But welcome. Although a humble player might wonder what monarchs would make of him."

Elizabeth glanced at her sister queen and smiled. *Clever boy.* Aye, and they both loved cleverness. Kit winked at Will over his Queen's diamond-studded shoulder, and Will's knees half melted before he quite forced his gaze back to Elizabeth. *Damn honor,* he thought. *And damn vows.*

Which was why Will had told Kit what he had, about Annie and his promise to remain faithful. Because he understood by now that Kit wouldn't offer where he wasn't certain of his welcome, and that as long as Kit didn't offer, Will could pretend he would refuse.

The world was full of other temptations, too—pretty, willing goodwives and tiresses and innkeepers—Mistress

Poley, who would gladly have him in Kit's stead, he thought, and Jenet at the inn he often overnighted in along the way to Stratford. But surely he could manage a little continence after fifty years in Hell.

The Queen looked back. "Your heart is divided, Master Shakespeare."

"As whose is not, Your Highness?" He'd scored. He saw it in the constriction of her mouth, and then the gracious tilt of her head, acknowledging the point. Somehow, the softness in her deep gray eyes was worse than censure or a Queen's cold wrath. "And yet I serve my Queen and Her England in all things," he concluded, making as pretty a bow as he could with his cane and his hat to contend with.

"In all things?"

"Over love or gold," Will said, and understood why he was being made to do this before Kit, and the Mebd. *So show the whole world where thy loyalty lies. And I am sorry.* It was true, what he said, as far as it went. Over love. Over gold. But not over the destiny of all Christendom.

And he could see from the smile in Elizabeth's eyes, the rapid flicker of her fan, that she understood. Understood, and approved? Will swallowed despite the lump that now always blocked his throat, and with a flash of the insight that had given him *Hamlet,* William *understood* his Queen in return. Not the ragged, painted, old woman before him, but the girl who had led a man like Francis Walsingham to beggar himself in her service, when with his dying breath he had known she could never show him gratitude. A woman who had given Kit Marley to the Faeries, when it would have been easier and safer to end his life and let him tumble into an unmarked grave. *It doesn't matter if Essex betrays her. It doesn't matter what Scottish Mary did or did not know when she was led to the block. Elizabeth understands that every drop of that blood stains her own hands. She knows. She knows she goes to judgement to face each life she's wasted. And she's always known.*

This is not a Prince who loves to kill.

His heart filled up with something vast and terrible at the realization, a shadowy whirl of wings and storm and light, and he knew why men died for Elizabeth. He would have died for Elizabeth himself. And he understood as well that there were things bigger than Elizabeth, bigger than England, for all they were things for which he did not have a name. *Faith. God. Liberty.* None of it was enough.

Worse things had been done in those names, than in Elizabeth's.

And yet—

"And what if thou didst think thou hadst choose between the Queen and thy England—no, do not answer, Master Poet. We would liefer know not. Little elf," Elizabeth said, turning to regard Sir Robert. "Thou hadst a question with regard to Master Shakespeare. Good poet"—she turned back to Will, and now her eyes sparkled—"you may speak now as if privily before ourselves."

Cecil smiled. *He's going to ask about the Bible,* Will thought at first, and then realized—*worse, he's going to ask about the plays. All the plays produced under Oxford's supervision, and subverting Oxford's control*—Will steeled himself not to dissemble or lie—

The high double doors behind him swung open, and a determined step hushed itself upon the carpet. Raleigh, Murchaud, and Kit moved as one man, coming around the Queens, rapiers hissing into a fence of steel between the women and the door. Will blinked even as he turned, realizing all three men had been armed in the Presence.

"Your Highness," the Earl of Oxford said, genuflecting as the door thumped back against its frame, "I must speak to you at once. This player"—a twitch of the head at Will—"is a traitor, and Your Highness is in very grave danger—"

Will glanced at Oxford and blinked as he understood a number of things. Including the cost of refusing to dance to Oxford's tune, and that *someone* considered Will troublesome enough to be cheerfully rid of him. And that it had not been happenstance that Raleigh himself had come so publicly to fetch Will from the press. *And what rumors and half-truths have the Queen and her elves been circulating?*

Enough to provoke de Vere into hasty action, for certain—

"Brave gentlemen," Elizabeth said. "We can be in no danger from so loyal a servant as our noble Oxford." She accepted Sir Walter's hand as he stepped back to her side and sheathed his blade. She stood gracefully, making her knight's gesture look like a courtesy, but Will saw him take the strain of her weight. And saw also the way her ungloved hand tightened on Raleigh's, until the pallor of her fingers matched the white lead on her brow. Saw the way Kit's rapier dropped until its point rested on the floor, though neither he nor Murchaud sheathed their swords or retreated behind their Queen. From his angle a little to the side of where Oxford stood, Will saw Cairbre slip a silver flute into his hand, and—*good Christ*—George Carey, Lord Hunsdon, draw a long-barreled pistol and conceal it behind Elizabeth's gilded chair.

I am on the wrong side of that dais. But Kit looked calm, and so did Carey. Sir Robert was actually smiling, one hand resting on the ornate back of Elizabeth's chair now that she had risen. He leaned forward to speak in her ear, and she smiled. "As you say, little elf." She gave Will a level, steadying glance before she turned her attention to Oxford. "What is it, sweet boy?"

Oxford looked from Elizabeth to the Mebd, still seated and anonymous behind her rich black veils and the bodies of her servants. "My Queen, I am not certain this is meet to discuss before strangers."

"Ah," she said, descending the steps coolly, her hand upraised in Raleigh's like a courting swan's neck. "But these are not strangers, my dear Oxford."

Will watched her come, amazed, as the Earl of Oxford chose his words, seeming to understand that he had made some sort of an error and seeking to understand how grave it was. Close on, Will witnessed the frailty of Elizabeth's neck, the hollows under her cheekbones, the lines of old pain set deep between her eyes. The scent of rosewater and marjoram surrounded her; he was reminded uncomfortably of Morgan and her eternal scent of rosemary. Elizabeth had nearly died—two years before Will was born—of the smallpox that had also disfigured her dear friend Mary Dudley, the mother of the poet Sir Philip Sidney. The candlelight outlined the scars on Elizabeth's cheeks through her paint, and still she presented—almost—the illusion of vigor.

"That will suffice, dear Walter." She tugged her hand from Raleigh's grasp, and she passed before Will and came and laid that same white, white hand on Oxford's cheek. He smiled at the touch, and the Queen smiled back. "What is it, Edward?"

"I am here to name this playmaker a traitor to Your Highness," Oxford said, on a breath that didn't quite manage the sneer he endeavored for. "I have evidence to present—"

Christ, Will thought, but Raleigh came to stand beside him as if about to take his elbow and block his route to the door, using the movement to cover a casual nudge.

"How convenient," Elizabeth said, turning her back on Oxford while Will marveled at her seamless courage and dignity. "When here we have a tribunal of sorts."

"A tribunal, Your Highness?"

"Of sorts," she repeated, withdrawing up the shallow steps. She paused before her chair, made a sweeping turn to accommodate her train, and did not take a seat. "We are here to consider the crimes of Edward de Vere, the Seventeenth Earl of Oxford. Would he care to make a defense?"

Kit shifted at the left hand of the Mebd, although his face seemed impassive behind the mask. Will saw her lay one black-gloved hand on the poet's wrist. Kit glanced down and gave her a smile as edgy as the rapier in his hand. Will stepped away from Oxford, giving Raleigh the room to step between them if he needed, conscious of his blocking as if he moved away from the principals in a scene onstage.

"My Queen." Oxford swept a low bow and stayed there, his hat in his hand as Will's had been. "May I hear these—charges?" He glanced sidelong at Will, already arranging his face into a mask of dismissive scorn. "What has this player told you?"

"*That* player has told us nothing," she said. Her hands looked terribly small against the massive white wall of her skirts; she folded them before the point of her flat-fronted stomacher and twined the fingers together. "For we have not yet taken his evidence." Disappointment edged her soft, sweet voice. "Edward. It has reached our ears that thou dost conspire with Catholic spies and agents, along with some others who are not presently welcome in our court—" She sighed. "Honesty may redeem thee, Edward. How dost thou answer?"

The look Oxford shot Will this time was nothing short of venomous, and Will had the distinct and elevated pleasure of smiling once and shaking his head with slow finality. *Nay. Not me, my dear Earl. I wonder if it was Essex or Southampton threw him to the wolves?*

One or the other. Elizabeth would not listen to many

men over—Kit's eye caught Will's again, and Will nodded so slightly he thought only Kit and perhaps Cairbre might catch it—*her own son.*

"Your Highness." Oxford had not yet risen. Will rather enjoyed seeing the back of his neck. "May I know by whose hand these charges have been leveled, then?"

"Mine," said Kit, and stepped forward with a naked rapier still in his right hand, and it struck Will abruptly that better than half the men in the room had drawn weapons in the presence of not one Queen, but two—and no one seemed to think much of it. Meanwhile, Kit's gloved left hand rose to strip the sculpted velvet mask from his face; he let it drop from his fingers to the floor behind, and smiled. "Hello, love. Art surprised to find me quick?"

Leaning on his cane, Will hitched himself back from the confrontation evolving in the center of the room.

Elizabeth's smile was a mask as unyielding of true expression as the one Kit had left lying at her feet, and Oxford's stiff-backed bow didn't survive the revelation. He straightened, reaching for the rapier he wasn't wearing, and took a slow step away from Kit and from the Queen as Raleigh edged between him and the door.

Oxford hesitated a moment when his hand brushed the richly figured cloth at his hip. Will saw his moment of decision, the squaring of his shoulders and the little grimace as he moved forward, past Kit as if Kit were insignificant, an inconvenience to be shrugged aside. "Your Highness," Oxford said, pausing at the foot of the steps and addressing himself directly to his Queen. "Surely you will not take the word of this"—his lip twisted, as if on words he would not say in the presence of a woman—"apostate, this perversion—"

Kit came the few steps back up beside Oxford on the left, and Will saw that his motion served to distract Oxford from Raleigh, who flanked the Earl on the right and just out of the periphery of his vision. Kit's voice stayed level, amused, but there was a honeyed rasp in it that Will knew for sheerest hatred. "Baines told thee not that I was living, Edward? I wonder what else he's kept from thee. Perhaps he reports directly to Southampton now."

"Thou shalt not *thee* me, sirrah."

Kit stopped close enough for Oxford to feel the heat of his breath, Will imagined, the naked blade angled between them as if laid down the center of a bed. "Or Essex; perhaps 'tis why Essex saw fit to set thee adrift—"

Oxford looked up at the Queen. "Your Highness would take the word of this common playmaker and, and—"

"—or perhaps 'tis Essex who wears Baines' rein. What thinkst thou? Thou hast been cut from their string, hast not?"

The Queen's smile was strained white under the carmine of fucus. She held her silence. The Mebd and the four black-clad men beside her might have been statues.

"—heretic, traitor. Catamite—" Oxford would not turn. Would not look at Kit, as Kit leaned closer. Will's stomach clenched in sympathy at the tightness that edged Kit's face, and never was heard in his voice.

"Ah."

"Your Highness?"

"Ah," Kit said a second time, and slapped Edward de Vere with the back of his gloved left hand.

It was a blow hard enough to turn the man's head and leave a welt burning red across the pallor of his skin, and Will flinched at the report. Oxford fell silent, didn't so much as raise a hand to cover the mark. Will imagined de Vere tasting blood, and the imagining troubled him not at all.

Kit tilted his head to one side like a crow thinking

which eye to pluck from a dead man's skull. He spoke clearly into the silence, and the knot in Will's stomach wrenched into a wild, braying kind of love. "I cannot fault thine own experienced testament, my lord—"

"Master Marlowe, I am certain—"

"Sir Christopher," Elizabeth said.

"Your Highness?"

"Sir Christopher," she said, as if reminding an idiot child. "Not Master. Sir."

Oxford's face went white before it went red. "Sir Christopher. I am certain I do not understand your implication—"

"Implication? My lord Oxford, I will *testify*." The poet stripped his gloves off with an elegantly negligent gesture and smiled up at the Queens. Will wondered if anyone else could see what Kit's smile cost him.

Oxford looked appealingly at his Queen, who ignored him in favor of gracefully resuming her seat, her skirts hissing about her like the foam on a moonlit sea. Oxford must have heard the rumors that the veiled blond beauty was the legendary Anne of Denmark, Queen of Scotland. Will could almost see the false assumptions heaping high in Oxford's thoughts.

"Sir Christofer," the Mebd asked in measured and musical tones, "are you suggesting that this my royal sister's subject has made improper use of thee?"

Elizabeth glanced up from fussing her skirts, but it was Kit she looked to. "Sir Christopher?"

Kit smiled green poison, not at the Queens but at Oxford. "Oh, he made rather a proper job of it, I'd say. May it please Your Majesties."

"Thou'lt burn with me." Hissed, and Will rather thought it was meant for Kit's ears alone, but in the still room it carried. Oxford flinched.

"I'm subject to another Kingdom now," Kit answered, and gently reached up and kissed Edward de Vere on the

cheek still reddened with that blow. Will bit his lip on a
cheer, turned aside before it could bubble out of him,
and met Raleigh's amused and savage grin. *He approves
of our Kit too,* Will thought, and gave the Queen's "Sir
Walter" back a flash of a smile as Kit stepped back. *Will
wonders never cease?*

"And more," Will said, understanding what he was
here for, and where Cecil's questions would have taken
him. "From his own lips, I heard the Earl suggest that
Your Majesty's continued good health"—a bow to
Elizabeth—"might be an impediment to the successful
future of England."

Kit stepped back and turned his sword so that the
blade cast reflected light in a moving bar across Oxford's breast and throat, all his polite attention to Will.
The band of Kit's mask had disarrayed his hair into fine
tangled elflocks, and Will folded his arms to keep from
brushing them straight.

"Have you proof, Master Shakespeare?" Raleigh's
voice. Oxford jumped at its closeness.

Will shook his head, pressing his arms against his
chest, his cane dangling from his fingertips. "Only mine
own sworn testimony, Sir Walter. Which will I give."

Kit cleared his throat and addressed himself to Oxford, not Raleigh. "I also have heard with mine own ears
that thou didst plot my murder, and treason against your
anointed Queen. And I also will swear to it and give par-
ticulars. My lord."

Raleigh looked across Oxford as if he were not there,
catching Kit's eyes. "Good to see you well, Kit—" He
cleared his throat and grinned. "Sir Christopher. I suppose that's not for bandying about?"

"Good to see you at all, Walter." Oxford moved, as
if to shift from between them, and Kit halted him with
a negligent tap of his blade. "Tut. None of that. And no,
officially I'm quite dead and likely to remain so."

Raleigh stepped closer. Kit moved back toward the dais, sheathing his blade as if Oxford were beneath concern. Oxford's expression of thwarted wrath lightened Will's heart, but the Mebd's voice broke through his delight; soft and amused as Kit came back to her side, stooping only to retrieve his discarded mask. "Dost regret now how fine a gift thou hast given us, sweet sister?"

"Oh, sister," Elizabeth answered, her voice rich and low over the colors of a grief Will imagined was almost like an old, familiar friend, "I've always been weak in the face of these rash, these beautiful boys." Kit hid a laugh to hear himself so described, but Elizabeth's eyes were on Raleigh and her face offered Oxford no sign of her pain. *She'll weep later,* Will thought. *She wept for Mary, they say, even as she signed the death warrant—* "My sweet Sir Walter. Sir Robert, my elf. See that our darling Edward tells us what he knows. Everything."

Raleigh took Oxford by the elbow; the Earl gave him a glance that might have melted glass. "Unhand me, popinjay." He pushed Raleigh back with the flat of his hands; Raleigh bore it like a standing stone, though pearls rained from his doublet like hail.

"As my Queen commands," Raleigh answered, one hand upon his sword. "Your Highness, when he has told us what he will?"

Elizabeth's fan moved idly, crimson and alabaster feathers trembling above a grip made of gold set with mother-of-pearl. "I do not wish to set eyes on him again."

Act IV, scene xiv

Since thou hast all the Cards within thy hands
To shuffle or cut, take this as surest thing:
That right or wrong, thou deal thyself a King.

—CHRISTOPHER MARLOWE, *The Massacre at*
Paris, Act I, scene ii

The two Queens removed themselves before Sir Walter or Sir Robert returned, and Lord Hunsdon and Cairbre went with them. Kit breathed a sigh of relief to be alone with Will and Murchaud in the mirrorless, close-tapestried retiring room. "I don't suppose there's a bottle of wine on a sideboard somewhere?"

"I'll find a servant," Murchaud answered, stripping his mask off and tossing it on the red velvet cushion of the Mebd's gilded chair. "Thou wert brave, Kit—"

Kit shrugged. "One down," he said, crossing glances with Will.

Will dragged a stool away from the wall and sat himself on it, balancing his cane carefully against his knee.

A liveried servant arrived with the wine; Kit intercepted the tray before Will could try to rise and serve his betters. The tightness in Will's narrow shoulders pained him; the hesitant, calculated step and the nearness at hand of that cane broke his heart. He poured wine into a softly swirled blue glass and pressed it into Will's hand, then did the same for Murchaud.

"And thou wert very brave indeed," Will finished, tasting the wine. "It cannot have been easy, what thou didst—"

"What, admitting my poor taste in lovers before every person who's ever treated me with a scrap of dignity?" It had been humorous in his head; on his lips it tasted of bitterness.

"Not everybody," Will said, while Murchaud bumped Kit companionably with a shoulder. "Tom wasn't here—"

"Oh, and I thank thee for that comfort. . . ." But Kit smiled, despite himself, and felt some of the painful unease in his belly loosen.

The door opened again and he looked up, expecting another servant, perhaps, or a summons. It was Sir Robert Cecil, his canine mask pushed up over his hair and his limp pronounced with tiredness. "Master Shakespeare—"

"Sir." Will stood, bracing himself with the cane. Kit stepped forward and relieved Will of his wine cup as the playmaker went to greet the Secretary of State.

Will didn't lean on the cane heavily so much as balance with it, but his step was halt and his right hand trembled. *Christ, how does he write?*

Kit felt his face pinch, his eyes begin to burn. He looked away and caught Murchaud's sideways glance. And knew that, too, for what it was, and shook his head slowly in the realization.

Slowly, aye. But Will was dying.

Sir Robert came forward and fell into step by Will, two men limping in unison. On stage, it might have been funny. "Master Shakespeare, I'll need you to write out and sign a deposition."

"Regarding the Earl of Oxford? I'll do it gladly, Mr. Secretary. Will he . . . ?"

"—go to the Tower?"

A pleasant euphemism, Kit thought.

Sir Robert shook his head. "No, but I doubt you'll see him in London again. Master Shakespeare, if you will?"

Will nodded in amusement at the pun, glancing over his shoulder to Kit. Kit waved him away with a pang, conscious of a breathless, drowning sort of agony filling his throat. *Eight years and I've managed the downfall of Edward de Vere. And now—*

Christ. I can't stand watching this. What will it take? Half a decade? Two? I should have stayed in Faerie. I should have—

—let Baines have his way with Will?

Murchaud's hand pressed the small of Kit's back as Sir Robert steered Will out of the retiring room. Kit didn't move away from the touch, for all it felt like sandpaper through his doublet and his shirt. The door closed behind Will and Sir Robert. Kit turned and looked up at the Prince, who pulled him into a stiffly awkward sort of one-armed hug. "It gets easier eventually."

"When they're all dead?"

It was an idle, bitter comment. Kit was not prepared for the placid irony with which the Prince said, softly, "Yes."

"Murchaud, why art thou kind? What dost thou wish of me?" It wasn't quite what Kit had intended to ask, and he stiffened, but he still didn't step out of the embrace, for all it was like standing among nettles. Murchaud turned his face into Kit's hair, and Kit was suddenly giddy with sorrow and frustration and something that hurt sharply, a pressure under his breastbone he didn't have a name for.

"Idiot. For I love thee," the Prince said, and kissed the top of Kit's head before he let him go. "What word hast thee of conspiracy, Kitling?"

For I love thee. Kit stared after the Prince, wondering if those words were true or calculated, or whether they could be both. "That depends of which conspiracy thou speakst, my Prince. This one or that one? I think we pulled a tooth of the dragon in London today—"

Murchaud shrugged, pouring more wine. "Something was accomplished, in any case. And Oxford's face when thou didst draw off thy mask was a worthy sight. With Oxford and Essex both out of court, that's a little breathing room for Gloriana."

"Will thinks the Puritans have gotten to Archbishop Whitgift."

"The Puritans, or the Prometheans?"

"Is there a difference?" Kit leaned against a leather-topped desk and watched Murchaud pace. "Essex's Prometheans have their fingers deep in every pie. They play politics layered on politics, and their goals are opaque to me."

"Their goals are very simple," Murchaud replied, turning as if startled. "Power, earthly and divine. Revolution, and the overthrow of the old ways."

"And our ways are better than theirs?" Kit breathed a little easier, the knot under his breastbone easing at having successfully diverted Murchaud. *Robin, I do not know how long I can protect you. I do not even understand why it is that I choose to do so.* Except Kit had seen men drawn and quartered for the sin of appearing on a list of names that he, Kit, drew up and provided. He thought of Will's new play and grinned. *To choose not is a choice.*

"Our ways are what we have," Murchaud said, reminding Kit of his own words to Will, so many years ago. "I wonder, sometimes, if a compromise could be reached—"

"Like the compromise with Hell?" Kit refreshed his own cup and Murchaud's as well. He leaned back against the desk, turning the glass between his hands. The pale blue spirals running up the sides caught the light; the room seemed very rich and lush in half darkness.

"I should hope not," Murchaud answered. He paced the edge of the room, letting his fingers wander over surfaces. "If the Archbishop of Canterbury is weakening, can the Church of England be far behind?"

"Murchaud"—a swallow of wine to loosen Kit's tongue—"why has the Mebd come here? Not for a play. And not merely for my little masque and unmasking."

"Oh, aye, for a play. And to discuss Elizabeth's succession with her. And Elizabeth's legend—"

"Ah." Kit set the glass down on the leather-topped desk and stretched his fingers, working the ache out of them. "Edward has a jaw like an anvil."

" 'Tis well thou didst not punch him, then. Is't broken?"

"Only strained. Bruised a little."

"Would kiss it well—"

"Would that thou couldst." Kit sighed. "What next?"

Murchaud shuddered. "We try to keep Gloriana alive as long as possible. We rid ourselves of as many of the false Promethean agents as we can find. Oxford is an excellent start. Skeres, not the victory I would have chosen, but something nonetheless."

"We discover—" Kit coughed and lowered his voice. "We discover why Sir Robert is protecting Poley and Baines."

"Is he?"

"There's no other explanation." Kit nodded with conviction. It came more plain to him even as he sought to explain it. "He sends Tom and Will to frame Baines, but it's not Baines who takes the fall. He allows Will and I to remove Oxford, but only once Essex has discarded him.

He opposes Will's plan for a new Bible, and I would not be surprised if there's more we don't know. Yes, I think Robert Cecil is playing a very deep game indeed. And I think I need to talk to Sir Walter about it—"

"Sir Robert," Murchaud said, still pacing, "believes in what he can grasp and hold. Sir Robert may already have plans for Elizabeth's successor. Sir Robert may see a weakening of Faerie as bending to his advantage."

"I can't imagine that he doesn't. I'm not sure that he understands that the Prometheans are something other than another chess piece—"

"He doesn't see them as players?"

"Does he see anyone else as a player? I think he imagines that some tokens merely move themselves about the board when his hand is not on them." Kit's own hand was swelling still. He frowned at it. "I did hit Oxford harder than I intended. At least the fingers work."

"Thou shouldst get Morgan to see to it—"

"Will Morgan see me?"

Murchaud's lips twitched. "Aye, I imagine she would. There's more we need to finish before Elizabeth passes—"

"Besides the Prometheans?"

"I set thee to find those who would conspire against my wife. I need names, Kit."

Kit closed his eyes. "I suppose thou wouldst not believe me an I lied to thee?"

"Your heart is divided," Murchaud quoted, and came to him. "Thou dost know something, and thou art loath to tell."

"I know many things I am loath to tell, lover. . . ."

Murchaud smiled at the endearment, but Kit could tell it would not encourage him to relent. He set his wineglass down. "Kit. It is my safety that thou dost put at stake. Mine, and Cairbre's, as well as the Mebd's. Thy friends and protectors. Hast thou no loyalty?"

"I have no wish to witness any more hangings in my lifetime, Murchaud."

"Hah!" Murchaud stepped back, and as he stepped back he reached out with both hands and cupped Kit's cheeks ever so gently. Kit steeled himself and bore the touch, and managed even not to flinch. "Kitling, we do not hang Faeries."

". . . we don't?"

"We haven't enough Faeries to hang, my love. No, the punishment will not be fatal. Or even, perhaps, painful, although the miscreants might find themselves sporting a pig's head or a cow's filthy tail. The Mebd has her own ways of enforcing obedience."

Or ass's ears, Kit realized, and then put his hand to his mouth as he realized also that he'd said it aloud. His expression must have offered whatever confirmation Murchaud needed, because the Prince nodded once, judiciously, and leaned close to kiss him on the forehead.

"Who else?"

"Geoffrey," Kit answered, his voice helpless in his own hearing. "Geoffrey and Puck, and the Faerie oaks. That's all I know."

"It's enough," Murchaud said. "They can be made to tell."

Act IV, scene xv

*O sir, we quarrel in print, by the book; as you have books
for good manners: I will name you the degrees. The first,
the Retort Courteous; the second, the Quip Modest; the
third, the Reply Churlish; the fourth, the Reproof Val-
iant; the fifth, the Countercheque Quarrelsome; the sixth,
the Lie with Circumstance; the seventh, the Lie Direct.
All these you may avoid but the Lie Direct; and you may
avoid that too, with an If. I knew when seven justices
could not take up a quarrel, but when the parties were
met themselves, one of them thought but of an If, as, "If
you said so, then I said so"; and they shook hands and
swore brothers. Your If is the only peacemaker; much
virtue in If.*

—WILLIAM SHAKESPEARE, *As You Like It*,
Act V, scene iii

Spring came late in 1600; Will spent Lent in Stratford
and returned in late March to his haunts in London. One cold rainy afternoon shortly after Easter,
he leaned back on his bench at the Mermaid and rattled
the dice across the planks to Thomas Nashe, who was

leaned forward inspecting the backgammon board set between them. "I should have made you play chess."

"You win at chess," Will answered complacently, reaching for his wine.

"Then perhaps we should alternate. I shouldn't play at dice with you, Will. No one should. You've the Devil's own luck—"

"If I have it, then he doesn't. When you meet him, be sure to challenge him at dice."

Nashe laughed, delighted. "I can count on you, Will. Have you seen Ben lately?"

"He's still not speaking to me over the poet's argument," Will answered unhappily. He steepled his fingers in front of his nose. "Burbage has hired Dekker to take a few cuts back at Ben. It's all childishness; I have plays to write. And you—I hear you've given up playmaking and pamphleteering entirely, Tom."

"Poetry for private patrons pays better," Nashe said without rancor, rattling the dice on the tabletop. He swore softly and moved his chips with a hasty hand. "And poetry seems less likely to find me in jail again. Or my work burned in the market square—"

"At least you brought Harvey down with you—"

"A minor victory. It's not hard to be funnier than Gabriel Harvey. Hullo, George."

"Good afternoon, gentlemen." Chapman patted Will on the shoulder and settled his bulk onto the plank bench beside Nashe. And then looked up, exasperated, and started to heave his stout graybearded self up again. "Damme, I forgot I wanted sack."

"I'll get it," Nashe said, pushing himself to his feet with a hand on either side of the board. "I wanted another ale. Mind you keep Will from 'repairing' the board while I'm up—oh, look. The Catholics are here again."

He jerked his chin, and Will followed the motion. Robert Catesby caught Will's eye and smiled; Will didn't know the big, well-favored redhead beside him, but the ridges of muscle on his arms and the scars on his hands said *soldier,* and he carried himself in the same manner that Ben did.

"At least we're unlikely to see Puritans in a poet's bar," Chapman answered, stretching his feet toward the fire. "And Catesby's a good sort."

Nashe snorted and went to find the landlord. Chapman turned and offered Will a considering look. "Does your offer still stand, Master Shakespeare?"

Will blinked, trying to remember what offer he might have made, and shrugged. He pulled a tiny bottle from his purse and shook Morgan's poisoned medicine into his wine cup, counting the droplets that fell from the splinter imbedded in the cork. "Which offer is that?"

Chapman glanced over his shoulder. "I've thought better of your idea. The Bible."

Will swirled the wine to mix in the bitter herbs, aware of Chapman's interest. "It's a tincture for my palsy, George."

"Oh." Silence, as Will drank and felt the tightness in his muscles easing. "The Bible," he reminded.

"Ben's not speaking to me."

"Ben thinks highly of himself," Chapman commented dryly. "We were young once too. It passes."

Will laughed, tidying counters on the board. "I'm uncertain I was ever so young as that. The Bible's been slow going. What changed your mind?"

Chapman shrugged as Nashe came back, juggling two wine cups and a mug of ale. He placed the cups before Will and Chapman, and settled in again, leaning forward to look at the board. "I bid you not to let him move my counters, George—"

"I was only straightening," Will protested. "Thank you for the wine, Tom."

"I was up." Tom brushed it aside as unworthy. "I interrupted."

"Not at all," Chapman said. "We were discussing the foibles of Master Jonson—"

Will sighed and nodded, glad that Chapman had failed to answer his question once Nashe returned. *Jonson owes too much to Tom Walsingham to give away what he knows of our tasks. But I cannot help but wonder, sulky boy that he is, if I made a mistake recruiting him. Still, it wouldn't do to have Tom Nashe wondering why I've cut him out of Bible study.*

Nashe rolled his eyes. "Ben's all wind and no rain," he opined, toying with his ale.

"Easy to say, when you're not somebody he's brawled with or cudgeled with his own pistol. Ask John Marston what he thinks of Ben's lists."

Nashe grinned at Chapman. "He'll wind up stabbed in unsavory circumstances. Mark my words."

Will marked them, all right. And, sitting at the table between two other friends and collaborators of Kit Marlowe's, found them less than comforting. *Well, if I can trust anyone with the news of Kit's survival, it would have been smarter Tom Nashe or George than Ben, now that I think on it. Oh, hell.* He caught Chapman's eye and nodded while Nashe was fussing with the dice, and Chapman returned the smile and sipped his wine complacently.

Act IV, scene xvi

She whom thy eye shall like, thy heart shall have,
Be she as chaste as was Penelope,
As wise as Saba, or as beautiful
As was bright Lucifer before his fall.

—CHRISTOPHER MARLOWE, *Faustus,*
Act II, scene i

K it walked down the sweeping greensward below the Mebd's gold-turreted palace and stopped on the bluff above the sea. A strange white tree grew there, where the lawn gave way to coarse and knotty salt grass. Kit let his viola swing from his hand, kicked the tree's trunk with the side of his foot, and arched his head back to look up into the branches.

Murchaud told him it was a New World tree, or perhaps one native to Cathay. It flowered heavily, hung with white petals thick as paper and soft as the skin of a peach. A thick honeyed scent the sea breeze couldn't leaven floated under the branches, cloying Kit's throat.

It wasn't what the tree was that interested Kit. It was who the tree had been. "Well, I hope thou'rt enjoying thy penance, Robin," he said. "Can think of worse prisons—"

The branches whispered one on the other. Kit freed the bow and lifted the viola. "I came to play thee a tune. I thought it might lighten the weary hours...."

There was no answer, of course. But still he settled his instrument and played for an hour or two, there at the border between the sea and the land, with the tree reaching up to scrape the sky. He would have played longer, and perhaps stayed to watch the sunset under the white tree's branches, but the heavy slip and sway of a caller's approach across the grass distracted him.

He lowered the instrument and turned. "Good evening, Lady Amaranth."

"A beautiful evening, Sir Poet," she answered. "Play on, and lull me to sleep in this forgiving evening air."

"Do snakes sleep?"

She smiled, that strange flat rearrangement of her face. "Snakes sleep with their eyes open, who was Christofer Marley."

"Please," he said, laying the viola down in a flat, dry patch of grass. He leaned back against the bark of the tree, wondering how long the Mebd would leave Robin stranded so before she deemed her lesson taught. "Call me Kit."

"Kit." Her snakes moved like a lovely woman's hair, tossed by the sea breeze. For a moment, he could almost imagine curls caught on her collar, limned like sculpture in the low angled light. "How likest thou the answers to thy questions?"

"The answers you're guiding me to?" He laughed. "Don't think I haven't noticed. Mehiel. The oaks. Puck. Other things ..."

She inclined her head, smile broadening, the picture of womanly waiting except for the flicker of her tail tip.

He pushed a hand into his hair, as much to hide his

shaking as to hold the wind-tossed strands out of his face. "How do you know what you know, Amaranth?" He'd meant to ask the question more subtly, to dance up to it.

She coiled aside and smiled, rising up to pluck a palm-broad blossom from the branches overhead. She buried her face in the flower, inhaling deeply, and then tucked the twig behind her ear. Threadlike serpents coiled over the petals as Kit watched in fascination. She leaned back, as if considering.

Kit straightened against the tree and folded his arms across his breast. "You are more patient than I, my friend. Older and more knowing—"

"But thou'rt more stubborn, and I should take it into account?" She showed him a bit of fang when she smiled this time, and fussed the lace on the cuff of her flowing white shirt. "I know because I know, Kit. Because serpents are for knowing things—"

"And sharing them with mortals to their detriment?"

Oh, that was fang indeed, and the flicker of a long forked tongue in silent laughter. It brushed his cheek as she swayed forward, and all her hair hissed in sympathy. "If thou knowest thy scripture. Or all the myths of all the world."

"Is there a difference?"

She settled back on her tail, watching him with an arch assessment that left him quite unsettled. "No. Now that thou dost mention it, there's not."

Something—the stubbornness she'd named, or just long-smoldering rebellion, flared in his breast. "And hast come to send me on the next errand of discovery, then, my lady?"

"I haven't. I came to hear thy music, Kit."

He stepped away from the tree, brushed past her—not roughly, and not within reach of her hair—on his way out of the bower. "There's my instrument. Be so good as to lay it by my bed when thou hast done with it—"

"And where goest thou, Sir Poet?"

Kit laughed and turned back over his shoulder. "I'm going to see a witch about a boy."

Geoffrey, who was currently too much a stag to be much use for conversation, had said of Morgan's cottage that one could only find it if one knew already where it was. Kit found it true: he found his way to the stream and across the bridge—after no troll appeared to greet his hail—and down among the roses without difficulty. If it were spring on the bluff above the ocean, it was high summer at the witch's cottage, and the roses hung damasked red and white beside the door like a lady's mantle thrown over her shoulder to display the embroidery. The red wooden door was propped open, and Kit heard a familiar voice raised in song over the splash and clatter of washing.

As homely a sight and sound as he'd ever imagined. He let his feet crunch on the gravel path as he came along it, and on a whim raised his voice in harmony. The clinking of pottery stopped, but the singing continued, and a moment later Morgan le Fey poked her head around the corner and smiled. And Kit blinked, because her hair was as red as the red roses that grew by the door, and her skin gone as pale as the white.

"Morgan?" He stopped and blinked, midverse, his hands hanging limp by his sides. "You've changed," he said, and walked closer when she summoned him.

"It happens," she said, tugging a long red lock out to inspect it. "I blame Spenser. All Queens are Elizabeth, now—"

"Really?"

"No. Only in stories. I imagine Arthur's still blond in his bower, though. Isn't he?"

Rather than answer, Kit reached with numb fingers to lift the curl out of her hand. The hair felt coarse and real, not harsh with dye. He fought the sudden ridiculous impulse to lift it to his lips and taste it; instead he said, "You knew about Mehiel."

She smiled and flicked her curl out of his hands, as Lucifer had flicked his wing. "Yes, Sir Poet. I knew about Mehiel. And I've underestimated thee, I see now." She stood away from the door, gesturing him into her house.

He followed. "I scream within," he assured her. "How knewest thou?" It was strange to speak to her so again, after such a long time, but he bit back a smile and thought, *If thou canst thee Lucifer, Prince of God's Angels, then thou canst thee Morgan le Fey.*

"I have my sources." She smiled mysteriously and went to stir something in the kettle over the fire, while he tried to decide if he liked her hair that brilliant shade.

"Morgan—" He had layers and layers of questions. Careful, teasing questions that he'd written out and memorized before committing the sheets to the fire. He had a thousand interrogations troubling his soul, and moreover, he thought he had the right to know the answers. And what he said was, "My Queen, what is it thou dost desire?"

It was the right thing to ask. God help him. He knew it by the way she straightened, and wouldn't look at him, but dipped a wooden mug in the spice-scented decoction seething over the fire and stood and stared at the mud-chinked wall while she drank it. "The impossible, Kit."

"How impossible?" He came to her, his slowly lengthening cloak brushing aside the rushes on the fresh-swept floor.

"Time to add another layer," she said. "Or thou'lt find thyself tripping whenever thou dost step back."

"Then I'll have to learn not to step back," he said, and touched her wrist with three fingers. "Answer me, Morgan."

She turned her head away. Her throat had a fine,

strong line, flowing into a stubborn chin. He lifted the hand from her wrist, caught that chin, and turned her face back to him, amazed at his own audacity. More amazed when he felt her shiver, before she brushed his hand aside and stepped back. "Peace. I want peace, Christopher Marlowe."

"I'll offer thee no war if thou wilt offer me none." She smiled, but he knew from the way her breath fell that it wasn't what she meant, and he returned her smile with a slight, thoughtful nod. "Thou'rt correct. It is impossible."

"Most things worth fighting for are."

"And is there anything thou'rt not willing to sacrifice to get it, my Queen?"

"Thou shouldst know the answer to that by now, Kitten," she said, and stood on tiptoe to kiss him on the mouth. "And the more we love it, the more likely it becomes that it will be stripped from us."

"Oh, *that* I know." He stepped back and bowed, a practiced gesture with his cloak. "May I be of service to a lady, then? What may I do?"

She laughed. "Don't look back. Don't step off the path. And never trust the guardian."

"I've heard that somewhere before," he said. She nodded.

"I know. I imagined he would tell you."

"Geoffrey?"

"Geoffrey the Hart." She smiled, and reached out to brush his lips with her fingers, and very carefully reached out and opened his collar to expose the brand high on his chest.

Her touch burned, but he bore it irritably. *Thou dost inflict this pain thyself.*

"It's inevitable now, what happens, Kitten. The wheels are in motion. But I managed a little trick you might approve of—"

"Yes?"

"The battle—"

"The one when Elizabeth dies?"

"Not when Elizabeth dies any longer," she said, and dragged her fingers through her long, red hair. "It cost me something of myself, though it was Spenser op'ed the way. The Prometheans will have to manufacture their rift in the collective soul of London themselves. Elizabeth's legend will linger past her death. Gloriana will not die with the Queen—"

"Gloriana," he mouthed, and cocked his head at her. At the fine hooked arch of her nose and the cheekbones like panes of glass, and caught his breath.

"Elizabeth the First," Morgan le Fey said on a breath like awe. "England's greatest ruler. So shall she be remembered." The sorceress offered him a bittersweet smile, and he knew that what she gave herself was not just peace, but a suitable sort of vengeance, after all these endless years. "A mere woman."

Kit studied her. "There are no mere women."

Her eyes shifted green to gray, smile rose-pink as her lips compressed. She said nothing, amused.

He liked her in triumph. "It's your revenge on Arthur."

"Arthur and not Gwenhwyfar? Art certain?"

He was. He wondered, for a moment, what the legends might have been if this woman, and not her half brother, had been King. "Does the Mebd know what you've done?"

"She'll learn soon enough. Come. Sit and have tea."

Act IV, scene xvii

Some say that ever 'gainst that season comes
Wherein our Savior's birth is celebrated,
The bird of dawning singeth all night long;
And then, they say, no spirit can walk abroad;
The nights are wholesome; then no planets strike,
No fairy takes, nor witch hath power to charm,
So hallow'd and so gracious is the time.

—WILLIAM SHAKESPEARE, *Hamlet*,
Act I, scene i

Will had learned by now to recognize the tingle of lifting hair at the nape of his neck that presaged Kit's sudden appearances. The specter showed first flat as a painting or an image in a glass, and then stepping forward as if he rose through water into three-dimensional reality. Will didn't move from his place by the fire—hard won, in Tom's cold parlor, and he wouldn't sacrifice it willingly. Tom himself only nodded, but George Chapman—

Will hid his laughter behind his sleeve as Chapman turned to face the outlandish figure of Kit Marlowe—

who had just materialized before the big window in his gaudy cloak—and dropped his half-empty goblet on the floor. Tom didn't even try to conceal his mirth as straw-colored wine spilled over the rushes and Chapman's jaw fell open, a red cavern within the bramble of his beard. He never even glanced down at the wine soaking his shoes, but when Kit smiled kindly at him and said, "Oh. Hullo, George. I hear you've been expurgating my poetry," his eyes rolled up and only Tom Walsingham's swift intercession kept him from dashing his brains out on the sideboard.

Kit considered the tableau for a moment, and then glanced over his shoulder and raised both eyebrows at Will. "He's a prankster, our Will."

Said direct to Will's face and not in Tom's direction at all, but it was Tom—tipping Chapman into a chair—who answered. "He is at that. Happy birthday, Kit—"

"Is it?" Kit glanced out the window, as if expecting rain and buttercups, and blinked at the cold gray slates and February darkness.

"February sixth, sixteen hundred."

"It is," Kit said wonderingly, putting his hand on the glass. He pressed the other against the center of his breast in a gesture that was becoming a habit, and one that quietly troubled Will. "Is't afternoon or morning?"

"Before sunrise," Will said. "We've been waiting up for thee—"

"And didst not tell poor George I was coming. Shame, William."

Will grinned. "Congratulations, Kit. You're thirty-seven."

"Strange, he doesn't look a day over twenty-nine." Tom finished settling Chapman into the chair and pushed one long hand through hair that was streaked with gray now, like a careless daub of whitewash at the temples. Will's attention was more on Kit, though, and he saw Kit flinch when Tom continued, "Worry not, Kit. Forty's not the end of the world, for all they say it's middle age and death on the horizon."

"Aye, Sir Thomas," Kit said, and crossed the room to crouch by Chapman's chair. "Thou'rt forty now? It cannot be. 'Twas only yesterday thou wert outriding and outshooting me day in and day out, and soon thou'lt be as toothless as old Chapman, here"—he chafed Chapman's wrists—"George, wake up. That was a cruel trick Will played thee—water, Will. If thou hast stopped the old man's heart I shan't forgive thee—"

"Old Chapman," Tom scoffed, standing back. "Aye, he's two entire winters on me—"

Will had left his cane by the door, and managed with some pride to fetch cold water and a cloth for Kit without stumbling. "As the youngest and baldest of the lot of you," Will said, "I feel I should contribute, but—alas—I find myself at a loss to compete with elder wits."

Kit snorted and ignored him, applying the cold soaked cloth to Chapman's neck until the woolly poet opened his eyes and groaned. "Kit. A ghost? It can't be Kit, so unchanged after a decade."

"Not a decade, George," Kit said, rising to his feet. "Eight years, a little less—"

"Near enough a decade," George answered, struggling upright, and Will saw Kit flinch again. "And not a wrinkle on thee—"

"Death is kinder than aging in that way," Kit said, and walked to the sideboard to pour himself wine and sugar it lightly. "I hear a rumor thou'rt holding Ben's pen for us now that the bricklayer has gone on to greener pastures."

Chapman blinked, and cast about himself for the cup that he'd let fall. Will took pity and retrieved and refilled it, to Chapman's effusive thanks. "Shall we begin?"

Kit sipped and laid his cup aside, turning to retrieve

the precious Bible from its shelf while Will dragged a low table with ink and paper between himself and Chapman. But Tom raised his hand and cleared his throat, and Kit paused before he was properly begun. "What is it, Sir Thomas?"

Tom smiled at Will. "You didn't tell Kit about his birthday gift, Master Shakespeare. . . ."

A blush turned Will's face hot.

Kit looked up, frowning. "Will . . . ?"

Wary as a stag at bay, and Will couldn't blame him. "Supper at the Mermaid," he said. "Everyone will be there. Tom Nashe, Mary Poley, and the lot—" *All that are left living. And let him look on young Robin with his own eyes, and make his own decisions, then—*

Kit's eyes grew wide. "Her Majesty would never permit it," he said, when he finally found something to say at all. "Christofer Marley must stay dead, Will—"

Will grinned. "Aye, but Thomas Marlowe of Canterbury, a young man of, oh, perhaps twenty-five, might just be of the age to have finished his prenticeship and come to London to meet the men his brother knew. What better excuse wilt thou ever have, my Christofer?"

Kit blinked and swallowed. Will saw his eyes too bright and his throat swelling above his collar, and hoisted himself out of his chair again. He crossed the floor and draped his arm over Kit's patchworked shoulders, damning the trembling in his limbs for an inconvenience and a bother. He was as proud of Kit for not pulling away as he had ever been of anything, and prouder still when his friend leaned into the embrace.

"How didst thou know I had a brother?"

Will grinned to stop the sharpness that would have filled up his own eyes, and found himself supporting Kit as much as clasping him. "I wrote thy mother, fool, to tell her the rumors attending the ignominy of thy death were false, and that she could be proud of her eldest son. We've had quite the correspondence, since—"

Then Kit did pull away, and set the Bible down, and hid his face against the window glass. No one spoke for long moments, until he straightened his shoulders and forced his voice steady. "What time is supper, then?"

Will had to encircle Kit's shoulders with his arm again to chivvy him through the Mermaid's door: the fair-haired poet froze with one hand on the door pull as if it were he and not Will who were halt. "Come on, Tom," Will said, tapping the side of Kit's shoe with his toe. "Your brother's friends are waiting to meet you."

"Tom," Kit said softly, and shook his head. "I always was beset by them. A veritable thicket of Toms—Will, I cannot go in there and pretend to be mine own brother."

"Hush. No one questions a truly outrageous lie. 'Tis the niggling inconsistencies 'twill trip thee." Will shifted his clasp to Kit's elbow, fumbling the cane in his other hand to free fingers for gripping. He grinned, and reached past Kit to open the door, pausing for one last inspection of his victim.

Kit wore the ill-fitting brown doublet that Tom had loaned him as if it pained him, constantly tugging at the too-long hem. His child-fine hair was twisted into a club and greased so not a trace of curl remained, and Will had brushed blackener through both it and Kit's fair reddish beard. The effect was to make Kit's dark eyes unremarkable rather than startling, and a subtle blur of kohl underneath had made them seem deep-set and a little sullen. He was thinner and fitter than he'd ever been in London, every inch the hard-muscled tradesman.

He looked at Will pleadingly, and Will shook his head.

"Come, love. Put on a demure demeanor and keep the pipeweed in thy pocket, and no one will know thee for a Marlowe at all."

"That's half what I'm afeared of," Kit answered, but he let Will bring him through the door.

A cheer went up as they entered. Will supposed God would forgive him for concealing from Kit the sheer number of well-wishers, nostalgic friends, and curious bystanders who might be expected to populate the gathering, but his friend's white pallor under wine-red cheeks made him wonder if *Kit* would do likewise. "See, Tom?" Under his breath, leaning close to Kit's ear as Kit tugged back, edging for the doorway. "Your brother did have friends."

Will thought he might need to interpose himself physically between Kit and the door, but then Tom Nashe extricated himself from the gawking crowd and hurried over. As one fish slipping through a weir is followed by a school, suddenly every body in the room moved toward them, and the erstwhile Tom Marlowe was surrounded and embraced and drawn into the center of the crowd so thoroughly that Will wondered if he would ever escape.

Nashe claimed Kit with a firm arm, introducing first himself—"Kit's school friend, also Tom, he'll have told you what we got up to at Cambridge with that play that almost got us all expelled. And why, when in London, didst thou to that hack Shakescene and not thy brother's old friend Tom!"—and then every member of the great and varied crowd. Burbage neatly cut Philip Henslowe off Kit's other arm, and between him and Nashe they got Kit seated and feted and served with warmed wine.

Will himself smiled and tucked his hands into his pockets, and went to slouch at the fireside beside Ned Alleyne, who looked tall enough to have been leaned there for a prop. "We don't see you out much these days, Ned—"

"I've money enough not to miss slogging through the mud behind a cart on tour. Why are you still at it, Will?"

Will paused and stretched his shoulders against the rough fieldstone chimney. Robin Poley brought him a cup, and Will ruffled the boy's hair before he remembered that Robin was too old for that now. "It's in my blood," he said at last, hopelessly. "The playing and the poetry. I'll be too sick to tour soon, I suppose—"

"Aye," Ned answered. "Enjoy it while you can. I hope poor Master Marlowe doesn't think his brother always received so warm a reception."

Will shrugged. "Let him take the news home to Kit's parents. It can't have been easy on them." He fell into the role of innocence so easily that it took him a moment to remember that the dark-haired young man holding court in the corner, looking charmingly flustered and confused by the attention—and then perhaps not as shocked as he should have been when Mary Poley all but slid into his lap in a tangle of dark hair and kilted skirts—wasn't Tom Marlowe at all, and wouldn't be taking any tales home to Canterbury.

Will watched Kit's face as Mary introduced him to Robin, and saw Kit's eyes narrow a little before his brow smoothed, and he took the young man's hand in a firm, unhesitant greeting. And then Burbage was leaning forward into the conversation, and Will caught enough of his shouted anecdote to know that he was telling "Tom Marlowe" an embellished version of the story of the ghost of Kit Marlowe accosting his killers on a rainy street—

To which Kit responded with startled and delighted laughter. And Will sighed, contented, and went to see the landlord about bringing out the feast.

It being a Friday, alas, they would eat fish. Not out of Papist superstition any longer, ironically, but of Elizabeth's desire that the good fisherfolk and fishmongers of England not be put out of trade by something so frivolous as a change of religion. Still, as befitted the name, the Mermaid was known for its fish in pastry, so all was not lost.

Will encountered his brother Edmund returning across the hall, and made it back neither to Ned Alleyne's side nor the table where Kit and Mary and Nashe and Robin and Burbage formed the focal point of the party. Rather he found himself standing in a little enclave with Edmund and John Fletcher, haphazardly snatching bites from passing trays and laughing as he hadn't laughed in—

—months.

An abundance of food lowered the rumble of conversation to a contented mutter, and when Will turned to check on Tom Marlowe né Christofer again, it took a moment to locate him. Finally, Will raised his eyes to the gallery and saw Kit standing with young Robin Poley, leaned against the railing like old friends, the boy pointing down and across at something that the man had leaned close to comment on. Kit caught Will's eye, and the smile he sent down might have melted Will like a candle end.

Lovesick fool, Will thought, and looked down before someone could notice his silly grin and draw an entirely correct conclusion.

A bustle near the door drew Will's attention from the careful study of his boots and the much-trod rushes. Will turned, hoping with all his heart that it wasn't Ben Jonson intent on troublemaking, but instead it was a pair of tall young men, one fair and one dark, each better favored than the other and both fabulously clad in white and gold. The blonder and taller was Robert Catesby, dressed as a member of a Lord's retinue. The darker and broader wore a Baronet's ruff and a knight's chain about his neck, as if they had just come from court or some festivity.

The sight of the two of them there, in the Mermaid, killed Will's smile and had him moving toward the door, his cane hitting the floorboards in steady staccato as he closed the distance. Edmund fell into step, the amiable redheaded hack John Fletcher on his other side.

"Will," Edmund asked, "what's Will Parker doing here?"

Will shook his head. "I don't know. He's Baron Monteagle now, though—" *And Essex's man, knighted by him in Ireland along with the rest of the useless retinue.*

"Who's Will Parker?" asked Fletcher, blinking.

"Francis Tresham's brother-in-law. Which makes him Edmund's and my cousin by marriage," Will said, and somehow despite his limp outpaced Fletcher and Edmund enough that when he bowed before Parker the other two were half a step behind him. "Lord Monteagle."

"Cousin," Monteagle addressed him, in that rich dark voice that the player in Will had always envied. "I have a business proposition for you and your partners in the Globe. Perhaps we could discuss it in private?"

"A business proposition?" Will smiled, the fearful tautness in his chest easing. For one mad moment he had thought something had gone terribly wrong, but if it was only a favor to a relative, even if he was a peer— "We have a patron, cousin."

Catesby fell in beside them as they turned. Edmund led Fletcher aside, and Will caught Burbage's eye, and Will Sly's, and summoned them over with a stagy jerk of his head.

Monteagle laughed. "Oh, no. It's just, I had planned a party tomorrow for a friend, and the arrangements. Well. Your Globe rents for performances, does it not?"

Burbage joined them, Sly a half step behind. Will

opened the door to one of the private dining rooms at the back of the Mermaid and poked his head inside; a quiet conversation broke up and a group of players made themselves scarce for the unexpected appearance of a peer. Places were exchanged, and Sly shut the door firmly.

"Can you three speak for the Lord Chamberlain's Men, Master Players?" Catesby, his voice not so rich and refined as Monteagle's, but clearly precise. Monteagle wandered away, trailing a white-gloved finger along the woodwork like a master of servants in search of dust.

"I can," Burbage said, with a smile that softened it. "As much as can any man speak for a parcel of rogues."

Will exchanged glances with the other two players. "What do you need, Master Catesby?"

He cleared his throat as if to answer, but it was Monteagle who spoke, cleaning his fingertips daintily on a lace-edged handkerchief as he turned back. "A command performance? On a bit of an extreme schedule, I'm afraid."

"Extreme?" Burbage, in charge.

"Tomorrow," Catesby clarified, looking uncomfortable. "The facilities we had planned to use became unavailable."

"Tomorrow!" Sly touched his lips with his fingertips, and cleared his throat. "I mean, sirs, it would be a challenge, may it please my lord."

"It would have to be a play in repertory," Burbage said thoughtfully.

"Richard the Second."

"Oh."

Will laid a hand on Burbage's shoulder. "The Master of Revels—cousin, Her Majesty has let it be known that she is not overfond of that play—"

The Baron smiled. "The Earl of Southampton will be in attendance, dear cousin, and he is very fond of *Rich-*

ard the Second. Surely, for our family's sake, you could see your way to a private performance."

And will a gang of players, sturdy villains all, deny a request on behalf of an Earl? Burbage moved a half step back; Will recognized the gesture. Richard was giving him the floor.

"Cousin. We could play something fashionable, and give better value."

Monteagle smiled. "It's Harry." Meaning Southampton, of course. "You know how he is when he has his heart set on something."

"We'll pay forty shillings more than your ordinary fee, cousin," Catesby added.

Again the look, Burbage to Sly to Will.

An Earl and a Baron. There's no way to refuse without risking the company.

For forty pieces of silver.

Indeed.

"All right," Will said, and Burbage nodded.

It wasn't until Catesby had counted the silver into Will's hand that Monteagle added, "Of course, you must include the scene in which Richard loses his crown."

Act IV, scene xviii

I know sir, what it is to kill a man,
It works remorse of conscience in me,
I take no pleasure to be murderous,
Nor care for blood when wine will quench my thirst.

—CHRISTOPHER MARLOWE,
Tamburlaine the Great, Part II, Act IV, scene i

M ary Poley's voice had never been musical. It was as gypsy-wild as her mad black hair, but she leaned close to Kit now and leveled it as she laid a hand on his arm. "Thou didst send Will to look after us, Master Marlin."

I told Will this was a bad idea. He turned to look her in the eye, his back to the gallery railing. "Mistress Poley, I'm not certain I take your meaning—"

She looked up at him and shook her head. "Can't fool old Tom Watson's sister, Kitling. Shall I kiss each of thy scars to prove I know thy body well?"

She dropped her gaze from his eyes and seemed to be looking past him, but he didn't turn to see where. "Mary—"

"Hush, Kit. I'm grateful. And Robin is too. He's courting his master's daughter, you know. She's to go in service at the end of the year, but I do think he'll marry her when she returns and his apprenticeship is done—"

"He seems a fine lad."

"For all his looks, Kit, he's a sweet soul. More like thee than my husband, damn him to hell."

"I'm working on it," Kit answered dryly. She laughed, and closed her hand around his arm. "Thou hast nothing to justify to me, Mary."

"Not all men would see it so. Why didst thou not get me word thou hadst lived? I hope it was not that thou hadst no trust in Robert Poley's wife."

"I told no one. I was on the Queen's business."

"And now art home?" There was hope in it, like a razor dragged lightly over Kit's skin. He lifted her chin and looked into her eyes. She blinked. "Christ. Thou hast aged not an hour."

"Not home," he said. "Christofer Marley is as dead as Tom Watson, I fear."

"Then why hast thou returned?"

The railing was rough against his back. He turned to lean forward, looking down over the Mermaid, the bustle of poets and players and drunks. He rubbed fingers over the time-polished dark wood of the railing and lost an argument with a frown. "To say good-bye."

"Ah." She stepped up beside him and snuggled close, a compactly elfin warmth. No great beauty, Mary Poley, but a comforting sort of fey. He bent and kissed the top of her head; there weren't many women Kit was tall enough to perform that office upon. "Wilt pass Will somewhat of interest for me, Kitling? I've had no luck in cutting him out of the crowd for a privy conversation."

"Aye, I will." *Will.* A name that still had the power to stop his breath. *Aye, and I'd traffic with Hell for thee all over again, for moments such as this.* Kit searched the crowd below, but there was no sign of Will. Or, come to think of it, Burbage. There stood Edmund Shakespeare, talking with Henslowe and Alleyne, John Fletcher watching with interest. Ben Jonson had finally arrived and was carrying on a conversation with Chapman that looked at once animated and hushed, involving much waving about of hands.

Mary gulped breath; he felt it swell her slight body where she curled under his arm. "Robert's about something."

"Not Robin your lad?"

"No, Robert my husband—"

" '—damn him to Hell.' "

"Precisely."

"What is he about, Mary?" She had Kit's complete attention now, but he maintained the casual pose, a man in flirtation with a likely woman, both of them watching the flow and ebb of the gathering below.

A grunt, her little noise of frustration. "I know not. Mistress Matthews at the Groaning Sergeant is a friend of mine, and she says Robert and Richard Baines were in there of a morning, well pleased and talking of duping some Earl."

"That could be important. What Earl, and how duped? Dost know more?"

"The Queen's old favorite, I think, from what Mistress Matthews overheard. Essex, I mean. Robert Devereaux. I do not know what it is they mean to have him do, but she said that Baines was positively gloating about compelling such a man to do his bidding."

Kit shuddered, having some experience with Baines' compulsions. Even the quiet ones. "What else did she say?"

"Only that men and prentices came and went and met with the two of them all the morning, and a good deal of silver seemed to change hands—"

She stopped speaking suddenly. Kit knew from the way her breath halted that his own body had gone entirely rigid in her offhand grasp. *It could be but a resemblance,* he cautioned himself. *Especially from this angle.* "Mary," he said carefully. "What is the name of that man, the blond one coming out of the back room beside Will and Dick?"

"Why, Robert Catesby," she answered, all innocence.

His left hand tightened on the railing. His right pulled her close. "Oh, holy Hell," he blasphemed. "Mary, thou'rt a princess among women, and a canny one at that. I'll carry my affection for thee to a second grave, if I get one. So please, please, do not take it amiss that I needs must talk to Will on this instant, my dear, and that I may not have the chance to bid thee farewell again."

He stepped back. She caught his coarse linen shirt collar in her reed-fine hand and tugged him down to lightly kiss his mouth. "Go with God."

He laughed as he turned away. "Oh," he said. "If only."

Act IV, scene xix

Was it the proud full sail of his great verse,
Bound for the prize of all too precious you,
That did my ripe thoughts in my brain inhearse,
Making their tomb the womb wherein they grew?

— WILLIAM SHAKESPEARE, Sonnet 86

"This can only end ill," Kit said.

Will, hurrying fresh-barbered and clean-scrubbed through the streets to the bank where he meant to hire a wherry to Southwark and the Globe, glanced over at his friend and nodded. "Aye, there's no clean way clear of this mess, love. But then, we knew the truth of that when we stepped into it." Sudden worry diverted his conversation. "Kit, this is thy second day out of Faerie—"

Kit smiled, a steadying hand on Will's elbow as they clambered down the steps to the bank. The Thames had never frozen over, this winter, and the banks were clear of ice by now. A sign, perhaps, that Baines' Prometheans were losing ground at last.

"I've one more at least before it troubles me. What

concerns me more is that I've dreamed of Catesby—my ill dreams—and I've verily seen him in a room, talking privily with Baines. I can't think but that his presence on this errand with Lord Monteagle means that there will be trouble over this play."

"Trouble for the Lord Chamberlain's Men—" Kit handed Will into the boat as if Will were a lady in a farthingale, and Will glowered at him but didn't resist. *Mind thy limitations, Master Shakespeare. Or like as not thou'lt tumble into the muddy brown Thames and drown.*

"Aye," Kit continued once they were seated, leaning close that the boatman wouldn't overhear. "And intentionally so. They know your strength now."

They were silent then, as the river flowed under them.

"Kit," Will murmured, and coughed to ease the scratch in his throat. "I cannot think but there's more to it than that. If Baines is gloating that Essex has done something foolish—"

"Something foolish that Baines has directed him to do," Kit amended, paying the boatman as they reached the opposite bank. "It must be more than a play."

"Aye. It must. And we must find out an answer quickly." *Before it finds us out.* The earth was thawed beneath a layer of frost, crunchy-sticky underfoot. Kit helped Will up the bank and made no comment when Will struggled.

Kit had not seen the Globe before, and Will paused to let him tilt his head back and take in the scope of the massive whitewashed polygon. "It's built on timbers over a ditch to keep the footings dry," Will explained. "I stayed in that little house beside it a while last year. 'Tis very snug—"

"Clever," Kit said. "There were times I swear the groundlings at the Rose were to their knees in mud and worse things. The south bank's very wet—" He paused and lifted his chin in the direction of a tall woman swollen with her babe, her hair modestly covered and her skirts kilted to the ankle to keep them out of the mud. She was making for Will and Kit with grave determination, and her stride was not that of a work-worn goodwife. "Marry, Will. That woman hurrying to meet us—"

"Aye?"

"I know her."

And a moment later, Will did too, for all he had met her only once before, in a little room where her father lay rotting alive. "Frances Walsingham Sidney Devereaux," he said under his breath. "I never did understand what Walsingham's daughter and Sir Philip Sidney's widow could see in that strutting popinjay Essex."

Kit gave him a sidelong look. "She married him to inform on him to her father, Will. Shortly after Sir Francis faked his death. There was rather a lot of suspicion in our group that it was Essex behind the . . . 'poisoning' attempt. Much as he was behind the hideous death of the Queen's physician, poor Doctor Lopez."

"She married the man she thought tried to kill her father?" Will felt a chill that had nothing to do with the wind or the half-frozen earth underfoot settle into his belly.

Kit shrugged. "She's a Walsingham, Will." Will stared at him, and Kit folded his arms and continued, "Tom's no different when you scratch him deep enough. All for Queen and country, and not even honor for themselves. Perhaps thou shouldst see what she wants, thinkst thou not?" And Kit clapped him on the arm and moved away, leaving Will leaning on his cane and awaiting the attentions of the Countess of Essex.

She came before him bare of face and with her luxuriant dark brown hair coiled in demure spirals below a stolidly middle-class headdress. The style reinforced the prominence of the Walsingham nose: a convincing portrait of a housewife, but she didn't remember to curtsey. "Master Shakespeare."

"Mistress Sidney," he answered, and was rewarded by a sparkle of a smile. He stepped closer and bent his head down beside her bonnet, leaning propped on his cane. "If your purpose is to warn me off the misguided performance upon which I am about to embark, by all means, Madam, consider that I am as forewarned as a man might be. And as entrapped—"

She took his elbow lightly and walked with him toward the playhouse. Will was conscious of Kit a few steps behind and several yards off to the side, seemingly out of earshot and varying his distance to look unassociated. "My father thought highly of you. And I have been unable to speak to my cousin—"

Tom, of course. Will nodded, brushing beads of sweat from his forehead with his gloved left hand. "You know something the Queen needs to hear?"

"Aye," she said. "The Earl of Essex plans a rebellion tomorrow. He means to ride through London in a grand procession, if you can credit it, and exhort the people to rise and make him King. Your play, of course, will make them ready to accept his glorious reign—"

Will snorted laughter, and regained himself only with effort. "And he thinks this will work?"

"He thinks it will work. Southampton, Richard Baines, and Robert Catesby convinced him it would work. That their—*magic*"—as if the word filthied her mouth—"would ensure it."

"Christ on the cross," Will swore. "That's insanity. He'll be beheaded."

"I know," she said. "And you will be imprisoned at the least, and very likely hanged, unless you have resources of which I am not aware."

"I have Tom," Will said, and turned his head to cough thickly.

The Countess of Essex squeezed his arm. "Tom might suffice. And you might have Cecil as well, and perhaps the Lord Chamberlain. I'd say you have me, but as I am shortly to be widowed a second time"—there was no regret in her voice when she said it, only a kind of military firmness, and Will remembered her iron control as she bent over her father's deathbed—"I believe mine energies will be quite well spent in keeping mine own head."

"See that you do," Will answered, feeling a sudden rush of affection for this woman. "Do you know what Baines and so forth are about?"

She shook her head, already moving away. "My husband's downfall is a blind for something; he's a stalking horse, as well as a peacock. Where, and what, I have no better information than I have given you. And now, Master Shakespeare, I have three children and one unborn who very much need not be in London when the sun rises."

"Godspeed," he said, because there was nothing else to say. She turned and walked away, and stopped a few short strides up the verge.

"Master Shakespeare?"

"Yes, Mistress Sidney?"

"Did you really see the Devil by my father's deathbed?"

He sorted and discarded answers long enough that her eyebrow rose. He gave it up for a bad business and spread flat the hand that did not hold his cane. "Yes, madam."

She tilted her head charmingly. Her eyes were large and dark, dewy and doelike: the eyes of a young and beautiful girl. "Hmm," she said, turned her back on him, and walked away without another glance.

Will sighed on a long ragged breath, and turned to Kit as he came up. "Is that what Tom Walsingham does to you?"

Kit grinned and shook his head, very slightly. "*He* does it without trying, damn his eyes. Come on—" He tugged Will's sleeve, very slightly.

"What?"

"I contrived to eavesdrop, and make sure no one else was doing so. You have a play to perform. And we have an appointment with history, my love."

The performance, to neither poet's reassurance, went off without a bobble. When the body of the players retired to the Mermaid Tavern, Will—coughing—pled pain and exhaustion and Kit excused himself with an invention about a long ride home to Canterbury on the morrow. Later that evening they presented themselves to Sir Thomas Walsingham with news that all three men deemed of interest to the Queen.

"Thank you, my dears," Tom said, and seated himself right before them in order to pen a hasty message to Cecil.

Accounts varied as to whether three hundred men rode through London with Essex or only one hundred, but Robert Catesby and the Baron Monteagle were indubitably among them. Will himself could not attest. Kit had returned to Faerie via the mirror in Tom Walsingham's study, and Tom—over Will's feeble protests—had put the playmaker to bed in a spare room. Will's brother Edmund came to help nurse him in the morning, for there Will remained, sick with a fever and a heavy cough.

Act IV, scene xx

View but his picture in this tragic glass,
And then applaud his fortunes as you please

—CHRISTOPHER MARLOWE, *Tamburlaine the*
Great, Part I, lines 7–8

K it had come to think of the Darkling Glass as a sort
of convenience, reliable as a faithful hound, and it
annoyed him to no end to find the thing suddenly
misbehaving. He'd long ago ascertained that it couldn't
be used to spy over the shoulders of Richard Baines or
Robert Poley, who must have warded themselves from
its power somehow. Nor was it useful in the Presence of
Elizabeth herself, or in any of her palaces—a wise pre-
caution, he thought, and one he wished to apply himself
to solving when he found a quiet moment—

He was accustomed to its vagaries, and resigned to
them. But today, when he needed it most, the thing's
damnable unwillingness to hold a single steady image
frustrated him to swearing, and he had to restrain himself when he would have driven his fist against the glass.
He hit the wall instead, which was less satisfying and

hurt more, but had the advantage of not putting a price-less magical artifact at risk.

A priceless magical artifact which gave him *nothing,* except the useless information that Will was still abed in a darkened room, and Edmund and Jonson and Tom talking quietly in the withdrawing room hard by it. He looked for Baines, Catesby, Poley—and got only flick-ering darkness and useless pictures. A flock of ravens circling the Tower of London—a cold chill touched him at the image so reminiscent of his dreams—the sound of chanting men, and a swirling flicker that resolved into the streets of London strangely silent, every ear tuned to the ringing hoofbeats of some hun-dred or hundred and fifty horse. Essex, all in white, was unmistakable at their head.

They vanished as they headed for the palace and the Queen, and Kit's vision resolved on the old monastery, later playhouse, currently vacant hall of Blackfriars on the west end of London, just inside the city walls. Men filed into it, men in monk's robes, as they should not have been in Protestant London. As they should not have been in the second playhouse owned by the shar-ers of the Lord Chamberlain's Men, which those Men had never been able to use as a theatre because of the opposition of its neighbors, although Ben Jonson's plays were performed regularly by the boy players at Paul's.

And isn't that a little odd? Kit asked himself. *That there was no such opposition to another such establish-ment almost across the street?* Kit pressed both hands against the glass as the image swam again. He pushed it back toward Blackfriars, but it slid through his control like the reins of a fractious horse, leaving him grasping after nothing.

Baines must be there. This is whatever Essex's stupid-ity is intended to conceal. It is a juggler's flourish: while all eyes are on the Earl, Richard Baines sweeps a treasure into his pocket. And odd that Will should come down hard sick this day of all days—

And anything at Blackfriars, which should be closed tight and all but abandoned, is another chain linking the Lord Chamberlain's Men to Essex. Layers and layers deep, this: better than anything Poley could have managed on his best day.

God in Hell, I wish I knew what was going on. Who does any of this benefit? Not Essex, not Southampton. Baines?

There had been eight or ten robed men, he thought, although he'd only had a glimpse of them. There was no way one lone Elf-knight and sometime poet could manage so many, but Walsingham's London residence wasn't far from Blackfriars, and there were Tom, and Ben, and Edmund too—*if Edmund can be trusted. If Ben is not a member of two conspiracies at once.*

Kit shrugged at his own suspicions, and pushed through the Darkling Glass.

It wasn't as bad as he'd feared. Edmund—obviously already nervous in the presence of a knight—stood blinking by the window as Kit appeared in the center of the room, and Jonson broke off midsentence, glowering, reaching across a belly grown as mountainous as his self-importance to grasp his swordhilt. But Tom turned away from the two of them and smiled. "Welcome back," he said.

Jonson grudgingly released the handle of his weapon as Edmund found his voice. "T-tom Marlowe? What sorcery—"

"No time to explain," Kit said, his eyes on Tom Walsingham. "Does it seem strange to you that Will should be taken so ill yesterday, immediately *after* he gave the performance he had to give to suit the Promethean's plans?"

"God," Tom said. "Yes. Essex rides—"

"I know—"

"—What must we do?"

Kit swallowed and glanced from Ben to Edmund. Edmund looked at Jonson, who nodded. "Baines is at Blackfriars," Kit said. "With eight or ten magicians. Whatever happens, happens now—"

"And thou mean'st to interrupt?"

"Aye, Sir Thomas. If I can request a few able-bodied men."

"There's that in this room," Jonson said. "All this keeping secrets is hard on the use of hirelings."

"That it is."

"I've a few sturdy souls about the house who would suffice. Kit—"

Edmund glanced over his shoulder once, at the door into Will's sickroom. His head snapped back at the name Tom used, and his eyes widened. Kit bowed, his arms spread wide under his cloak. "At your service, Master Shakespeare. There's still no time to explain. What seems to be the problem, Sir Thomas?"

"The sturdiest of those souls is one Ingrim Frazier."

Kit's stomach clenched. From loose readiness for action to seasick horror in a second, but he gritted his teeth and kept his voice level. "As he's earned your forgiveness, Tom, I'll live with it. But—" *But I want to talk to him first.* Except there was no time for recriminations now, was there? Not with Will's life and Elizabeth's crown on the line. "I'll endure," he said, and ended whatever comment Tom might have made next with an abrupt flip of his hand.

Edmund seemed still at a loss. He tapped his fingers on the window ledge, his voice level and calm. "Will's told me a bit of these poet-wars, and that they have been quiet of late. His sickness is related?"

"To these sorcerous doings? Aye."

"Then I will come." He paused. "If I may consider your presence an invitation."

Kit laughed and turned to follow Tom as Tom moved toward the door. "Stuff your Warwickshire politeness, Ted. It's time to go to war."

It wasn't any easier to turn his back on Ingrim than he'd thought it would be. And Ingrim was keeping a weary weather eye on Kit as well, and Tom's broad shoulders between them. Kit thought, if Frazier could manage it, he might have turned invisible, or hidden himself behind Ben Jonson's bulk completely.

Ben, bless him for a foul-tempered young mule, was having none of it. He walked alongside Kit, an outward show of alliance that left Kit puzzled and looking for the trap, but the possibility existed that Jonson saw in Kit a more likely ally than Walsingham. Or possibly he just didn't care to run shoulder to shoulder with the servants, and wanted the buffer of Kit's velvet doublet and hooded cloak.

Kit sighed and turned away from another sidelong glance of Frazier's. *And the whole world knows Kit Marley lives. Thou couldst just have hired a herald to cry it through the streets, Kit—*

Seven men, including two servants whose names Kit had failed to overhear, walked swiftly west on Cheapside, which had begun to bustle again in the wake of Essex's dramatic ride. It didn't matter, to Kit's way of thinking; it wouldn't be long before Essex was riding back again. He overheard talk in the crowd: witnesses reported that Essex, due to a delay over choosing his outfit for the revolution, failed to prevent Sir Robert Cecil from publicly proclaiming the insurgents traitors, and that the people of London likewise failed to rise and make Essex their King.

The crowds made way for the seven afoot; Tom's height and Ben's sheer bulk were impressive, and Kit expected they all had the look of men with intention.

They were almost in sight of Newgate (where Kit had once spent an unpleasant two weeks, detained on charge of murder) when their route turned south; in a matter of minutes they drew up under an overhang a few hundred yards from the playhouse. Kit stripped his glove off his right hand carefully, lest it interfere with his grip on his rapier.

"Well," Jonson said in his incongruous tenor, "time's a-wasting—"

"Aye," Kit answered. "Shall we be clever about it?"

"You're too clever by half, if you ask me—"

"Which no one did."

"Gentlemen." Tom didn't bother to glare, but Kit subsided like a chastised schoolboy and Jonson fell silent too. They both had cause to know that tone. "The time for subtlety is past," Tom continued, and drew a snaphaunce pistol from his belt. "I wish we had Will or Dick here. It would give a little more credence to the story that we shot ten men for looting if one of us had somewhat to do with the property."

Kit shrugged. "Forgiveness is cheaper than permission. And we're unlikely to shoot more than one or two at the most unless you're handing out petards, Tom."

"Aye," Tom answered. "Sadly, I've but the one. Come on then; let's bloody our hands."

It wasn't exactly a charge: more a concerted rush. Jonson reached the door first and—to Kit's surprise—merely tried the handle. Tom, nervy as a colt, jumped when the hinges creaked, and Ben stopped with the portal open no more than a quarter inch. "Dammit, Ben—"

"We'll be silhouetted against the street when we open the door," Jonson said with a soldier's calm. He braced the door with his toe to hold it in place while he drew, cocked, and primed his own pistol. "We have to enter quickly, divided to each side, and fan out in case they have firearms within."

Edmund shot him a glance with a question behind it, and Ben shook his head. "Fought in the Low Countries," he murmured. "Ready, lad?"

"Aye."

"Good. Stay at my shoulder. Keep moving. Master Marlowe? Sir Thomas?"

Kit nodded tightly, not sad to see Jonson take control. As much as he bragged on his brains, Kit thought, drawing his sword, Jonson was very much in his element as a man of action.

"Go, Ben," Tom said over the hammering of Kit's heart, and Jonson shoved the door open and went in, head down and shoulders hunched like a charging bull. The rest rushed through behind, slipping aside like court dancers into the dimly lit interior. Somehow, Kit wound up pressed against the wall beside Frazier, shoulder to shoulder, but neither had a glance for the other now as their eyes strained into uncandled dimness, searching for a flicker of movement that might reveal the shift of a pistol or a blade. To Kit's *otherwise* sight, the figures of any conjuring sorcerers should have stood out plainly, but he saw nothing in that breathless moment but a few dust motes hung on a crack of light.

And then Jonson cursed, moving forward, and bent over some dark shapes outlined on the floor. Kit moved away from Frazier and the wall, deciding there was no need for quiet and that he was damned if he'd let Ingrim rattle him badly enough that Kit wouldn't turn a shoulder on him with five other men there to ward his back. Kit crossed to where Ben crouched. "Master Jonson?"

"Too late," Jonson said, and used the blade of his rapier to prod a pile of sad-colored cloth. "Monk's habits. Theatre costumes, I think, and quite abandoned. Are those your robed men, Master Marlowe?"

"Fuck me for a whore," Kit said, turning his head to

spit on the floor. "I just played right into his god-be-damned hands. Again."

Tom turned to search his face, and Kit forced himself to meet the expressionless gaze. "What meanst thou, Kit?"

"I mean this was a feint as well, a trap laid for any that might have followed Baines or sought to scry after him. And while we were here, and the Queen's troops distracted by Essex, and Will struck down sick in his bed, Baines and his fellows have been about whatsoe'er they wishcd to be about, utterly undisturbed."

"Ah." Tom braced his hands before himself and settled back against the wall. "So what do we do now?"

Jonson, strangely, clapped a hand on Kit's shoulder—and drew it back again, quickly, as if scorched. "Wc go back to your house, Sir Thomas. And we fight like cats to save our Will, and pray we make more of a success of it than we did with saving Spenser."

Kit flinched. "And Lord Strange. And Walsingham."

Act IV, scene xxi

For why should others' false adulterate eyes
Give salutation to my sportive blood?
Or on my frailties why are frailer spies,
Which in their wills count bad what I think good?

—WILLIAM SHAKESPEARE, Sonnet 121

In his fever, Will dreamed that Elizabeth attended him. He dreamed her long fair hands, her hair like ruby glass when the light shone through it. He dreamed Elizabeth, but her breath was sweet as a maiden's and her eyes as much green as gray.

His flesh burned until he thrust the blankets aside, and then he shivered with the cold. He was distantly aware that he whined like a child and fussed at the tender hands restraining him, while voices gentle, cajoling, and bitterly frustrated by turns spoke over him. One voice—"Annie?" It could have been Annie—and then a second.

There was a rhythm to that other one: halting, hiccuping, but a meter and a tenor he knew. "It's not the King's Evil," the voice said pettishly. "The touch of a Queen's hand won't heal him—"

Linen abraded his skin like coarse wool. His muscles ached as if knotted. Sickly sweet fluid trickling past his teeth made him gag, and he batted the hands that wrung a damp rag into his mouth and other, stronger hands that held him down. He screamed when they covered him, but it was a mew weak as a kitten's, and he shivered when they did not. He clawed at a blanket with a texture that puzzled him, for it was sometimes velvet soft and sometimes silk-slick under his hands.

The rag was withdrawn. Someone leaned into his ear and whispered poetry. A thread of logic and meter and beauty wound through the madness of the fever and the visions and the knotting pain—

"Come live with me and be my love

"And we will all the pleasures prove—

"As hills and—dammit. Dammit, William, thou'lt not be quit of me so easy. These words thou knowest. There's virtue in them. Say them with me, damn you to Hell, just a little breath—"

Dear voice, and so frightened, so thick with frustration and hurt. He reached for it, or tried to reach, tried to do what it bid him and shape the words, find the power behind them. There was nothing, no movement, no reach.

Such a dear voice.

And so far away.

> *There will I make thee beds of roses*
> *And a thousand fragrant posies,*
> *A cap of flowers, and a kirtle*
> *Embroider'd all with leaves of myrtle.*
> —CHRISTOPHER MARLOWE, "The Passionate
> Shepherd to His Love"

Kit pressed the heels of his hands to his eyelids to keep the tears locked in. A terrible odor rose from Will's papery skin. Kit wiped his nose on his cuff and looked up at Morgan hopelessly. "I don't know what to do."

"Keep fighting." Succinctly, and not looking up from whatever she was steeping by the fire. She stood and came toward him, the steaming cup held in her hands.

Kit reached to restrain Will's hands, so Morgan could again trickle her medicines into him. Will's skin felt thin enough to crackle to the touch, hot as the side of a lantern.

Morgan shook her head. "Kit, 'tis for thee." She held the mug out and he took it, cupped it in hands too tired to lift it to his mouth.

"Thou wert wrong about me, Morgan."

She nodded, straightening Kit's cloak across Will's breast as he tossed and shivered. They did not know if its magic would help Will, but there was no harm in trying. "I underestimated thee."

Somehow, Kit got the cup to his mouth. Perhaps even the steam was fortifying. It tasted of bitter earth and summer sun and the unshed tears still clogging his throat. "What if he dies?"

"What if he dies *now,* thou meanest?" She bent and kissed Kit's hair as if he were a child. "We endure."

> *No, I am that I am, and they that level*
> *At my abuses reckon up their own . . .*
> —WILLIAM SHAKESPEARE, Sonnet 121

Will fell deeper. Sometimes it seemed those hands held him, caressed him, cooled his brow. Sometimes he thought he plunged through darkness eternally and heard nothing but the Devil's amiable laughter, and knew nothing but the heat of his own Hell. Nothing could touch Will in the void; he knew somehow that he needed poetry, needed the power of his words, but in his jumbled consciousness he could not put one line of a poem with another.

But through the darkness came that dear, distant voice again, and that voice gave him poetry. "Thy gift, thy tables, are within my brain, full charactered with lasting memory—"

Will turned to the faint glimmer of sound, if turning it could be called. Heat cupped his body, pressed his skin. He writhed away from it, sure that there were flames and that the flames had seared his eyes from his head, because surely there could be no such agony in darkness.

The pain left him amazed.

"Which shall above the idle rank remain, beyond all doubt ev'n to eternity—"

Iambs.

Not blank verse though, and blank verse was important. Blank verse, the enjambed line, the rhythm of natural speech carrying an incantation's power.

"Or at the least so long as brain and heart have faculty by nature to subsist—till each to razed oblivion yield his part of thee, thy record never can be missed."

A sonnet.

It's a sonnet.

A sonnet he knew, although he could not remember from where. He swam through blackness, pushed and pulled, following the thread of that voice—a voice that cracked with weariness or emotion, and in cracking broke Will's heart and made him strive the harder, because he knew, somehow, that the pain he heard could somehow be healed if he—

"That poor retention could not so much hold,"

—could only—

"Nor need I tallies thy dear ... dammit. Thy dear love to, to score,"

—pierce—
"Therefor to give them from me was I bold,"
—that—
"To trust those tables that receive thee more."
—blackness.

The heat was more. The pain, the burning. Will pressed at it, and it was not like walking through flames, because flames cannot push back. His body trembled, and he understood that it was his body, suddenly, soaked in sweat, cloyed under blankets in a room where the fire roared beyond all sense and the bed was pulled so close beside it that the bedclothes smelled scorched where they weren't soaked in sour sweat and stinking fluids. And he was cold, shivering cold, and Kit was bent over a book beside the bed. Kit was wiping away the sweat that must be stinging his sleepless eyes, then angling a tablet in dim light to read the poem in a voice that creaked with overuse.

Will's hand darted out like a snake, all his reserves gone in one flash of motion, and he caught Kit's wrist, and Kit's eyes came up, widening.

"To keep an adjunct to remember thee," Will finished, or tried to finish, because coughing racked him into an agonized crescent. Kit steadied his head, pressed a handkerchief to his mouth, which filled with ropes and clots of something that had the taste of iron and the texture of boiled brains. Will choked, coughing until he would have vomited if there were anything in his belly but bitter yellow froth, until he sobbed, half wishing for death.

He would have curled up again in misery, but Kit held his shoulders until he finished, and wiped his mouth again, and touched his forehead, which was slick and wet.

And then Kit smiled, and said, "Were to import forgetfulness to me," which Will understood was the end of the invocation, the end of the poem. And then Kit finished, "Thy fever's broken. Praise God," and hugged him hard enough to make his bones creak.

"I'm *hot*," Will said petulantly, and Kit burst out laughing with relief and got up to knock the fire apart until it died down a little, all the while shouting for Morgan.

> *A gown made of the finest wool*
> *Which from our pretty lambs we pull,*
> *Fair linéd slippers for the cold,*
> *With buckles of the purest gold.*
> —CHRISTOPHER MARLOWE, "The Passionate
>   Shepherd to His Love"

After the fateful ride, the Queen's men escorted Essex, a wounded and dignified Catesby, a profusely apologetic Monteagle, the estimable Francis Tresham, and a few dozen others to their temporary quarters in the Tower of London, from whence they would be tried. The revolution ended, most said, more or less as ineffectually as it began. And it was Richard Burbage who brought the news to Tom Walsingham's house, where he had come in search of Will.

"It's good that thou'lt live," Burbage said, perched on the stool at Will's bedside as Audrey Walsingham spooned broth into the sick man, out of mercy for his shaking hands. The bed had been pulled back from the fire and Kit's cloak aired and returned to him. Will himself was sitting up against pillows, the crusted lesions at the corners of his mouth almost healed and his eyes their normal calm blue, not dull with fever.

Kit leaned back on a settee against the wall and cupped between his palms the mulled wine that Morgan had given him. His voice at last had failed him utterly, and he drooped, inches from sleep, in a warmly contented state of exhaustion that was too pleasant to abandon for bed. *Beside that,* he thought, *I'd rather sit in a corner and watch that man make faces over unsalted bouillon than ever sleep again. Even if the whole*

room draped in red cloths to combat fever does make of
this place a scene out of Dante.

Morgan and Tom and Ben Jonson had crowded into
the tiny sickroom now, Tom by his wife's shoulder, Morgan not far from Kit, and Jonson as geographically distant from the slumping Marley as the closet's confines
would allow.

Will, concentrating on swallowing the soup without
choking, did not answer.

" 'Tis good thou hast survived," Burbage repeated,
"because Her Majesty would be most wroth with me if
thou hadst not."

"Her Majesty?" Will's voice was weak but clear.
He laid a hand on Audrey's wrist to restrain her when
she would have poured more sustenance into him, and
turned to Burbage. "Richard, what meanest thou?"

Burbage sighed. "She requests the Lord Chamberlain's Men perform for her on the twenty-fourth of the
month. Shrove Tuesday. That's thirteen days hence; thou
hast lain fevered for three. And the play she wants is
Richard the Second, and she very especially mentioned
your name among the company of players she wishes
to see perform it. I was half afeared"—Burbage's hand
on Will's thin shoulder belied the brusqueness of his
tone—"I would have to send word you were detained
in a churchyard."

"Not dead yet," Will answered before taking more
soup. "Thirteen days. *Richard the Second.* I may be able
to do it—"

"I won't have you killing yourself over a play, Will."
Jonson, forgetting himself, moved from his nervous
post by the door and then stopped. He cast a wary
glance at Kit, who knew his chin had started sagging to
match his eyelids, and Kit struggled with a half-formed
understanding.

Christ. Ben Jonson is scared of me. Scared I'll seduce

him? Or scared I'll overpower him and have my way with him?

Now *there* was an image incongruous enough to send an exhausted poet giggling, and giggling touched Kit's ravaged throat and turned to a hacking cough, which drew the worried glances of everyone in the room.

"Kit, thou'rt sickening—" Will, ignoring Jonson's command.

Kit saw another measure of hurt cross the ugly young man's face, and the half-formed understanding crystallized into pity. *Oh. Ben—*

But there was nothing to be done for it, was there?

"No," Kit managed, a stage whisper that almost started him coughing again. "Just talked raw. Will, Ben is right." Morgan brought Kit more wine, and he drank it, enjoying Ben's surprise at his intercession.

Will shook his head, looked up at Burbage. "Richard, why the twenty-fourth, precisely?"

The room got very quiet. Kit glanced from face to face, and realized everyone assembled knew the answer but for him. Like Will, he waited, calm enough in the knowledge that they would live. It was satisfying enough that he and Morgan and Tom—and Audrey and Jonson and Burbage and most of all, Will—had *beaten* Baines' worst. No answer could trouble him.

It was Tom who cleared his throat, and answered, "Because Essex is to be executed on the twenty-fifth, and Her Majesty wishes to see the play before she has her old friend drawn and quartered."

Silence, as Kit struggled upright against the sugared grip of gravity, and his gaze met Will's across the room. "Oh," Will said. "Oh, poor Elizabeth."

Act IV, scene xxii

The play's the thing,
Wherein I'll catch the conscience of the king.

—WILLIAM SHAKESPEARE, *Hamlet,*
Act II, scene ii

The Queen in her goodness commuted Essex's sentence from hanging and torture to a simple beheading; it was rumored that he had been reproved to choose his wardrobe the night before, and Will imagined he might be about his task even as *Richard the Second* wound to its close. Will's hands shook as he sponged the makeup from his face.

The dates of the other executions had not yet been set, and Will wondered if they would be, when news from across the Irish Sea had Spanish Catholic troops again landing in alliance to the Catholics of that emerald isle.

A genteel cough at Will's shoulder alerted him to the presence of a page. Will turned. "Yes?"

"Her Majesty wishes to see you, Master Shakespeare. In the red withdrawing room. Her Majesty said you would know it."

"Aye," Will said, wiping his hands again to be sure he was free of paint, and reaching for his cane. He should have felt apprehension, he knew. But when he reached for emotion, there was nothing there at all. "Please tell Her Majesty I'll be along presently. My balance is not what it was."

Which was the curse of this disease; his strength didn't leave him, or his intellect. Just his ability to make his body obey his lawful commands.

When the page opened the door and gave him admittance, Will was startled to realize that the Queen was alone. The page slipped out behind him and the door latched shut. Will suffered a second realization that *he* was alone with the Queen.

Elizabeth stood by the far archway, a single candle warming her ice-white ceruse. "Master Shakespeare," she said, as he began to bow awkwardly. "Rise. 'Twill be enough of that. And find a chair, young man: I can see thy legs are about to desert thee and I have no mind to pluck thee off my carpeting."

"Your Highness," Will said, and sat awkwardly although the Queen did not. *I, she said, and not we. How interesting.* "I am honored to be in your presence."

Her lips assayed a smile and almost managed it. "I'll kill a man tomorrow."

"Yes, Your Highness." Trying to keep his Christian pity for Elizabeth from his face, and, he suspected, failing.

"I waged rather a grand battle to save him, Master Shakespeare, and failed. Why do you suppose that is?"

"Why you did try to save him, Your Highness? Or why you did fail?" Greatly daring, he thought, but she seemed to invite it. Indeed, she inclined her head under its great jeweled tire and made a come-along gesture with one gloved hand. Will watched her face, trying to judge how bold he might be, but her ceruse made a mask. "I think you did try to save him for you loved him. And he failed to be saved because he loved himself."

"Ah," she said. "Thou art a poet indeed. When I am gone, wilt make a play of me as thou didst my royal father?"

"No mere play could capture Your Highness, and no boy could play you. As well set a pussycat to play a princely lion."

"Flattery." But she smiled, a real smile this time. Her voice was low and very sweet. "So in honesty, as a poet, and with no ears to hear but mine—what think you of this latest string of murders upon which I will filthy my hands?"

Will examined her face, and knew by the way she stood that she meant to seem only a woman. He could not trust that, however. *Kit would be proud.* "Monteagle's just a foolish young gallant, Your Highness. Southampton—" Will shrugged. "Led astray, perhaps. Perhaps leading. I don't know that they deserve to swing. Unlike Essex—"

"Who won't. Swing, that is. He'll get a clean death. My last gift. Perhaps I'll spare the other two, if it pleases thee." She cast about herself for a chair; Will hastened to rise and fetch her one, and she pinned him down with a look. "Obey thy sovereign."

"I was there when they hanged Lopez," Will said, once she had settled herself. "I was there when Sir Francis died."

"Meaning?" Perhaps dangerous, those folded hands, that softly arched brow.

And what will she do? Cast thee in the Tower? "It seems, if it please Your Highness, that your enemies sometimes get the gentler side of your hand than your loyal friends. My Queen."

"It does not please me," she said. They faced one another across the dark red pattern on the carpet, faces dim in shifting candlelight. Will forced his hands to stay smooth on his thighs and swallowed against his worry that he had overstepped. "But it is true. And thou art correct in other things as well. I am sick of politics, Master Shakespeare. I am deathly tired."

It was an understatement. He saw it in her face, heard it in the timbre of her voice. An old woman, Queen before Will was born and—he realized with a shock—not likely to be Queen much longer. Elizabeth had been eternal. Elizabeth was England.

Elizabeth was deathly tired. *Perhaps this was Baines' goal all along,* Will realized. *To force her hand to kill Essex, whom she loved for all his faults. It's broken her at last.*

"Your Majesty—"

"Aye?"

"Did anyone among your servants ever love you as much as you loved him? Or did they all betray you?" Will almost clapped a hand over his mouth when the words came out, but it was too late and they were flown. He watched them hang there in the candlelight, wishing them recalled, and did not look at the stunned placidity of Elizabeth's face.

Until she laughed. She threw back her head and roared like a sailor, one hand clutched to her breast, her eyes squinted tight and tears of mirth smearing her kohl into her ceruse. Her mouth fell so far open in her laughter that Will saw the wads of batting that padded out her cheeks where her teeth were gone. "Oh, William," she said. "Oh, you ask the finest questions. I should have made thee my fool—"

"Your Highness, I am sorry—"

"Apologize not." Suddenly serious, as she dabbed the corners of her eyes. She sat and thought a little while, and smiled. "I think I have been loved," she said at last. "Aye, my Spirit loved me—Lord Burghley, to thee. And

Sir Francis, for all I was very wroth with him. And my good Sir Walter; caught up in his games, but I do think his love is true. It's these others I cannot seem to choose with any—" Her voice cracked, and she waved her hand as if to show that the word eluded her, but Will thought it wasn't tears of laughter that showed now in her eyes. "I am Great Harry's daughter, Master Shakespeare. Great Harry, I am not," she said simply. "I am not my sister. I am what I am—"

"You're England, Gloriana," he said, and rose—against her command—and with his cane as a welcome prop he kneeled down at her feet.

Act IV, scene xxiii

Strike off their heads, and let them preach on poles.
No doubt, such lessons they will teach the rest,
As by their preachments they will profit much
And learn obedience to their lawful king.

—CHRISTOPHER MARLOWE, *Edward II,*
Act III, scene ii

Thomas Nashe was buried on the last day of July 1601, some five months after the execution of the Earl of Essex. They had been quiet months, and Kit Marlowe (or Marlin, or Merlin) had a sense that both sides were holding their breath, waiting for the next sally to follow the removal of Essex.

There was no question anymore that Baines would sacrifice anyone without a thought, and no supposition that he had any allies among his pawns.

Kit Marlowe (or Marlin, or Merlin) attended Nashe's funeral in a plain brown cloak and a workman's tunic. He stood well toward the back, his hood raised in a manner inappropriate to the heat, supplementing the illusions with which he had veiled himself. He left before the body was lowered into the grave.

He felt Will's eyes upon him as he left the church, but Will didn't turn to follow, and Kit thought they'd meet later in Will's rooms, anyway. Maybe. Kit wasn't sure he wanted to talk about Tom, thought maybe he wasn't ready to talk about Tom. Tom who had been acerbic, witty, abrasive—and Kit's oldest friend.

Tom, who alone among his friends Kit had managed to keep clear of the damned war with the Prometheans and its black world of espionage and sorcery and murder. Tom who should have grown old and fat and retired none the wiser, and raised up babies and perhaps named one Christofer.

Tom, who had not even died for a cause—of poison, of sorcery, of a knife in the eye—but who had died simply because he'd tripped on a paving stone and been crushed to death under the wheels of a carter's haulage.

Kit wandered London like a homeless man, a sturdy vagrant or a tradesman out of doors. He startled a feral hound or two and smiled at a feral child, who was equally startled. Slow clouds came over one by one, but none of them promiscd any rain, and his cloak was stifling. His feet baked inside their boots. *St. Paul's,* he thought, the churchyard where the stationers had their booths. But something drew him west instead, beyond the old cathedral, until he stood in the shadow of Newgate and then passed through. Prisoners were being loaded into a cart outside the walls of London; Kit spared them a sideways glance and barely prevented himself from stopping in his tracks.

One of the men on the cart, his hands bound with rope and his face pinched with privation, was Nicholas Skeres.

The cart lurched as one of the oxen shifted. Skeres fetched up against the rail and yet did not look up, and the milling guards largely ignored him. Kit tapped one on the arm.

"What?"

Kit showed the man a pair of silver shillings, cupped in his palm. "Those prisoners there. Where are they bound?"

The guardsman grunted and glanced over his shoulder to see if they were observed. He held out his palm, and silver jingled into it. "Bridewell," he said. "Questioning and execution. Counterfeiters and a cutthroat or two, not that you asked."

"No," Kit said. "I didn't. Thank you." *Questioning and execution.* Torture and execution, more like. Kit stepped away from the guardsman and kept walking, putting a few hundred yards between himself and Newgate before an ox lowed and the rattle of the cart alerted him that the prisoners were moving. He stepped to the verge and waited.

Nick Skeres, the little bastard. And Baines and Poley throw him to the wolves as well, and the rescue Will and I expected unforthcoming. I wonder how he outlived his usefulness. And then a softer thought, hesitant. *I could do somewhat. I could find a way to rescue him. Sorcery is good for something. . . .*

Who was Christofer Marley, is that a glimpse of forgiveness I see in thee?

Kit poked it, considering, and shook his head within the mantle of his hood. *No,* he decided, and slid his hood down before the cart reached him, stepping forward to draw Skeres' eye. The little man looked, and startled, and looked again. Kit left his hands folded tidily under the cloak and lifted his chin, meeting Skeres' eyes, watching the condemned men pass.

There, he thought, when the press of bodies kept Skeres from turning to watch him out of sight. *There was a touch of fate in that one.*

Something witnessed.

* * *

Later that evening, he leaned forward on the floor before Will's chair and gritted his teeth. He bundled his shirt in his arms and held it to his chest, covering the scar there, as Will ran cool hands that almost didn't tremble down the length of his back. The touch itched; Kit forced himself to think of it in the same terms as that long-ago evening, when Morgan had painstakingly stitched the wound over his eye.

"Kit, does it hurt thee?"

"It makes me want to crawl over broken glass to escape, but no, it does not hurt me. And it may, perhaps, be better than last time." *A little,* he amended, forcing himself not to cringe as Will laid his palms flat on the tops of Kit's shoulders. A simple touch that should have been warming, and it was all he could do to permit it.

"If it doesn't help," Will said, "we won't do this."

"I don't know yet if it helps," Kit said. "Distract me. What shall we talk of? Not poor foolish Tom—"

"No, not Tom. Essex? I didn't attend the execution."

"Nor I. But our Sir Francis and poor Lopez are avenged."

"Some vengeance," Will answered, pressing harder. The firmer touch was easier to bear. "Elizabeth didn't commute *Lopez's* sentence from hideous torture to clean beheading."

"There's a moral there, my William." Kit flinched away finally, the need to withdraw too great to bear. He hugged his shirt tighter and bent forward, fighting useless tears. Will poured him wine, and he dropped the shirt in his lap to take it. They had swept the rushes aside, and a splinter on the floorboards snagged Kit's breeches.

"What's that?"

" 'Tis better to be pretty than to be skilled."

Intra-act: Chorus

In the forty-fifth year of Elizabeth's reign, twenty-five months to the day after the Lord Chamberlain's Men performed *Richard II* before her on that Shrove Tuesday in 1601, Will leaned over the garden gate of the house on Silver Street. Snowdrops bloomed in profusion about his boots, but Will was insensible to them. Hands folded, head cocked, he listened to the amazing present weight of something he had never heard before and would never hear again.

Silence in the streets of London Town.

The church bells hung voiceless. The criers and costermongers and hustling shoppers had deserted the streets. The playhouses stood empty, the markets deserted, the doors of every church open to the cold and any in need of refuge, or of comfort, or of prayer.

Elizabeth of England was dead.

Act V, scene i

But Faustus' offence can ne'er be pardoned: the serpent that tempted Eve may be saved, but not Faustus.

—CHRISTOPHER MARLOWE, *Faustus,* Act V, scene ii

My dearest Kit:

I hope this finds thee well, & her Majesty the Mebd recovered from her weary illness when Gloriana passed. I have thought of her often, although I have refrained from offering prayers on her behalf, as she will no doubt understand.

As for myself? I am thick with news, & will make haste to lay it before thee. James of Scotland & England is King, & all is not well, my love.

Ev'ry bell in London tolled his welcome.

The King landed at the Tower of London on eleventh May, having taken some care to ensure his progress from the north would be suitably stately that his arrival would not encroach on Elizabeth's state funeral. Ben designed the triumphal arch through which he entered the city, and Ned Alleyne, a bit coldly clad, delivered a speech penned by Tom Dekker. The poets will have their say—and Ben got a charm into his working, which may help or it may not. Sir Robert Cecil came with him, having ridden north to York to greet our new Monarch. I did hear later that the ravens at the Tower flew up to greet the King's barge, & that the small zoo of lions within that ancient stronghold's precincts roared him welcome from their cages.

Gossip has been running through the streets on a river of wine & ale, &—between performances—I soak it in from my accustomed chair at the Mermaid. I am become quite the fixture there; thou wilt be pleased to know I have made a fine recovery of my fever, & in fact feel stronger now than I did before it.

Sadly, the same cannot be said for London. James has been crowned in a time of plague such as London has not suffered since thy murder, dear friend. Almost a decade since, & again crosses mark doorboards & whole families sicken. 'Tis not, methinks, auspicious.

One of the dead is Ben's son. Still when they cannot have us, they strike at our children.

Ah, but on to those gossips. They say, dear friend, that the new King is as great a hunter & lover of sport as the old Queen. They say 'tis time England had a man's hand on the tiller again. They say James dances at court & tumbles with his children: he has three, & another in his fair Queen's belly. They say that that Queen loves dancing as well, & plays— which bodes well—& the masques of Ben Jonson.

Moreover. They say she is Catholic, & her husband the King Protestant. & I am not the only one who has breathed a low sigh of relief & permitted himself a giddy measure of hope at that small truth.

We players wore scarlet for the coronation: we are the King's—rather than the Lord Chamberlain's—Men now, & Grooms of the Bedchamber. Which one would suppose might give me some greater power to tug the King's earlobe & press the suit of our Bible, but alas, 'tis the Great Chamber only, and not the Privy—'tis but a ceremonial toy, as someone I know was wont to say. And James has adopted Cecil, & raised him to the peerage no less, & Cecil will not see it done.

I've managed to remind Monteagle of my assistance in seeing him & Southampton released from the Tower, & that may serve us well. Elizabeth's good Sir Walter, I fear, has taken their place in duress, for James does not trust him. Many changes are afoot, & I for one shall tread most carefully.

Still, Annie is well, the girls tall as trees. Tom sends his affection, & Ben has rejoined our fold along with Chapman. All of us would like to see thee come again to our evening's entertainments, if I may call them that. Well, all but Ben perhaps, & he will endure. I cannot say age has settled him, precisely, except it has. After a fashion. Or it may simply be that his wife is in London now, and it may be that they will reconcile. And if she will not content him, he has the wives of other men to hawk after—

Have a care. The Prometheans are very quiet. The plague notwithstanding. Young master Benjamin Jonson buried at seven years notwithstanding, as well. Though, if anything, that has made our Ben more determined. He speaks not of it, but he's cold with purpose now.

We have that in common.

Oh, Kit, shouldst see what I am writing. Our adventures in Lucifer's demesne—I know do nei-

*ther of us talk of them o'ermuch, but the plays I
am making now, daresay, are not like anything thou
hast seen before—*

—nay, shall not tease thee.
But come, love.
I have things to show thee.

thy Will

The door of the library swung open, and Kit looked
up from quiet conversation with Amaranth to see Murchaud framed against its dark red wood. "Kit," the Prince
said, smiling, "a moment of your time?"

"Your Highness," Kit answered, not unironically. He
made a bow over Amaranth's hand and turned to follow
Murchaud. They went in silence up the stairs; Murchaud
led Kit to his rooms and unlocked the door with quiet
concentration.

Kit followed calmly. *Oh, won't this inspire gossip in
the court.* "Murchaud?" he asked, when the door was
latched again.

The Elf-knight's shoulders drooped like wings as
soon as their privacy was assured. "She's no better," he
said shortly, and went to pour wine for them both.

Kit followed at his heels, trying not to think that he
must have looked like a faithful cur at his master's boot.
"Is she worse?"

"No. I've never heard of anything like. 'Tis possible
the Faerie Queen grew so linked with Gloriana in the
minds of England's folk that Gloriana's passing could
take the Mebd with it. And if the Mebd dies without
loosing her bonds, all those Fae who are knotted in her
hair die with her."

"Would she do that? Take you all to the grave?" Kit
was unprepared for the barb of panic that stabbed his
breast; he took the wine—littered with bits of peppery

nasturtium flowers like confetti—and covered his face with the rim.

"Come, sit." Murchaud gestured him to one of two chairs on either side of the low table near the window. There was a chessboard set up, and beside it lay a book marked with a ribbon that Kit had been reading—

—before Will came to Faerie. *And Murchaud has not seen fit to return it to the library.* Kit planted himself in the chair and set his glass down. Murchaud settled opposite. "She might," the Elf-knight said, nodding judiciously. "Wilt fight for her, Christofer?"

"Poetry?"

"Aye." Murchaud swirled his wine as much as drank it, seeming to savor the aroma.

"I will," Kit answered. A familial silence fell between them, and at last Kit succumbed to the siren song of the book on the table. He picked it up and thumbed through, trying to see if he remembered what led up to the place where the ribbon lay.

Murchaud let the quiet linger long enough that his voice startled Kit when he spoke again. "Dost trust me, my Christofer?"

Kit raised his eyes over the top of his book and met Murchaud's gaze. "Thy Christofer? Surely not—"

Murchaud braced his boot on the low table between them, turning a black chess knight between his fingers. "Then whose else art thou?"

Which gave Kit pause. "The Devil's. I suppose."

"And not thine own?" Murchaud stood, a movement too fluid to seem as abrupt as it was, and began to pace, revealing to Kit that this was not an idle conversation.

"Had I *ever* that luxury?"

Which made Murchaud turn his head and blink softly. "Does any man?"

"Or any elf? No." Kit sighed. "Aye, my Prince. I trust thee as much as I might trust any Elf-knight."

"Which is to say not at all."

Kit shrugged and set his book aside, then reached for the wineglass on the table. He raised it in salute, watching Murchaud roll the chess knight across the back of his fingers, as Will was wont to do with coins. "Why all this sudden concern with trust?"

"There is a wound festers in thee."

"Who, me?" Kit sipped his wine and managed an airy dismissal with the back of his left hand. "I assure thee, I am festerment-free."

"Not that *I* distrust *thee* . . ." Murchaud smiled and closed the distance between them. He dropped the chessman into Kit's wineglass, where it vanished with a plop and a clink, and crouched beside Kit's chair. When Kit turned to him, startled, Murchaud knotted Kit's hair tight in both hands and kissed him fiercely, with a seeking tongue.

Kit bore it as long as he could, but couldn't stop the sudden backward jerk of his head—a painful yank against Murchaud's grip on his hair—or the sharp, humiliating whimper.

"Aye," Murchaud said, breath hot on Kit's ear before he sat back on his heels. "Thou'rt perfectly fine. Stubborn fool."

"Murchaud—"

"Silence. I can heal thee, Kit."

"Heal?" His heart accelerated; he drew back the hand he had braced on Murchaud's chest and brought his wine to his mouth. The chessman bumped his lips as he swallowed.

"Heal thee or break thee."

"That is curiously like what Lucifer said." The wine was gone, except for a little pool under the ebony horse's head at the bottom of the glass and bits of orange petals adhered to the rim. Kit set the goblet on the table. "What dost thou propose?"

"There's a ritual of sacred marriage," Murchaud offered slowly, after a long pause.

"A barren marriage 'twould be, between thee and me." Kit shook his head. "My problem is Mehiel. I think I could bear mine own discomfort, to speak quite plainly. His—the distress of angels—is something else."

"And what would it take to free Mehiel, then?"

Kit leaned forward. He pulled the chess piece from the glass and sucked the wine from its surface, then polished it dry on his handkerchief. He set it down on the tabletop with a pronounced, careful click, amazed at his own calm. "He'll have to come out sooner or later, I suppose. And it would frustrate all our enemies enormously—Lucifer, the Prometheans, the lot."

"Kit?"

"My death, Murchaud. It will take my death, I am told."

Act V, scene ii

Some holy angel
Fly to the court of England and unfold
His message ere he come, that a swift blessing
May soon return to this our suffering country.

—WILLIAM SHAKESPEARE, *Macbeth*,
Act III, scene vi

Alas, my Romeo—

—the Mebd is no better; I have visited her with poetry to comfort her weary hours, & she seems somehow . . . faded. We must contrive to convince the world of the currency of Faerie Queenes. I don't suppose a revival of thy Midsummer Night's Dream *might be possible?*

I hear what thou sayest of James; I suppose thou knowest there are rumors that he finds his favorites among the young men at court. It might be worth thy while to befriend such, as they will have His Majesty's—attention—& if the Queen is so fond of

Ben's work, then it may well be that Ben can find succor for our projects with her.

You might visit Sir Walter in his immurement, if he is permitted guests—I know Southampton was—for if he be nothing else, Raleigh is a poet and a poet sympathetic to our cause. & clever in politics. Gloriana is gone: we are not just for England now, but for Eternity, our little band of less-mad Prometheans.

I will rejoin your Bible studies, of course. Even working piecemeal and catch as catch can, methinks we've accomplished too much to abandon our plans now.

My kindest regards to thee and to thine Annie, to little Mary and her Robin, to Tom and Audrey and George and Sir Walter should you see him. And my love most especially to Ben.

—in affection,
thy Mercutio

Will made his final exit on cue and elbowed John Fletcher in the ribs in passing as he quit the Globe's high stage. "By Christ," he said, as Fletcher slapped him across the back, "another plague summer. I can't bear touring another year, John. On top of learning six new plays in repertory. Ah well. At least they've more or less mastered *Timon,* which has to recommend it that 'tis not *Sejanus* again. Gah—" Will scrubbed sweat from his face on a flannel and tossed it away. "How are we to endure it?"

"Because we have no choice." Fletcher tucked a stray strand of hair behind his ear, revealing a half-moon of moisture under the arm of his shirt. In the unseasonable June of 1604 he'd left his habitual crimson doublet thrown over the back of a nearby chair. "Speaking of *Sejanus,* at least Ben is behaving himself of late."

"If thou deemst getting himself fined for recusancy again *behaving*."

"At least he's not getting the playhouses shut down."

"No," Will answered bitterly, thinking of Baines' faction and the endless stalemate fought back and forth between the groups of Prometheans. "The plague manages that just fine." He unbuttoned his doublet, opening the placket to entice some breath of cool air in. "Come, Jack. I'll stand thee a drink."

John caught up his doublet and regarded it with distaste. "Tell me it will be cooler in the Mermaid and I'll follow thee anywhere." He took Will's arm, steadying him down the stair.

"I doubt it's cooler in the Thames. Or any better smelling. I wonder what Ben thinks he's about. I should not like to be Catholic in England under James." Will bit his lip in silent worry—for Edmund more than Ben. Ben wasn't the only one who could stand to hide his sympathies a little better.

" 'Tis true. It's hard to believe it could be worse than under Elizabeth. . . ." They came out into the sunlight, and John looked doubtfully toward the crowds along the way to London Bridge. "By water?"

"Indeed." Even with his cane to steady him, and the new strength in his strides that led him to believe there was something more sinister than merely an unfortunate patrimony behind his palsy, Will didn't intend to brave the long walk in the afternoon heat. "I suppose bankrupting the Catholics with fines is one way to deal with it. Still, Ben's tastes in religion don't seem to affect his popularity at court. Well, now that the problem of *Sejanus* is settled." It had, Will must admit, been in questionable taste to deliver a play on the downfall of a sodomite Emperor's favorite to the stage just as a reputedly sodomitical King was coming to the throne. Still, it wasn't as if James could claim to be the target of the satire, and Ben had weathered the inquisitions well enough, all wide-eyed pretense at innocence.

"There is a divide," Fletcher noted, "between Queen Anne's entertainments and King James' policy." And that was where the conversation ended along with their privacy to speak freely, for they embarked on the wherry to cross the Thames.

The Mermaid *was* cooler than the Globe, in fact, and if possibly not cooler than the Thames, fresh rushes and sawdust on the floor assured it was better-smelling. And—as if Will's very conversations were attaining some magic with the raw new power that charged his poetry—the tavern was empty of all save the landlord and Edmund Shakespeare, who sat on a bench against the wall, pushing turnips about in his stew.

"Ted!" Fletcher pushed Will unceremoniously toward his brother and went to ask the landlord for dinner and ale.

"Jack," Edmund answered. "Will, come sit."

Will remembered something and turned over his shoulder. "John, I said I'd stand the meal—"

"Stand it tomorrow," Fletcher answered, juggling two tankards as he returned. "Henslowe paid on time, for once. Ted Shakespeare, that's an interesting expression thou'rt wearing. What news?"

Will blinked, and glanced back at his youngest brother. It *was* a knowing expression, as catlike smug as anything Kit might have worn. "All right, Edmund." He tasted his ale, which was dark and sweet. "Fletcher's right. I can see the mouse's tail through thy teeth. Out with it."

Edmund let his grin broaden until it stretched his cheeks. He took a swallow of his ale and waited for silence, then fixed Will with a steady gaze. "Edward de Vere is dead."

Edmund's timing was precise, and Will sprayed ale

across the table. "Oxford?" he spluttered, reaching for his handkerchief.

"Aye."

"How?"

"Plague."

Of course. Will dabbed his chin and the table dry, and picked up his ale again. *When one outlives one's usefulness to the dark Prometheans, they are not shy about making it plain.* Will hefted his tankard thoughtfully and clinked it against Edmund's.

"To the former Earl of Oxford," Edmund said. "And not a moment too soon. They say he died very nearly in penury: he's had to sell all his properties, and left almost nothing to his son." His eyebrows went up; he looked to Will. And Will sucked his own lower lip, thinking that those who played politics danced with a snake that swallowed itself.

"I didn't know you were acquainted with the Earl," Fletcher said, as the landlord brought their supper to the board.

"Aye," Will said. "Unpleasantly so." He wished he found the news more comforting: the end of an old enemy. But all it confirmed was what he had suspected. The Prometheans were moving—again—and Will hadn't the slightest idea what about, or how to stop them.

This was easier when I had someone to tell me what to do, he thought, and picked up his bread and his spoon. And laid them down once more, hands shaking with the realization that it wasn't necessarily the Prometheans who were responsible for the death of Edward de Vere, now that the Earl was utterly without the royal protection that had kept him alive so long.

Kit would have told me if he were contemplating cold-blooded murder.

Wouldn't he?

Act V, scene iii

As for myself, I walk abroad o' nights
And kill sick people groaning under walls:
Sometimes I go about and poison wells.

—CHRISTOPHER MARLOWE, *The Jew of*
Malta, Act II, scene iii

Edward de Vere, Kit thought with a certain cool satisfaction, did not look well at all. But he didn't think the man was sick with plague, as had been put about. Rather Oxford looked ... shrunken, against the rich brocades of his sweet-smelling bed. He seemed as if he dozed, a book open on his lap, and he did not look up when Kit stepped through the Darkling Glass and into the shadows at the corner of the room.

Kit cleared his throat, right hand across his waist and resting on the hilt of his rapier. "How does it feel to be ending your life on charity, my lord?"

The Earl of Oxford awoke with a start, the book snapping shut as his body twitched. He blinked and struggled to push himself upright against the pillows as Kit came out into the sunlight, but his arms seemed to fail him and his face contorted in pain. "Kit Merlin," he said in wonder, his voice unsteady. "Of all the faces I did not look for—"

And even he cannot recall my name.

"I wasn't looking for thee either," Kit admitted, lounging against the bedpost. He let his hand fall away from his hilt. The carved wood wore into his shoulder, a reassuring discomfort. He pressed himself against it, parting the bed curtains, and with his right eye saw the light of strength draining from a man he used to fancy was his lover. "The Darkling Glass sent me here."

"Sent thee?"

Kit took pity on the struggling Earl and moved forward, propping the pillows behind thin shoulders. It was like touching a poppet, a bundle of kindling wrapped in a silk nightgown. "Aye." Grudging. "I was looking for Richard Baines. It showed me thee."

Oxford nodded weakly. "He's warded against thee—"

"He's warded in general." Something stirred in Kit's breast. He closed his eyes, leaning heavily on the head of the bed as a wave of dizziness exhausted him. "Edward, how dost thou bear the weight of thine own skin?"

"My skin, or my sin?" It was a weak chuckle, barely an effort. From his right eye, Kit could see how the darkness within Oxford seemed fit to devour the fragile, flickering candle flame that was his life. "It matters not. Baines is consuming me."

"I see that." Kit tugged Oxford's covers higher, then wiped his own hands fastidiously on his breeches. "Thou wert never better than an adequate poet, Edward. What made thee think thou couldst turn thy back on Prometheus, and live?"

"Kit," Oxford said, and held forth a knotty hand. Kit took it, oily paper over bone. "Why thinkst thou I meant to *live*?"

An excellent question. Kit sat himself down on the edge of the bed and laced his fingers around his knee. "I loved thee, thou bastard," he said in what was not meant to be a whisper.

"Pity, that."

"Thou'lt never know how great a one. I hope thou knowest what thou spurned, my Edward."

Oxford's mouth twisted; Kit thought it was pain. "A bit of a poet and a catamite?" de Vere asked, and Kit flinched.

"Christofer Marley," he said. Naming himself as if the name meant something. "A name to conjure with, or so I am assured."

"Why didst thou come here? To mock me on my deathbed?"

Kit bit his lower lip savagely. *This is not going well.* "To discover why thou didst appear in my glass when I sought Richard Baines."

Oxford laughed. It might have been a cough. "Because I can tell thee something about the Prometheans."

"Aye?"

"Aye," de Vere said. "What is Prometheus but knowledge?" He coughed, and had not the strength to cover his mouth with his hands. "What is God but mercy?"

"Is God that?" But the light in his breast flared into savagery, and—unwitting—Kit laid a hand on Oxford's shoulder. It was not his own hand, quite: he could see the glare and the power gleaming behind the fingernails. *Mehiel. God's pity, at least. Does Oxford deserve that?*

"When we need him to be." Oxford smiled, his teeth white as whittled pegs behind liver-colored lips. "Those that steal from the gods, those that defy God, they are punished. How couldst thou, with the divine fire of thy words, expect to escape?"

Kit thought of Lucifer's exquisite suffering, and nodded. "Aye. Punished."

Oxford smiled, and Kit still knew him well enough to read the pleasure in his eyes. The pleasure of a chess player who has successfully anticipated his opponent. Kit blinked. "You summoned me."

"Did I?"

"Aye."

"Aye—" Oxford's cough racked Kit as well, and both of them pressed their fingers to their mouths. "I summoned thee. I cry thee mercy, Kitten."

"I owe thee nothing."

"Except revenge?"

"It's no longer worth it to me." *Vengeance is mine, sayeth the Lord.* "Thou'rt dying."

"I never said," Oxford answered, his gaze perfectly level on Kit's, "that thou shouldst seek vengeance on me. But there are other purposes my death might serve."

Baines is consuming me. Kit nodded, understanding. Then gasped as Mehiel answered Oxford's words from within, a flare of panicked strength that Kit thought might stream from his fingertips, halo his head like the inverse of Lucifer's shadowy crown. The angel—was afraid. And moved to pity, both. *Don't you remember how this man used us, Mehiel? How he plotted to have us slain?* "Thy death might serve my purposes quite well, Edward."

"Didst ever ask thyself what Prometheus might want?"

"Other than a new liver?"

"Thy wit has always been thine undoing," Oxford said tiredly. "Kit, mock me not when I have the will to aid thee, this one last time. Baines has used me as much as he has thee—"

"How fast they run to banish him I love," Kit said, just to see Oxford wince. "What, Edward? What does Prometheus want?"

"It's a riddle. It depends on when thou dost meet him.

Is he climbing to the heavens, or is he hurled back down? Is he chained on a rock, moaning for release? Would he seek immortality, or would he entreat thee take it from him, and make him but a mortal man again?"

Kit shook his head. Oxford was always one to speak in riddles, enjoying teasing others with what he knew and they didn't, and Kit had no stomach for it now. "What vile task wilt thou bid me to? Why is't I should not break thy wretched neck?"

"No reason," Oxford answered. "Do."

"Do what?"

"Do break my neck. If that is how thou preferest to end this." Oxford's hands pleated the blankets across his thighs. "I did serve England—"

"Thou didst serve thyself and thine own futherance. The Prometheans were meant to seek God and the betterment of Man, thou bastard. Thou—" Kit swallowed the shrillness that wanted to fill his voice. "Thou wert nothing but a spendthrift, a wastrel, a posturing cockerel."

"Think it as thou wilt." A sigh, exhaustion. The traceries of light that tangled Oxford were nothing like the dull red of the fever that had so nearly killed Will. "I will not serve *Master* Richard Baines, once ordained a priest. Kill me, Kitten."

A blatant request, and Kit blinked on it. "*Kill* thee."

"Aye." Fumbling, Oxford tried to pluck the pillow from behind his neck. Kit helped him with it, careful not to touch the Earl's fevered skin as Oxford lay back flat. Kit stepped back, the pillow clutched to his chest. Oxford closed his eyes. "Wilt let Baines have the use of me, Kitten? Kill me tonight."

God, Kit thought. *I'd imagined this as somehow satisfying.* He looked down at the pillow in his hands and closed his eyes.

*   *   *

Amaranth's touch did not trouble Kit in the slightest, perhaps because she was more beast than woman. So when he was done with Edward de Vere and had left the Earl of Oxford's body laid out tidily under the coverlet of his borrowed bed, it was Amaranth that Kit sought.

She lay on her back on the grass under the honey-scented tree that had been Robin Goodfellow, the creamy white scales of her belly exposed to the dappled sun and her slender, maidenly arms stretched high over her head. She wore a shirt of thin white lawn spotted with embroidered violets, startlingly feminine on a creature that was anything but. Kit dropped into the grass beside her, far enough away that he wouldn't startle her hair, and crossed his legs, leaning forward with his elbows on his knees and his chin in his hands. She twitched her tail, acknowledging him without opening her eyes, and tapped a coil against his hip.

"Thou'rt pensive, Sir Poet."

"I am more than pensive. I am troubled."

Her scales were soft and leathery, warmer than the grass when he ran his hands over it. As comforting as a hot-sided beast in a byre, and she smelled of autumn leaves or curing tobacco, musky as civet; mingled with the sweetness of the flowers, it put Kit in mind of expensive perfume. He lay down on the grass, his head propped on his knuckles, and sighed. She reached down lazily and stroked his hair. "And what troubles thee, Kit?"

"Prometheus," he said, leaning into the luxury of a touch that did not make him cringe. She shifted to pillow his head on her coils, the gesture more motherly than predatory. "Someone has made an interesting suggestion to me, just now."

"Interesting?"

Her voice was drowsy in the warmth; it relaxed him as smoothly as if it were a spell. "What if Prometheus—as in, the Prometheus Club—were a person, an individual.

A role. As much as he is a symbol of what they intend to accomplish, that is to say, stealing fire from the gods? Or God? And if so, what are we to do about it?"

"Sss." A ripple of muscular constriction passed down her length. Her hand stilled in his hair for a moment, and then resumed smoothing the tangles that always formed at the back of his neck, where his hair snagged on his collar. "Comest thou to a snake for sympathy, Sir Poet?"

"I come to a snake for information. Which may be equally foolish."

She laughed and levered herself upright without disturbing the section of coils upon which Kit rested. He rolled on his back, her wide belly scales denting under the weight of his head, and looked up her human torso as she rose. Sunlight shone through the cobweb lawn of her shirt; it bellied out on a breeze, offering him a glimpse of her maidenly belly and the underside of her breasts, the embroidered violets casting shadows like spots upon her skin.

"Come along," she said, and gave a little shudder to shake him to his feet. He rose, dusting bits of grass from his doublet, and fell into step beside her.

She led him down the bluff by the water, holding his hand—her arm extended to keep him well away from any aggressive gestures from her hair—and across the sand. "Wait," he said, and stripped off his boots and ungartered his stockings so he could feel the sand between his toes. Amaranth didn't stop, but slithered forward at a stately place, leaving a wavy line through the sand. Kit had only to walk a little faster to catch up. "What is it thou dost not wish the Puck-tree to overhear, Amaranth?"

"There is a Prometheus," she said, and turned to look at him through matte steel-colored eyes. She smiled liplessly. "Ask me another mystery, man."

He swallowed. The sea broke over her bulk and

foamed around his bare feet, drawing the sand from under his soles as if sucked by mouths. "Where do I find this Prometheus?"

The white foam ran down her dappled sides. She bent to trail her fingers through the waves. "In the mirror, Sir Christofer. In the eyes of a lover. Under an angel's bright wings. All of those places and none. One more question. Come."

I've fallen into a fairy tale. "How did I earn three questions of a serpent, my lady Amaranth?"

"Is that the question thou wishst to waste?" But her voice was kind, a little mocking. "I shall not count the answer, though. The answer. Which is, thou hast earned nothing, but this I give thee as a gift. Ask."

Another wave, and this one wet him to the knee, spray salting his cheek and lips. The flavor was as musky as the lamia's scent, salt and depth and thousands of deaths over thousands of years, all washed down into the endless, consuming sea. Kit shivered. *And if everything has a spirit, what do you suppose the ocean's soul is like?* His chin lifted, as if of its own accord, and he turned to look out over the sea and its breakers like white tossing manes on dark stallions' necks.

Amaranth coiled around him, an Archimedean screw with Kit the column at its center, and rested her seashell fingers on his shoulder, her head topping his by two feet or more. "Ask," and the hiss of her voice was the hiss of the waves.

"What magic is a sacred marriage capable of, Amaranth?"

"Ah." She settled in a ring about him, a hollow conduit with a poet at its center, sunlight glazing her scales as it did the dimples on the surface of the sea. "A grave risk, such a ritual. To work, it would need to be more than a ritual sacrifice. Thou wouldst die of it, who was Christofer Marley."

"A grave risk. And?"

"A potential triumph. It could be salvation: it's so hard to tell. So much depends on—"

The waves came and went.

"Circumstance?"

"Mehiel," she answered. "Mehiel, and how badly tormented the heart or the soul of an angel might be."

"Badly," Kit answered, but he was thinking of Lucifer Morningstar and not the sudden, fearsome heat and pressure in his chest.

Act V, scene iv

To this I witness call the fools of time
Which die for goodness, who have lived for crime . . .

—WILLIAM SHAKESPEARE, from Sonnet 124

William held his wrist out, turned over so the unworked buttons showed. "Ted, couldst see to these? Thank thee—"

"Court clothes," Edmund said. "So high and mighty is my brother now—"

"Hah." Will picked his wine up with his other hand and drained the goblet down to the bitter, aconite-flavored dregs. He polished the cup with his handkerchief and set it on the trestle, upside down. "I am summoned to attend, is all. The King's Men are no different at court from drawing-room furniture: meant to fill up the corners, but hardly of any real use. Hast thou any news for me?"

"Robin Poley," Edmund said, fastening the final button on Will's splendid doublet.

"Robin Poley? Or Robert Poley?"

"The elder."

"What of him?"

"Is a Yeoman of the Guard of the Tower of London now."

Will paused in the act of tugging his sleeve down over his shirt cuff. ". . . *really*."

"Aye. Cecil's doing, again. Although I suppose I must call Cecil the Earl of Salisbury now—"

"Where ears can hear, you must. Christ on the Cross. Sixteen hundred and five, and I have no better mind what old Lord Burghley's second son is after than I did twelve years ago, Ted. He plays the white and black pieces both, a double game that defies all understanding. But he has got himself raised an Earl, so I suppose whatever his game might be, he is winning it. Do I look grand enough for church with a King?"

Edmund stepped back, sucking on his lower lip until he nodded once, judiciously. "Cecil's at odds with the King, they say—"

"Aye." Will checked the mirror over his mantel, and ran both hands along the sides of his neck to pluck what remained of his hair from his collar. "Well, is and is not. The King wants Scots around him, but he *needs* Salisbury. What he's got is good Calvinists, and he's still urging that the Bishops be diligent in their pursuit of Catholics." *For all his own proclivities are not so Calvinist as that. Gloriana's failings were what they were, but she was never a hypocrite.* Will stopped, and fixed Edmund with a look. "I wrote to Anne and told her to see she got herself and the girls to church, Edmund. And I want to see thee in attendance too."

"Will—" Edmund sighed. " 'Tis my faith thou dost so lightly dismiss."

"Aye," Will answered. "And I am eldest now, with Father gone, and thou dost owe me that much duty. Thy life is worth more, and thy family's safety. Catholicism has been *outlawed*, Edmund. Recusants are not tolerated now. You will obey me."

"What's a life worth without faith?" Edmund looked Will square in the eye, but Will would not glance down.

"I won't forbid thee whatever—diversions—thou dost seek," Will said. "But thou wilt to Church. I'll not see thee stocked or hanged."

His brother matched gazes with Will for what seemed like an hour, but Will—frankly—had the weight of experience. And the authority of the eldest son behind his edict. Edmund dropped his eyes to the floor.

"As you bid." Edmund glanced up again as a church bell tolled the hour. "And now thou must hurry. Or thou wilt be late for thy King."

Infirmity, if not age, granted Will the consideration of a stool in the corner near the fire, but he found it rather warm for a midmorning. Especially when Burbage, also resplendent in James' livery, had cleverly staked out the corner nearest the wine on the sideboard—incidentally doing his usual fine job of framing himself against dark wood that showed off his fair curls to advantage.

If it weren't for the King's scarlet, however, Will would vanish against the paneling like a ghost. Which suited his mood admirably, come to think of it; his mood was fey, and dark lines of poetry taunted him.

Burbage refilled his goblet a second time before Will could think to forbid it, and Will swore himself solemnly to drink no more after this last cup. "Thou'lt have me drunk before the King, Richard," he said from the corner of his mouth.

"Matters not," Burbage answered. "I'm drunk every day, and it's done me no harm—"

"Not until thou diest of yellow jaundice," Will said dryly. "Or thy belly swells up like a berry full of juice."

"Well, a man's got to die of something." That bit of philosophy accomplished, Burbage turned to check Will's reaction. "The King," he hissed, and dropped a flourishing bow even as Will was turning to make his own obeisance.

"Your Highness," Will and Burbage said, speaking in unison as if rehearsed. *And after fifteen years playing together, 'tis no surprise if we pick up the cue.*

"Master Players." James the First of England had ruddy cheeks, contrasting with slack, pale skin and a sad-eyed, wary expression. Will thought he looked hunted, and he had not lost a trace of his thick Scottish accent in two years in the south. "Can we hope you are about plotting some new masterwork to entertain us with?"

"Always plotting," Will answered. "What would please the King?"

James made a bit of a show of thinking. "You know our Annie loves masques and divertissements. We had Ben Jonson's *Masque of Blackness* at court just this winter past. But perhaps something a little more exciting, for the lads. I worry a bit at their mother's influence: women are such frivolous things, and she has her ideas."

"Ideas, Your Highness?" Will was grateful that Burbage spoke to fill the King's expectant silence.

"I fear being so beset by witches as we were at our old lodgings has made her dependent on Papist rituals to keep ill spirits away," James said frankly, dropping into the informal speech that was his habit. "Silly conceits, and a woman will have them. But I do not want her leading my boys from good Protestant ethics. I'll see my little Elizabeth crowned queen before Henry or Charles king, if she turns them Catholic." The King shrugged, carelessly tipping some drops of wine over the edge of his cup. "So perhaps something with Scottish kings and the mischief of witchcraft—"

"Do you have a plot in mind, Your Highness?"

"We saw a Latin trifle at Oxford at the beginning of the month. That Quinn fellow. You know him?"

"*Tres Sybillae.*"

"That's the one."

"Your Highness wishes a play about King MacBeth."

"The usurper, rightfully deposed." It was a gentle re-
buke, as such things went, delivered with a smile. The
King turned to acknowledge Robert Cecil as the new
Earl of Salisbury came up alongside him. "It will serve a
welcome distraction in a time of plague. I've prorogued
Parliament for fear of it: we'll meet in colder weather.
And a good morning to you, my fine Earl Elf. What
think you of the fifth of November?"

"It's a fine day for a hanging, I suppose. Or did you
have something else in mind, Your Highness?"

"Parliament. We'll have some bills come due that
must be paid, sooner rather than later—"

"Ah, yes." Salisbury nodded an acknowledgement as
Will filled a cup for him and dropped a bit of sugarloaf
in. "Thank you, Master Shakespeare. I think we must
talk a bit about expenditures too, Your Highness."

The King snorted. "A parsimonious elf. Canst not
transform some oak leaves to gold, Salisbury, and refill
our coffers?"

"Alas—" Salisbury laid a hand on the King's elbow,
and the two men turned aside. But Robert Cecil's last
tenacious glance told Will there would be another conversation, later, out of earshot of the King.

"Is he still opposed to thy Bible?" Burbage asked
quietly, when the King and his minister were very well
out of earshot.

Will blinked. "How didst thou know about the Bible,
Richard?"

Richard Burbage paused, his cup frozen halfway to
his mouth as his attention turned inward. He pursed his
lips, and answered at last, "Mary Poley mentioned it to
me as if it were common knowledge. I thought she must
have had the word from thee."

"No," Will said, feeling his blood drain from his limbs. "I told her no such thing."

Will wrote by candlelight, late into the warmth of the evening, and was not surprised when a familiar cough interrupted his study. "Good evening, Kit."

"Hello, my love. I brought thee supper—"

Will glanced at the window, surprised to see that twilight had faded to full dark. "Thou'rt considerate."

"Thou'rt like to starve to death, an I did not. What is it has thy fancy so tightly, Will?" Kit laid his bundle on the edge of the table, well away from Will's papers, and unwrapped linen to produce a pot of steaming onion soup and a half loaf of brown bread folded around a still-cold lump of butter that was just melting at the edges.

"Fey food," Will said, and pushed his papers aside. "Or the homely sort?"

"Both," Kit answered. "Morgan's cooking. Thou didst not answer my question—"

"Oh, a tragedy," Will answered. "Something to catch James' fancy. Witches and prophecies. We have problems and problems, Kit. Thou didst not speak to Mary Poley of our testaments, didst thou?"

"Nay," Kit answered. He pushed the crock of soup in front of Will, and laid a spoon alongside it. "Talk while thou dost eat."

"Someone did." The soup was good, thick with onions cooked transparent. Will reached for the bread, which he could manage more comfortably through his stiff throat if he soaked it well in the broth. "Or worse, she heard it from Robert Poley and his flock."

"How would Poley know?"

Will shrugged, surprised at his own appetite. "Salisbury? They've made Poley a Yeoman of the Tower, Kit."

"They?"

"Salisbury. Who was Sir Robert Cecil."

"Thou sayest it as it were a refrain."

"More and more it seems to be. And I am at a loss to ferret out why. You probably haven't heard that Essex was the Master of the Armoury before his ill-fated ride."

"Master of the Armoury, and then beheaded there." Kit propped a hip on the window ledge, his back to the embrasure, and adjusted a folded-back cuff as if hiding his pleasure at the irony. "Hast spoken with Sir Walter?"

"Words in passing, only. I'll see if I can bring this play to him for comment before I make the fair copy. It might cheer him." Will pushed the soup away, his appetite fading. "He needs cheering, Kit."

"Shall I steal him away to Faerie, then?"

"Would he go?"

"Not unless he could conquer it for England." Kit grinned. "So ask thyself what Cecil wants, Will."

"What Salisbury wants."

"Whatever."

Will sighed. "I'd like to stamp him as his father's son, and a servant of the Crown even when he does not agree with the Crown's objectives. But I think he has been unafraid to manipulate even Princes, when it serves his goal. And his goal may be no more than ambition."

"He's Secretary of State. Surely that's enough to satisfy any ambition."

"I am not sure that's so. In any case, he's ordered Ben Jonson and me to infiltrate the Catholic underground in London." Will looked up in time to see Kit flinch. Kit drew his knee up, bootheel hooked onto the window frame. "That means Catesby and Tresham."

"Catesby is cheek by jowl with Poley," Kit commented. "If Poley is truly such a fine friend of Ce—of Salisbury's, then one would think he could get Poley to risk himself playing intelligencer in this case."

"Except Salisbury knows Poley's linked to the Prometheans through Baines—" Will shrugged. "I'll be damned if I understand it, Kit. Mayhap Salisbury expects to see the whole mess of them eradicate one another. And—" Realization stopped his voice.

Kit leaned forward. "Will?"

"—Poley must have heard about the Bible from Salisbury. But Salisbury is not supposed to know it's being writ. Tom Walsingham would never tell him."

"Tom Walsingham doesn't tell his teeth what they're chewing," Kit said fondly. "So from whom would he have heard it, then?"

"Christ," Will said. "I hope not Ben. But more on Catesby—now, it seems, is the ideal time to move. There is a rumor he's looking for men of strong Catholic belief to join some agency of his. He's been seen about with Poley, aye, and Richard Baines as well. And Salisbury says he has a letter from a Captain Turner that says Catesby and a fellow named Fawkes are planning what he ever so helpfully terms 'an invasion.' The good Earl wants Ben and me to play at being disloyal Catholics."

"Baines is ordained a Roman Catholic priest, Will, for all I think his faith plays the hypocrite more even than mine own. If Catesby wants Catholics— Well. Poley and Baines both know thou art more than a mere Catholic."

Will nodded. "But Poley also knows"—a pressure in his throat, but he did not let it change his voice—"how Hamnet was buried, and how often my family's been fined. Monteagle will vouch for me, in any case: he owes me his life after that damned stupid rebellion, and he knows it. A new King, and worse times for the Catholics, and things change. Men change their opinions, and all Catholics are not Prometheans."

"Any more than all Puritans are." Kit nodded, as if

seeing the logic. "Your opposition is not to Catesby. Only to those who use him, so unwittingly."

"As they used Essex, and discarded him when they were done."

"Hell," Kit said. "As they used and discarded one Christofer Marley, playmaker—" He stopped, fingers tight on the cloth of his sleeves, and closed his eyes for a moment. "I beg thy pardon, Will. Pray continue."

I made the right choice not to ask him what became of Oxford, Will thought. "Catesby had been imprisoned for recusancy again, but he's out, and building a ... congregation."

"A congregation and not a private army?"

"Is there a difference, in this age?" Will sighed. "I haven't a choice. Remember old Sir Francis and his damned lemons out of season?"

"It was a good conceit." Kit stood and crossed the rush-covered floor in a few short strides. "He swallowed enough bitterness for his queen to know the taste of it. I do not think Robert Cecil is such a civil servant as that. But be cautious, Will: it's easy enough to hang for treason even when one acts on the orders of the crown. I've seen it happen, King's Man."

"Queen's Man," Will corrected, with a smile. "I'm only a player for James."

"Good," Kit said, and laid both hands carefully on Will's shoulders, with a precision that belied the force of choice behind that action. "I'd hate to think I had to defend thy virtue from a king."

"He suits my fancy not at all," Will answered, and let his head fall back against Kit's belly. "I'd find something better to be forsworn for, if I were of a mind to be forsworn."

Kit bore the touch for a moment and stepped back. "I dreamed of thee again. Thee, and a pouch full of silver coins, every one of them tainted in poison. I knocked them from thy fingers—"

Will pivoted on his stool, away from the table, so he could watch Kit pace. "And?"

"And a flock of ravens arose, startled by the sound, and then the ravens dove on the coins and were transformed into magpies. And the magpies touched the silver—it was shillings, all shillings. Forty of them." Kit's face went dreamy as he pressed a palm to the window glass.

Will stood, a bit unsteadily, and came up beside him. "And then what happened?"

"The magpies died. Every one. And turned into gray-feathered doves as they fell. Damned if I know what to make of that for a prophecy." Kit's shoulders rose—slowly—and then dropped.

"I do," Will answered, shaking his head just a little, remembering the weight of a pouch of coins in his fingers on the eve of the Essex Rebellion. Remembering Robert Catesby's considering glance as Will took it from his hand. "The plague. And that sickness that almost killed me, four winters back."

"And did kill Spenser and Walsingham. Aye."

"Coins. It's spread on coins, Kit. Ensorcelled silver, that taints any hand that touches it."

Kit turned to him and blinked, candlelight cupping his cheek like a hand. "By God," he said. "Thou'rt right. Thou must be." And then he stopped and crossed his arms before his breast, and visibly swallowed. "How does a man fight something like that?"

Will just shook his head. "I do not know."

Act V, scene v

But while I have a sword, a hand, a heart
I will not yield to any such upstart.

—CHRISTOPHER MARLOWE, *Edward II,*
Act I, scene iv

"She's asking for you," Murchaud said from the doorway, and Kit laid down the book, open to a page he'd read three times over and never seen.

He stood and twisted his rapier back into place in its carrier. "The Mebd's awake?"

Murchaud didn't answer, only beckoned. Kit came to him and they passed through the corridors side by side, not speaking until they reached the threshold of the Mebd's privy chamber. He paused, his hand on the doorknob, and glanced over his shoulder at the Prince. "Thou'rt not coming in?"

"No," Murchaud said. "My royal wife said Kit, and Kit alone. So alone thou goest."

"What does she want of me?"

"Thy company, I presume." He smiled a worried

smile, one that made the corners of his pale, soft eyes turn down.

"It's the teind year. Sixteen naught five, and less than a month to choose the sacrifice—"

"No." Murchaud's headshake was slow. "Thy William went willing, Kit. Even though thou didst retrieve him— mad poets, the both of you—the debt is paid for seven times seven years. Go on, my love."

Kit shivered at the endearment, set his jaw, and opened the door.

A cool breeze ruffled silk curtains, admitting sunlight on dancing rays. The chamber smelled of lavender and peppermint, and thick rush mats muffled Kit's footsteps.

The Mebd lay on a daybed by the window, embroidered pillows behind her shoulders and her thin violet gown draped over one bent knee, a bare graceful foot showing beneath the hem. Her head was turned, her gaze trained out the window, her hair down on her shoulders in a thousand braids as fine as golden wire.

Kit bowed, then straightened when she summoned him with an airy wave.

"Sir Kit."

"Your Highness."

She smiled as he came closer, her eyes as violet now as twilight, matching the shadows that surrounded them and lay under her cheekbones. The lines of her collarbones glinted like knives, and he could see the rings of her larynx through the translucent skin of her throat. He thought the bones of her fingers might crumble if he simply reached out and took her hand; even her amazing hair was lusterless and dry in its floor-long braids. "Sit," she said. "I'm healing at last. England's King is secure upon his throne. Faerie will endure."

"Was it wise of you to risk Faerie so far?" Kit asked, because he felt secure enough in his Bard's patched cloak to do it. He reached out softly, and took a few of her long yellow plaits in his hand. "There are many lives braided here, my Queen. Lives that would be lost if you were."

"The war's not over," she said. "I understand thou hast been speaking with Morgan, yet."

"Aye."

"Her politics?"

"What are her politics, you mean, Your Highness?" When she nodded impatiently, he continued. "She says she wants peace."

"She does," the Mebd said. "But she's never understood that compromises can be required to assure it, and sometimes the Devil you know is to be preferred to the Devil you don't." She smiled into his eyes as he leaned forward, and turned her gaze out to the garden again. "I have a task for thee, one that shall burden thee a while, and one which I cannot ask my bounden subjects. And one which thou wilt never speak of, Sir Kit. I charge thee."

"And what task is that, Your Highness?"

And she smiled again, never looking back, and handed him a comb.

Act V, scene vi

These late eclipses in the sun and moon portend no good to us: though the wisdom of nature can reason it thus and thus, yet nature finds itself scourged by the sequent effects: love cools, friendship falls off, brothers divide: in cities, mutinies; in countries, discord; in palaces, treason; and the bond cracked 'twixt son and father.

—WILLIAM SHAKESPEARE, *King Lear*, Act I, scene ii

Just before dawn on September 17, 1605, Will was dragged from a companionable reverie in the garden of the Silver Street house by an urgent hand on his sleeve, reaching awkwardly backward. "Will," Kit said. "Look at the moon."

They were huddled under blankets, back to back on the bench. The wine was finished; the night's conversation drifted into sitting and dozing, watching the night. Will turned over his shoulder and gasped; the full pewter disk was eaten away on one edge, as if someone had taken a bite from the disk, and a dim red glow shone through it. "An eclipse."

"Not a full one, I think," Kit answered. "Remember old Doctor Dee, Gloriana's astrologer?"

"I remember his beard," Will said, picturing its white luxuriance. "The Queen used to ride out to his house on horseback and scandalize the court. He's still alive, you know, though James won't have aught to do with him."

"Is the old bastard?" Kit's smile shone through his voice. "I always liked him better than Northumberland. And he was right more often, too. Thou knowest his horoscopes for Elizabeth were sealed as state secrets?"

"Out of favor now, though."

"We could ride out and see him, as Elizabeth would have—" Kit's voice swelled, a momentary flight of fancy on what a pageant that would be. And then he stopped himself, and shivered. "Nay. Unwise at the extreme."

"So what would he say about that?" The moon continued to darken, even as the eastern sky grew pale. A third of the disc had vanished into shadow, and Will caught his breath at the beauty of it, and the danger. "That's a portent, Kit."

"The sky is full of portents." Kit stood, and walked from one wall of the garden to the other, studying the sky. "But that's an especially bad one. The moon is devoured in the dragon's tail, or so the expression goes— the moon, astrologically speaking, equates the psyche."

"What does it mean?" Will's voice, still and small. He moved to stand beside Kit, as if the warmth of another body in the chill fall air would make a difference to his pounding heart.

"It means," Kit said, "that the Mebd is right. And the war is nearly on us. And everything we have believed in, fought for—Gloriana, England, Faerie—is coming to an end." He dropped his eyes from the sky; Will could see the yellow witchlight gleaming behind his right eye when he turned. "Will, just remind me. What day did Elizabeth die?"

"March twenty-fourth," Will said. "Very early. Or perhaps late the night before."

"The last day of the year," Kit said softly. "The sun would have been at fifteen Aries when she died if she had held on one day longer. The brave old bitch almost made it." Tears clotted whatever he would have said next.

"Kit?"

Nodding, a sniffle in the darkness as the moonlight reddened and dimmed.

"I don't know what that means," Will said at last, plaintively, and was relieved when Kit laughed and threw an arm around his shoulders, as if they both needed the support.

"Fifteen Aries is when you sacrifice a King," Kit answered. Whispered, really, though it had almost the quality of a pronouncement to it. "So that his blood may replenish the land, and make it strong."

"Oh," Will said, only half understanding the shiver that rocked Kit's body. "You're saying she died for England."

"I'm saying she tried her best." Kit folded like a dropped marionette and sat down on the ground, his knees drawn up and his arms wrapped around them to pull them close. "I'm saying we're losing, and there's our proof. That"—a shaky hand waved at the setting, half-eaten moon—"means the end of an old way, and violence, and upheaval...."

Will sat down too, and cleared his throat. "Couldn't the end of an old way mean the Prometheans, just as well?"

"It means Elizabeth," Kit said with quiet conviction, both his fists pressed against his chest as if his heart might burst right between his ribs, and there was no arguing then.

* * *

Will had cause to remember those words a fortnight later on October the second, when broad noon turned to darkness over London Town as if a tarnished silver coin had been slid across the disk of the sun. A strange twilight strangled the city's voice to desperate murmurs as every foot paused, every voice hushed, every eye lifted and then quickly fell again, unable to bear the light of even a half-occluded sun.

Will shaded his eyes with his hand, pressing his forehead to the rippled glass and lath of Tom Walsingham's casement window and tilting his face to the side. "It seems a year for ill omens," he said softly, and did not look down until Tom came to draw him away from the window.

"What, a cloud across the sun?" Kit came up too—the three of them were alone, Ben and George having been left home from this particular council of war—and glanced through the window. "Ah. I don't suppose I missed a rain of fire while I was away?"

"Nay," Will answered, and pulled Tom toward the door. "That's a terrible sight."

"Don't look upon it," Kit warned. "Wilt burn thine eyes. Tom, have you smoked glass?"

"Nothing so useful," Tom answered as the three men emerged from the garden door into a world that seemed to Will even stranger and more alien than Faerie. In those places where gold and auburn leaves still clung to the trees and bushes, the dappled shadows moving underneath them formed diminishing crescents, layer on layer of moving images.

Will thrust his hand under the branches of an oak, watching the gleaming crescents shrink upon his skin. The air seemed thicker in its darkness, and hung with sparkles like a summer night. "Camera obscura," he said, gesturing Kit and Tom to join him. Somewhere beyond the garden wall, he heard someone sob and the sound of a window

breaking. "Look at this. The leaves make the pinholes."
He almost fancied he could feel the light brushing his skin
as the leaves tossed in time with the breeze.

"Sweet buggered Christ," Kit said. "I need my
books."

"What books?" asked Tom alertly.

"Oh, I had—" He paused, as if considering. "A Ptolemy, and Brahe's *Die Stella Nova,* an Agrippa, some of
Dee's work—" Kit stopped and looked around, realizing that Tom and Will were staring. "Research," he said.
"*Faustus.* In any case, I loaned them all to Sir Walter
and he never gave them back. A most notorious thief of
books, that one—"

Tom coughed into his hand. "I have some volumes of
Ficino."

"Please?" Kit looked up, exactly as he had admon-
ished Will not to, and closed his left eye. He seemed to
pay no notice as Tom returned to the house.

Will cleared his throat, the unease swelling in his
belly. "Kit?"

Kit looked down and smiled at Will. "Fear not," he
said. "I doubt an eye that won't be damaged by a knife
will be blinded by the light of a half-dimmed sun."

"What art thou seeking?"

"The way the moon moves," Kit said, taking the book
from Tom's hands when Walsingham returned with it.
He angled the pages to catch what light he could, but
read with ease words that Will would have found incom-
prehensible in the unnatural twilight. He watched as Kit
riffled pages, seeming to know what he was searching for
even if he did not know quite where to find it.

"Sidereal," Kit murmured, and some other words
that meant nothing to Will. Tom watched with interest, hands on his hips, head cocked to one side and
the wind ruffling his silver-streaked auburn hair. The
strands too made pinholes as they rose and fell; as the

eclipse ground toward totality, Will watched the tiny crescents scattering Tom's face first fade to nothingness and then reemerge as twisting rings of light.

Will risked a glance upward and caught his breath at the image of the sun occluded, a jet-black round crowned in twisting fire that reminded Will of Lucifer's writhing, shadowy tiara in reverse. "Sweet Christ," he swore, but it was more of a prayer, really.

"Ah," Kit said, and clapped the book shut like a pair of hands. "No," he said. "Not good at all."

"It's an omen, then?"

"Yes, and as ill as you'd like to make it. 'Tis, again, a marker of the end of things, and an overthrow of balance and harmony. If Elizabeth and her famous temporizing were a force to keep England in symmetry, and in accord with God and nature—"

"Aye?" Will's feet would not quite hold him steady.

Kit shrugged, and handed the book back to Tom. "You are witnessing the end of her power, gentlemen. And the death of whatever peace our sufferings, and those of the poets and intelligencers who came before us, and the Queen's cool brilliance at the chess of politics, bought for Mother England." Kit swallowed and looked down. "The sun will be in Sagittarius at the end of this month and the beginning of the next."

"And?" Tom and Will, as one voice.

"And," he said. "The best date for a sacrifice would be November fifth, I think. Fifteen Sagittarius."

"That's when Parliament is to meet," Will said, as the sun began to emerge from its enshadowment. "They were—"

"That late in the year? That's—"

It was Tom who finished, both hands raised and bound tight in his hair. "They were prorogued," he said. "The session bound over. On account of plague."

"Plague," Kit said, looking at Will for confirmation.

"Aye," Will said, abruptly sick with exhaustion. "I heard the King discuss it with Robert Cecil, not two months since."

It was a week later, only, that a sturdy tapping at his door drew Will's attention and he rose. "Who's there?"

"Echo the Nymph," Ben answered deadpan. Will lifted the latch and stood aside to let the big man into the room.

"Thou lookst more like a Narcissus to me," Will said. "What brings thee to my humble doorway, Ben?"

"Thou'rt invited to a gathering," Ben answered, shaking rain from his cloak. "A party of sorts."

"Tonight?" Will gestured to the leaves of paper spread over his table, where they would catch the watery light from the window. "I've too much work."

"Thou'rt only the most-sought playmaker in London," Ben answered, careful not to drip on the papers as he bent to inspect them, his massive hands laced behind his back. "Surely thou canst pass a night with friends—"

"I owe Richard a fair copy by Monday—"

"Five days," Ben said. "Thou dost work too much, Will. And how canst thou refuse an invitation from Robert Catesby, to dine with him and his recusant friends on a cold Wednesday night?"

Will set the latch with a click. "I beg thy pardon?"

Ben turned, his homely face unimproved by his grin. "Call it luck or call it happenstance. I've been working on Catesby and Tresham six months now, Will. And been overheard to mention once or twice that thou—and thy brother Edmund—had once or twice missed out loud the more permissive ways of Warwickshire, with regard to the old religion. If thou takest my meaning. And they did."

Will pinched his lower lip between his teeth and ran his tongue across it, forcing himself to stop when he remembered it would chap. "Catesby is one of Baines'. He'd never believe I'd welcome any Promethean plot. Not after twelve years fighting them, and all the advances I've spurned."

"Not to hear him talk about it." Ben shrugged. "Not Promethean, anyway. Catesby's aims are strictly political, and he'd love the great William Shakespeare to come in under his banner of revolution. I suspect if he knew the sort of black sorcery his friends get up to he would be even more appalled by them than he is—for all he's willing to compromise and let politics make what bedfellows they will, he's a good Catholic, and wouldn't be damned for sorcery. I think they mean to use him as they used Essex before him, as a sort of stalking horse. Come, get thy cloak."

"Thinkst thou to educate him, then?"

"I'll tell thee more on the way to the tavern," Ben said, and handed Will his shoes. "No, I don't think so at all. Not that he's uneducable. If anything, he's a good man, strong in his faith, willing to die for it. A fighter for freedom, and his two chief lieutenants are also quick and true."

"And they're plotting against the King." Will latched the door behind them when they went. "What way are we going, Ben?"

"To the Irish Boy. Age before beauty, gentle Will. Lead on."

"Then we shall have to wait for a handsome passerby, or we shall never get anywhere," Will noted, but he did not tarry. The afternoon was cold, the rain something more than a drizzle. "Ben, it pains me to ask this of thee—"

"Aye, Will?" The banter fell from Ben's tone like the stagecraft it was; Will could feel the weight of his expectancy.

"It wasn't thee told Salisbury about our Bible-crafting, was it? When thou wert so unhappy with me?"

"Nay, I'd never do such a thing. Slather thy name in mockery and eat it with relish, aye—"

"It was mustard, not mockery," Will said. "And the coat of arms was my father's conceit, in any case."

Ben laughed. "But something that could bring thee real harm? Never, my friend."

"That's bad," Will answered. "Because if it was not thee, then Chapman has spoken more than he should, and where the wrong ears could hear it."

Ben grunted, tugging his hood up higher. "I would not be startled to discover it. In any case, I think thou shouldst consider what the Catholics offer," he said with a wink. "Thy family will thank thee for supporting the old faith. And with such men as Catesby and Tresham, and Guido Fawkes—who thou wilt meet tonight. He was a soldier in the Low Countries when I was, that last."

"Fighting for the Queen?" Will asked, and Ben shook his head.

"Fighting for the Spaniards. A man of strong convictions. They call him the soldier-monk, of all things."

There was a throb of admiration in Ben's voice; Will sighed to hear it. *Nothing worse for an intelligencer than to come to admire the men he will betray.*

Aye, and nothing more vital for his credibility with those men. "I'll make thee proud enough, for a soldier-bricklayer," Will said, and Ben laughed at the subtleties behind that statement as they passed under the sign of the Irish Boy.

The tavern's common was bigger than the Mermaid's, but not overcrowded. Will counted eleven men drinking by the fire, a hum of cheerful conversation flagging only a little when he and Ben entered. Catesby stood, his golden-blond locks glowing like the sun, and came across the rush-strewn planks to greet them. Another man rose as well, a walrus-mustachioed redhead Will had seen somewhere before, not quite so handsome as Catesby but broad-shouldered and nearly as big as Ben, though not so portly.

Catesby introduced the redhead as Fawkes. Will shook his hand—switching his cane to the left to do so—while Ben dragged a bench over and repositioned a table to make room. Will was seated and introduced about; he was amused to note he'd come far enough as an intelligencer in twelve years that he felt secure in remembering each name and each face without the need to scribble notes.

The evening's entertainment was much as promised, the playmaker finding himself wined and dined by men who were—for a change—more interested in his personal and political leanings than in his celebrity, and who gave very little away. The role came to Will with enough ease to unsettle him, and it unsettled him more when he remembered that some of the men he sat beside were relatives, acquaintances.

Acquaintances who plot against the throne, he reminded himself. And then he sighed, and thought of Edmund or Annie hanged for no more sin than clinging to the Catholic faith, and wondered if he had chosen the right side after all.

It's not the side that's right, he reminded himself. *It's the side you're on.*

And thank you, Kit, for that piece of intelligencer's wisdom. Will felt queasy with more wine than he was accustomed to drink. He looked up at Ben, who was regarding him with a knowing sort of pity, and Ben nodded and stood.

"Gentlemen, thank you," Ben said. "I fear Master

Shakespeare is a bit poorly, and perhaps I should escort him home."

"No, Ben," Will said, although he accepted help to stand. "I'll manage. You stay for the evening. I'm just tired and in pain."

"Art certain?" As Ben led him toward the door. "The streets are not as safe as they were—"

Aye, which is saying something, as they were never in particular safe. The King's Peace doesn't hold much sway in London any longer. "I'm certain," Will said.

Fifteen minutes later, when unseen ruffians dropped a bag over his head and hustled him into a carriage, he had wit enough left to find a measure of irony in those words.

He kicked rather helplessly, but whoever held him— a big man smelling of mutton and damp leather—had every advantage, and Will found himself shoved unceremoniously to his knees, his fingers numbed from a thin cord wrapping his wrists. *Helpless as a jessed and hooded hawk, damn them all.*

The carriage lurched and rattled on for a little while, and he was just as casually carried out of it and up a flight of stairs, and deposited on a mattress. Still blindfolded, Will heard another scuffle, but was able to do little about it with his wrists bound behind his waist and his vision baffled. He knew Kit's voice when he heard it, however, and shouted, trying to shove himself to his feet and measuring his length instead on the rush-covered stones.

The fall knocked the wind from him, a spasming pain that wouldn't let him fill his lungs. He wheezed, worming forward on scraped knees and bruised chest, and then grunted once as someone dropped a knee between his shoulders and pinned him hard. "None of that, old man."

The scuffle ended abruptly enough that he knew it

was not Kit who'd won it. *Oh, bloody hell,* he thought. *Damn-fool Kit, when wilt learn to bring friends on these missions of mercy?* Will did not hear Kit's voice again, but he heard a man grunting with effort as if he lifted something unwieldy, and then the slamming of a heavy, strap-hinged door. *Damn it. Damn it. Damn it to Hell—*

Act V, scene vii

This dungeon where they keep me is the sink
Wherein the filth of all the castle falls.

—CHRISTOPHER MARLOWE, *Edward II*,
Act V, scene v

Kit woke in absolute blackness, with a ringing head, and tried to remember how he had gotten there and why he was lying on a dank, lumpy surface with the taste of earth on his lips. He summoned a witchlight first, wondering that the darkness was so complete that even he could not see through it, and when the hoped-for blue glow failed to materialize around his fingers he swore softly and rolled onto his back.

He lay on earth, he decided, burrowing his fingers into it. Packed earth, and foul; it reeked of sweat and filth and the long tenancy of terrified men. He cast his right hand out, and his left, and found stone blocks on either side. The walls of his cell, if it was a cell. He snapped his fingers again, to spark light, and nothing answered his murmured incantation except a strange clatter and a heaviness, a constriction on his fingers. His head throbbed as if John Marley were on the inside, banging Kit's skull with his tacking hammer, and Kit hunched forward between his knees and tried to take some inventory of the situation.

Feet, bare. His head swollen as a broken fist, and oozing blood from a welt on the left side. His cloak was missing, and his sword—he chuckled under his breath in recognition of what was gone. No external sound reached him—

—No. Not quite true. Somewhere far above, he heard ... not so much the sound of footsteps as the echo of the sound. "I might as well be at the bottom of a well," he said out loud, to hear something besides the half-panicked rasp of his own hurried breaths. His voice echoed too, peculiarly: from above, rather than from any of the sides.

Carefully, wary of his head and his dizziness, Kit stood in the darkness and extended his arms. His palms lay flat against the walls on either side—masoned stone, he thought—and whatever rings encircled his fingers clanked on the blocks. A harsh, heavy clank, and not the ring of silver or the clink of gold.

He lowered his hands, feeling the moist earth under his feet—heels, ball, toes—and drew another deep breath. The stench of a place men have died in, aye.

And something else.

Thick and raw, the stench of the Thames.

"The Pit," he said, and sat down on the floor again, shaking his head. "I dreamed this."

He knew where he was now, and he knew who had him. He was in the oubliette at the Tower of London, and he was in the power of Robert Poley. And by extension, of Richard Baines.

In absolute blackness, Kit paced the cramped circle afforded him. His right hand trailed on the damp stones of the wall. He had no fear of tripping; his feet knew the path, and the dank earth was where he slept when he grew too tired to walk. *Wasting energy,* he thought, but he could not sit still. "The sink wherein the filth of all the castle falls," he mumbled, but it wasn't, quite. More an old, almost-dry well, lidded in iron as much to keep light out as the prisoner in, for the sides were twenty foot and steeply angled.

He had paced forever.

He would be pacing forevermore.

The iron rings—or so he thought them, groping in the darkness—on his hands wouldn't come off. He'd tried, and all he'd gotten for his trouble was a clicking pain as if he were trying to yank each finger individually from its socket. Upon pulling harder, there had been the stretch of tearing flesh and a slow, hot trickle of blood, but the rings had not shifted.

A strange sort of irritation, first an itching and then a raw, hot pain, grew in patches on his torso and his thighs. To pass the time and to stave off whatever sorcery Baines might be working, so far out of reach above, he told himself stories. Bits of verse—Nashe's plays, half memorized, Kyd's *Tragedy,* Will's *Titus,* and Kit's own words. The Greeks and the Romans and the Celts. The Bible.

Anything to keep from thinking of his own predicament, and worse. To keep from remembering how he had failed Will. Because when the throbbing in his head had subsided, he'd remembered how he'd been surprised.

Coming to Will's rescue.

Just as Baines would have known that he would, having seen it before. *Stupid, Kit, to leave anyone alive who knows what William means to thee—*

He'd stepped from the Darkling Glass, his sword in his hand and witchcraft on his lips—and straight into a sorcerer's trap.

*   *   *

He slept twice more. His belly cramped with fear more than hunger, and his dry throat turned his recitations into a mumble. He dragged his ringed fingers along the stone, and thought to dig through the floor with his fingers, but all he did was tear his nails and score his fingertips on buried rocks. He came to know his domain intimately, an oval four feet by five feet, with a slimy, echoing drain that stank even worse than the earth but at least ensured he wasn't sleeping in his own piss.

The cramping belly reminded him of something, and he smiled. *If Baines plans to use me for whatever blackness he had planned on the fifth—*

—won't he be surprised when Faerie kills me for my absence in a couple of days?

Kit closed both eyes. It made no difference: he walked, and turned, and walked, and turned in a blackness as deep as if his eyes had frozen into ice. He hadn't seen real darkness since Hell; he barely remembered it, but whatever bound his magic bound his *otherwise* sight as well.

Mehiel's brands burned on his chest and sides. "All very well," Kit said to the angel, a whisper like a rasp dragged over his throat. "Couldst speak to me, thou knowest. Would help to pass the hours. And 'tis not as if we're unacquainted." A cracked-lip grin, blood paying for a pun. *And not a good one at that.*

The chafe of unoiled hinges served his warning of the shaft of light that seemed to boil his eyes from his head. Kit covered his face in his hands, swearing, and hated it that he knew who saw him cringe.

"Art yet hungry, puss?"

Sweet God in his heaven. Kit could never speak loud enough to be heard from the depths of the oubliette, with the fire in his throat. And damned if he would plead and whisper. He stood, looking up, and shaded his left eye with his hand. *Nay,* he thought, wishing he had the wherewithal to speak. *But could use a drop of wine, hast it to spare—*

Things dropped. A cloth-wrapped bundle, a wineskin—*praise Christ*—something round and heavy that Kit's blurry eyes could not quite make sense of. The objects variously thumped and clanked; Kit blinked back tears. "Good puss," Baines said. "Make it last a day or two. I'll be back for thee when I can."

Dignity, Kit. It was what he could do to walk to the edge of the pit rather than scramble. He reached for the wineskin and paused, fingers trembling like Will's.

The scold's bridle lay beside the skin, tilted on its side, a maniacally grinning iron skull face that gaped open, unlocked.

Ignoring it, Kit reached for the skin. It sloshed, and he hoped it was water or ale, and nothing stronger. Still, he wouldn't drink in front of Baines. *A few more minutes.* His hands ached with desire. *Puss, be brave.*

Oh, that turned his stomach enough to give him strength. He looked up again. Baines—resolving now as Kit's eyes adjusted to the light—leaned down, his hand on the enormous lid of the oubliette. "Hast made the acquaintance of thy friend Edward the Second's ghost yet, pussycat? They tell me he still screams."

Stupid bastard. Edward died at Berkeley.

Kit made a rude gesture and swore without breath. Baines grinned—a white flash of teeth—and lowered the lid silently, without even the catharsis of a ringing slam. The silence lingered. Kit lowered his head in the darkness. His laugh came forth a voiceless sob.

He sat on the floor and drank half the lukewarm small beer, rationing it, then laid his face down on his arms and cried.

I have to get out of here. The bastards have Will.

Act V, scene viii

*What a piece of work is a man, how noble in reason,
how infinite in faculties, in form and moving how ex-
press and admirable, in action how like an angel, in
apprehension how like a god.*

—WILLIAM SHAKESPEARE, *Hamlet,* Act II, scene ii

It was Robert Poley who unhooded Will, much later, in a candlelit room with an arrow slit that showed only blackness but admitted the stink of the Thames. There was a narrow pallet on the floor, a straw tick and some blankets, and a single sweet-smelling beeswax pillar flickering in the embrasure.

Will didn't speak at first. Poley stepped back, a rough dark brown woolen sack dangling from his fingers, and gestured with his other hand to the oversized roaring boy holding Will's elbow. Thick fingers released the knotted ropes at Will's wrists; he gasped at sudden prickles, white-hot pins and needles jabbing his finger-tips and palms. "I beg your pardon, Master Shakespeare, for the undignified circumstances of your appointment here," Poley said.

"Appointment?" Will pressed his useless hands together, trying to squeeze blood back into the veins. "In absolute precision of language, Robert, thou must admit this is an abduction, and not a social call."

Poley smiled when Will thee'd him. "As it may be."

Will swallowed and let his aching hands fall to his side. He wobbled, and the big man grabbed his elbow again to steady him. "Where's Kit? What dost thou plan to make of me, thou cur?"

"I'm sure I don't know what you mean," Poley answered. "You will be quite well and safe, Master Shakespeare. My lord Salisbury would never permit you to come to harm; you are one of England's treasures in your very own person. But simply too much trouble to be left lying about until things are more certain."

Will turned his head and spat, though it took him a moment to work enough saliva into his dust-dry mouth to manage. "Cecil. I should have known—"

"You'd be surprised how little you know." Poley rested his knuckles on his hips, the image of a fighting cock. "Then again, perhaps you wouldn't. In any case, you'll be safe and sound here until it's possible to set you at liberty. You might try to get some sleep, and I beg your pardon for the rudeness of the accommodation. There are better rooms available, but I am not prepared to explain your presence there."

"Kit . . . ?" Will asked, and Poley shook his head even as he moved toward the door.

"There are things we're not prepared to discuss," he said. "That's one. A pleasant night, Master Shakespeare. Anything you have need of, simply ask my friend Allan here. I'm sure you will have company from time to time."

Will looked up at the big, balding blond, who offered him an amiable and gap-toothed smile. Allan, now named, turned to follow Poley from the room, leaving the candle behind.

The heavy door shut behind them, and Will turned to examine his cell. The room was cold through the unglazed window. He was glad of his winter cloak and doublet; some thoughtful person had tucked his gloves into his cloak pocket, and he drew them on. There were blankets enough on the bed, he thought, although he had not been laid a fire and the room, in fact, was hearthless. *Perhaps they'll permit me a brazier when it grows colder.*

A thought which almost paralyzed him, when he realized he'd accepted that he might be trapped here for some time to come. *No resignation,* Will told himself, kicking his boots off and sliding chilled feet under the rough but warm woolen blankets. The straw tick smelled clean, at least; he hoped that meant it wouldn't be crawling with lice and bedbugs.

He pinched out the candle and composed himself for sleep.

Morning came slowly, after long hours of tossing and worry. He sat up and shuffled to the embrasure in stocking feet, unmindful of the chill. His bones ached of a morning, winter and summer, these days; it was only a matter of degree. "God protect the halt and the lame," he muttered. "Also the purblind fools. And one Kit Marlowe, wherever he may be."

The slit would have been just wide enough to get his head into. A black bird the size of a small dog perched inside the opening, eyes gleaming like jet beads pressed into the black cloisonné of its plumage. "Good morning, Master Raven."

It cocked its head at him as if it understood, and fluffed its wings. The right one hung at an angle, broken once and healed askew. Beyond it, Will could see sunlight on gray-white walls, and beyond them the rippled expanse of the Thames.

"I seem to have a problem," he remarked, and tightened his grip on the ledge. "I don't suppose *you* have any bright ideas?"

The raven tilted its head the other way, and then departed in a flurry of feathers and cawing when the door clattered and swung open behind Will. Its flight wasn't quite level either, and Will frowned as he turned to face whatever the morning might bring.

While Thou art looking out for the halt and the stupid, Lord, let me put in a word for a crippled bird, as well.

And as the Earl of Salisbury limped into the doorway, Will laughed and amended his prayer. *All right, Lord. Mayhap not all the lame.*

"My lord," Will said, more aware than he liked of his uncombed hair and stocking feet. He stopped himself from pushing a hand through his curls to settle them, and fumbled in his pocket for a coin to fuss instead. *Not long now, and that trick won't steady thy hand any longer.* He could tell from the trembling in his fingers even as he rolled the shilling across their backs. "What is the purpose of this outrage?"

Salisbury pushed the heavy door a little more open and came forward, the sleeves of his black robe rippling in the cold breeze from the window. "This will never serve," he said, casting a disdainful eye over the cell. "I will not have your health at risk."

"My lord—"

"Peace, Will." The Earl drew himself up to his full, slight height as if the gesture pained him. "Thou'rt here for thine own protection."

Will swallowed, knowing how hoarse he must sound. "You'll risk Ben Jonson on a fool's errand—"

"Master Shakespeare," Salisbury said. "Thou needst ale before thou dost speak again, to judge by that throat.

Come, let me see thee breakfasted." He stood aside, gesturing to the door through which he'd passed.

Will hesitated, and then stooped painfully to pick up his boots. He hadn't time to work his feet into them, and his previous night's captors had taken his cane, but he hobbled along as best he could.

"Master Jonson's more Walsingham's than mine," Cecil said while they walked, as if speaking to an old companion. "Although I will admit I haven't my father's sense of which of you intelligencers and agents is playing what end against which. No, Jonson's not reliable enough to suit. But which of you sturdy scoundrels can choose a side and stand with it? My men, Baines' men, Walsingham's men, Poley's men. Who can tell one from the other?"

"And what side do you support, my lord?" Will pitched his voice low, a servant's deference, and hoped Salisbury's expansive mode continued, although he dreaded to learn the source of it.

"Mine own, of course. Which is to say, England and her crown, and the best way to assure a strong England is to assure a decisive King. Thy Walsingham doth consider these Catholics and Puritans and Prometheans are the threat ... the *Prometheus* Club? As ridiculous as Raleigh and his School of Night. Like boys playing at capture the fort, and they have no concept of what's truly at stake."

Will did not pause his stride. He noticed with amusement that his limp and Salisbury's matched admirably. Will trailed a hand along the wall as a substitute for his cane, in case his balance should desert him. "And what's that, my lord Earl?"

Salisbury brushed Will with a sidelong glance as if to see if he made mock. "Sovereignty," he said. "Do not think that England's is by any means assured."

"My lord?" Will almost skidded to a stop in his stockinged feet as Salisbury turned on him. Something filled the Earl's eyes—not fury, precisely, or desperation, but whatever it was the player's part of Will's mind saw it and recognized it as *motivation*.

And saw in that silence the thing that Salisbury wouldn't say. *James is a terrible King.*

"Let us merely say," Salisbury continued, in the teeth of that long hesitation, "that the Scottish influence among the courtiers does not serve to unify us, and leave it at that. In any case, Master Shakespeare, I would see thee safe—"

"I will be missed."

"Thine absence will be explained. 'Tis not as if thou wert not noted for the occasional abrupt disappearance."

"And Kit Marlowe?" Will interrupted, and then held his breath. "The Prometheans who worry you so little, my lord, have taken him hostage as well."

"Not on my orders."

"No," Will said, remembering the sound of a blow, a skull thumped hollow as a melon struck with a knife.

The Earl pressed his lips together and considered long enough that faintness made Will light-headed. And his words sent Will's stomach plunging hopelessly. "Regrettable," Salisbury said. "Truly regrettable. But I need them more than I need Marlowe, Master Shakespeare, for the next month or so. Conspiracies are useful—a force that may be directed to profitable service, like a waterfall through a millwheel, but I learned well from my father that they must not be plucked before they are ripe. I mean to use these conspiracies as he would, to secure the future of the realm."

Will closed his eyes and dropped his chin, hearing finality in the tone. "My lord."

"I'm sorry," Salisbury answered, and Will almost thought he meant it. "Come. Thou knowest Sir Walter Raleigh, dost not? He's a guest here as well—in a pleasanter section, although his teeth are quite pulled these days. I have no doubt he would welcome a little company. Shall we call on him?"

Will nodded, smoothing his face so his panic would not show before this man. *I'm safe. One problem attended to.*

But Kit and Ben are not, and neither is Tom.

Act V, scene ix

Can there be such deceit in Christians,
Or treason in the fleshly heart of man,
Whose shape is figure of the highest God?
Then if there be a Christ, as Christians say,
But in their deeds deny him for their Christ,
If he be son to everliving Jove,
And hath the power of his outstretched arm,
If he be jealous of his name and honor
As is our holy prophet Mahomet,
Take here these papers as our sacrifice
And witness of thy servant's perjury.

—CHRISTOPHER MARLOWE,
Tamburlaine the Great, Part II, Act II, scene ii

Kit sat in that darkness too deep for his witch's sight to pierce, even had he the use of it, and ran his fingers over the rugged surface of the scold's bridle Baines had left to keep him company. He'd thought at first he might force it to pieces and use the cast-iron straps to dig, but the welds proved strong. He knew every inch of the thing's surface by now, had bloodied his fingertips with worrying at it, with picking at the spikes on the mouthpiece and exploring the curve of the cheeks. It weighed as much as a small child in his arms, resting against his knees, and holding it close to his breast was the only thing that silenced the savage pain in his brands any more.

The wrenching in his belly, the agony that told him he must return to Faerie sooner rather than later, or die in pain he wouldn't have to find unimaginable—

—there was no help at all for that.

Kit sighed, and curled his fingertips into the earth, pressing his matted hair back against the stone. A lump like a church door had risen and fallen on the side of his head, and Baines had not returned.

Another spasm dragged at his belly; he wondered if it was what a hooked fish felt, or a man who suffered with the stone. *"Christ,"* he prayed wetly. The agony pressing his brands out—until he would have sworn they bulged redoubled—arced, flared, and settled.

Kit caught his breath and took another slight sip of beer, before resuming his interrupted monologue. "Well, Edward? You know, Your Majesty, I have to imagine it can't have hurt that much. I mean, at first, certainly. But not like slow impalement, or breaking on the wheel. Hell, probably not so much as—"

Oh, shall we not think about that? He wondered if Mehiel's thrashings were like a breeding woman's experience of carrying a baby under her heart. *Pregnant by God. But 'twas not God that knew me—mayhap when 'tis born, 'twill be an Antichrist.*

Pity thou'rt not Catholic, Kit: couldst ask the Virgin Mary.

Pussycat, thou'rt raving.

Why, so I am. And knowest thou reason why I should not rave?

Aye. The small, still voice inside of him. The one he'd known with such certainty once. *Thou'rt scaring the baby, puss.*

Meaning Mehiel. Meaning the thrashing thing within him, terrified—*terrified?*

Angel?

Mehiel?

And somehow, as if in response to the suddenly gentle tone of his questions, the tearing sensation faded. And Kit clenched both hands on the straps of the scold's bridle and cursed himself for a fool who would whip a failing horse until it fell over dead in the traces. *Aye, and he's torn from God's mercy and rammed up the arse of a sodomite, tortured and raped, and what do you get him?*

He couldn't quite hold back the giggle as he laid his forehead against the straps of the bridle and clutched it tight against his breast. *Why, fucked by Lucifer. Of course.*

"Mehiel." A tentative whisper. "Angel, dost hear me?"

:And angels of the Lord are *thee*?:

A voice for a moment he mistook for his own defiant tones, the spiked irony he saved for moments of abject vulnerability. *This one is—oh. Mehiel?*

A flicker, a suggestion of bright yellow wings barred in black. A voice that was not the voice of his conscience or the voice of his faith, but was very much his *own* voice after all. A sense of a head upraised, and hesitance. Kit thought if the angel stood before him, it would have cringed, and then forced itself upright. :Greetings, who was Christofer Marley:

"Thou knowest I can't stand to be called that," Kit said, but he said it wryly. "Why speak to me now, angel of the Lord?"

A soft silence, with a small voice following. :Thou didst never listen before:

Which wasn't something he could answer, exactly. And no excuse he could make.

:And now: Mehiel barely whispered :thou must listen all the closer, or we will be lost eternally, and hope lost with us:

"Can I be more damned than I am now?"

:Always: the angel answered, and Kit sighed and set the bridle aside.

"All right," he said, before another blade of agony curled him to his side, gasping until the spasm had passed. There was no hope in his breast, but he grimaced in determination and cracked his bleeding fingers one by one. Despair was a sin, after all. "Never say die. What happens if we climb? There's always a way out if you look hard enough. Canst fly?"

:My wings are bound in thee—: the angel began, but the rest of his comment was lost.

:Ah, Sir Poet: A voice like brushed silk, and there would have been no mistaking this one for his own, or for that of Mehiel. :Is *always* a way. Come to me, my love; I am the way:

There was light, suddenly. Light cast from over his shoulder, and as he found himself standing he turned to it, turned into it. The scent of pipe tobacco surrounded him, a comforting memory of Sir Walter Raleigh's chill parlor and many late nights.

Mehiel?

:Do as you must: the angel whispered in his ear, and folded himself taut within a flurry of remembered golden feathers.

Kit took a deep breath, and walked into the light.

Act V, scene x

For thou wilt lie upon the wings of night,
Whiter than new snow on a raven's back.
Come, gentle night; come, loving, black-brow'd night,
Give me my Romeo: and, when he shall die,
Take him and cut him out in little stars,
And he will make the face of heaven so fine
That all the world will be in love with night,
And pay no worship to the garish sun.

—WILLIAM SHAKESPEARE, *Romeo and Juliet,*
Act III, scene ii

The crippled raven found Will in his new room and seemed well pleased with the wider window, for all it must rattle the glass for attention. Will didn't think this typical behavior in a raven, but perhaps the pampered birds at the Tower had been hand-fed into audacity. He opened the casement, despite a cold, sharp wind that whittled past the edges of the palm-sized panes: the bird hopped into the air as the frame swept the window ledge and then settled again in its own footsteps. It cocked its head at him, wise-eyed and glossy, and fluffed its lacquered feathers. "Is a predilection for charity branded on my thumb?" Will asked mildly, and flicked the raven a bit of boiled egg, trying not to think how it resembled a plucked-out eye. The ravens had their reasons for staying close by the Tower.

The bird pecked it up and looked for more, and Will laid the next crumb closer and stepped away from the window. Southampton had had a cat for company. *I'm not certain a raven is much of a companion, but it's either that or tap out messages to Sir Walter on the wall in code.*

By the fourth bit of yolk, the raven was crouched on the lip of the window frame, its peaked head bobbing between heavy, crookedly spread wings. Will tossed the fifth bit on the floor and held his breath. The bird's black cold-chisel beak dipped once or twice as it examined the room, Will, and the bit of egg with suspicion. Will chirruped as he might to a chicken, feeling foolish. It crouched, about to hop down onto the floor—

—and vanished backward in a tempest of black feathers, shocked into flight by the clatter of the bar outside Will's door being drawn from the braces and hurled unceremoniously to the floor. Will startled, turned too fast, and fell sprawling, forearm and hip slamming the floor near hard enough, he thought, to strike sparks between bone and stone. It hurt too much for him to manage a shout, or more than a rasping whimper. The door burst open, wide strap hinges creaking, and Will pushed himself to his knees with the arm that wasn't numbed from fingertips to elbow.

And then he blinked, and sat back down among the rushes and herbs strewing the floor, because it was neither Salisbury nor Allan the guard who entered, but Ben Jonson, Tom Walsingham, and Murchaud, the Prince-Consort of the Daoine Sidhe.

"Will!" Ben was the first to start toward him as he sat foolishly blinking, cradling his injured arm in his left hand and hugging it close to his chest. "Thou'rt hurt. And it's freezing in here, the barbarians—"

"Nay," Will said, shaking his head. "Just a fall. Just a tumble—" He wiggled his fingers slightly, to show the arm unbroken, and panted in pain. "Robert Poley took my cane, damn him to Hell."

Murchaud had turned with Tom to brace the doorway, both of them facing the hall, and the Elf-knight's blade was drawn. "Master Shakespeare," he said; Will heard tautness of emotion in his voice. "Where is Sir Christopher?"

Will swallowed a whimper as Ben lifted him to his feet as easily as swinging a girl across a threshold. "I know not, Your Highness," he answered. He leaned on Ben's arm while testing his leg and decided it might almost hold his weight. "You could not find him in your Glass?"

"No," Murchaud said without glancing over his shoulder. "Hast a looking glass?"

"I have a window."

" 'Twill serve. . . ." Murchaud stepped back, tapping Tom on the shoulder as he moved into the room. Tom followed without taking his eyes from the hall until Murchaud stepped in front of him and swung the heavy door shut. "Sir Thomas, if you would be so kind as to drag that table over?" A moment later, and they had it barred from inside, while Will clung to Ben's arm.

"Damn," Tom said, turning to face Will. "Damn. I'd hoped we'd find Kit if we found you—"

"How did you know I was missing?" Will's eyes followed Murchaud as the Prince moved to the casement and dragged it shut. He sheathed his sword and tugged two-handed to be sure the frame had latched.

"When"—Tom glanced over at the elf—"His Highness noticed Kit was missing, he sought you. Realizing your circumstances, he came to me. Ben was my idea."

Ben grunted. "And still we have no Marlowe."

"No," Murchaud answered in a low and worried tone. "And he'll be dead with Faerie-sickness if we do not find him soon. Come along, mortals—"

"Wait," Will said. "Sir Walter Raleigh is in the next chamber. Should we see to his liberty too?"

Rather than meeting Will's eyes, Tom looked at Ben. "Sir Walter's a legal prisoner of His Majesty's," he said. "And not a loyal subject held illegitimately. I cannot countenance it, I fear—and every minute we tarry here is a minute Kit is dying."

Regrettable, Will heard Salisbury say again, and nodded while Tom lugged a footstool toward the window. "Right. 'Tis the side we're on."

Murchaud held a hand out, ready to pass him through the glass, and Will limped away from Ben's steadying hand and went.

Act V, scene xi

Oh, thou art fairer than the evening air
Clad in the beauty of a thousand stars;
Brighter art thou than flaming Jupiter
When he appear'd to hapless Semele:
More lovely than the monarch of the sky
In wanton Arethusa's azured arms:
And none but thou shalt be my paramour.

—CHRISTOPHER MARLOWE, *Faustus,*
Act V, scene i

Kit stepped through the light again, but this time there was nothing beyond to support his bare, bruised feet.

He fell.

Into infinite cold and blackness, tumbling hopelessly, arms windmilling, the scream in his throat vanishing into silence as it passed his lips, his fingers freezing so they might shatter and—

Lucifer caught him by the wrist, pulled him close, cradled him in the warm snowfall of wings. Breath hissed

into Kit's lungs, the frozen tears melting on his cheeks.
"Christ!" he wheezed. "Christos!"

:Kepler: Satan answered, and flung his wings wide. He
held Kit's hand in his strong, perfect fingers, though, so
that Kit scrolled out alongside him like a ribbon let flap
in the wind—but Kit could feel no wind pressing at him
as they fell. They tumbled in preternatural calm, or perhaps Kit's initial impression had been wrong, and they
merely floated like puffs of thistledown in the air.

Except that what surrounded them was blackness,
velvet and complete between the pricked-out diamonds
of a thousand million stars, and they swam among those
stars like dolphins sounding the deeps. "Strange fish,"
Kit said, and shook his head. "Kepler. The German
astronomer."

:Aye: Lucifer answered, and Kit could hear the pleasure in his "voice." *I've passed a test?* :This is his universe, my love, as before I showed thee Ptolemy's. Is't
not lovely?: His hand tightened on Kit's, squeezing the
iron rings around Kit's fingers.

The poet winced in pain, but Lucifer took no notice.
Rather, he lifted his right hand to point. :See Mars?:

A racing red pinpoint, a droplet, a globe. Kit focused
on it and grinned in dumb wonder as his eyes seemed
to adapt, his focus grow closer. He saw veils of mist and
shining white glaciers on the surface of the round ochre
world, and two moons no bigger than afterthoughts
tumbling like puppies through the red planet's sky.
"Oh, Lucifer," he said. "Which is the truth, then, my
lord? This, or what thou didst show me before?"

:They are both true: the Devil answered. :All stories
are true. But this story is becoming more true than the
other. Look thee; there is thine earth:

Kit blinked through watering eyes. The soft blue-and-
white sphere spun like a top far beneath them. He could

see the hurtling globe of the moon arcing about it, and a smaller body sharing Earth's path that seemed to play a flirtatious dance, approaching and retreating. "What is *that?*"

:Ah: Lucifer answered. :She'll not be discovered for four hundred years. They shall name her Cruithne when they do. A moonlet, a captured wanderer fallen into the orbit of some greater, brighter thing:

"Strange," said Kit, "that such a thing should have a name, when I myself do not."

:Dost mourn thy namelessness, who was Christofer Marley?:

And Kit blinked, hanging there among the stars, watching the world spin like a top with his fantastically powerful vision. And thought of Will saying that he had never had time to tell Amaranth about the oaks.

:I could protect thee. Take thee from that place where they have thee so sorely imprisoned. Save thy life:

"Aye," Kit said, tugging his aching fingers firmly out of Lucifer's grip. He floated, hugging himself, and took a miraculous breath of nothingness. "I've been lucky at the brink of death before—"

Lucifer chuckled like breaking glass. :So say you:

"Thou sayest otherwise?"

It was a spectacular thing, to see an angel shrug. :The blade entered your brain, who was Christofer Marley. It broke through bone and severed the great artery above and behind the eye. You *died*:

"But I—"

:You died:

He would not let Lucifer see him tremble. "The Devil asks me to believe him."

The Devil . . . winked. :The Lord works in mysterious ways. When he works at all:

And Kit, quite suddenly, saw through him. He swallowed. *How have I been so blind so long?* "But couldst protect me, Light-bringer?"

:Lightborn, aye. I never liked that role so well as the others thou didst grant me: Lucifer smiled, that glorious expression that turned his crown of shadows into the gentle darkness of a moonlit night.

Kit looked up, regarding the serpent for a long, long moment before he answered. "What sort of apples are you peddling this time, old snake?"

"The same old apples every time," Amaranth answered, her hair twining out of the shadows around her face, her heavenly blue eyes gone the flat color of steel. Kit forced himself to watch the transformation, clenching his fists until blood broke around his rings. The image lasted only a moment, and then the twisting tail was wings, the crown of snakes become a crown of shadows once again, and Kit's breast ached with the beauty of the angel who reached to take his crimsoned hands.

"Oh, yes. Thou always wert the teacher, wert thou not? The seducer with truths, the bestower of knowledge and power. The rebel condemned to torment. Mankind's scourge and seducer, warden and guiding star," Kit said. "The serpent and the apple. The gift of terrible knowledge. The light-bringer, the fire-bringer. I know thy name, my lord."

:I have many names, my love:

Kit drew a breath that hurt. "Prometheus."

:All stories are one story: Lucifer said, and drew Kit—unresisting—close, and kissed him with a lover's passion. :Come now, love, and I shall free thee from thy prison, and thou shalt dwell with me:

The kiss was a brand on Kit's mouth before he pulled away, and he felt the wild tumult of Mehiel, within. He reached for poetry, and could not find his own, but there was other verse would serve. Kit drew breath and quoted his old friend Sir Walter Raleigh into Satan's face—*"If all the world and love were young, and truth in every shepherd's tongue, these pretty pleasures might me move to live with thee and be thy love."*

And the devil laughed. :Doth thy shepherd lie to thee, Sir Poet? It is the way of shepherds. Lying creatures, the more so when they talk of God:

"Father of Lies," Kit answered, with a shrug.

:But all my lies are Truth. Dost love me, Kit?:

Kit edged away from the angel, and found his back scraping the rough damp wall of the oubliette. Dirt moved under Kit's feet, a transformation sudden enough to dizzy him. Lucifer's halo filled the grim little room with light, and he seemed suddenly more beautiful than ever. Something fragile and almost mortal, unreal, outlined against the sweating stone.

"How could I ever love anything else, once having been loved of thee? I can't comprehend thy logic, Father of Lies. Both ends against the middle. Like a two-headed serpent devouring itself. Christ. What canst thou hope to obtain?"

Lucifer smiled only, and in the sadness of that smile Kit knew the answer. "Oh. For the love of God." *Oh, he is right: we are more alike than not, my lord Morningstar and I.*

:For the love of God. One way or another. Dost judge me? Begrudge me?: Lucifer beckoned, cupping feathers brushing the stone.

Kit shook his head, and did not come closer. "What would I not give for the same?"

:Mortals are *ever* so clever. And you tell stories. Sooner or later one of you will tell the story that will set me free. That will make Him to love me again, for He cannot forgive me my trespasses as He is, and I cannot be content without Him: The angel sighed and looked away. :Why should such as I care what story that is?:

"A lover's quarrel, Lucifer? That's all?"

:What is more divine than love?:

Kit hadn't an answer. He balled his fists again, freshening the drip of blood, and came to the center of his prison. "Forgiveness," he said, and smiled. "Forgiveness is more divine than love, my lord Lucifer. That was Faustus' fatal flaw too, thou knowest. I'm always startled how few understood."

:That Faustus could not be forgiven? Mustn't the fatal flaw come from within and not without?:

"No," Kit answered. "He could have been forgiven. Anyone can be forgiven, who repents. Faustus had opportunity, time, and chance to repent, again and again and again. But he never meant to. Never meant to repent, my lord Prometheus."

:Then what was his fatal flaw, Sir Poet?: Lucifer's eyes sparkled. He tilted his head aside, lovelocks drifting against the exquisite curve of his neck. Enjoying the game.

" 'But Faustus' offence can ne'er be pardoned,' " Kit quoted. " 'The serpent that tempted Eve may be saved, but not Faustus.' Faustus' flaw was the sin of Judas, who deemed his transgression too great to repent of, and thereby diminished the love of God, who can forgive any offense, so long as the sinner wishes forgiveness. Faustus sinned by hubris. I for one had always thought it plain, but they say the playmaker is the last to see the truth in any play—"

:Hubris, my love? And is that thy sin as well?:

Kit laughed. "No, not my sin. My sin is not hubris. My sin is love, in that I love my sin too well to wish to repent of it. I am not Faustus." He looked up into Lucifer's cerulean eyes. *Read my mind now, Lucifer Morningstar.*

The angel blinked once, considering, and the barest part of a frown creased the corners of his mouth. His wings expanded on a breath, a slight wind stirring. He nodded once. :Wilt come with me, then, Christopher Marlowe? And comfort one another in our exile, until the world shall change?:

Kit's laugh hurt, sharp edges that cut the tender inside of his throat. "Even thou—"

:Even I?:

"Even thou hast forgotten my name."

:Come with me. Let me be thy shepherd, and bring thee from this dismal place:

Kit turned in the open circle of Lucifer's wings and let his eyes rove over the seeping stone walls of the abandoned well, the rough round shape of the scold's bridle kicked into the corner, the dank and odorous earth under his feet. "No," he said thoughtfully.

:Kit?:

"No." He couldn't quite manage the defiant glance over his shoulder and the lift of his chin he would have liked, but his voice stayed steady and that was a victory in itself. "No, my love. Thank thee. I'll do it on my own." And then he turned away again, blood oozing from his fingers and the flutter of Mehiel's approval like a heartbeat in his breast, and waited for the light to fade around him.

The first touch of returning agony came as the darkness told Kit he was alone. Golden wings, golden eyes, a dream of memory and warmth as Kit dropped to his knees, body clenched around a scream he was still too proud to give voice. :God loves a martyr, Sir Poet:

God's welcome to get himself fucked too.

Act V, scene xii

Came he right now to sing a raven's note,
Whose dismal tune bereft my vital powers,
And thinks he that the chirping of a wren,
By crying comfort from a hollow breast,
Can chase away the first-conceived sound?

—WILLIAM SHAKESPEARE, *King Henry VI*
Part II, Act III, scene ii

Ben and Tom were shuffled back to Tom's study—over predictable protests, for which Will felt a great deal of sympathy. But he would not permit them to stay in Faerie without the assurances that he held, when any amount of time might pass them by in the mortal realm.

Once they had parted company and Murchaud had brought Will through to the Mebd's palace, Will slumped to the floor of Murchaud's night-shadowed chamber and buried his face in his hands while the Prince went about, lighting candles that failed to lift the gloom. Murchaud unlaced his outer sleeves and drew them off. He tossed them carelessly across the foot of the bed and began unbuttoning his doublet with fingers he stopped to massage now and again, as if they ached. Will watched in fascination a Prince—still moving like an old man—playing his own body servant. "Your Highness, are you well?"

"Iron-sick," he said, in a tone that brooked no more questioning. "London is full of the stuff."

Will nodded. "What do we now?"

The Prince shrugged on a woolen jerkin in deep blue, with golden knotwork. He leaned back against the wall. "We beg my mother for help."

The white tree on the bluff over the ocean was hung with icicles like curtains of glass, creaking faintly in the wind. Morgan's cottage, once they passed through the icy, snowless beech wood, was white as bone and black as aged oak among the weathered stems of the garden. The gnarled canes of ancient roses twisted about the crimson door, woven tight as the withy hurdles the farmers of Will's youth used to keep sheep properly divided in the pastures.

Despite the biting cold, the door stood open and a big, shaggy copper-colored dog lay across the threshold, the crochet-hooked tip of his tail flipping deliberately. He rose as Will and Murchaud approached and ambled into the cottage, turning once to glance over his shoulder and prick alert, shaggy ears covered in the same luxurious coat that swayed about him when he moved. A moment later, Morgan stood framed in the doorway, the dog leaning his cheek against her hip and watching with gaze bright through a fall of hair. She shaded her eyes with her hand against the wintry sunlight and called out. "I was not expecting thee this morning, O son. And in such company."

"We have a bit of problem, Mother," Murchaud interrupted. "Master Shakespeare has witnessed Sir Christopher taken captive by the Prometheans. We must find him—"

"—quickly, if he is to live. Thou didst try with seeking-motes? And consult the Darkling Glass?"

Murchaud pursed his lips at her, one eyebrow rising. Will made himself meet Morgan's eyes past the Prince's shoulder. "Thank you your tisanes and tinctures, madam," he said. "They have made a difference."

She met the gaze for a moment, then snorted and dropped a restraining hand to the dog's neck. "Come in. Come in."

Will followed Murchaud through the doorway and was most thoroughly inspected by a canine nose along the way. Inside the cottage it was warm as summer, despite the open door—another touch of Morgan's homely magic—and sweet-smelling cakes were baking on the hearthstone, their crusts just golden-brown on the side closest the coals.

Morgan crouched to turn them, moving quickly to keep her fingers from scorching, and stayed crouched by the fire long enough to fill a kettle and hang it on the kettle-arm. She stood and turned around. The dog observed her from his post by the door, whining a little.

Murchaud rattled down three mugs and set them out on a bench while Morgan measured herbs into them. "Scrying by water, do you think? Or by the cards?"

"If the Glass won't show it, water won't," Morgan answered, measuring herbs into the mugs. "And the cards are not suited for questions with—definite—answers. So I fear we will have to find someone to ask."

"Ask?" Will said. The trickle of steam from the kettle's spout became a jet that stood out eighteen inches. He moved forward, taking a square of toweling from a wall peg to shield his hand, and poured for all three of them, ignoring the twinge from his bruises.

"Aye," she said, as Will hung the kettle up again. She stirred honey into each mug, and handed him one. He cupped his aching hands around the warmth and cradled it to his chest.

"Whom do we ask, my Queen?"

She smiled at Will over the rim of her mug, flecks of mint dappling her upper lip. "The things that listen in the crevices and quiet places, of course. And the things that listen to the things that listen there."

Morgan led them speedily over frost-rimed beech leaves, to the edge of a talking brook that trickled between glassy walls of ice. She turned at the frozen bank and followed it upstream; Murchaud steadied Will as they scrambled in her wake. Despite his worry, Will straightened his spine and breathed the cold scent of crunching leaves, drank deep the welcome air of Faerie and felt its strength fill him up.

They came up to a little plank bridge with darkness beneath. The icy brook chattered louder there, echoing from the underside of the arch. Ridiculous in the season, but Will could have sworn he heard a frog chirp. Morgan stopped short where the slick silver boles of the beech trees still broke the line of sight into slices. "Go on ahead, sweet William," she said, tossing her long red hair over her shoulder.

"There's something across the bridge?"

"Perhaps," she answered. "But thy business is with the one who lives under it."

With one doubtful glance at Morgan, and ignoring the low, uncertain noise that issued from Murchaud's throat, Will shuffled down the bank. The slope was rocky and slick with frost. He clung to flexing twigs and underbrush to steady his uncertain descent, his bruised hip aching when he slipped.

And faintly, over the singing of the brook, he heard other singing: "For thy delight each May-morning, hurm, If these delights thy mind may move, harm . . ."

"Come live with me and be my love," Will finished, under his breath. *Strange he—it?—should be singing that.* "Hello, the bridge!" he called, feeling silly. Icy silt crunched under his boots.

"Hurm, harm," a slow voice answered. Something shifted in the dark archway. It might have been mottled a greeny-brown like weedy water, shining with healthy, slick highlights in the reflected light. "Master Poet," it said, in reedy tones of slow delight, "have you also come to offer me a poem for passage?"

"No," Will said. *A bridge-troll. What else could it have been?* "What would you take in trade for the answer to a question?"

"Ask me the question and I will tell you the price."

"Tell me the price and I will tell you if I wish the question answered," Will said, having some little idea of how such bargains worked.

"Hurm," the troll said. "Very well. 'Twill serve, 'twill serve. Quest your question, then."

Will drew a breath. "Where is Sir Christofer Marley, that I may find and rescue him?"

"Ah. Harm. No charge for that one, Master Poet. No charge. For knolls troll what trolls know, and I know I cannot answer it: there is no person by that name."

Will let his head fall back upon his shoulders. "Too late," he said. "Kit's dead."

The troll coughed, and Will got a glimpse of long fingers as it demurely covered its gaping, froggy mouth. "Perhaps a different way of phrasing the question, hurm?"

Will blinked. *Never ask me,* Kit had said, and now Will thought he understood. "Where is—" *my lover?* But that was a question with too many answers to serve Will's purpose, to his sudden chagrin. "Where is the poet whose song you were just now singing, Master Troll?"

The troll chuckled, seeming pleased at his care, and trailed long fingers crooked as alder in the water. "And on to the matter of payment, froggily froggily. Would give me a song?"

"Any song I have," Will said without hesitation.

"A bauble?"

"Nothing could be as precious to me as Kit's life, Master Troll." Will thought of Hell, and a quiet garden, and tried not to let the troll see the cold sweat that dewed his forehead. An animal was picking its way cautiously through the brush not too far away. Leaves crackled while Will waited.

"Hurm, harm." The troll lifted a crooked finger and pointed. "Give me the ring in your ear."

Automatically, Will reached up and let his fingers brush the warm, weighty gold. "It's magic," he said, though he was already fumbling with the clasp.

"Trolls know what trolls know."

"It lets me stay in Faerie without being trapped here."

"Then you'd better hurry home, hurm."

Farther upstream, beyond the bridge, a stag crashed out of the underbrush and paused at the top of the bank. It gave Will a wild look, then bounded through the stream.

"Stag," the troll said, following his gaze. "Good eating. The earring, harm?"

Will tossed it gently, underhand. The troll picked it out of the air like a flycatcher after gnats and popped it into his mouth. He belched a moment later—a toadlike, bubbling sound—and croaked: "Look down wells and look in the dark wet places. Look in forgetful places, and for forgotten things. Ask those that know the secrets whispered under earth and between stones."

"That's all?"

"That's all I know," the troll said. "Don't drink the water, mortal man. Go home now."

Will refused Morgan's tisane, over her smile, when they had returned to her cottage. She said nothing about the troll's pronouncement, but Murchaud grumbled. "He told us nothing but riddles." He rubbed his hands as if they still ached.

Will shook his head. "Nay. He told us everything he needed to. *Ask those that know the secrets—*" He stood. "He's a Faerie. Do *you* expect him to play straightforward?"

Murchaud looked up. "Where are you going now?"

Will smiled. "To strike a bargain with a snake."

Act V, scene xiii

*Faustus: When I behold the heavens then I repent
And curse thee wicked Mephostophilis, Because thou
hast depriv'd me of those joys.*

*Mephostophilis: 'Twas thine own seeking Faustus,
thank thy self. But thinkst thou heaven is such a glorious thing? I tell thee Faustus it is not half so faire As
thou, or any man that breathe on earth.*

—CHRISTOPHER MARLOWE, *Faustus,* Act II, scene ii

When the rasp of the hinges heralded Baines' return, Kit was again huddled around the rough, round shape of the scold's bridle. He'd lost track of the comings and goings, the feedings and tauntings, and could now think only of the ever-rising pain, and wonder when it might release him. Curled tight as a caterpillar, his fingers laced through the bridle as if the touch of iron could ease his agony, he still flinched when the light struck his face. "Puss," Baines said. "I've bread and cheese and a little ale for thee."

Kit whimpered. The thought of food made burning bile rise in his throat.

"None of that, puss." A gentle voice, as something struck the floor far enough away to pose him no threat. "Mehiel won't let thee perish. And thou'lt need thy strength for our little ritual, wilt thou not?"

He did not want to cringe in front of Baines, skin welting and hair matted with filth. He got a fist against the earth and shoved himself to his knees, raising a face that Baines grimaced to see. "And I see thou'lt need cleansing beforehand."

"It's a hazard," Kit mocked, finding the ghost of his voice, "of residence in a filthy dungeon. What day is it?" Then—"Oh—!" a cramp like an uppercut to the belly doubled him over. He bit down on a whimper and a flinch.

"Near on Hallow's Eve," Baines said. "Only another week or so of our hospitality to look forward to."

"And then what happens?"

"Nothing thou hast not already proved thou canst withstand, brave puss," Baines said. "I imagine it might even be less unpleasant than Rheims, if thou dost cooperate a little."

"And then the sacrifice." Every word like speaking broken glass. Kit shivered and dropped his gaze to the floor, wondering if they'd let him die cleanly, at knifepoint, or if it would be something drawn out and ugly.

"Peace, pussycat." There was—*Christ*—pride in Baines' voice; the tone was enough to make Kit wish he had something in his gut to vomit. "I'd rather burn a cathedral than see thee come to any lasting harm. What a waste of eighteen years' work *that* would be."

Kit bit down on his lip to stop the whimper, and managed only to convert it to a whine. *Mehiel,* he thought, like a prayer. *Mehiel, Mehiel, Mehiel—*

"Rest well," Baines said. "You'll need your strength." And gently closed him in.

The darkness was complete. Kit bit his fist against a

rising wave of pain and nausea, his teeth gritting on the iron bands. He tasted his own clotted blood, the rank sickliness of the infected, swollen flesh on either side of the immovable rings. It hurt to bend his fingers; he wondered how long he had before gangrene started to claim them, one by one.

Mehiel.

:Sir Poet: A stirring, as of distant attention drawn close. *Is't true what Baines said, just now?* Kit reached out in the darkness and found the scold's bridle, lifting it with battered hands. The touch of that iron soothed his pain, just a little. Enough to almost concentrate, even in the unhelpful dark and quiet of the pit. The effect of iron on Faerie magic, perhaps. *Art keeping me among the living, angel?*

The angel hesitated. :I bear a little of thy hurt: Mehiel replied. :As much as I am able:

Ah. Kit stroked the scold's bridle with the flats of his palms. He wondered if it was the same one, if his own blood seasoned that rusty metal. He did not stop to think what his suffering might have been without the angel's intervention. *Morgan's words were truth, all those years ago. I would not survive this separation from Faerie.*

"And Deptford? Didst aid me there, as well?"

:Did what I might: Shyly, as if his questions embarrassed the angel. :Not what I might have managed once, by the grace of God:

Kit's hands bled again, but at least it smelled of copper and not pus. They knotted tight on the bridle; it fell open on his lap. "Baines will— Baines will hurt us again."

Silence, long and bleak. :Aye:

"The Morningstar said it was our own fear that crippled us."

:The Morningstar: Mehiel said wryly :wounds with truth:

And tempts with the thing you long for most. There was regret in that thought. *Like not living alone, Kit?*

Aye. And isn't that the thing that frightens thee most, as well?

Kit weighed the instrument of torture in his hands. "How brave are we, Mehiel?"

:We are a very small angel, Sir Christofer:

He breathed through clenched teeth. "It's all right, Mehiel. We're a very small poet, too. And call me Kit, an you will."

It was dark enough that Kit didn't bother to close his eyes before he lifted the scold's bridle and—hands moving as jerkily as if an inexpert puppeteer were at his strings—fitted it to his face. He had to wet his tongue on the flat, warm ale that Baines had left, and began to work the bit into his mouth. Dull blades pressed his tongue and palate, not quite sharp enough to prick blood to the surface if he didn't fight the thing.

His hands shaking, the hinges rustling rather than creaking, he closed it around his face and sat there in the darkness, holding the edges together for a full ten counted seconds before he permitted himself to fling it away. It rang from stones on the far side of his narrow prison.

He wasn't sure if the salt and iron he tasted was blood and the bridle, or Mehiel's tears.

Or his own.

But the pain *was* smaller.

Kit crouched in darkness, stronger for the bread and ale he'd forced over his iron-numbed tongue, his trembling hands pressed to the iron bands across his cheeks, below his eyes. *I can do this.*

We can do this.

Mehiel, coiled in a tight, black-barred ball of misery, shivered and did not answer.

*We can endure this. We endure. We live. We cooperate
if we must. And then we find our vengeance.*

:Vengeance is mine, sayeth the Lord:

As thou wishest it. We will live, *Mehiel.*

"Froggy frogs," someone whispered. Kit startled, felt
about him. He tore the bridle from his head again; it
rolled and rattled in darkness, a heavy iron jangle, but
his hands brushed nothing that felt like flesh, slick or
otherwise. *Losing my mind. And who could wonder?*

"Master Troll?"

"Froggy frogs. Froggy frogs. Froggy frogs—" Faint as
an echo up a drain pipe.

"Master Troll! There's a way out, sir?"

"Hurm. And *harm."* Something that luminesced
faintly *squeezed* itself from a narrow space in the floor,
expanding like a rose from a stem, and loomed over
Kit.

"Sir Poet," the troll said, a green-mottled pattern of
dim light against the darkness of the cell. "There's no
way out but through," he answered, and reached a long
hand through the darkness. Spatulate fingers rasped
against Kit's filthy hair, found his earlobe, and tugged.

"What? *Ow!"* A wincing pain to add to all the greater
pains, and suddenly the sensation of a small thing burrowing out of Kit's intestines ceased.

"A gift," the troll said, sounding inordinately pleased
with himself, and sat down beside Kit with his back to
the wall, still glowing faintly.

"And now we escape?" Kit said hopefully, raising his
fingers to touch the heavy warm circle throbbing in the
lobe of his left ear.

"And now we wait," the troll answered complacently.
"Tell me a story, frog-and-prince."

Act V, scene xiv

I durst, my lord, to wager she is honest,
Lay down my soul at stake: if you think other,
Remove your thought; it doth abuse your bosom.
If any wretch have put this in your head,
Let heaven requite it with the serpent's curse!

—WILLIAM SHAKESPEARE, *Othello,*
Act IV, scene ii

Amaranth was easy to find. Her long green-and-silver body lay like a jeweled ribbon dropped on the dust-colored winter grass near that strange white tree; her woman's torso rose among the ice-covered branches, her hands upraised like a supplicating sinner's.

Will glanced over his shoulder at Murchaud as they came up the hill. "Shall we interrupt?"

"Go thou on," Murchaud answered. "She likes thee better. I'll stay for thee here."

Will dug his toes in to climb the slick bank, leaning on a birch limb he'd liberated from the wood—a temporary walking stick—as he climbed. Amaranth heard him coming, of course, or perhaps felt the vibration of his footsteps through the ground. She turned from the waist, the flakes of ice she had been brushing from the tree's pale branches dusting her arms and shoulders and the complaining mass of her hair. Thread-fine snakes coiled tight against the warmth of her skull in the Novembery chill.

"Good afternoon, my lady," Will said. A silvery tone came to him on the same cold breeze that snapped the brave green and violet banners on the Mebd's shining turrets: the cry of a fey trumpet, climbing the rise.

"Hello, William," she said. The trumpet sounded again, burying her words under a landslide of music. "The Prince is going to be late for the rade if he lingers here."

"Rade?"

"The Faeries ride on London," she said. "Time's slipped past thee while thou wert in the wood, I fear."

"What day is it?" Thickening worry, as his hand rose to his naked ear. *I could have lost a lifetime in the time it took to walk back from the troll's bridge. And think you not that the Prometheans will kill Kit out of hand, should they find the Faerie court tromping through London?*

"In the mortal realm?" She dusted ice from her hands. It fell like snow through still air, sparkling on her scales where it landed. Looking up, Will could see that she'd cleaned half the boughs already. "It is Hallow's Eve."

"Damme," he said. *Almost a month gone.* The knowledge made him reconsider his fear for Kit, as well. *And if Kit be not dead already, so long out of Faerie, it is only that something is protecting him.* Will would have swallowed, but his throat was too tight. He would not bury Kit before he saw the body. Not a second time. "Thy help, Amaranth—"

"All thou needest ever do is ask," she answered, lowering her human torso so that he looked her directly in the eyes. Something flickered across their opaque surfaces, a blue so bright he thought first it was the reflection of the unreal sky of Faerie. "Although"—a tongue-flicker of a pause—"I will not vouch that the answer will be always 'yes.' "

He laughed despite the worry gnawing in the pit of his belly. "Why art thou so willing to help a poor poet?"

Dead grass hissed against her scales as she shifted, swaying. "A snake never shares what she knows unless it serves her own purposes. Thou shouldst comprehend such things by now."

"Aye," he said. "I should. And she never shares her reasons, either."

"Perhaps because we have friends in common, thee and me."

"...perhaps. How is thine eye for a riddle, Amaranth?"

"If 'tis a riddle with an answer—"

Will sighed. "I asked a troll where to find Kit, who is held captive by the Prometheans. Wilt help me for his sake?"

"Aye," she said, "and thine own sake as well. Tell me thy riddle."

Will closed his eyes, blessing a memory drilled into sharpness by grammar school and years of playing thirty scripts in repertory. "Look down wells and look in the dark wet places," he repeated. "Look in forgetful places, and for forgotten things. Ask those that know the secrets whispered under earth and between stones." And then he peeked through half-closed lashes, hoping to see some sign of enlightenment cross her face, and half afraid that he would not.

"A snake should know such things," she said, and seemed to consider. "An oubliette," she said at last. "Forgetful places and forgotten things. An oubliette that used to be a well, perhaps? Is there such a thing in London?"

Will's held breath rushed out of him with the words. "There is indeed, and a famous one," he gasped. "Lady, if it would not kill me, I should kiss thee."

"If it should not kill you," Amaranth replied, "I would like that. And now?"

"And now," Will said, "I must discern how I may invade the Tower of London, from which I have myself only recently escaped. And I must convince Murchaud to stay his mother's ride until we have safely recovered Sir Christopher."

Act V, scene xv

What is beauty, saith my sufferings then?
If all the pens that ever poets held,
Had fed the feeling of their masters' thoughts,
And every sweetness that inspir'd their hearts,
Their minds, and muses on admired themes:
If all the heavenly Quintessence they still
From their immortal flowers of Poesy,
Wherein as in a mirror we perceive
The highest reaches of a human wit:
If these had made one Poem's period
And all combin'd in Beauty's worthiness,
Yet should there hover in their restless heads,
One thought, one grace, one wonder at the least,
Which into words no virtue can digest . . .

—CHRISTOPHER MARLOWE,
Tamburlaine the Great, Part I, Act V, scene i

The troll's company kept him sane, and the earring—
Will's earring, Kit got the troll to admit in its usual
circuitous manner—kept the agony at bay. The news
of Will's escape was enough to grant Kit new strength of
intent. *He'll come for me. He won't leave me here.* He knew

it, with the same calm certainty with which he'd known that he could not leave Will to take his own place in Hell.

Somehow, whenever they heard the sounds of the bolts being shot above, the troll always managed to squeeze its enormous bulk into the handspan-wide clay drain before Baines could lift the lid and see it. Kit wondered, and chalked it up to magic, and didn't try to touch the troll after the time his iron bonds raised blisters on its slick, shiny hide.

On All Saints' Day—the troll said—Baines came back with more food and water. "Only a few more days until we're needed."

"Fifteen Sagittarius," Kit murmured, taking no comfort in having been right. He gritted his teeth, knowing that he had to get out of the Pit if Will was to have a chance of finding him. "I'm ready to bargain, Baines."

A chuckle. "Not faking your death of chills and ague any more, I see. What do you have to bargain with, then, Kitten?"

Edward de Vere's old nickname for him. Kit clenched his aching hands against his thighs. "Myself," he said. "You said you wouldn't kill me. After."

"No," Baines answered, leaning down with his hands on his knees, like a man bending to converse with a very small boy. "In truth, puss, I'd hurt you as little as I know how. I'm not without pity or heart."

"Does it mean the irons again?" Strange, how he could think of that so calmly, when his mind skittered away from the rest.

"Not as bad—Kit, give me thy parole that thou wilt not fight nor try to flee, and I'll bring thee up so we can discuss this like civilized men."

:Kit, what art thou about?:

He tasted the angel's fear. *Stalling.* "Come and get me."

Baines let a long ladder of rope and dowels unwind down the side of the oubliette and stood back from the edge. He must have had it ready there by the rim, just in case Kit broke. It galled Kit to know how predictable he had been. "I can't climb with these hands, Dick." They were better than they had been, but still swollen and infected around the bands.

"Thou'rt scared of a little pain, puss?" A pause. "Aye, and tie the bridle to the bottom of the ladder before thou dost ascend. I should not like to have to climb down after it."

Wishing the troll still stood beside him, Kit did as he was bid, and then made his laborious way up the height of the ladder, his fingers leaving streaks of bloody lymph on the rungs while he prayed thanks to the troll for its company, and to Mehiel for his strength.

"See?" Baines grasped Kit's wrist in a hand like a manacle and almost lifted him over the edge of the pit. He tugged the ladder up behind, and tipped the lid shut with a booted toe. Kit stood, examining his hands in the light, and did not realize that he might perhaps have tackled Baines and plowed him into the oubliette until Baines turned back to him. "Let me have a look at those hands, puss."

Mutely, Kit held them out. Baines clucked. "They need cleaning, aye. But I think thou wilt not die of poisoned blood, for all it hurts thee. Still, thou art brave, puss. Art not?"

Despair crushed the breath out of Kit. :This is what moves mortals to suicide, Kit. Is it not?:

Kit nodded mutely, an answer to Mehiel more than it was to Baines. "What will you have of us?" And then realized too late what he'd said, when Baines quirked a little smile and examined him from filthy toes to matted hair.

"Nothing until you're bathed," he said. "Then you may rest until Tuesday."

"And what happens on Tuesday?" *15 Sagittarius.*

"Parliament meets," Baines answers. "The old King dies, and his sons and his peerage with him, and we take Princess Elizabeth and make her Queen."

"Elizabeth's a girl in short skirts—"

"The better to raise her as she should be raised," Baines answered. "Mr. Secretary—the Earl of Salisbury—will be Lord Protector. And I can control Salisbury."

And I'm sure Salisbury thinks he can control Baines. "Salisbury knows of this? You would murder a *King* and shed that sacred blood on England's stones?"

"As Edward the Second was murdered?" Baines smiled. "Sacrifice, puss. A murder serves no purpose. The sacrifice of the head of God's Church in England, along with his Archbishop, timed to coincide with the subjugation of an angel—"

:Kit!:

Not now, Mehiel.

"I see," Kit said. "How can you be so sure of Mehiel's subjugation, Dick?" His arms itched, but he would not scratch the filth on his skin before Baines.

Baines smiled. "Walk with me. I think I know just the room to keep thee in. It will be barred, I fear—"

"It would not be like you to be negligent with trust."

"No. 'Twould not. This is where the choices enter into it. Thy choices as well, puss. Oh"—interrupting himself—"I'll have someone fetch thee a salve for those hands. Poor puss. As I was saying—as Mehiel does, so must do God. Especially once we have weakened the influence of the Church of England so, and here on British soil, where the Catholic dogma has already been broken."

"I know," Kit answered. He let Baines open the thick ironbound door and hold it for him. Together they paced the corridors, Kit so weak with exhaustion that it was all he could do not to stagger. He knew better than to humiliate himself by trying to escape.

"The angel can be influenced by thee. By what thou dost. Willing or unwilling."

"Willing is better."

"Of course."

"And that's all you want of us? And then we're free?"

"Us, is it now?" Baines sounded pleased, and Kit shuddered.

"As you wish," he answered, biting his tongue on everything sharp he wanted to say. *Stay alive,* he reminded himself. *Justice later.* He studied his feet, the skin red and irritated under a layer of dirt.

"Not free, perhaps. Not at first. But eventually, it could be aspired to. Thy very existence, Kit, and that angel in thy bosom, binds God to earthly will as he has not been bound since the Archangel impregnated Mary. We've counterfeited a prophet."

Lucifer, Kit thought, in pain. *Oh, Morningstar. Thou art as clever as thou art beautiful, my love.* He swallowed. "The Christ preached tolerance."

"Aye, and the God we'd give the world is much the same. A God for the common man, rather than a God for Popes and Kings. Is that so wrong?" Baines' voice almost took on a pleading note. "It's peace we offer the world: an end to the black sorceries that foul men's minds, an end to the power of Faeries who steal babes from cradles and poets from graves. A Senate like Rome, perhaps, or a democracy like Athens. Peace. An end to tyranny."

A Senate whose power is founded in blood. Kit closed his eyes. *As the power of the Tudors and Stewarts is not?* Baines fell silent, and they walked together—slowly, in deference to Kit's weakened state—until they came to a barred oaken door. *Can there be an end to Kings?*

"Your quarters," Baines said, lifting the bar.

Kit paused in the opening. *Morgan wants peace.*

The Mebd wants peace. Baines wants—ha!—peace. The King's peace? Or the peace of Rome?

Who would have thought three separate peaces so irreconcilable? "I've thought on what you said."

"Aye?"

He nodded. The words that he forced out were the most difficult he'd ever spoken.

"I'll cooperate."

It was almost worth it, he thought later, to be clean and cleanly dressed, and to lay himself down in a bed furnished in white sheets and woolen blankets, while a cold November rain pearled on the glass. A crooked-winged raven huddled in the embrasure beyond, and Kit remembered the story he'd spoken of with Murchaud, by the bier of Arthur, King of the Britons. *I wonder if the legend that Britain will fall if the ravens ever abandon the Tower of London is linked to the story that Arthur's soul became a raven when he died?*

But the story's not true. I know where Arthur lies.

:All stories are true: something whispered against his ear. He meant to answer the angel, too, but the last thought he managed before warm old sleep claimed him was that his pillow smelled strangely of Will Shakespeare's hair pomade.

Despite everything, it helped him sleep.

Act V, scene xvi

Knock, knock; never at quiet! What are you? But this place is too cold for hell. I'll devil-porter it no further: I had thought to have let in some of all professions, that go the primrose way to the everlasting bonfire.

—WILLIAM SHAKESPEARE, *Macbeth,* Act II, scene iii

"There," Murchaud said, tapping the cool surface of the Darkling Glass. "There is your cellar, Master Poet, and there is your oubliette."

"Not mine, surely." But Will stepped closer, leaning forward over Murchaud's shoulder. "Can we see inside?"

" 'Tis dark," Murchaud answered. "But fetch a lantern and I'll send you through to have a look."

"Fair enough," Will answered, and went to find a page. He returned with the requested lantern, as well as a pry bar and a rope. "How do I get him back?" *If I can get him out at all.*

"I'll come with you," Murchaud said gently.

Will swallowed, his pulse dizzying. "Just as well," he said, hefting the silver crowbar in his hand. "There's no guarantee I can lift that lid alone." He hesitated, and looked up at Murchaud as Murchaud took his hand to lead him through the mirror. "Does a Prince of Faerie love a mortal man?"

"It's not encouraged." The Elf-knight stepped forward, and Will went with him.

Faint light filtered into the rough, cold chamber. Will's breath smoked in raw air; he was surprised to notice that Murchaud's did not.

The Elf-knight stayed close to the unfinished stone wall, as far from the massive iron cover of the oubliette as practical. He was dry-washing his hands as if they ached, until he noticed Will looking. Then he folded his arms one over the other and waited in a stance as falsely relaxed as parade rest.

Will leaned on the pry bar and bent over the oubliette, worry pressing like a thumb into the hollow of his throat. The chisel tip of the bar left a paler gouge in the floor when he lifted it again. "It's unlocked," Will said. "That likes me not."

"Can you lift it?"

"No."

The Elf-knight came forward, tugging black hide gloves over each long finger.

"Take the far end," Will offered. Murchaud bent down beside him and grasped the butt of the bar once Will had seated it under the lip. With a well-oiled creak, the cover lifted a few dark inches. Will gagged at the reek that filtered out. He and Murchaud shared a grim look, and Will said, " 'Tis recently occupied."

"We must look," Murchaud answered. "Hold the bar." He took his hands away slowly enough that Will, sweating, could take the strain. Will's forearms trembled with effort, but for once his hands weren't shaking—with palsy or with fear.

"Your Highness," Will said. " 'Tis steel—"

Murchaud ignored him, squatting with easy strength and slipping his gloved hands into the crack. He grunted—once—his only outward sign of pain. And stood and raised the lid as if it weighed nothing, laying it open so gently as to make no sound. He leaned it back against the hinges and pressed his hands together, palm to palm, and then he turned away. "Lower the lantern, Master Shakespeare."

Will sighed, tied the rope to its handle, and slowly let it drop into the pit, terrified of what he might find. He struggled to let the rope out smoothly so that the candle wouldn't flicker. "Leaving me to face this alone?" he asked Murchaud when the lantern was two-thirds of the way down.

"Nay," the Elf-knight replied, returning. He'd stripped the gloves off, and Will could see the blistered and peeling flesh on his hands. "Perhaps," he said, in a tone that made Will pause and look up.

"There are reasons it's not encouraged," Will said, understanding.

"What is not encouraged?" Murchaud was looking down now, leaning ever so slightly forward into the pit and watching the light flicker on its damp mortared walls.

"For elf-Princes to love mortal men." The lantern swung lower, revealing a blessedly empty pit. Will breathed a shuddering sigh and let the rope go slack, his hands falling to rest at his waist.

A faint smile softened the elf-Prince's face, half concealed by his fine black beard. "So our Kit is learning," Murchaud said, turning to look at Will. "You are breaking his heart, Master Shakespeare."

Will began pulling the lantern up. "And I should leave such tasks to you, Your Highness?"

"It's a heart, I think, has been broken enough."

"Ah." The lantern retrieved, Will turned away. "Shall we search the cellars for him?"

"He *was* here. But he is long gone."

"How do you know?"

"The troll told you. And besides"—a delicate wrinkling of that aristocratic nose—"I can smell him."

"Can you smell where they *took* him?"

"Alas." Murchaud stepped back. "The trail is cold."

"I'm a fool," Will said suddenly, dropping his left hand from his earlobe. He looked up at Tom, who leaned in silent contemplation against the casement, frosting cool glass with his breath. "A fool and twice a fool."

Ben closed Kit's Greek Bible carefully over the ribbon and set it aside. "How a fool, Will?"

"Because here we sit, wracking our brains on how to save Kit and thwart Salisbury, the Catholics, *and* the Prometheans, and the answer is in our very hands." He reached for his cane and struggled up before Tom could help him. "My cousin William Parker. Baron Monteagle. Who owes me his life, I might add, and is close with Catesby and his lot."

Tom blinked. "How does that assist us, Will? Perhaps if we could sort one plot from another we would stand half a chance of averting them, but they're intertwined as nettles, my friend."

"Look at what we know." Will raised his left hand and ticked off points. "Kit saw signs in the heavens that the fifth of November was the day on which the Prometheans would arrange their sacrifice. He saw the downfall of old ways, the death of Kings."

"The King has been useful to Salisbury," Ben said. "I do not think Robert Cecil stands to overturn the monarchy."

"No," Tom answered. "But the Catholics do."

"And the Prometheans," Will answered. "And knowing how they operate, we must assume that Baines and Poley and their lot are using my Catholic cousins as some sort of a stalking-horse or distraction—"

"Fawkes and Catesby have been fussing about Westminster a great deal lately," Ben said, leaning back in his chair. He lifted his enormous hobnailed boot and propped it on the low bench before the fire. "And they've been less than forthcoming of late. Parliament meets in four days. I imagine what happens will happen then."

"What if they assassinate the King?"

"Hell," Ben answered. "The King, the Queen, and both their sons will receive the House of Lords that day. If anything happened, it would be all England's peerage and the royal family down to Princess Elizabeth—"

"Who is all of nine years old." Tom laced his fingers together as if he really wished to strangle something.

"Aye," Ben answered. "Well, there's your Catholic plot. What do the Prometheans want?"

"The Prometheans have Kit," Will said, "and the Fae have been intending something for a long while now, and biding their time. Both sides treat Kit as if he's some sort of a—counting piece. And I swear he knows why, although he will not tell me."

"What about thy Prince? Or the Fae Queen who came to nurse thee in thine illness?"

"*My* Prince?" Will smiled at Tom. "Kit's Prince, you mean. You know, I rather suspect he's watching us now: I would be, were I in his place." Will glanced up and around, and calmly addressed the air above his head. "Prince Murchaud? Are you listening, Your Highness?"

A shimmer hung on the air, and Murchaud stepped through it. "You know me too well, Master Poet. And Kit is not a counting piece to me." The Prince nodded to Ben and Tom once each. Ben swung his boots down to the floor.

"No. But he is important to your plans. And those of your wife." Will lifted his chin to catch Murchaud's gaze, thinking *when did I grow so comfortable challenging Princes?*

"Valuable," Murchaud answered. "I can tell you what it is my wife seeks: sovereignty for Faerie, and freedom from old bargains."

"Lucifer," Will said. "Everyone wants to remake the world."

"Indeed. And the Prometheans' ritual will give them the power to do it. Or us, if we manage to take that power from them. Since you discovered where they are holding Sir Kit, and we failed to retrieve him, the Mebd has decided that the Faerie Court will ride to the Tower of London on the fifth of November, shortly before dawn." Murchaud folded his arms, the green silk of his sleeves draping heavily. His brow creased; Will thought the expression was disapproval. "Once the Promethean ritual begins at which Kit's presence is so necessary."

Will glanced at Tom for advice. Tom merely inclined his head slightly. *Continue.*

"We wait until they begin? Is that not dangerous?"

"I do not know where Kit is," Murchaud answered. "I can make a strongly educated supposition as to where the ritual will be held."

Will sighed. "Kit. I'd not see him endure torture."

"The Mebd is unimpressed by suffering. The Daoine Sidhe ride at dawn; I cannot stay them longer. There will be power raised that dawn, and all are loath to miss it. And—"

Will waited the Prince's hesitation through. "Aye, your Highness?"

"—once the Prometheans' power is raised, and linked to Kit, he becomes the keystone to their ritual. If the Queens come to his rescue then, once the power is in him—"

"You mean, once he's raped and savaged."

"Yes." Silence, as Murchaud turned and met their eyes. "If my mother or my wife can command Kit, then, then they can command all of that strength, and claim a victory over the Prometheans. They hope."

"And we leave Kit trapped a few more days, under who knows what sort of duress—"

"They must bring him from his cell to complete the ritual," Murchaud said. And then he cleared his throat, after a long pause. "It will likely be in the Roman chapel that's buried under the Tower precincts. Some of us ... some of us might choose to arrive a few hours early."

Will chewed his lip. "I shall be there. I'm sure Sir Walter would not begrudge a companion or two to keep him company in his captivity, and a late night of drinking and dicing is not unheard of among men who have no business in the morning, except with their prison walls."

The Prince nodded to Will's cane. "Thou'rt not going. Thou hast not the strength."

"You could barely stand the iron realm long enough to see me freed. What if there's bars? An iron gate? I'd hate to explain to your mother how I permitted you to burst into flames in a mortal prison."

Ben snorted laughter, and a smile even lifted the corner of Murchaud's mouth.

"Thou'lt walk back into a prison after we risked our lives to get thee out?" Tom asked mildly.

"There's a difference between being kidnapped and held in secrecy," Will said, "and walking in the front gate in plain view of everyone. Salisbury wouldn't dare hold me publicly, especially not were I in the company of Sir Thomas Walsingham and the esteemed playmaker, Ben Jonson, a favorite of Anne of Denmark's. I'm a Groom of the Bedchamber, a King's Man. And His Majesty is *very* fond of my plays."

"If His Majesty survives Tuesday night," Ben said.

Will shrugged. "Two can play at Salisbury's game. He as much as told me England needed a King who was willing to make decisions, or let them be made for him by competent advisors. I cannot guess what his disposition of events is likely to be, if the King does die at Westminster, or even if he intends the King to die or merely to shock him into action rather than this endless equivocation, at which he does not excel as Elizabeth did. But if several upright citizens can all attest that Salisbury knew treason was planned in advance—"

"Then he can hardly hope to benefit from it, if it is carried out successfully," Ben finished in Will's silence. "And so he must prevent it. Your logic's sound, I wot."

"I'll attest it," Tom said. "I've not much to risk. My star at court is less than bright these days, in any case—and I do not find James' entourage as much to my liking as Elizabeth's."

Ben rose, slowly, and turned to Will. "With Chapman having been in Salisbury's pay, it's likely the Earl knows us well enough to anticipate every move we make, Will."

Will shook his head. His bare left ear felt strange. "In any case, we can only do our best."

"It will mean Catholic heads when the plot is discovered." Ben sounded resigned rather than angry. He pressed the meaty, branded heel of his right hand to his eye socket.

"It may help a little," Will answered, without real hope, "that the warning comes from a Catholic mouth."

Will himself went to see Monteagle, wearing his scarlet livery, his thinning hair tied back with a ribbon to match. The Baron was at home, and Will was shown in at once and offered mulled wine and ale with spices, which he accepted gratefully. Then he stood beside the fire in the parlor, warming his chilled toes and fingers, and awaited his host's convenience.

It was not long in coming.

"Cousin," Monteagle said warmly. "Thou comest at an interesting hour."

"So I've heard," Will answered, making as much of a

bow as he felt capable of just then. "What do you know about Robert Catesby and Westminster, Cousin?"

Monteagle blanched. "Are you here as a King's Man?" he asked carefully. "Or on behalf of the Earl of Salisbury?"

"I'm here as a loyal subject of the crown," Will answered. "You do know something, then."

"I've told Salisbury everything I know," Monteagle answered. "I should not tell you this, Will, but I trust your motives—Francis Tresham is Salisbury's man too. The King's advisors are well aware of the plot. I take it they have not yet spoken to the King?"

"I do not know the answer to that for certain," Will said, but he thought perhaps he did. "Will you do me a favor, Cousin?"

"Anything." Monteagle's voice was serious, his face calm. A steadier man, Will thought, than the foolish boy who had ridden with Essex only four and a half short years before.

"Let Salisbury know that if he does not approach the King by the end of the day—"

"Someone else will?" The Baron nodded. "Aye." And sighed. "I like it not, Will. We're hanging men we grew up beside. It does not seem—meet—to choose sides against them."

Will shook his head. "It is neither meet nor fair," he answered. "But it is politics. What's the nature of the treason? Do you know?"

"Aye," Monteagle answered. "There's thirty-six barrels of gunpowder concealed in the cellar under the House of Lords. Catesby and his friends planned to blow the whole damned Parliament to Glory."

Act V, scene xvii

What, Mortimer, can ragged stony walls
Immure thy virtue that aspires to Heaven?

—CHRISTOPHER MARLOWE, *Edward the*
Second, Act III, scene iv

On his second night in his room in the Salt Tower, Kit had tried to make his escape through the reflections in the narrow windows; he'd been unable to touch the power of the Darkling Glass at all, and he had wondered at how easily the iron rings on his fingers quelled all the strength he knew he had in him.

He had no clock. Nor was he vouchsafed candle or paper or anything to read. And so he paced, from the bedstead to the window and the window to the bed, pausing occasionally to pick a splinter of the rush matting from the tender sole of his foot or to trace the old markings scraped into the wall—a pierced hand, a pierced heart. Symbols of the passion of the Christ, etched there by Jesuit prisoners who had inhabited his cell before him. At least Kit was fed—what he could force himself to eat of it—and twice a day had a moment's glimpse of another human face when Baines—or Poley, in his Yeoman's livery—came to see him cared for.

Two nights later, Kit was simply *bored,* and sick unto madness with waiting.

"And yet like Faustus in his final hour I count the seconds," he muttered. He leaned against the embrasure, supported on his forearms, and pressed his forehead against the glass. Baines would come for him before midnight, and then the ritual—he couldn't bring himself to think of it in more concrete terms—would begin.

:And thou'rt willing to submit to this for a little less pain, a scrap more of dignity?:

When rape is inevitable— Kit answered, and told himself he didn't remember the exact timbre of Baines' voice, asking *didst thou like it, puss?*

I'm willing to submit if it means I'll get a better chance at Baines, he answered. *It's not as if I could avoid—*

:There's always a way:

And then Kit realized the angel was looking at the window.

"If we lived, we would be crippled."

The angel bowed his head. :Kit, we would not live:

And damn myself for a suicide? Or wouldst thou keep me from dying again, Mehiel? 'Tis not so far to fall, methinks—

:'Tis some twenty-five feet from thy window, onto cobblestones. It should suffice. Thou wouldst die with thy brands intact—:

Die, damned a suicide.

:Thou who so boldly defied Lucifer, and told him thou wouldst not repent thy sins, for they were sins of love?:

Kit paused. Slowly, he raised his hand and opened the window latch, then pushed the glass wide and laid his hand on the rough mortared stones of the wall. He leaned out into the icy night air. The windows were small, but a small man might slide through them. Far below he could see lights scattered around the Tower precincts like flower petals on the sheets on a marriage bed. "Die with my brands intact," he whispered, as a clock struck half eleven. "Then thou wouldst—"

:It is suicide for me as well: Mehiel said calmly. :I will cease to exist. And thou wilt be damned. But Lucifer and the Prometheans both will be thwarted:

The cold wind tugged Kit's hair, a sensation like the caress of Lucifer's feathers. The crippled raven who always came to visit at suppertime landed on the window ledge, strangely awake in that midnight hour, and on an impulse Kit reached out tentatively and touched its black jet wing. He felt the slick surface of feathers, the deeper warmth of the flesh, and wondered if he'd been a fool to send Lucifer—and Lucifer's promises of love— from him. The raven endured his caress, and Kit stifled an impulse to gather it up in his arms and cradle it close like one of his small sisters with a poppet.

"Mehiel," he said, softly. "Art become so tainted by mortality, after twelve years my companion, that thou shouldst preach suicide?"

:An it save God, I am prepared to make the sacrifice:

"Despair is a sin, angel," Kit said, and closed the casement frame.

Baines came for them as the clock struck eleven.

> *Look, here's the warrant, Claudio, for thy death:*
> *'Tis now dead midnight, and by eight to-morrow*
> *Thou must be made immortal.*
> —WILLIAM SHAKESPEARE, *Measure for Measure,*
> Act IV, scene ii

A heavy bell tolled midnight, and Will laid his cards face-up on Sir Walter's ornately carved black wooden desk and raised his eyes.

"It's time," Murchaud said from his place against the wall. Light-colored stone with the look of hasty mortaring and great age caught the candlelight, outlining his dark-clad frame.

Will nodded and stood, resting one hand on smooth waxed wood. "You know where the magic will be worked, Your Highness?"

"There's a temple under the Tower," Murchaud said, straightening away from the wall. Unlike Will, Ben, and Tom, he had arrived by unusual means, and still wore his rapier at his hip. "More a chapel, really. 'Twill be not a comfortable place for me, but I am content to suffer it."

"Sir Walter," Tom said, rising and bowing. "I am afraid we must then bid you adieu—"

"Go," Raleigh said graciously, rose, and tapped on the door, summoning the guard to inform him that the guests were ready to be excused and that he himself was ready to go up to bed with his wife, Elizabeth.

If those guests managed to vanish into the shadows between the Garden Tower and the gate, how was he ever to know?

Accurs'd be he that first invented war!
They knew not, ah, they knew not, simple men,
How those were hit by pelting canon-shot
Stand staggering like a quivering aspen-leaf
—Christopher Marlowe, *Tamburlaine the Great*,
                                     Part I, Act II, scene iv

This isn't so different from climbing down to Hell, Kit thought, balancing himself with a hand on one wall of the ragged stone stairwell. His shadow writhed before him, cast by the torches Baines, Poley, and the four others walking behind carried.

All in all, he would have preferred the demon with the glowing maw.

He was exquisitely careful how he placed his bare feet on the ragged stone, annoyed all over again that Baines hadn't given him back his boots. He had to give the bastard credit: on a floor like this one, it was an effective means of keeping him from running.

At least his skin and hair and clothes were clean, and the puffy flesh around his rings was peeling with eczema now rather than infection. Which was an improvement of sorts, and so was the cloak warming his shoulders. Not his own fey cloak—this one was as white as the woolen doublet and breeches that would have made it all that much harder for him to run. If he had planned to. *And where would I run?* Or perhaps all that white served to mark him a virgin sacrifice, which was a thought worth a slightly hysterical giggle.

"How far down are we going, Richard?"

"All the way," Baines answered.

The wall grew moist under Kit's fingertips, wet, sandy earth gritting between his skin and the mortared stone. "It's a wonder the river hasn't washed these tunnels away," he commented. "How old are they?"

"Since Arthur's day."

Which was a strange choice of words. Kit almost wished they'd bound his hands, but then he probably would have fallen down the stairs. *Essex refused the blindfold,* he thought. *Can Marley do less?* "These must be Roman ruins?"

"Puss, must you chatter so?"

Kit shivered at the fond correction. "I am understandably somewhat nervous, Dick." The quaver in his voice was less showmanship than he would have wanted it to be.

:Be bold: Mehiel chanted in his ear. :If thou hadst listened to me, thou wouldst be beyond this fear and pain:

Aye, and on to others.

:I still fail to comprehend thy plan:

That's because I do not have one, other than that I will not die tonight, but live, and thwart Richard Baines another day.

:And if he has remade our God into the image he pleases—:

Mehiel, Kit reminded, *my power may be chained and my magic shorn from me, but I am a bard, a poet, and a warlock too. And there's a half-completed Bible in Tom Walsingham's study that says that my God has as much claim on the world as the God of Richard Baines and . . . Lucifer.*

:Prometheus, thou meanest:

Aye. Kit steadied himself against the wall and stretched over a step too crumbled to be safe. "Watch your step, Richard."

:Hast thou the power to do this thing?: Wonder on the angel's voice, those golden eyes shuttered by dark lashes.

You never know until you try. Kit swallowed dryness, and tried to hush his thoughts so the angel would not overhear his fear. *The force of will to defy Richard Baines, and wrest his own greatest sorcery away from him? I can't even best the man in a verbal jousting match. What think I that I can take control of a sorcery in which I am only the catalyst, the sacrifice?*

:Sir Poet: the angel reminded gently, :thou art the man did tell the Prince of Darkness where to take his blandishments:

From the way his shadow stretched before him in the fluttering light, Kit could see that they were coming to the bottom of the stair. A low tunnel vaulted with Roman arches stretched away before them.

Aye, Kit answered. *But Lucifer Morningstar doesn't frighten me like Richard Baines.*

Now entertain conjecture of a time
When creeping murmur and the poring dark
Fills the wide vessel of the universe.
From camp to camp, through the foul womb of
*   night,*
The hum of either army stilly sounds,
That the fix'd sentinels almost receive
The secret whispers of each other's watch: . . .
—WILLIAM SHAKESPEARE, *Henry V,* Act IV, chorus

The Earl of Salisbury limped up the stairs with a half-dozen men-at-arms at his back. "Your Highness," he said, raising his chin to look over Will's shoulder. "Master Shakespeare—"

"Stand aside, my lord," was Will's answer as he continued his descent. His cane clacked staccato on the steps as he stumped downward.

Salisbury did not move. "I will not have thee risk thyself in this," he said. "Thy King needs thee to shape what will follow, Will. There's nothing thou canst do to help Marlowe now. They will have already begun."

Will stopped, one step above Salisbury and leaning forward. He wanted to close his eyes at the declaration, remembering the heat of a crimson iron close enough to curl his lashes. The hand that did not hold his cane tightened on a bit of silk in his pocket, and something pricked him. The enchanted nail Kit had given him, and Will drew strength from it.

He could have glanced over his shoulder, but he knew what he would see: three big men standing shoulder to shoulder, Murchaud with his blade catching lanternlight, the others half crouched and ardent for whatever might come. Tom cleared his throat but held his tongue, granting Will precedence this once.

"Then have your men run me through, Mr. Secretary," Will replied. He drew himself up, balancing against the wall so he could lift his cane off of the step, and looked down at Salisbury from his greater height and the advantage of the stairs. "Because if I am alive, I am going down these stairs, and I am going in the service of England."

The man Elizabeth had called her Elf never glanced down. His eyes sparkled in the lanternlight as he rubbed a gloved forefinger against his thumb, and visibly came to a decision. "The treason is safely under control," Salisbury argued, his soldiers shifting impatiently behind him. "Fawkes will be arrested tomorrow, Catesby as soon as suits us. They'll give evidence that I can use to bring Baines under control once and for all, and their networks with them. The Baron Monteagle has been most forthcoming—"

Will almost dropped his cane. "That's what this has been about," he said, and shook his head. "You still think you can rule the Prometheans. *Rule* them?"

"Every man can be ruled," Salisbury said, provoking a dry laugh from Ben. One of the men-at-arms started forward; Salisbury halted him with a flick of fingers so slight that only Will's training as a player let him see it. "Baines is too useful to waste."

Will swallowed dryness. *The trick with the pewter coins. Of course. Blackmail, plain and simple: Salisbury never intended to see Baines hang.*

Merely to let him know that he could see him hang, if he so chose. "If every one could be ruled," Will said softly, "Lucifer the Prince of God's angels need never have fallen into darkness, my lord Salisbury."

"We have the conspiracy dead to rights." Such hubris, such arrogant certainty. "The realm's ire will rise against the Catholics and in defense of the King. James will move from upstart crow to beloved monarch, and the royal family will regain public sympathy. Baines will perform his Black Mass in front of my witness, and I shall own him. And England will be strong and united again in the mind of her people."

"In front of your witness?" *Not Kit, surely. He would not permit himself to be so used—*

"Robert Poley," Salisbury said with a satisfied smile, "works for me."

Will set his cane back down on the step and leaned on it, dumbstruck. His mouth opened, and closed again; he felt as breathless in air as the fish he was certain he resembled.

Tom caught Will's elbow in passing, and shouldered Salisbury aside. Murchaud and Ben fell in behind, and Will was never certain whether it was something in their eyes or Salisbury's stunned failure to issue a command that kept them all alive.

"Sir Thomas!"

Tom's auburn head swiveled on his long neck, fixing Salisbury with a glare. "Perhaps you should look to your own nest, cousin. That seems to me a cuckoo's egg you are roosting there," he commented. A pause, a dismissive, calculating glance. "Sir Francis thought the same thing, once."

The Earl just stood with his arms akimbo like wings, watching them squeeze past. Will patted Salisbury's black-robed shoulder as he went by. "The Faerie will be here at dawn," he said helpfully. "Expecting a skirmish with the Prometheans. Perhaps it would be well for you to decide which side you wish to be on when they come, my lord. Incidentally—"

"Master Shakespeare?"

Will narrowed his eyes and offered Salisbury his coldest, most stageworthy stare. "—I will not fail to see that the King learns of your hesitance to interfere with this autumn's treason at your earliest convenience, despite having all the knowledge in your hands. If you should choose a side other than the one I find myself allied upon."

> *See, see where Christ's blood streams in the*
>   *firmament!*
> *One drop would save my soul—half a drop! ah,*
>   *my Christ!—*
> *Ah, rend not my heart for naming of my Christ!—*
> *Yet will I call on him!—O, spare me, Lucifer!—*
> *Where is it now? Tis gone; and see where God*
> *Stretcheth out his arm, and bends his ireful*
>   *brows!—*
> *Mountains and hills, come, come and fall on me,*
> *And hide me from the heavy wrath of God!*
> —CHRISTOPHER MARLOWE, *Faustus,*
>   Act V, scene ii

Kit hesitated in the half-crumbled archway, the torches failing to illuminate the darkness beyond. "There's a step down," Baines said behind him. "Have a care among the rubble."

"Perhaps if I had a light—"

"Perhaps if you had a weapon, puss?" Baines came up beside him, a hulking form, breathing softly. He smelled of soap and wine and rosewater and lightly of fresh sweat. "You wouldn't club me with a torch and make your escape, would you?"

Barefooted over broken stones? Kit didn't dignify the comment with an answer. "Cleaned up for the ceremony, Richard?"

A companionable hand on his shoulder made him shiver. "I thought thou wouldst prefer it." Baines brushed past Kit, ducking to pass through the arch, and stepped down. He paused, holding his torch high, and surveyed the chamber beyond.

Kit caught the glitter of firelight on marble, heard the slow drip of water spattering against stone. He grasped the wall with his left hand and stepped carefully onto damp, slick stones outlined with jagged shadows, expecting at any moment to slice his bare sole open. Richard Baines turned back at the sound of stones shifting lightly and held up one meaty hand to help him over the rocks, handing him down like a lady out of a carriage.

Kit gritted his teeth and accepted the assistance.

The chamber didn't quite look Roman, he thought. Admittedly, the once-frescoed ceiling was matted with mold and dangling roots, and the flickering torchlight showed mineral streaks and water damage on walls that might once have been painted plaster. The floor was slimy with ash-fine mud; it sucked between Kit's toes, and under the surface he could feel a hard, pebbly surface that must be tile. He wondered what design the mosaic would have shown if black silt had not occluded it.

"I can think of more pleasant places for an assignation," Kit admitted, drawing his white wool cloak tight in the raw underworld cold. Dripping water freckled his shoulders and tapped against his hair. He pushed damp strands off his forehead, wiping water from his eyes with the back of his hand.

"But few with older power," Baines answered. "And none of those in London. Come on, puss. We'll need a canopy to keep the brazier dry. Come and help me set it up. Pity it's my lord and master who will have the shaping of thy power tonight: I would have liked it for myself, thou knowest."

Baines moved toward the wall. Kit followed carefully as Poley and the other robed men scattered around the chapel. *Nothing like last time,* Kit told himself. *For one thing, all of those men are dead. Either hanged as Catholic traitors, or on the end of my knife.* The memory of de Parma's sticky lifeblood spilling over his hand warmed him; his rings clinked as he rubbed his palms together.

Something rustled in the darkness, disturbed by the torchlight. *Bats,* Kit worried, and then he saw a row of wire cages tucked behind a pillar and a slumping arch, and a dark lantern with the aperture turned toward the wall. The gleam of a too-blond head, and capable shoulders straightening.

"Good evening, Robin," Baines said over the hollow plink of falling water. "Is everything in readiness?"

"Every raven in the Tower," Catesby said, resting a hand on the hilt of his sword. "I'm just about to leave for Westminster: one last meeting with Guido and a check of the powder barrels. I don't *like* this, Dick."

"None of us *likes* it," Baines said softly, as Kit came up beside him like a dog at heel. "But we do what we must, for God. Innocents will die—"

"Aye. And you'll avail yourself of black arts for power." Catesby cast a pitying glance at Kit. "Is this our poet, then?"

"I am," Kit answered, before Baines could do it for him, and extended his right hand.

"Christopher Marlin, Robert Catesby," Baines said, stepping back to keep the hissing torch clear of a stream of water. Catesby slid Baines a sidelong glance and opened his mouth.

Kit cut him off. "You were about to say that I am a bit unprepossessing, Master Catesby?"

A startled glance back. The torchlight made Catesby's nose look long and beaked. "How did you know that, Master Poet?"

Kit smiled. "Words are what I do," he answered. He stepped past Catesby, stubbing his toe among the jumbled stones but doing himself no serious harm. A row of unhappy black birds huddled on a long iron bar within, crouched shoulder to shoulder with their feathers ruffled against the cold. Despite himself, Kit looked for one with a twisted wing, but couldn't see it. "What are the birds for, Dick?"

The torch bobbed and guttered as Baines coughed into his hand. "The sacrifice," he answered.

> *What is your substance, whereof are you made*
> *That millions of strange shadows on you tend?*
> *Since every one hath, every one, one shade,*
> *And you, but one, can every shadow lend.*
> —WILLIAM SHAKESPEARE, Sonnet 53

Will paused in Murchaud's shadow, half wishing he had a weapon in his hand and half glad he did not. "Downward?"

"Ever downward," the Elf-knight answered, glancing over his shoulder for Tom and Ben before he started moving.

"There'll be an echo," Ben murmured. "Keep your voices soft. And we shall have need of a light."

Murchaud blinked. "Of course you will," he said. "How foolish." Of himself or of them he did not say, Will noticed, but he waved his left hand in an airy arc, swarming green motes flickering into existence in the path of his moving fingers. They scattered, swinging low to the ground in twining pursuit, and illuminated the ground by Will's feet, and Ben's, and Tom's. "Master Shakespeare," he said, "can you manage the steps?"

"I'll manage what I have to," Will answered. "Could we make more expedience? Every moment we hesitate is a moment that Kit is in danger."

"By all means," Tom said, setting his boot down carefully among a school of witchlights that danced about his feet like minnows in shallow water. "Let us make our way underground."

So, so; was never devil thus bless'd before.
— CHRISTOPHER MARLOWE, *Faustus,*
Act III, scene ii

He was thankful for so many things.

That it wasn't Baines who undressed him, but two of the other men, and that they did it with impersonal disinterest. They stripped him only to the waist, and left his feet free when they bound him standing between two pillars, and not helplessly prone on some clammy altar. That there was wet stone giving steady purchase under his bare feet instead of the greasy mud, and that the lengths of white silk binding his arms wide as wings were soft around his wrists, and tied so he could clench his hands tight about them, his fingers leaving rusty stains of blood where they had cracked around the iron rings.

Poley's men had set up a rough pavilion not too far away, and the warmth of the braziers protected by its span just reached Kit. A warmth that he was also thankful for, because the water that dripped slowly onto his hair and shoulders, leaving delicate branching trails of silt down his skin and slowly soaking the waist of his breeches, was so cold it burned. A cut he hadn't noticed stung on the bottom of his right foot, and he could feel the warm stickiness of a trace of blood.

He tossed his head to flick his dripping hair from his eyes, and then wished he hadn't, because Baines climbed up the three swaybacked steps to the dais and smoothed the muddy locks back with thick, gentle fingers. Kit flinched from the touch as if it burned him, and in his heart he heard an angel whimper. "You could have lent me a hat."

"Sorry about that, puss," he said. "The roof leaks a little. You're all over gooseflesh. Shall I fetch your cloak for now, until we're ready to begin?"

"It's past midnight and gone," Kit answered, gritting his teeth so that they would not chatter. "What are we waiting for?"

"The man of the hour," Baines answered, and brought the white wool cloak to drape over Kit's shoulders. He drew the hood up to shelter his head and settled it carefully. "'Twill soon be over, and then we can all get good and thoroughly drunk."

Poley emerged from the shadows on the far wall, carrying an end of one of the long iron cages Catesby had been tending. Kit watched, idly twisting at the lengths of cloth restraining his wrists. He should thank Baines for that, he supposed. The bindings were calculated to do him very little harm, no matter how he struggled.

Baines turned and walked down the steps to Poley, and Kit tried to relax into a state of waiting readiness, calling poetry to mind. *What a pity thou hast ne'er written a comedy. If ever, now would be the time for a happy ending—*

He smiled to himself, and quickly dropped his head to hide that smile behind his hood and the fall of his hair. If his own work wouldn't do to hold him together through this, he knew the play that would. *Even if I "like this" not at all. Thank thee, Will. In mine extremity, I knew I could trust in thee.* He drew a long, slow breath, tasting mold and wet upon it, and shaped the well-loved words. *As I remember, Adam, it was upon this fashion bequeathed me by will but poor a thousand crowns, and, as thou sayest, charged my brother, on his blessing, to breed me well: and there begins my sadness. My brother Jaques he keeps at school, and report speaks goldenly of his profit: for my part, he keeps me rustically at home, or, to speak more properly, stays me here at home unkept—*

He closed his eyes and leaned into the poetry as he leaned into the cloths that bound him, and his lips moved silently. *I can bear this. With Will's help.*

I can do this.

I can—

:Kit: A low urgency like panic in the angel's voice that wasn't quite a voice, and Kit looked up, his mute recitation stumbling when he saw who had entered the crumbling chapel, his brow ringed in shadows and his wingless body wreathed in light. Lucifer Morningstar had eyes only for Baines, sparing Kit not so much as a glance.

"Prometheus," Kit whispered, leaning forward to see the red slick stain wetting the left side of the devil's silken shirt.

"As I am summoned," the fallen angel said formally, tilting his head so that the torchlight and the brazier light and the light of his own pale halo reflected on his hair in red and golden bands, "so have I come."

His voice was a bare whisper, resonant of violoncello and the wind through midnight trees. It pressed Kit's heart to thunder in his chest; all pretense of ignorance forgotten, Kit hurled himself backward against his restraints. "I told thee *no!*" he shouted, fabric burning his skin. His feet went out from under him with the force of his struggle, but the cloths held him upright. He sagged against them—*like Christ from the cross*—his arms lifted and spread wide, his shoulders bent open by the weight of his body, the bad one wrenched to pain. The cloak dropped to tangle about his ankles, leaving his bare back cold, the ghost of warmth fled. His hair hung in his eyes. He sobbed in pain and got his feet under him.

Lucifer did not turn his head, but Baines did, and

smiled. "Hush, puss," Baines said, a low tone that nevertheless carried. "Or I'll yet see thee in that bridle thou dost so hate."

Kit permitted his head to tip back onto his shoulders, and let his lashes shield his eyes from the dripping water, and the cloth hold his body up. He was too tired to fight further.

Outmaneuvered, he thought, listening to footsteps approach. Lucifer stood beside him, then, and Kit could imagine the rustle of wind from his wings. He pictured the slightly crooked, narrow-bridged nose, the golden skin and hair, the strong line of Lucifer's jaw. :Thou didst give thy consent, Sir Poet:

"Because I thought it would thwart thee," Kit answered aloud, refusing to look into those still, blue eyes. He didn't want to encourage the false intimacy of Lucifer reading his thoughts. There would be enough false intimacy soon.

:I am rarely thwarted long. Dost thou never lose thy power to intrigue?:

"Get it over with," Kit said. Not an answer but a command.

:Master Baines: Lucifer continued, as if Kit's answer meant nothing to him. :Do see about removing those rings—:

"The rings keep his power in check, my lord Prometheus."

:His power is mine: Lucifer answered, and that was all. Baines obeyed, the rings that Kit could not budge sliding smoothly into his captor's hands. Kit kept his eyes tight shut, unsurprised when they cut his remaining clothes away. He could smell the coke, the tang of the hot irons, and knew he would soon smell his own cooking flesh.

The thought troubled him surprisingly little.

Not nearly as much as the soft touches of a paintbrush

on his skin, marking his body with intricate warm symbols. He did glance down then, and saw Baines crouched beside his feet, delineating sigils in a medium Kit knew by its sharp coppery smell was blood. The blood, he realized, of the first of the three dozen birds that fluttered in Poley's long cage. The brush Baines used was a carefully pared raven's quill.

"You're killing the Tower ravens," Kit said foolishly.

Baines glanced up at him and smiled. "Very clever, puss. Would you care to tell me why?"

"England will fall."

"Leaving one less faith in Europe," he said, dipping his brush. The blood had clotted, and he set the basin aside as Poley brought him the death of another sacred bird in a little white stoneware cup, a fresh trimmed quill balanced across the top. "Before you know it, everyone shall believe as Prometheus' children will them to."

You were halfway kind to me, Kit thought, with a sidelong glance at Lucifer. "Was my consent so important to you?"

:No man can be damned without consent: the Prince of Lies answered. :Nor saved neither:

That will teach me to say yes to anything.

"That doesn't explain your kindness. Or that you promised me the power to deal with mine enemies."

:All stories are true: If Lucifer had been wearing his wings, they would have flicked tight shut just then. Kit found the fallen angel somehow—diminished—without them. Iron jingled in his hand. :Where are thy rings now? Where is thy cloak? Where are thy boots and thy blade? Where is thy name?:

You have them, Kit answered.

Lucifer laughed, and let the rings fall like drops of frozen blood, to ring on wet stone. :No power left but thine own, and that of my beautiful brother. All thy hoardings and borrowings stripped away. And yet though thy power will not be enough for thy purposes, it will suffice for mine:

"How can you be so certain you can use my strength?" *If I cannot outwill Baines, can I be certain I can outwill Lucifer?* Somehow, the dripping water did not carve runnels in the patterns Baines painted over every inch of his body. Kit mourned the ravens, surprising himself, gritting his teeth as Poley brought Baines a third bowl of blood.

"Because my story is truer than thine," Lucifer answered, "and because thou didst give thy consent." Kit hissed in shock; the voice shook his body like a hard-carilloned bell. Then he hissed again when Lucifer bent down and kissed his open mouth, and Kit felt the rustle of wings within.

Kit was bloody to the hollow under his chin. Cold water dripped from his hair, beads trickling between the bumps of gooseflesh. He watched the conspirators move about the chapel, seeing plainly in the darkness again now that the barbed rings were off his hands. The cessation of that pain alone was such a relief that he could not stop flexing his fingers against the silk, leaving smears of color upon it. He didn't look at Baines, even as Baines leaned close enough to him that Kit felt his breath hot on his skin.

Instead, Kit looked out into the darkness, wincing as Poley drew the very last raven from the cage, mastering its struggles as easily as Baines—time and again—had mastered Kit's. He wrung the black bird's neck and it fell limp in his hands, relaxed. Kit winced in grief.

"Last one," Poley said, after he had drained the blood from the bird and brought the vessel up to Baines. "He looks—interesting."

Kit turned his eyes away as Baines patted him on a

red-daubed shoulder. He watched Lucifer poke idly at a coal-filled brazier, the rod stock in his hand brilliant red at the tip.

I've played into his hands. Again.

Gold and black. :I told thee so:

Kit didn't think the angel really deserved an answer.

Duke: *There rest. Your partner, as I hear, must die*
   to-morrow,
And I am going with instruction to him.
God's grace go with you! Benedicite! [Exit.]

Juliet: *Must die to-morrow! O injurious love,*
That respites me a life, whose very comfort
Is still a dying horror!
                    —WILLIAM SHAKESPEARE, *Measure for*
                              Measure, Act II, scene iii

"There must be something," Will said tiredly, leaning back against the dank stone wall. His shaking hands ached with the cold; his feet were numb things at the bottoms of his legs.

"Nothing," Murchaud answered, both hands raised over his head as he pressed the blank stones of the wall near a trio of identical arches. His sword, still clenched in his fist, caught the light of Tom's lantern and reflected it back through cold drips of water.

Will tugged the hood of his cloak up and stepped away, back to the edge of the inadequate puddle of light.

"There is a taste of sorcery," Murchaud said. "But it's shielded and dark. I don't know which of these paths to take."

"I thought you knew where the chapel was. Your Highness."

"Have you ever stopped to consider what a ridiculous

honorific that is, Master Poet?" Murchaud moved slowly along the wall, trailing his hands over the stones nearest the dripping ceiling as if they might whisper something in his ear if properly coaxed. "Your *Highness*. Higher than what? At least *Majesty* or *Grace* are admirable traits to wish on a ruler—" His voice, softly cultured as ever, showed little sign of emotional strain until he dropped his hands to his side and swore. He turned his back to the abutment between two of the archways and leaned back on the dank stones, careless of his silk and velvet, his rapier angled across the front of his legs. "I can't smell anything but mold and what magic they used to hide their trail."

"Let me have the lantern, Sir Thomas." Ben came forward, a hand on Will's shoulder, and lifted it out of Tom's hand. He crouched so the light was concentrated on the threshold of the first door. At the second he paused, running a finger over the stones, and at the third he bent very close for long seconds and then shook his head, finding nothing. "There's a trace of blood through that second doorway, and what looks like a bare foot-print on the stone—"

"But?" said Tom, coming to retrieve the lantern.

"—but I think 'tis not the way they walked."

"Why not?" asked Will quietly, fiddling with the iron nail in his pocket to stop his hands trembling. He hated his hesitant steps for slowing them, hated the querulous nodding of his chin that he could not seem to stop.

Ben looked up, shook his head. "That, I know not." Broad hands spread wide. " 'Tis but an intuition."

"We should follow the blood," Tom said, and Murchaud nodded. "Or we could split into pairs—"

"Aye, and be murdered all the more easily for our troubles," Ben scoffed, standing.

It was Will, standing a little back from the other three

and their conversation, who heard the rustle. "Gentlemen," he murmured, amused when they all three fell silent. "Tom, a little light over here, an you please."

Tom turned with the lantern just as Will turned, and
a dark shape bigger than a terrier hopped awkwardly
across the time-heaved floor toward Will. He crouched,
drawing his cloak tight so it would not flap and frighten
the raven, and held out his hand. "How strange," he
said.

It fluttered into the air and landed on his fist, dry feet
pinching and the impact as if somebody had smacked
his hand with an overhand blow. He cushioned it, bending the elbow to take the weight, then standing with the
assistance of his cane.

The bird cocked its head left and right, black eyes glittering in the lanternlight. It opened its beak and cawed
once, harshly, with a tone of entreaty, and then stiff pinions brushed his doublet and chest as it lifted again and
flew to wait in the third doorway, the one that Ben had
hesitated by.

Will knew it by its twisted wing.

"Gentlemen," he said. "I think we have a guide."

They hurried.

The raven was impatient, and Will thought at one
point that Tom was about to order Ben to *carry* Will.
But somehow, four men and a bird managed to move
through the low, tumbledown corridors in almost complete silence until the low murmur of voices and the
flicker of torchlight ahead alerted them.

Ben and Murchaud went first while Tom hung back
with the hooded lantern, one steadying hand on Will's
shoulder. The playmaker and the soldier moved forward
with cat-footed softness, stopping well inside the mouth
of the tunnel. Will saw them silhouetted against the dim
moving light beyond, and smiled. The darkness was their

friend, the torchlight their ally; it would turn the mouth of this particular tunnel into a well of darkness for anyone in the open space beyond.

Will's heart dropped into his gut at the expression he read on Murchaud's face as the Elf-knight leaned heavily on the wall, visibly restraining himself. Ben turned back to Tom and Will, waving them forward, and Tom left the lantern behind as he came.

The raven was heavy, rustling on his fist. Tom steadied him, but it was Ben's big hands that almost lifted him up the last rubbled slope to the crumbling entryway, that turned his head with a gentle touch to see—

—Kit.

Naked. Wet. Shivering. A few steps up a raised dais on the far side of the red-lit space, his feet planted shoulder-width apart as if he held himself upright out of sheer defiance, his arms spread and bound wide. Shuddering visibly, even from fifty feet away, every time the two figures who stood beside him touched the skin of his face with the quills they held.

Will knew them both, and one of them was anything but a man.

Braziers bristling with the handles of irons stood under an improvised tent at the foot of the dais, and torches guttered here and there, but Kit's flesh was redder than the firelight should paint it, and it took Will a moment to understand why.

"Holy mother Mary," Will said. "Is that all his own blood?"

"I think," Murchaud answered softly, "that we should make haste to intervene, or our timely arrival will be wasted after all. Leave the Devil to me. Master Poet, if you would see to Kit's freedom?"

Will lifted the raven off his fist and set it down on a high point of the rubble as Lucifer and Baines turned away from Kit and started toward the braziers. He drew his belt knife into his right hand and nodded, forcing himself not to think of what he was about to do.

"Ben and I will see to the rest of the rabble," Tom said. "Baines is the one to watch. We three will go first and clear your path, Will—"

Don't underestimate Robert Poley, either, Will thought, but all he said was, "Aye." He took a single deep breath and nodded, his eyes trained on Baines as Baines and Lucifer separated, Lucifer climbing the stairs again and Baines moving toward a darkened corner of the chapel. "Go if you're going, gentlemen—"

He was speaking to their backs. Murchaud's silver rapier gleamed when the torchlight touched it, made itself a brand of darkness in between. The Elf-knight slipped forward, half invisible in the shadows, and Ben and Tom flanked him. Will watched, fascinated, as Ben came up behind the lone man tending the braziers and broke his neck.

Kit, standing like a statue between the pillars, did not move. But Lucifer did, leaning close to Kit with a heated iron held negligently in his hand. He had not even time to turn to face Murchaud as the Elf-knight's advance metamorphosed fluidly into a tackle. "S'wounds," Will muttered, limping forward, his knife concealed in the fall of his sleeve. "This is a fool's errand if ever I've seen one."

> *It's no sin to deceive a Christian;*
> *For they themselves hold it a principle,*
> *Faith is not to be held with heretic . . .*
> —CHRISTOPHER MARLOWE, *The Jew of*
> *Malta,* Act II, scene iii

In a moment, the heat would touch him. Kit braced himself for the pain, tilting his chin down to his chest

and imagining that his weight flowed like water through
his pelvis and down his legs, anchoring him to the floor.
He closed his eyes—a blessing anyway, as they tended
to fall on the heap of mutilated ravens at the foot of the
steps—and drew deep, heavy breaths. Mehiel stirred, so
close to the surface that he could feel the muscles under
his skin that would move the giant wings. He heard the
rustle of feathers, smelled their warmth.

We've done this before, Kit assured the trembling
angel. *It's only the fire.*

One breath and then another, and then again. The air
filling his lungs was thick and sweet, invigorating, full
of the scent of fresh blood and hot metal. Very similar
scents, some part of his brain mused, looking for a fresh
conceit. Anything to distract himself upon. *Mehiel. What
are we going to do?*

:Endure: the angel answered.

:Be strong, my love: Lucifer whispered in his ear.

Kit readied himself as best he could, gritting his teeth
as if sheer willpower could keep him silent against what
was to come. The fine hairs on his back melted under
the nearness of the iron. The Morningstar's long fingers
tangled in his hair.

Something that Kit did not see struck Lucifer from
the side, knocking him away, and the iron rang on the
stones and then sizzled. The blow thrust Kit forward
against his restraints, shoulders wrenched as his feet
came out from under him. He yelped, a startled sound,
and struggled back upright, twisting in futile desperation to seek the source of sounds of swordplay and a
struggle. He couldn't turn his head far enough to see
anything of use.

But a moment later a hand was on his shoulder, and
that he could crane his neck to see, and gasped in shock
at the worry in blue eyes and a tight, hopeful smile. "Kit,
can you hear me?"

"Will!" Kit glanced around wildly, glimpsed shadowy combat through blurred vision. Recognized Murchaud's dark hair and nimble grace circling a laughing Prince of Hell, saw Ben Jonson brandishing a red-tipped iron poker he must have snatched up from a brazier, and shook his head in wonder. "Will, they'll be slaughtered—"

The playmaker shook his head. "Your Prince assures me he can handle this, here, now. How badly are you hurt?"

"Not at all," Kit answered, and then saw where Will's eyes rested. " 'Tis not my blood." He pointed with his chin, while Will produced a dagger from his belt and sawed at taut-stretched silk. Something about the wasted slaughter of all those birds made his breath catch in his throat, and he choked on it, refusing to cry now that he could almost taste safety. "They slaughtered all the ravens."

"Not all."

Kit sagged as Will severed the left-hand restraint, surprised by Will's strength as his friend hauled him to his feet. Kit looked up, trying to catch Will's eye, but Will was moving hastily to free Kit's other hand. "Not all?"

"I left a friend in the hallway ..." Will's sawing dagger parted the final shred of cloth. He glanced sideways as silver rang on steel. "Murchaud could use thy help, I imagine."

Kit looked down at his naked, blood-covered body, the short lengths of gossamer trailing from his wrists. At his fingers, swollen and raw. And bare of their restraining rings.

He smiled. "I don't suppose thou didst bring me a blade, sweet William?"

"Alas," Will said, and stooped slowly. When he stood, something long and dark speared from his hand: a length of twisted rod stock, drawn to a fine sharp point. It steamed slightly in the torchlight as Will reversed it in his hand and offered the looped butt to Kit. "Thy rapier, my love."

It weighed more than a rapier, and would be useless for a cut. But the point was sharp, and the iron was heavy. He glanced over Will's shoulder to where Murchaud fought Lucifer, falling back steadily before the Devil's laughing, casual advance. Lucifer had drawn a blade from somewhere, a shadowy thing that flickered like his crown and rang like steel on Murchaud's silver rapier. None of the others came near them; Tom and Ben stood back-to-back at the foot of the stairs, guarding Will and Kit. Ben still held the poker, Tom a brace of pistols. Between them they had three men at bay, a fourth one bleeding among the murdered ravens. Neither Baines nor Poley was anywhere in sight.

Kit snickered. The improvised weapon in his hand, the comfort of his friend at his side, were all the strength he needed. "Now all I need is a pair of breeches."

Will pointed at a dead man, falling back a step. "That one looks about thy size."

Lucifer's dark blade struck sparks from a pillar as Murchaud ducked and cursed. Kit's head turned. "And boots moreso," he growled, and sprinted barefoot and unclad over wet stones and slick mud to reach Murchaud's side.

A moment's eagerness for battle might race his heart and pulse false strength along his veins, but his long confinement had left him unfit and he knew it. Four steps down, a wave of vertigo caught him like a trap. He stumbled, expecting the hard stones on knees and forearms, the skitter of the iron bar on the tiles. There was shouting, nearby. The clash of iron on steel, blade on bar. Tom's voice, Ben's. A grunt, the sizzle of coals on wet tile as someone kicked over a brazier. Kit heard it all, scented, tasted. Pushed it away and *dove*.

And something caught him falling, a hard slap like wings cupping air, a jerk like a harness, a blaze of light around his hands and under his skin, silhouetting the crimson sigils painted on every inch of his flesh black on hot sunlight.

He sailed forward, the dark iron in his hand burning like a spear of light, a voice like a choir of falcons bellowing Lucifer's name somehow rising from his throat, and everything a fury of gold-barred black and searing light. "Behold!"

Mehiel?

:Be not afraid, my friend:

Except Lucifer straightened, that dark sword still in his hand. Kit saw through the haze of Mehiel's wrath the edge smeared red with blood, the blade itself bottomless dark: a cut in reality, whatever lay behind it gleaming with silver motes like stars. "Murchaud, *strike* him," Kit cried in his own voice, but the silver blade was falling from the Elf-knight's fingers, and he was settling slowly, breathlessly back against the fluted pillar he stood before, both hands clutched across his abdomen and red welling through fisted fingers.

:Be not afraid: Mehiel said again, and—wearing Kit's body like a suit of armor—raised his sword of light and purity to parry Lucifer's blow.

But Lucifer barely tapped the blade, teasing, and stepped back, opening his guard to all but bare his chest. :Brother: he said mockingly, :how it pleases me to fence with thee. Come, strike:

His words resonated in Kit, and Kit shook his head, knowing that the words were meant for Mehiel. Mehiel, who knotted Kit's fist on the butt of the poker and slipped steadily to the side, tapping lightly not at Lucifer's breast but at Lucifer's blade.

:Come: the Devil whispered. :This is not stage fighting. Strike at me:

And Mehiel did, but it was a wild blow and Lucifer deflected it without obvious effort. The angel in Kit said nothing, but Kit felt his confusion, his passion—

—his memory of Lucifer's fingers lovingly carding Kit's hair. *Strike him!* Kit urged, and Mehiel swung again.

Inadequate. And Lucifer did not strike back.

Mehiel lowered his sword and stepped away. :I cannot:

Mehiel!

:I cannot: the angel repeated. :I cannot strike. God forgive me. I pity Lucifer:

Then let me strike him, Kit replied, and lifted the iron poker in his hand.

Come not between the dragon and his wrath.
—WILLIAM SHAKESPEARE, *King Lear,* Act I, scene i

Kit moved like a serpent, Will thought, and not a man. No. Not a serpent.

A dragon.

Will almost saw the massive wings that hurled him forward, *did* see the halo of light that curled and flickered about his head and hands, the power and fluidity in his gestures as Murchaud fell and Kit lunged toward Lucifer. Will had just enough time to hear weapon crash against weapon once and then again before a hard arm clipped his neck and he found himself dragged backward, too startled at first to react.

"Master Shakespeare." Robert Poley's voice. Robert Poley's broad-palmed hand and rough fingers clenched upon Will's jaw, stretching the tight muscles of his neck. He dragged Will backward, off balance, far stronger than Will. His other hand caught Will's right wrist in a numbing grip, immobilizing the knife Will hadn't had time to resheathe. "Do you suppose Master Merlin would surrender to ensure your safety?"

" 'Tis possible," Will admitted through gritted teeth, determined not to give Poley the satisfaction of hearing his fear. Foolish, he thought, as his heart raced dizzyingly. He bit his lips and let his body go slack, trying to roll and fall forward to the water-slick tiles. Poley kept him upright with ease, his livery stiff against Will's back, the ornate buttons gouging Will's skin through layers of cloth. Lucifer was laughing, defending himself delightedly from the slender light-wrapped figure who pressed him only tentatively. "But I do not think Master Merlin is in command, at present."

"Pity," Poley said, his grip tightening. At the foot of the dais, Will could hear Tom and Ben engaged in a passage of arms with whatever men remained. Poley sneered, still backing away, still dragging Will. "Then I'm afraid I have no use for you—"

Will heard another set of wing beats. Smaller, lighter, a cracking sound like paper shaken in the air. He ducked, bruising his throat on Poley's thumb, and kicked back hard against the side of the other man's knee just as something black and heavy barreled shrieking into Poley's face.

Poley swore and pressed his face to Will's shoulder, protecting his eyes. A good conceit, except his right hand's grip loosened on Will's wrist, and Will was ready for it. He ducked under the buffet of the raven's wings and slammed the dagger into Poley's right thigh. Poley staggered backward, fingers clenching on Will's jaw, and Will clung to the dagger and let himself fall forward, shielding his face with his flat left hand.

Hot, raw-smelling blood spurted, soaked his sleeve to his skin, sprayed his breeches and the back of his calf. He went to his knees and then forward as Poley fell.

The stones slammed the wind from Will, and somehow Will kept his dagger and rolled. He came up, saw blood fountaining, and backed away on his hands and knees until he was out of range. Somehow, the dagger remained in his hand. The pommel scraped on stone harshly enough to make him grit his teeth.

Will had opened a gash like a gaping mouth in Robin Poley's inner thigh. Poley twitched and kicked on the stones, groaning as if he'd been kicked in the gut, red blood spurting between his clutching fingers and his other hand raised in a futile attempt to keep the croaking, stabbing raven from his eyes.

Will scrambled to his feet, spitting blood, wiping blood from his face with blood-soaked hands, and turned to go to Kit—

—just as Lucifer saluted with his star-black blade, chuckled, and vanished like a cloud blown to tatters across the moon. Kit, committing to a lunge behind his poker as if behind a rapier thrust, measured his length on the silted tiles.

Poley fell slack, bubbling. The raven raised its head, jet eyes gleaming in the darkness, blood and vitreous fluid dripping from its beak, and regarded Will with feral intensity. Will looked away with an effort, eyes seeking Ben, or Tom.

Or Kit, who pushed himself up onto his hands and knees—naked again, no longer clothed in light, the bloody patterns marked on his skin blurred with effort—and swore most vilely. He turned over his shoulder, and met Will's eyes. "I swear to God he planned that," Kit said, and flopped over like a fish thrashing on a deck.

"Does that mean you know what he's playing at?"

Kit shook his head, modesty abandoned. "Unless he was trying to awaken Mehiel," Kit said, holding up a hand that briefly flickered gold. "In which case, he's succeeded admirably. I don't honestly believe he wants the Prometheans in power, though. Otherwise he wouldn't keep interfering with their plans for him."

Will saw movement alongside the shadows near the far wall. A lean figure in dark clothing, forcing himself to his feet. "Your Prince is still bleeding, Kit—"

"Murchaud!" Blinking, startled, as if he had utterly forgotten the Elf-knight's existence, Kit turned away from the mortal men and hurried to Murchaud's side. Kit pulled Murchaud upright, checking his injuries with a fussiness that left Will tasting bile and jealousy. "Art well?" Kit answered, and even by torchlight Will didn't miss his hopeful smile.

"I'll live," the elf answered, straightening. "There is no iron in Lucifer's blade, and naught else can harm me for long." He glanced about the room, squeezing Kit's hand before he let it fall. "It will bleed, but that is all. In any case, the Faeries will be here shortly, and even if Baines' plans for Kit have been altered, there's a scene or two yet to play."

Will dragged himself up and staggered away from Poley's corpse, threw his own blood-slaked cloak over Kit's bloody and goosefleshed body. Then he sank down on the wet tiles beside Kit and Murchaud, crossed his legs, leaned his elbows on his knees, and pressed his forehead into his hands. "This is all too complicated for me."

Kit dropped down beside Will and lay back on the floor as if he reclined in a featherbed, drawing the cloak around him. Tom and Ben staggered over to them. "A timely rescue, gentlemen. Now find me a pair of trousers, and we'll see if we can manage a timelier one."

Ben limped heavily, blood staining the outside of his

breeches. "Can't find Baines," he said, bending down to brace his hands on his knees, breathing like a runner.

"Bloody buggered Christ," Kit answered, sitting up so Will could see the long curve of his back. "I imagine he'll find us before the evening's out. It's all for naught. The war's over for England and James anyway: the portents have spoken, and the Tower's bastions are breached with the deaths of the ravens—"

The heavy beat of wings interrupted Kit. He looked up as the crippled raven rowed heavily through the air and landed on Will's automatically upraised fist.

Kit blinked. "A raven. Unwounded and alive."

Will smiled, and Tom Walsingham coughed into his hand. "Just one. But one's enough, isn't it? All stories are true stories, or so Will tells me."

"All stories—" Will and Kit shared a glance, and it was Will who looked up first. "Kit, should we be asking ourselves what Lucifer wants?"

Kit shook his head. "I wonder if we should be asking ourselves what 'tis he wants to *become*. He's Prometheus, thou knowest. And the serpent Amaranth too."

" 'Twas Amaranth told me where to find thee, Kit," Will said. He held out his hand to help the other poet to his feet. "I don't understand—"

"Surely you don't think the Father of Lies is limited to one shape only," Kit said dryly, once his feet were under him. "You know how you said of Salisbury, he plays his game as if there is no other player, only pieces that sometimes move themselves?" His voice was quiet, his gaze hooded, as if he directed his commentary not to Will and Tom and Ben, but someone closer still.

"Aye. . . ." Will glanced at Ben for assistance. Ben looked up from binding his leg.

"Sir Christopher," Ben said softly, "are you suggesting that Lucifer is playing both sides of the board?"

"I'm saying that his opponent is refusing to move, and he's attempting to provoke—something. A commitment. Possibly just a response. We've walked into a lovers' quarrel, gentlemen."

"Walked, or been dragged?" Will shook his head.

Act V, scene xviii

We are no traitors, therefore threaten not.

—CHRISTOPHER MARLOWE, *Edward II,*
Act I, scene iv

It might lack of warmth, comfort, and sartorial splendor, but Kit was happy simply to be clothed. He'd resumed the white breeches—grimy enough now that they would be slightly better suited to skulking in the darkness—and pulled his shirt back on over the bloody sigils that patterned his flesh. He scrubbed the cloth against his skin to smear the marks, and looked up to see Will watching with an inscrutable expression twisting his mouth.

"What happens next?" Will asked, when Kit would not look down. Will's fingers idly stroked the rainbow-dark plumage of the raven that perched on his wrist, and Kit's fingers itched with the memory of feathers. If he closed his eyes, he was sure he would feel those enormous wings again, lifting him, bearing him up—

He was glad Mehiel hadn't struck down Lucifer. Glad, and furious. *Conflict is the essence of drama.* He shrugged and turned to seek Murchaud, but the elf-Prince was in conversation with Tom. "I'll find a pair of boots," Kit answered, and went to pull Poley's off his dead feet.

They were too soaked with blood to wear, which was a pity, because they would have fit, unlike the too-large ones Kit liberated from the corpse of the man Ben had killed, which rubbed his feet to blisters as the five of them wound back through the tunnels to the surface, a straggling line lit by two lanterns.

Ben took the lead on the argument that Baines was still ahead of them somewhere, and neither Kit nor Will in any condition to fight. Kit, leaning on a captured poker as he walked, raised an eyebrow at that, but the big man shrugged. "It looked from my vantage as if Lucifer made a point in failing to injure you, Master Marlin."

"Aye," Kit said. "I'm untouchable. Pity your charge is not, Will." He gestured to the raven, who seemed quite content to nestle against the curve of Will's neck. "I think I recognize that bird."

"He's prone to keeping company with the prisoners in the Salt Tower," Will said, craning his head with amusement to see the witchlights that flitted from Kit's hands, and Murchaud's. "We made an acquaintance while I was there."

"That is no natural raven," Murchaud said from the rear of the group.

"Aye," Will answered. "I had come to suspect as much. Some form of Faerie creature?"

"Some such thing, Master Shakespeare."

Will staggered in exhaustion. Tom put a hand on his shoulder at the same instant that Kit caught his arm. The raven beat its wings heavily, but seemed loath to abandon its perch; Will yelped as its talons pinched. "And the sole thing betwixt England and destruction, if the legends of ravens and the Tower are true. We cannot even bring him away for the danger: he must stay in the Tower precincts."

"That bird on your shoulder is the reason behind the legends," Murchaud said.

Kit glanced over his shoulder at the elf-Prince. Murchaud moved wearily, as if his bones ached, frowning as Kit met his gaze. "Too much iron?" Kit asked.

Murchaud nodded. "London is full of it."

"The reason behind the legends?" Will's voice, considering. He leaned heavily on Tom's arm now, to Kit's concealed annoyance. "That seems to me a statement that begs an explanation, Your Highness."

Kit coughed, every breath still carrying the metallic reek of the ravens' blood crackling and itching on his skin. He stopped with his hand across his mouth, his feet suddenly too heavy to lift, and turned to Murchaud in speechless amazement. His mouth worked once or twice. "But he lies in Faerie," Kit said. "Thou didst show me his bier."

"Beg pardon," said Ben, at the front with the lantern. "But all this talking will make it certain that if Baines *is* ahead of us, he'll hear us coming."

"Wait, Ben," Tom answered. "I have a feeling we'd do well to hear this out. Kit, of whom dost speak?"

Kit didn't look, didn't lower his eyes from Murchaud's. The Elf-knight shrugged. "Aye. He sleeps in Faerie as well, but—"

"All stories are true," Kit finished, and craned his neck for a better look at the raven. The bird cocked its head at him, a sideways twist like a girl tossing her hair, and Kit laughed low in his throat. "I'll be buggered," he said, and angled his gaze to meet Will's eyes.

Will shook his head. "Thou'rt insane."

"Arthur Pendragon," Kit said, and so saying made his nagging suspicion crystallize with a sound like cracking ice. He turned to face Murchaud, and bit his lip on the smile he wanted to taste. "Turned into a raven when he died. Murchaud—"

"Aye?" The Prince did smile. "It changes nothing. We protect the bird, and we climb."

"Oh," Will said, craning his neck to examine the profile of the black bird on his shoulder. "And when we get to the surface?"

"We deal with my mother and my wife," Murchaud answered. "We save the life of a mortal King. We do not let England or Faerie fall."

"That's something I'm not sure I understand," Will said, still idly caressing the raven's head. "What is it that they hope to accomplish here tonight, Prince Murchaud? Why are the Fae in London at all?"

Murchaud shrugged; Kit felt the heavy lift and drop of the Prince's shoulders, the swing of his cloak, and spared a moment wishing for his own patchwork cloak. *Baines probably burned it.* The imagined loss stung. "It's an auspicious night for the overthrow of regimes. Baines' plans are not the only ones coming to fruition on November fifth."

"No," Kit said. "Lucifer's as well—" He was struck by a sudden, vivid memory of the Mebd's golden hair spread between his fingers, the cool, smooth surface of a tortoise-shell comb, and he stopped and lowered his voice so that only the Elf-knight would hear. "Morgan's. What's Morgan after, Murchaud? I remember when first I came to Faerie, it was her ear thou didst whisper into, and not the Mebd's."

Murchaud rested a hand on his elbow, almost lifting him up the ragged stairs. Only pride kept Kit from leaning hard on Murchaud's arm. "Thinkst thou so little of me, Sir Poet, that I must serve the agenda of my mother or my Queen, and have no passions of mine own?" The hand squeezed, pulling the sting from the words.

Kit shot Murchaud a sideways glance, and realized it

was true. Exactly and precisely: he had indeed assumed that Murchaud served Morgan's whims, and to a lesser extent those of the Mebd. "Very well," he said. "What is it that thou dost seek?"

"Freedom," Murchaud answered succinctly. "We all have our own purposes in seducing thee, Sir Poet. Thee, and that which thou dost harbor."

"Seducing me." He laughed. "In Morgan's case, breaking me into a shape of which she approved. She told me she thought I was the one who could reconcile Faerie and Hell, England's crown and the Prometheans."

"Aye. And the Mebd thinks that thou—and Mehiel— are the ones who can burst Faerie's bond with Hell, can destroy the Prometheans so that we no longer need Lucifer's protection from the avenging spirit the Prometheans would set as the Divine."

"Lucifer *is* Prometheus," Kit said. "I do not understand why he takes payment to protect us from himself."

Murchaud laughed softly. "An old acquaintance of Robert Poley's, and thou dost not understand how extortion works? Besides"—a modest pause—"Lucifer no doubt has plans of his own. Which he has not seen fit to share."

"He maneuvers all the pieces," Kit answered, climbing. Will slipped on the stairs. Kit reached up to steady him, and Murchaud steadied Kit. Above them, Ben kept climbing, inexorable as a Jewish *golem,* and at the rear, Tom followed. No one spoke, and Kit realized they were all listening as intently to his quiet conversation with Murchaud as if they leaned close over a candlelit table in some tavern, whispering conspiracies. "I believe I know what he wants, Murchaud."

Murchaud turned his head. "Aye?"

"The love of God," Kit said plainly, and winced at his own forgetfulness when Murchaud flinched and stumbled.

"Thy pardon, Kit—"

"Nay," Kit said. "Thy pardon, I cry. But that does not answer the question that holds me most."

"Aye?"

"What is it that *thou* seekest, Elf-knight? Thou hast not made that plain to me, but thou must have some use for me, or thou wouldst not have been so kind, so long."

"I—" The Elf-knight hesitated. "I am Fae."

It was not an excuse, but simply a statement, and Kit nodded agreement. " 'Tis so. So tell me now."

A low, solemn laugh. "Thou didst never ask before."

"I make no argument. And I am asking now."

"Faerie," Murchaud said. "Sovereign." He looked pointedly at the raven huddled on Will's shoulder. "I would like to see the ghosts and legends settled. I'd like, perhaps, to know for a day what story I might walk through—"

"You want what Baines wants," Kit said coolly. "You want to choose the nature of the Divine."

" 'Tis futile," Murchaud answered. "Say rather I'd prefer that some stories were just stories. That a legend could change without changing the world. Call it the inverse of the Prometheans' goal—if they wish to shape the stories, I wish to not be shaped by them."

Kit considered that in silence for a moment or two, and found himself in sympathy. *Mehiel?*

:Ask me not about morality: the angel said unhappily, :when I, an Angel of the Lord, find myself in love with Lucifer Morningstar—:

Kit blinked at the words. *In love.*

:Hast another name for it?:

Slowly, thoughtfully, Kit shook his head. *If I found a way to free thee, Mehiel—*

:Thou must not: the angel said. :Thou must not give thy life up needlessly. We will endure:

—*regardless. If thou wert freed, what wouldst thou do?*

A hesitation as the angel pondered his question. Fleetingly, Kit wondered if an angel could lie.

:Go home: Mehiel answered, after a little while.

Return to God's embrace. Go back to Heaven, and out of Hell. Despite thy love for the Morningstar.

:Wouldst not thou? Wouldst choose love over Heaven?:

Kit chuckled softly. *Mehiel.* He laid a hand on Murchaud's arm, and Murchaud gave him the edge of a worried smile in the inadequate, flickering light. *I have.*

Another pause for thought. :Wouldst choose love over duty, then? Over remaining true to thyself?:

And Kit thought of Edward de Vere, and shook his head. *Thou art right. But what wilt thou take home to the Lord thy God that thou hadst not when thou wert taken? Thou, Mehiel. Thou who art a piece of God?*

:Thee: the angel answered without hesitation. :Man, mortal and fragile. I know thee now, and thou art more worthy of brotherhood than I had realized. And I will take in that brotherhood all thou art, and thy true-love's grief and pity over his son, over thy pain. I will take the Fae in all their sorrow and bitterness and their solemn pact with Hell:

And the love thou hast for another—

Silence. And then the angel, wondering, the flex of black-barred yellow wings. :Love. For the Morningstar. Yes, I will bear that home as well:

Aye. Climbing still.

:Sympathy:

"Simple," Kit said dryly. "Or sympathetic magic, rather."

"I beg thy pardon, Kit?"

"Nothing, Will. I don't think we need to worry about the Morningstar further, fellows. Lucifer has what he came for." *All my life is stairs, Mehiel.*

:Better stairs than falling: the angel answered, but he did not sound convinced.

There were no torches lit in the Tower's great courtyard when the ragged, soaking little party emerged from the bowels of the earth. No mortal lights illuminated the scene: not even a few candles flickering dimly in the windows of the White Tower. There was only the ethereal moonlit glow surrounding the court of the Daoine Sidhe, who waited on their Fae steeds like so many ghostly riders on a procession out of Hell.

The Mebd sat her black horse sidesaddle in the center of the procession, and on her right side, on a milky gray the shaded color of alabaster, Kit was surprised to meet the eyes of Morgan le Fey. Cairbre the bard rode beside them, and a half dozen other Fae Kit knew more or less well—

—and, on a shaggy, floppy-eared pony no taller than Kit's breastbone, the gawky figure of Robin Goodfellow, elbows akimbo and knees disarrayed.

Kit felt Murchaud drawing himself up tall, and laid a hand on the Prince's elbow. "Puck?" A stage whisper, and Murchaud looked at him and shrugged.

"She knows thou dost care for him," Murchaud said. "Perhaps his freedom is a gift to thee, to reassure thee of her good will. They're waiting for us, Kit—"

"No," Will said, even more softly, raising one knotted, trembling hand to point to a figure clad in raven-black, a gold chain glinting at his shoulders as he entered the spill of Faerie light. "They're waiting for the Earl of Salisbury."

Act V, scene xix

March all one way, and be no more oppos'd
Against acquaintance, kindred, and allies:
The edge of war, like an ill-sheathed knife,
No more shall cut his master.

—WILLIAM SHAKESPEARE, *Henry IV Part I,*
Act I, scene i

"Jesus wept," Kit said, and started forward. Will held on to his sleeve and followed; Ben, Tom, and Murchaud paced them a little behind. *Given pride of place by a Prince and a Knight,* Will thought, amused despite the worry seething in the pit of his belly. *Or perhaps they're simply willing to let us be the ones to beard the lions. And the lionesses.*

Salisbury turned as they came up on him, a double-dozen guards and yeomen ranged at his back. He considered and dismissed first Kit and then the rest of the party—their bruises and scrapes, their mud-spattered rags. "Gentlemen," he said, in a tone that didn't mean *gentle.* His black robes rustled as he turned, and Will fought the ridiculous desire to step behind Kit like a child twisting himself in his mother's skirts.

Kit, whose battered dignity as he limped forward to face Salisbury lifted Will's heart into his throat and brought tears to his eyes. Will blinked against sharpness, glanced over Salisbury's shoulder, and caught the considering gaze of the Queen of Faerie on her horse that might have been carved from jet. The Mebd blinked once, long violet eyes closing like a cat's, and Will dropped his gaze to the silent consideration between Kit and Salisbury.

Kit's mouth was half opened to speak.

Even now, Will realized, he could sense Kit's movements with a lover's awareness. He wasn't sure if that comforted or troubled him, but he stepped closer because he could, and raised one hand to touch the hackled raven crouched on his shoulder. A cold breeze coiled around his ankles with a physical weight, heavy with moisture from the wet paving stones. "My lord Earl," he said, in his most carefully measured tone. "Your timing is impeccable."

"Master Shakespeare?" Salisbury's eyebrow rose at Will's impertinence.

Oh, I'm making no friends tonight, Will thought, and didn't care.

"What is that on your shoulder?"

"The salvation of the realm," Will answered. He squeezed Kit's elbow and felt Kit lean against him—not so much relaxing as seeking comfort and perhaps warmth, despite the way he almost flinched away from Will's steadying touch. The air above ground was colder than in the tunnels, and Kit shivered violently. Will remembered the blood on his foot.

"Please," Kit said wearily through the chatter of his teeth. "Let us pass, my lord."

Salisbury glanced from Kit to Will and back again,

sparing his final glance for Murchaud. Tom and Ben were silent, tall pillars on either side of the poets and the Prince.

"If we're all nominally on the side that does not look forward to a Promethean conquest of England and the Church," Will said, lifting his chin, "I must agree with Sir Christopher. You misjudged Baines and Poley, my lord, and it is only through the bravery of these men behind me that the King and the crown were saved tonight."

"Misjudged?"

Will smiled. He imagined it wasn't a pleasant one, and thought the glance Kit angled him was proud and amused. "This raven on my shoulder is the last raven at the Tower, my lord. All the rest are dead."

He wished he'd seen Salisbury take that short, ragged step back under circumstances where he could appreciate the victory. "Where are Baines and Poley?"

Will gathered his thoughts, but Kit beat him to the answer. "Poley is dead," he said. Will admired the lack of apparent relish in his voice, and then blinked, startled, when he saw the golden earring wink in the shadows under Kit's tangled hair. *I'll be damned*— "Baines has perhaps gone to join Catesby and Fawkes and their friends. I can't say—"

"Fawkes is in custody," Salisbury said, smoothing the front of his robes. The silence that followed was all but thick enough for Will to lean into. The harness of the fey horses creaked with their breathing; the eyes of the Faerie riders rested on himself, on Kit, on Murchaud. "Catesby and his bravos will follow before dusk, I warrant. We know his movements well, and their plot is ended, the gunpowder seized, the kingdom quite safe."

"Quite safe from explosions," Tom Walsingham supplied, with a sideways glance at Will. Will nodded, sneaking his hand into his pocket to rub the iron nail in its silken pouch. "Safe from sorcery?"

"Sorcery—"

"Scoffs a man with the Queen of Faerie at his back and a magician close enough to spit in his eye?" Kit said softly. He glanced at Will.

Will picked up the cue as smoothly as Burbage might have, and continued. "The astrologer Dee would tell you the same. 'Tis a night for the fall of kingdoms, Robert."

Will could see Salisbury's shock at his use of his Christian name, the ripple that spread through the guardsmen at his back. He bit his lips to keep from laughing at the casual way Kit pushed forward, all but disregarding Salisbury, moving toward the Fae. Will kept to Kit's elbow, grateful when Murchaud came along on the other side, and Tom and Ben stayed with them as if drilled.

Kit limped heavily now, and Will kept a hand under his elbow to support him, limping himself. Murchaud shot them a sideways glance, and seemed as if he might move closer. And then bit his lip, nodded, and looked away. Will was surprised to find himself grateful for the Elf-knight's looming presence.

It was the Puck who came to greet them, his lop ears lolling like his pony's, with the clop of unshod hooves on stone. Will took a breath in relief when Kit didn't shrug off his steadying hand, instead seeming to lean harder. "I see you are forgiven, Master Goodfellow," he said.

"Aye," Puck answered, his ears laid flat down the nape of his neck. "Art thou?"

Will squeezed Kit's arm, sensing some unspoken context. He glanced up at Kit, who frowned. "Thou art the one who can answer that, Master Goodfellow."

The Puck glanced from Kit to Will to Salisbury, sideways at Murchaud, and then over his shoulder at the silent, solemn Queens. "Yes," he said softly. "I suppose I am. Your steed is ready, Sir Poet."

"As long as it's not white," Kit answered, and followed where Puck led, toward the rear of the Fae guard. Salisbury stamped off in the opposite direction and stood, conferring with one of the yeomen.

Will hung back a little, with a glance to Murchaud. "Where are we going?"

"Damned if I know," the Elf-knight answered. "I suspect it will involve hunting Richard Baines to ground, but nevertheless we should ask the Mebd." With a single glance to see that Tom and Ben were following, he went to pay court on his Queen, taking Will's elbow as Will had been holding Kit's. Salisbury, still off to one side, didn't manage to intercept them and take precedence; Ben and Tom moved to block his attempt. *There'll be Hell to pay over that.*

The raven on Will's shoulder twisted its head to look back at the soldiers, ruffling its damaged wing as if the cold air pained it. "There'll be Hell to pay no matter what," Murchaud commented quietly, and smiled when Will raised an eyebrow at him. "You were thinking out loud, Master Poet."

"Ah—" Will raised his eyes to the impassive, alabaster masks of two women who had never looked so much like sisters as they did at this moment, for all the Mebd rode sidesaddle, swathed in layers of color-shifting silk, and Morgan wore those damned riding breeches that had once so discomfited Will.

"Master Shakespeare," Morgan said musically, patting a stray strand of hair back into her pearl-braided chignon. "It appears thou hast a thing which doth belong to me." She raised a hand imperiously, fingers balled loosely into a fist, and her eyes were not on Will's but on the raven's black ones.

Will told himself that the raven could not *smirk*. "He doesn't leave the Tower," Will said. "His life is England's, now." The poet rubbed his beard. Ice crystals were forming between the spiral hairs; they dusted his breast when he lowered his hand.

Morgan left hers upraised, her head tilted as if she, herself, were some strange new sort of raptor. The Mebd, still silent, turned only her head to regard her sister, her pale lips twitching toward a smile. The long, woven braids of her hair slid like a fisherman's weighted net around her shoulders.

Morgan did not return her sister's glance. "What wouldst thou see done with him?"

"I'd see him ensconced with Sir Walter, I think. The brave captain can see to his safety, can any man—and is conveniently unable to leave the Tower."

"I shall reclaim the bird sooner or later, sweet William."

"Aye," Will said. "But not until ravens flock these grounds again. Do we have an agreement, my lady?"

She bit her lip, ignoring the Mebd's arch amusement. "He's hidden from me for a thousand years," Morgan le Fey said at last, acquiescing. Her hand slid gracefully down to rest on her thigh, cupped inward, palm open. "A few more days mean nothing."

Will looked at the raven. The raven looked at Will. Their silent regard was interrupted by the measured clop of hooves.

Kit's horse wasn't white at all, Will saw with relief, but a sorrel gelding so red he gleamed like wet blood even by the cold fey light that surrounded them. His saddle and bridle were leather, even redder, a saber sheathed on the harness by Kit's left hand. A white blaze graced the animal's nose, dripping so low he seemed to drink it, and Kit's free hand rose again and again to stroke the coarse blond mane back from the crest.

The fond gentleness of Kit's touch contrasted harshly with the expression he turned on Morgan. Murchaud took a half step forward. Will shot a hand sideways and gripped his sleeve, staggering with the force it took to stop the Prince's movement.

"Will—" Tom said behind him, and Will shook his head just enough to make his hair brush against his collar.

" 'Tis his to play out, Tom," Will said under his breath. Ben grunted on Murchaud's far side, but stayed steady as if planted. "Stand fast, and be ready for whatever might befall."

"My kingdom for a good iron blade," Tom answered. Will grinned at the sideways flattery despite the tension in the air.

"Don't say that where the Fae can hear you," Will answered. "They've been known to take men up on bargains like that." He didn't take his eyes off Kit and Morgan, listening to the long silence stretch between them, wondering when it would break. He smiled to himself, and thought, *and now is the time to brace Salisbury, while he's still considering blackmail and England.*

Silently, controlling his limp as best he could, Will disengaged himself from Murchaud and went toward the thunder-browed Secretary of State.

Fie on that love that hatcheth death and hate!
—CHRISTOPHER MARLOWE, *Edward II,* Act IV, scene v

Morgan met Kit's gaze calmly, her eyes dark and mysterious as emeralds in the weird, cold light. Over her shoulder, the Queen of Faerie looked on. Beyond her, not even turning his head to the scene, Cairbre the Bard sat his saddle like a statue, a ruby gleaming in the tip of his pointed ear where it parted the black strands of his hair.

The sorrel's hooves were steady on the rimed cobblestones; nearby, Will and Tom and Murchaud and that damned self-satisfied Ben Jonson stood side by each, bloody and ragged and ready for more. Kit's breast filled up with a warrior's pity and indignation, that men so tired should be made to fight endlessly on—

Wrath held him silent long enough for the corner of Morgan's mouth to twitch with discomfort. Kit cleared his throat. "You lied to me."

"Sir Christofer?"

Such patent innocence, her hand raised to her throat. Kit turned his head and spat, the sorrel dancing a sidled step. A fragment of motion caught his eye: the flip of Puck's ear, where Puck sat his pony. "Such pretty nonsense you all told me—and chief among the liars, you, Morgan. Poets and rades and battles of song and powers and portents—"

"Dost see a rade before thee?" Morgan's gesture swept the gathered Fae, touched Murchaud and his mortal companions, swept up and dismissed Salisbury and his men.

Kit raised an eyebrow when he spotted Will, moving between the groups. The laugh he could not contain sliced like a fish bone at his throat. "Thou hadst no care for me, my Queen—"

"Not so—"

"—I was only the vessel. The container. The prison for the being thou didst truly wish to touch, to win—"

"—not so," she said again, even softer. The tone in her voice was too much.

He flinched, and stopped, the gelding shaking his mane as Kit's grip tightened on the bloodred reins. His nervousness affected the horse; he could see white traces of foam against the crimson neck, where the reins rubbed the animal's cold sweat into lather.

"We're here for thee," Morgan said, lifting her head on her long white neck. "We would not have permitted thee to be sacrificed—"

"No," Kit continued, finding his voice again. He shivered no longer, Mehiel's power warming his shoulders like a feathered cloak. "You did not come to fight a war, but to twist another sorcerer's magic to your uses. Baines would not have completed his ritual, had thou thy choice of events. But thou wouldst have waited until he had the opportunity to fill me up with his power and his plans, as if I were no more than a talisman, a crystal to be cut into a lens—"

"We could have used the power," Cairbre said quietly.

"I imagine you could," Kit answered.

"It does not mean that we have no fondness for you—"

"No, teacher." Kit's outrage and fury were failing him. The warm horse breathed between his legs, the ears swiveled one forward, one back, switching with every nervous ripple of the gelding's tail. "No, I know the Fae and their fondnesses. Fondness would not stop you from spilling my blood." He gave his attention back to Morgan. "What did they offer thee for thine assistance, my Queen?"

He didn't need her answer. He saw her eyes flick to the raven, and to Will. Murchaud stepped forward, away from Ben and Tom. "Mother," he said. "You should have trusted me."

A ripple of power, the sound of wings inside his mind. Kit forced his hand open, forced himself to stroke the sorrel's rough mane rather than knotting his fingers in it as he would have liked to as Murchaud walked calmly to his mother's stirrup and drew her down by her sleeve to whisper in her ear. The gelding turned his head slightly, enough to roll his eye at Kit. *Could you move this along, please? 'Tis tiresome, Sir Poet, standing here in the cold on rough cobbles.*

Kit bit his cheek on tired laughter, all his irritation

draining away. *Perhaps I've just been used too much to care any more,* he thought. *And also, I'm keeping this horse.*

"Trusted thee?" Kit asked the Prince, when Morgan did not comment. He wondered at the speaking look Murchaud gave him, and hesitated. Twisted the reins around his fingers until they cut his skin. Nausea twisted likewise in his belly; he caught himself looking after Will, bent in whispered argument with Salisbury, and away from Morgan and Murchaud.

'Tis time to pick a side. He touched the trusted sorrel's mane again. "I wish I knew your name."

"Gin," Puck said, having come up silently on his pony.

"Gin?" The sorrel's ears flicked back. "For Ginger?"

" 'Cause he's a rum one," Puck answered. His laugh smelled of juniper and loam, and Kit's confused expression showed; it made the little elf laugh the harder. "What will you do, Sir Poet?"

You, not thou. It stung, and Kit could not deny he deserved it. "What do you think the Prometheans' ritual, their capture of Mehiel, will mean over time, Master Goodfellow?"

Puck shifted on his shaggy pony's saddle. The barrel-bodied animal shook itself, its wiry upright mane rippling with the motion. "If the angels are clever, it means an end to miracles."

"And an end to martyrs?"

The little Fae's wide mouth twitched. "There will always be martyrs. You did not answer me."

"No," Kit said. "I did not. First we deal with Baines."

"And then?"

"This will never end," Kit answered, "as long as I live, and Mehiel lives in me."

"Aye. Shall I ask you a third time, Sir Poet?"

Kit lifted his reins. Murchaud stepped back from

Morgan's saddle and moved away. He caught Kit's eye under the arch of her horse's neck and mouthed something—two words. *Trust me.*

Ah, my Prince. If only. Kit's gaze slid off Murchaud's, and found the back of Will's head as Will laid his hand quite boldly on Salisbury's sleeve, demanding the Secretary of State's attention. Kit sighed. "Will is for England," he said with a tired shrug. "And I am for Will."

> *The devil knew not what he did when he made
> man politic; he crossed himself by 't: and I cannot
> think but in the end the villainies of man will set
> him clear. How fairly this lord strives to appear
> foul! takes virtuous copies to be wicked, like those
> that under hot ardent zeal would set whole realms
> on fire.*
>
> —WILLIAM SHAKESPEARE, *Timon of Athens,*
> Act III, scene iii

Salisbury looked up, still scowling, as Will closed the distance between them until he was close enough to the Earl that Salisbury visibly resisted stepping back. Will gathered himself, drawing on a player's dignity as he framed himself against the Tower wall and the Faerie lights behind. He waited a moment, until he was certain of Salisbury's full attention, and deepened his voice when he spoke. "I think I know what you want, Mr. Secretary. And I think I can give it to you."

Cecil paused, his head angling sideways on his short, wry neck. "What I want, Master Shakespeare?"

An attempt at coolness, and Will saw through it. For all his political savoir-faire, Salisbury was no player. "You wish English security," Will offered, smiling and holding tight to the sleeve of Salisbury's warm woolen robe when the Secretary might have pulled away. Will's hand trembled only a little. He leaned forward to make the nodding of his chin seem chosen rather than uncontrolled. His breath steamed in the air between them; he was grateful for the drama of the effect. "You wish the power of the Romish and Puritan factions lessened, the Prometheans brought to heel"—a gentle cough—"and your own, shall we call it, future assured."

"Very astute, Master Shakespeare," Salisbury said, lowering his tone. "You do not mention the King."

"No. My lord, I do not. But England—I mention her. Not the King. Not the Church. But the land, and the men."

"All this love for a spit of rocky land cast adrift from the Continent?" It was mockery, but not dismissal. Mockery that hid something else, something slick and sapient, and Will went after it carefully as tickling fish.

"All this love for Englishmen," Will answered.

"You expect me to believe that?" Low, intense, the man's teeth flashing.

Will smiled and stepped back, only half a pace. Eight inches, no more, and he knew Salisbury heard his foot scuff lightly over the cobbles. "And nothing for myself?" Will brushed a hand across the expensive, stained brocade of his doublet, the King's livery badge on his breast. "Haven't I more than any common man should dream? Both from James and from Bess?"

"Yes," Salisbury answered.

Will glanced over his shoulder, and saw Kit's eyes drop a second too late to hide the intensity of his regard. Relief and pity warred in him, and a cold white flame he knew for bitter, possessive love. *Frustrated love.*

Is love nonetheless. The raven stirred on his shoulder. Salisbury's eyes were drawn.

"We can be allies," he offered, striving to keep his tone generous. "Or we can be enemies. You are who you are, my lord, but Earls before you have found me a very bad enemy to have."

It was Salisbury's turn to glance over Will's shoulder, and Will wondered what he saw. "Are you going to threaten me again, Master Poet?"

"Not unless you force me, Mr. Secretary." Will looked down at his hands, let them fall, folded them in front of his belt. "Speak with our King. Talk to him about our Bible—"

Salisbury scoffed. "What purpose will that serve?"

Will raised his eyes again, held Salisbury's with his own practiced, disquieting gaze. "The power of the Romish and Puritan factions lessened, the Prometheans brought to heel"—he recited, the same tones as before—"and your own, shall we call it, future assured." A tilt of his head. "Believe in me."

Salisbury blinked. "We'll discuss it when the conspirators are captured—"

"If we live so long."

"Little danger of any other outcome," Salisbury replied. He paused, considering. "The King would wish to involve Bishop Andrewes."

Who had been Will's own parish cleric, after a fashion: the Bishop of Southwark, at Saint Saviour's. Will sighed, but nodded.

He'd worked by committee before.

Salisbury raised his head a moment before the clop of hooves alerted Will that they had company.

The Mebd's soft voice followed, furred like catkins, complex as honey. "Master Shakespeare," she murmured as Will turned and dropped her a deep and heartfelt bow, and another for the red-haired Queen beside her. A poet flanked them on either side—one dark, one fair and blood-smeared—and a Fool rode a pony between. "My Lord of Salisbury. Dawn is coming."

"Yes, Your Highness," Salisbury answered. Will stepped to the side. "I am at your command." With a sideways glance to Will—*this is not settled*.

"Ride," she said. "See to your Romish conspirators. You may find them more challenging to catch than anticipated."

"And your royal selves?"

She smiled, sunlight through the first pale leaves of spring. "We shall see to Richard Baines."

Act V, scene xx

Stand up, ye base, unworthy soldiers!
Know ye not yet the argument of arms?

—CHRISTOPHER MARLOWE, *Tamburlaine
the Great,* Part II, Act IV, scene i

Sir Walter welcomed the raven's company enough
that Kit rather suspected he would have been
happy to stage a small escape and come with them.
Unfortunately, Salisbury had been reluctant to let the
poets go up to see him alone, and so they had climbed
the stair—each limping, leaning on one another despite
the way Will's touch still made Kit's skin crawl—in the
company of four of Salisbury's guard, Kit's lacerated
and blistered foot as painful as if he had roasted it carefully over one of the braziers below. They climbed down
again poorer by one mythic raven, who seemed remark-
ably sanguine about being left behind with Sir Walter.

When they returned, they found Salisbury no longer
in evidence and his men more or less dispersed. Murchaud, Ben, and Tom had all been given Faerie mounts;
Kit wondered if they were real fey animals, or if they

would disappear into dried leaves and twists of straw with the dawn's advent. He checked the horizon, catching Will's bemused expression from the corner of his eye, and the rosy glow over the Tower wall told him if that were the case, they had best ride fast.

Puck came forward, leading Gin and a soft-eyed gray mare, but Will looked at the horse askance. "I'd rather ride pillion behind Tom or Ben," he said, hesitantly stroking her nose.

"Ride pillion behind me," Kit offered. Will glanced sideways and grinned, surprised. Kit hid his flinch as Will's gloved fingers tightened on his own. "I don't suppose you know where in Hell we're going?"

"Not Hell," Puck said. "Well, perhaps Hell, but I think it unlikely." He handed Kit the sorrel's reins, and Kit tugged his hand from Will's and leaned on the saddle instead.

"Where then?"

"We go a-hunting Richard Baines," the Mebd said, riding toward them, her horse's hooves making not a sound. Kit swore he saw her ears prick and swivel. "Welcome, poets. Welcome, bards. Master Shakespeare, I have a task for thee—"

Kit tightened his grip on the warm, smooth leather, fumbling for the stirrup as the gelding snorted impatiently but stood steady as a menhir. *Up, clumsy mortal! Up!*

"How does Your Majesty intend to find him?" Kit asked, pitching his voice in the courtly range. "He's warded against the power in the Darkling Glass."

He stilled his hand with an effort when he found his thumbnail picking flaked blood from his opposite wrist. Instead, he patted the comforting weight of the saber still slung from Gin's saddle. Will crossed to lay a hand on his boot; Kit reached down to help swing him into the saddle, and paused when the Mebd cleared her throat.

The Mebd glanced over at her sister Morgan, and

the two women shared an enigmatic smile. "Hounds," the Queen said, and reached out with one pale lily of a hand to touch Murchaud on the thigh. He startled, his clubbed hair bobbing as his head snapped up, his horse fussing at the sudden uncontrolled jerk on her reins. The Mebd let her hand slide down his thigh, turned, transferred the reins as smoothly as a trick rider and leaned perilously far from her sidesaddle to trail the other hand down Morgan's white-sleeved arm. "Hounds," she repeated, and—in a transformation that was over in an eyeblink—a red dog and a black-brindle crouched in the saddles where Morgan and her son had been.

Kit reached blindly for Murchaud, stunned, his hand trembling. The black dog showed teeth and laid his ears flat on his head, and Kit let his fingers flex softly and his hand fall to his side. He heard Will's startled gasp, the long slow rattle of his breath permitted to slide back out. "Your Highness." Kit raised his eyes to the Mebd's. "Change them back."

Her long nails scrabbling for purchase on the sloped leather of the saddle, the red hound hopped to the ground and wove between the horse's legs, sniffing intently. And the Mebd smiled. "We shall," the Mebd answered. "After we have your nemesis in hand, Sir Christofer. Surely thou hast ridden to the hunt before?"

"Nay," he said. "Surely you have other hounds, my lady. . . ." The black dog joined the red, sniffing, circling, wiry coat undulating in the cold gray predawn. Kit blinked, realizing how bright it had grown. He reached down right-handed to grab Will's fingers, still resting on his ill-fitting boot.

"No hounds such as these," she said. "Master Shakespeare, come forward."

Kit clutched Will's cold gloved fingers, but Will tugged them loose and moved three steps away. Gin shied and sidestepped away from the pressure of Kit's knee when he would have gone after, and he could only watch skinny, shiny-headed Will limp up to clasp the stirrup of the Queen. "Will—"

"Your Highness," Will said, quite ignoring Kit. The Mebd nodded to him silently and lifted her chin to stare Kit down.

He lasted perhaps a minute and a half. "Why these hounds?"

"They are hounds that have a certain link to thee which will help them find the sorcerer who used thee so badly, Sir Kit," she said, and smiled. Kit heard Tom's sudden indrawn breath, the creak of leather as he swung from the saddle of his own Faerie mount. Kit turned to fix him with a withering stare, but it was as if Kit had grown as invisible as Mehiel. The red hound craned her neck up to nose Kit's stirrup once.

"Your Highness," Tom said, raking both hands through his graying auburn hair. "If I understand you correctly, I would serve in this capacity as well." He looked at Will, as if for permission. Will tilted his head, smiling, and shrugged, and finally both men turned to look at Kit. Who looked down promptly, away from Ben Jonson's startled cough.

Kit turned to fix Ben with a glare, but the wry bemusement on the young poet's face turned a searing glance into a sideways shrug. One that made Ben cough again, and then burst out laughing, both hands over his face.

The Mebd laid her hands on Will's head, and Tom's, and flinched. "You have iron on ye," she said, leaning back in the saddle. The spare Faerie horses withdrew as she spoke, milling in back of the rest, docile as if led.

Kit watched as Tom divested himself of various things—boots and dagger and what else came to hand that might have so much as a flake of iron in it. Will did the same, but when he searched his pockets he paused and turned back to Kit. "Hold this for me," he said.

"Safekeeping." And pressed a silk pouch containing a bit of iron into Kit's palm.

"Oh, Will," Kit said, words forced past a wall of emotion.

Will just shook his head. And a moment later a tall, wire-coated gray hound and a blue-brindled one stood beside the red one and the black.

"Christ," Kit said, not caring that the Queen made a moue of distaste and the Puck clapped his hands over his lolling ears. "What sort of hounds are those?"

"Faerie hounds, Sir Poet," Puck answered, patting Kit's boot as he hung the little silk pouch around his neck. "With yawning mouths, sharp teeth, and wet lolling tongues. Fleet of limb, compact of foot, and tireless in the hunt."

The dogs circled, casting for a scent. Kit watched, slowly shaking his head, and bit his lip when the red bitch belled in a voice he would have known anywhere. A moment later and all four hounds gave throat, and Cairbre and the Mebd wheeled their steeds around.

"Come on," Puck cried to Kit and Ben, giving his heels to his shaggy pony. "Come on! We hunt!"

If the trail took them through London, Kit never knew it. He crouched low over the gelding's blond mane and watched the running hounds—their half-pricked ears, their wiry coats, their long muzzles and longer legs stretched out in flight. The gray limped, he thought, but it still outran the blue-brindle. Kit could not force himself to give them names. *Will. Tom.*

The horses' hooves might have flailed air, for all the sound they made, and Kit thought they ran through walls and buildings as easily as if they coursed along roads. The whole world went to shadows, rosy with the dawn and gray with winter, and all around was the silent rhythm of horses running like ghosts, their breaths

and those of their riders trailing back in plumes of white,
the pulse of air through their lungs, the creak of leather,
the bell of hounds the only sound. Ben's big bay surged
along on Kit's left; on his right side the Mebd's leggy
black outran the rest. Beyond her Kit glimpsed Cairbre's
mount steady at her flank, nose even with the post of
her sidesaddle, and when he ducked his head to glance
under his arm, he saw Puck's strange little pony striving gamely in their wake, almost lost amidst the Mebd's
flock of courtiers.

Kit pulled his eyes away, rocking with the motion of
the horse, wincing when his weight hit his injured foot in
the stirrup and fresh blood oiled the inside of the dead
man's boot, wetness soap-slick on the glassy surface of
sweat-cured leather.

The hounds ran on, and the horses ran behind them,
and the sun rose from behind the ghosts of houses and
trees. Glimmerings moved among the city's landmarks:
Gin ran through the shadow of a girl who stood one moment golden-haired and garbed in blue, laughing—and
the next sodden and dark, clad for mourning. It was a
dream of London, Mehiel told Kit. A dream of England:
not quite Faerie, but a place that was neither quite Faerie nor real. *So this is how Baines hides himself so well.
Except . . . how did he come here? How did he know of
this place? What is it, a shadow world, world of the half-
told stories?* Kit glanced sideways to catch Ben's face
over the lofting mane of his bay, saw the wonder and the
bitten lip and the big hands steady in concentration on
the reins.

Five hounds now, not four, Kit saw, and the fifth one
white as starlight on snowdrifts, running strongly alongside the others, close as if teamed. The fifth dog was
larger and more beautiful than the others, like an ideal-
ized alabaster statue rather than any real hound, even
a transformed one. Kit felt Mehiel's wings flutter, cup

air almost strongly enough to tear him from the saddle, more real here in this place of half dreams than elsewhere. *A caution, my friend.*

Kit's scars flared with pain, subsided. :He hunts with us: Mehiel said, wondering. :Can the Devil serve two masters?:

And Kit blinked, and raised his head to look at the red dawn spilling over the shifting landscape they ran through, sure-footed fey horses clearing withy hurdles that were jumbled stone-crowded stream courses when they landed beyond, charging up hills that turned into houses, and he understood. *Of course.*

:Kit, I do not understand:

Mehiel would not. For Mehiel was a creature of service, a creature under will, made to obey: a moral imperative made flesh. He could have no doubt, no hesitation, no regret, no hope. Except. Except he had stayed his hand when he could have struck Lucifer down. When Lucifer, mocking, had spread his arms wide and offered himself like a sacrifice. Like Kit. When Lucifer had come at the summons of those who had held Kit, who had treated them as a lord with servants, had sworn—

Had promised them everything they had asked him for.

And then ... led Kit's rescuers among his own servants, interrupted the ritual that would remake God in the image they desired? It made no sense, and Kit worried at it, shredding it like a falcon shreds a rabbit haunch. Because, because, because.

Because Lucifer was a legend too. A legend like any other, a construct, a fable, a myth.

And Morgan had had hair as golden as straw once, and she had been a goddess then.

:All stories are true: Mehiel said, comprehending. :He can be both things at once:

Not if Lucifer can help it, Kit answered, and crouched

back in the saddle as Gin collected himself to scramble
down a slope that was gravel, was slick mud, was trap-
rock, and scree. The five hounds ran before them; the fey
steeds strove beneath. The light shifted gold for crimson as the sun broke free of the horizon, and Kit leaned
closer to Gin's neck and held on for dear life. *Mehiel,
my brother, I dare say the one thou lovest doth care for
thee, as well.*

Act V, scene xxi

Be thy mouth or black or white,
Tooth that poisons if it bite;
Mastiff, grayhound, mongrel grim,
Hound or spaniel, brach or lym;
Or bobtail tike or trundle-tail;
Tom will make them weep and wail:
For, with throwing thus my head,
Dogs leap the hatch, and all are fled.

—WILLIAM SHAKESPEARE, *King
Lear*, Act III, scene iv

The scent is hot wine, acidic and intense. Spicy, irresistible. His legs move tirelessly, tremors stilled by the willow-being's magic, only a slight limp affecting his stride. The quarry lies ahead, the pack lies behind; the grass and gravel and tramped earth lie steady under his feet.

He follows that scent—that hated, enticing, bittersweet scent—to its inevitable conclusion. A man, a man who does not serve. A man who threatens something the hound holds dear. A man who will not be permitted to continue.

Close. So close. Running feet, the jostling shoulders of brothers and a sister beside him. Sweet motion, hot scent, follow it down—fox to his lair, wolf to his den, badger to his burrow. The scent hot, metallic as blood, bitter as the sap of monkshood dabbed against the tongue. The red bitch whines low in her throat, levels her strong, slender body. On his other side, a smoke-and-gold brindled dog bends low to the ground, hard into an angle, and runs.

Over hedgerow and ditch, down bank and through privet—it is not his concern how the horses will stay with them. That's a worry for the horses and their masters. His concern is to hunt, and to run.

The scent's hotter now, fresher. Borne on the wind as well as the earth. It's not a scent, precisely, more a contagion, a trace of the passage of the one they hunt. The one they hunt. And the ones they hunt *for* ride behind—

There! he shouts joyously. *There! There! There! There!* The quarry turns, a broad figure on a dark-colored horse, floppy brim of a thing on his head, gray cloak wrapped tight. A rogue wind swirls it about his shoulders, about his thighs.

The gray hound collects himself for the leap. His brothers, his sister, they gather themselves. The white hound who runs before them is gone, vanished, tattered and blown apart by the freshening breeze as if he had no more substance than a twist of smoke. The gray dog can already feel the panicked horse shying from his scrabbling nails, the way they'll furrow saddle leather and flesh, taste the man's blood hot over his tongue, muscle stretching and tearing between ripping teeth—

"Hold!"

Somehow he stops the killing leap, braces front feet hard enough to furrow turf, trips on the black-brindle dog who likewise struggles to a stop before him, and they go down yelping, tumbling one over the other, coming to their feet again almost under the horse's belly. It shies and dances a step, and the rider gentles it; deftly, not harshly, but the motion unseats his hat, and pale hair glitters in the strange sunlight.

The gray dog whines and crouches low, his limbs tingling uncomfortably, baring his teeth in a silent, warning snarl. Behind him, a woman's voice rises, fluid and mellifluous on words he does not understand, until Will pushed himself upright with both hands flat on the dew-wet grass and got his feet under him in a crouch. Around him, Morgan and Murchaud and Tom all stood as well, Murchaud rubbing a wrist that Will thought he might have rolled over when they tripped into each other.

Will stood, scrubbing his earth-stained hands on the front of his breeches, unmindful of a little more muck on the ruined cloth, and tilted his head back at Richard Baines. "Your master's thrown you to the wolves, Dick," Will said mildly as the horses came up behind him, their hooves that had been ghost silent clopping on the strangely solid turf. "Or perhaps I should say, the hounds. I suppose it's too much to ask that you would come quietly?"

"For the sparing of my life?" Baines chuckled, spreading his hands. Something glittered between them. Will stepped back. "Somehow, Master Playmaker, I do not think that is a vow you can make on their behalf—"

"Will!" Kit's voice, a startled shout as Baines moved suddenly. Will threw himself backward hard, scrambling to get out from under the gold-shot shadow that flared from Baines' hands like a fisherman's high-spun net.

He was not fast enough. What settled over him felt like the brush of a silk sheet down his skin. What followed that touch was blackness, utter and complete.

Act V, scene xxii

Talk not of me, but save yourselves, and depart.

—CHRISTOPHER MARLOWE, *Faustus,*
Act V, scene ii

The saber hung useless from Kit's hand as Baines spun light over Will and yanked it tight, his gestures efficient. Will didn't fall. He raised his hands and froze there, still as an oil painting, posed like a man shielding his face from divine light.

The same radiance that netted and shrouded Will twisted around Baines as well, knotted in his hands, drawn up to his chest. The dark bay gelding he rode stood steady, one white-stockinged forehoof cocked but not lifted. Kit froze where he was, half standing in the saddle, one hand upraised, the hilt of his borrowed saber warm in his palm, the red horse breathing convulsively beneath him.

He'd outridden the others on Gin's game back, just by a stride or two, and now he could feel Cairbre, the Mebd, Ben Jonson, the Puck, and the rest of the fey courtiers drawing up in a half circle. Murchaud had been standing closest to Will; both he and Tom stepped up beside the paralyzed poet, flanking him and facing down Baines while Morgan dusted her hands on her riding breeches and fell back to stand at Kit's stirrup. "Dick," Kit said, without lowering the saber. "Let Will go."

Morgan laid a hand on Kit's boot. Gin sidestepped, mouthing the bit, Kit's tension flowing down the reins like cold water.

"Why should I wish to do such a thing as that?" A timeless ray of sunlight singled Baines out, fingering his blond hair gold. *Perhaps we are in Faerie after all,* Kit thought, *and the Mebd has stilled time's passage.*

And then Will's lips moved. No, not precisely moving so much as compressing rhythmically, as if attempting to shape speech despite their immobility. Kit could read the panic in Will's eyes, the tightness in his face. *How hard is this for him, who lives with the fear of his body's rebellion every day?*

Poetry, he realized, watching Will's face. A furious brightness sparked in Kit's breast, equal parts pride and fury. *Even now, he comes back with poetry.*

Morgan did not try to move closer again. Murchaud's face stayed impassive; Tom's expression was that of a man who wished he had a pistol in his hand. Kit glanced over his shoulder, not certain what he was seeking besides reassurance, and found himself looking into the Mebd's swirling violet eyes. Somehow, she'd come up beside him on the side opposite Morgan, her mount shoulder to shoulder with his own.

The corner of her mouth quirked; it wasn't humor. " 'Tis in thy hands, Sir Poet."

"Sister, nay!" 'Twas Morgan's protest, and the Mebd silenced her with a glance.

Kit turned back to Baines and smiled like a small animal baring his teeth. "Let him go," Kit said, feeling

Mehiel's understanding and acquiescence. "And I shall go with you."

"*Kit!*" Murchaud and Tom cried in unison. Will's mouth also worked, his eyes squinting tight.

Fight it, William.

Morgan shook her head, sunlight glinting from her hair, but she said nothing. Kit sheathed his saber without looking, clenched his right hand on the nail in his pocket, his left hand tightening on the reins. Gin sidestepped, feeling Kit's tension, the hair on his neck drying into salty spikes where the leather rubbed them. *Trust me,* Kit prayed, catching Murchaud's eye for a moment before looking back at Baines. "Set him free, Dick."

"I know what thy parole is worth." Baines' smirk gave the words layers Kit did not care to think about. Baines jerked his hands as if tugging reins; the web of light around Will tightened. Will staggered woodenly, like a jangled marionette.

"I did everything I swore I would," Kit answered, refusing to flinch or look away.

Baines smiled, voice like a velvet glove across the back of Kit's neck. "Pussycat. Isn't it time thou didst admit where thou dost belong?"

"I'll do what you wish, Dick," Kit said, the words like grit on his tongue. He hated that he did not have to pretend to the fear and diffidence in his tone. "But let Will go, or you'll get nothing from me."

Kit closed his eyes, feeling Baines' consideration. Mehiel stirred restlessly under his skin. The man pushed the angel down, and waited. Morgan touched Kit's boot again, and this time Gin did not shy. Kit leaned down to her, never taking his eyes off Baines, and she hoisted herself on the edge of his saddle until she could speak into his ear.

"Is this the side thou'rt choosing, then, sweet poet? After all the kindness of the Fae to thee?"

"Kindness?" Kit snorted, not caring that Baines could see his lips. "Is that what thou callest it, my Queen?" He hoped she could hear the irony in his tone. He drew his hand from his pocket and let his fingers brush her hair behind her ear. *Trust me.* "Do not vent thy wrath on Will, when I am gone," he murmured, taking a chance and dropping his eyes for a moment to catch hers. "And trust us. I think, my Queen, at last we understand our destiny."

She chuckled. He straightened in the saddle, raised his head, and nudged Gin forward, aware that Ben had joined the Queens in flanking him. Kit warned the big man away with a glance, and turned his attention back to Baines and the tangle of light in his hands like so much knotted yarn.

"Well?" Kit said.

"I have your word, puss?"

"I have been many things," Kit answered, "but I have never been forsworn. I swear to thee that Christofer Marley will do your bidding, Master Baines, and do unto thee no harm."

"And your friends."

Kit pinned each one of them with a glance, registered their looks of protest, anger, grief, betrayal. "I give my parole for them," he said, not looking away.

Baines laughed low in his throat and opened his hands. "So mote it be." And boldly, calmly, he collected his reins and turned the bay gelding with his knees. "Thou'lt forgive me if I lay a compulsion and a binding upon thee, this time—"

"I'll forgive anything," Kit answered, and reined Gin up alongside the bay, leaving the Mebd and Morgan and Ben staring after him, and Murchaud's long fingers digging into Will's shoulder to hold the poet back. He clenched his hand tight on the nail in his pocket and listened while Baines whispered the words, made slow passes in the air. The two steeds maintained a stately pace, down the bank toward a river that might almost have been the Thames, or might have been the Stour of Kit's childhood memories: it twisted back and forth in his vision, from a broad tidal thing, green and brown with eddies, subtle enough to drown a man no matter how strong a swimmer he might be to a brook a man might ford on horseback and barely wet his boots.

Kit felt the magic clutch at his mind and heart and liver, a mindless obedience that would have sucked the wit and love and courage from him. He bit his lip, and let the ensorcelled iron pierce his palm until his own blood wet his hand and his hip through the fabric of his doublet. He heard himself whimper, and felt his own power flare and then slither back, pressed aside by the practiced might of Baines' sorcery. He quailed like a man slipping on ice toward a cliff face, clutching at slick grasses, and his fey horse shuddered beneath him. *Mehiel*—

:Hold fast: the angel answered, and quoted poetry. :Angels and ministers of grace defend us—:

The pain of the nail in Kit's palm was just enough to keep the laugh from bubbling from his lips. Baines' spell clutched his throat; he could not breathe; he dropped the reins and clutched his collar, tearing it open, sagging forward over Gin's blond mane. The pressure crushed him, swept him aside, rolled him under. *Shoved*.

And eased.

Baines' hand was on his sleeve, tugging him upright. "Sit straight, puss," Baines said, and Kit obeyed without thought. "Come along."

Kit opened his hand, the nail driven through his palm grating between the bones. He gasped and sat back in the saddle, feeling the eyes on his back. The eyes of his friends. *Trust me.*

Baines could destroy him in any fight. Sorcerous or physical, it mattered not. Kit had no hope of meeting him in open war.

Which left just treachery.

Kit gave Gin a little leg on the off side, sending him shoulder to shoulder with Baines' bay. Kit's knee banged Baines' calf; Baines cursed good-naturedly, raising his right hand to Kit's shoulder to ward man and horse away.

As he turned, Kit skinned the saber from its saddle sheath and put the whole curved, wicked length into Richard Baines' belly and out his back, low and angled for the liver, a kidney, both if Kit was lucky. His hand on the hilt, the iron nail in his palm, his blood binding him to the blade, Kit felt skin pop before the blade's knife tip—a slashing weapon, not designed to stab, awkward and unbalanced. But it went through.

He leaned across his saddle and *twisted* the weapon in Baines' guts, and the nail thrust through the back of his own hand.

Gin shrieked and planted both forehooves at the cataract of blood that drenched them both, and Baines' bay horse too. The bay reared; Kit yelped as the saber was dragged from his grip, Baines somehow staying in the saddle as his horse curvetted.

Staying in the saddle, Kit estimated, but not for long, with both hands folded across his belly like that, holding his guts inside like an overfull armload of mold-slicked gray rope. Gin's eyes were white-edged, his ears laid back hard as he backed away, one step and then another, his head down to protect his throat as if he faced a slavering dog.

"Puss—" Baines managed, more a bubble of blood on his lips than a word. He blinked, his expression the strangest blend of grief and hurt betrayal; Kit saw it with a clarity that made a mockery of the ten feet between them. "Forsworn?" And then his grip failed, and his guts slid out over his thighs and the saddle, and his body tumbled backward as his bay horse said *enough* and put its hooves hard to the ground.

Kit gentled Gin with a hand that left bloody streaks on the sorrel's blond mane, remembered a moment later the nail sunk into his palm. He picked it free while his gelding's quivering slowed, and bound the wound with a scrap torn from his filthy white doublet. He trembled like shaken paper, and it took all his concentration to wind the cloth around his hand. By the time he had the bleeding stopped, the Fae had joined him, and the mortal riders too.

Morgan got to him first, Will seated pillion behind her. She reined her mare in close enough that Gin could lean a shoulder on her to be comforted, and slid her own arm around Kit's waist, seeming not to notice that it took all of *his* flickering strength of heart not to shy and buck. "Clever," she said, and left it at that, leaning away.

He sighed, stealing another glance at the ruin of his worst nightmare sprawled messily on the bank. He couldn't quite look at Baines; nor could he—quite— look away.

"Kit." Will's voice, and Will's gentle hand on his arm.

Kit flinched, held himself steady as Gin tossed his head in protest of the blood and his rider's plain fear. "Aye, love?"

"You forswore yourself for me?"

Kit laughed, and looked up, feeling suddenly lightened. "No," he said, and shook his head, feeling how his hair gritted against his neck. "I told Dick that Christofer Marley would do as he bid."

"And?"

Kit shrugged, pressing his right hand to his thigh to slow the piercing agony in it to a throbbing ache. "There is no Christofer Marley any longer, Will." He picked flakes of blood off the back of his hand with a thumbnail and did not stop himself this time. "Come away, love. I want a bath. Come away from this place."

Act V, scene xxiii

And when he falls, he falls like Lucifer,
Never to hope again.

—WILLIAM SHAKESPEARE, *King Henry*
VIII, Act III, scene ii

Catesby would not be taken alive. Will heard later
that the chase led the King's Men as far as Warwickshire, his cousins gone to ground in a gate-
house and pried loose only at the cost of blood on both
sides. He heard, and nodded as if it had been no more
than he expected, and—wishing he had more grief left in
him—turned his face back to the fire.

There was an ugly bit of business when they returned
to London and learned that Salisbury had arranged to
have the recusant Ben arrested for questioning regarding the Gunpowder Treason. But he was pried loose
soon enough, following a renunciation of his convenient
Catholicism and a few earnest threats from Will and
Tom, and the comments of the Baron Monteagle, roused
from his bed at an inconvenient hour.

The following morning, Will took himself to Westminster in the company of Thomas Walsingham and that same Ben Jonson, where the three of them presented themselves again before the Secretary of State. Salisbury met them in a red-walled receiving room where Will had once been greeted by a Queen, and Will suspected the canny old Earl had chosen that location on purpose. There were wine and a fire; Tom and Ben availed themselves of the former, Will of the latter, and they stood in wolf-pack silence while Salisbury sugared a cup of sack for himself.

"Master Shakespeare," Salisbury said finally, turning to face the hearth and Will. "I've considered thy proposal, again. And I am afraid I cannot allow—"

Will drew a breath and raised his hand, not quite believing himself what he was about to say. "I'm afraid, my lord, that my request is no more negotiable than Ben's freedom."

"Not—" Disbelief. Salisbury set his cup aside.

"Would you care, my lord, to see my talents turned to the sort of satire our friend Ben is known for? To the odd anonymous broadside? The Devil makes work for idle hands."

"I have mine own resources," Salisbury countered, the threat patent in his voice.

Will laughed, crossing his arms in the King's red livery, trying not to show how much he needed the support of the wall he leaned back against. "What can you threaten me with? I am dying, my lord. Behead me tomorrow; you cost the world at most a few plays, and my wife the pain of nursing me through my decline."

Salisbury's mouth worked. He glanced at Ben, who remained perfectly still, a shaggy, menacing figure in incongruous wire-rimmed spectacles. Will did not need to turn to know that Tom Walsingham smiled. He could see its effect, the sudden nervous flicker of Salisbury's smirk. Tom's voice was light, level, and as sweet as a woman's when she has her husband dead to rights. "I too have *resources,*" Tom said. "And while I am not Secretary of State, my lord Earl, I *am* Tom Walsingham."

Will took his cue from the heavy downflex of Tom's voice, the emphasis of the accidental rhyme of verb and name. "And I dare say," he continued pleasantly, "that we three know enough of your dealings, and have enough trust from the King and Queen between us, to see you in the room beside Sir Walter's. No doubt His Majesty would not be averse to seeing one of his loyal Scotsmen in your place; you know how he prefers them to the English-bred men of the court."

The silence stretched taut. Salisbury's breathing slowed, a muscle in his jaw flexing in time. Will concentrated on that muscle, on Salisbury's eyes—so arrogant and full of the awareness of power—and almost winced and glanced down. Almost. And then he thought of Burbage, and he thought of Lucifer Morningstar, and Will Shakespeare dropped his hands and pushed himself upright, retrieving his cane before he shuffled forward. Rush mats crackled under the ferrule—iron, of course—but Will kept his eyes on Salisbury's. His two short steps framed him before the fire, and he lifted his head and crossed his arms once more, keeping a disinterested glare fixed on Salisbury.

Salisbury folded his arms, an unconscious mirror of Will's position. Will permitted himself a little smile of triumph, quickly quenched, as the Earl bit his lip and then sighed. "What is thy desire?"

"You'll convince the King that his legacy should be a new English translation of the Bible," Will said. "And you'll extend your personal patronage to Ben."

Salisbury coughed lightly against the side of his knuckle. "You feel entitled to a great deal, Master Shakespeare." But there was an echo of capitulation in his tone.

Will smiled. "Yes," he said, stopping his hand a moment before it could rise to tug his earlobe, where Morgan's earring no longer swung. "I will admit that failing, my lord Earl."

Salisbury sucked his teeth and turned his head aside quickly, raising one shoulder in a lopsided shrug, more at Ben than at Will. Ben chuckled low in his throat, but Salisbury's voice rose over it. "Thy judgements proved better than adequate this week past," he admitted at last, as if it pained him. "I will speak to the King. And thou wilt have a play for us by Twelfth Night."

"By Lady Day," Will corrected. "I am going home for Christmas, to see my daughters and my wife."

The New Place was warm despite the weather that heaped snow to windward until it touched the windowsills, and warmer still with the presence of the friends and family crowded between its thick walls. Will straddled a bench beside the fire, leaning back against the wall, and breathed Annie's scent as she leaned on his chest, her knees drawn up under her skirts. He closed his eyes and closed also his hand on her upper arm, drowsing to the sound of Susanna's voice raised in caroling.

"People will whisper of thy licentious London ways," Annie said sleepily, leaning her head on his shoulder.

Will turned his face into her hair, resting his cheek against the top of her head. He sighed, just slightly, and felt her stiffen.

"Art lonely for London, husband?" She pressed her shoulders to his chest, her tone light. "The applause of the crowds—"

"The rotten fruit hurled in our faces—"

She snickered. "Thou knowest, Susanna and Judith will be married before all that much longer."

"Aye," he said, although he wanted to deny it.

"I had thought . . ." She hesitated, leaned back harder.

"When the girls are gone, Will. There will be naught for me in Stratford."

Will held his breath lightly, trying to anticipate what she might be dancing up on with such intensity. He gave up, and blew some loose strands of her hair aside, trying to brighten her mood. "Out with it, my Annie."

She drew a breath. "May I to London with thee?"

He didn't hear her at first. The words were so entirely what he had never expected to hear, and all he could do was blink slowly and shake his head. "To London?"

"With thee. Surely thou couldst make enough room for a wife, and I'd not wheedle to be taken to court or interfere in thy trade. . . ."

"Oh, Annie," he said. He heard her held breath ease from her, then, and felt her shoulders slump in defeat.

"Foolish notion," she murmured. "Thou'lt to home for Lent, my love?" Just like that, forgiven for what she saw as a dismissal, again.

Will's eyes stung. "Silly wench," he murmured. "Thou canst not come to London with me, Annie. Because I'm coming home."

She sat up and turned, swinging her legs off the bench. Guests and daughters turned to look, then averted their eyes quickly as she leaned in close, her eyes on his. "Don't tease me, William."

"I'd never tease," he said. "I can make a play here as well as there, and playing's finished for me. I'm coming home. I love thee, Annie. . . ."

She leaned back, eyes wide, blowing air through wide nostrils. She studied his eyes for a moment, assessing, her spine stiff with wrath. Which softened, inch by inch, until she tilted her head to the side and blew the lock of hair he'd disturbed out of her eyes. "Thou daft poet," she said. "I know."

Act V, scene xxiv

*Why did it suffer thee to touch her breast,
And shrunk not back, knowing my love was there?*

—CHRISTOPHER MARLOWE, *Dido,
Queen of Carthage*, Act IV, scene iv

K it rose with the sunset and went to the window,
leaving his bed rumpled and unmade behind him.
The casement stood open; it might be winter in
England, but at the castle of the Mebd it was high spring,
and the wood was in leaf as gold as primrose blossoms.
He leaned a hand on either side of the window frame
and stared out, watching darkness unfurl along the
horizon.

:Sir Poet:

Mehiel? Feeling eyes on him, almost, Kit turned back
to the room. The way his shadow fell behind him was
warning enough. A glimpse of arched eyebrow, of swan-
white wing followed.

:Surely thou knowest my name by now, my love: Lucifer said, and opened his wings in welcome.

"What makes you think I would greet you, Morningstar?" Kit folded his arms, trembling in the warm spring breeze. The wall he put his back to was smooth as glass. He would have preferred the purchase of rough-hewn stone.

Lucifer tilted his head and smiled, and Kit felt his knees turn to water where he stood. The fallen angel wore a whiteworked shirt of ivory silk with sleeves that flowed like water, as full as a second set of wings. The crown of shadows that capped his golden hair seemed to draw a rich dark tint from the crimson velvet of his breeches, and his eyes caught more light than the sunset sky had to offer.

Kit held his breath as Lucifer came to him, tilted his chin up with a wing-tip touch, wordlessly eased open his tight-folded arms with the brush of gentle feathers. The Devil's lips hovered over Kit's, satin as rose petals, the warm brush of breath on Kit's skin and the warmth of a presence close enough to stir the fine hairs on his cheek.

Kit drew breath in an agony of anticipation, felt Mehiel's surrender in the coldness in his brands. The wall stood firm behind him; his hands flattened on the stones, but they gave him no purchase and less strength. The fire in his belly was chill.

"I could give thee wings," Lucifer murmured. His true voice rang Kit like a bell, with a sensation of flying. Of falling. Kit closed his dark, dark eyes.

Mehiel turned his mouth upward for the kiss.

And Kit's fingernails found a crack.

A finer and a smaller chink than he had picked away at during his confinement in the pit. But a crack nonetheless, and he drove nails into it, clutching, clawing. Drawing his own bright blood, feeling the pain of the nail bed tearing as the nail folded.

He turned his head away and pressed his fingertips to Lucifer's mouth, crimson staining palest dog-rose pink.

"I love thee," Kit whispered, and Lucifer smiled against his fingers.

"And I thee, poet and angel."

Kit shook his head, dropped his hand to Lucifer's chest, and pushed. The Devil stepped back smoothly, offering no resistance, and all Kit could see was the red of his own blood on the whiteness of Lucifer's breast. "I love thee," Kit said again. "And thou wilt destroy me. Be gone. And take thy witchery with thee."

Lucifer's wings cupped air, a sound like a backhanded slap. Kit flinched, but the Devil flinched moreso. And looked Kit in the eye. And nodded once, slowly, and closed his eyes that were bluer than the twilight.

And ceased to be where he had been.

Kit stood a moment in darkness, the sunset wind riffling the fine hairs on his neck, and slid down the wall until he could bury his face in his arms.

A tap on his door roused him. It seemed as if moments had passed, but as he stood the dawn air felt cold through his linen nightshirt. He limped across the chamber. The knotted red wool of the carpet pricked his bare soles and the tender flesh of his bandaged foot. He lifted the latch without asking a name, knowing from the sound whom he would see.

"My Prince."

The Elf-knight stepped past him and pulled the door from his grasp. "Kit, what hast done to thy fingers?"

Kit looked down, startled. "Split a nail or two," he said. " 'Tis nothing."

" 'Tis not nothing," Murchaud answered, relatching the door. "Let me clean it."

Kit followed in obedience, gasping at cold water spilled across his palms and wrists. And then marveling at the Prince-consort of Faerie, bent over his—Kit's—sad, calloused hands with a rag. "My Prince," he said again.

Murchaud dabbed at a bit of blood, and looked up. He'd dressed, but his hair was still tousled from the night and his eyes were so bruised with exhaustion as to seem kohled. "Is that all I am to thee?"

"No...." Kit protested, Mehiel silent within him. Murchaud took one step away.

"I came to bring thee something. I'll be quick. I did not mean to presume." Murchaud cast his eyes down, and Kit's breath snagged as he understood.

"Murchaud," he began, and couldn't find the next word.

The Elf-knight dug into his sleeve, unmindful of the water pink with Kit's blood that spotted it, and came out with a scrap of silk. He held the cloth out, and Kit numbly took it. It was like quicksilver, the highlights blue as shadows on snow and the shadows the color of twilight. Kit stared uncomprehending.

"For your cloak," the Elf-knight said, and turned away.

Kit's mouth worked, his tongue dry and dumb as un-inked paper. Murchaud crossed the room in five long strides, lifted the latch, turned the handle on the door, and opened it, unhesitating, back straight, lean and dark in the half-light so far from the window.

He stepped into the hall.

"Wait," Kit whispered, but the door was closing. *"Wait!"* he shouted, and froze, listening for the click of the latch.

Silence.

And then the door opening again, and Murchaud framed against the gold stone of the hallway. "Kit?" he asked, lifting his chin.

"Do—" Kit took up a breath, and his courage with it. "Dost love me?"

Murchaud considered the question, turning his answer over on his tongue. He dropped his eyes to his hand on the door handle, stepped back into the room, shut the door behind himself. Latched it, and leaned against the boards. "Can an elf be said to love?"

Kit nodded, his sore fingers knotted white on the bit of silk in his palm.

Murchaud did not leave the door. The air between them grew golden with the rising, indirect light. "Then as elves love, aye."

Kit closed his eyes on the fear, closed his heart on Mehiel's startled protest. "Wilt prove it?"

Mute, Murchaud nodded. Drew a breath and another, came one step toward Kit. "Anything."

Kit gasped, and laughed. "Thou swearest."

" *Anything.* I vow."

And Kit felt his own heart break.

"It is not fair or just, what I will ask of thee," he began, calm now that the die was cast. "I need thee to undo what was done."

It was the kiss that broke Kit. Not the kisses on his mouth; he lay still, hands clenched into fists on the cov- erlet, through those. Murchaud lingered over them, a hand on either side of his head, all that black hair freed from its tail and tumbling down around Kit's face, no contact between them except lips and tongue.

No, it was when Murchaud kissed his eyes closed that Kit knew he had made a mistake. "God," Kit said, and Murchaud flinched but did not draw away. Instead, he caught Kit's lip between his teeth, but Kit continued to speak anyway, his fingernails bloodying his palms as he struggled not to shove the Prince to the floor. "Mur- chaud, just finish it."

Murchaud gnawed at his own lower lip. "I said I will unbind thy angel, though it mean thy life. Wouldst have me misuse thee, also?"

It *would* mean Kit's life. But if the bonds that

trapped the angel in his body were severed first, then Mehiel need not die with him, but—when his cage was shattered—might go free.

Kit drew breath and said, "I would it were *done*."

Murchaud leaned down on an elbow, close enough that Kit could feel the heat of his body. He raised his right hand and outlined the scar over Kit's heart. Kit gasped as that scar and its brothers flared on his skin as if freshly seared. "Is there no means to make this gentle?"

Kit swallowed and closed his eyes. "It is mine to endure."

"If enduring is what thou chooseth."

I cannot do this. I cannot lie still for this. I cannot bear it.

:And thou wouldst have had no choice, were it Baines: The voice startled Kit, coming as it did with a sense of unfurling and a gazing awareness within. Eyes like a falcon's, gold as the sun, and wings whose stunning plumage was banded in black and gold, not swan-white at all. Mehiel.

A rape I could have endured, Kit answered. *And yet my lover will be kind.* "Murchaud," he whispered.

"Kit."

"Bind my hands."

"Love?" Honest dismay. "I will not—"

"Thou must." Kit drew a ragged breath. "I will refuse thee otherwise. I have not the strength of will for this. And I must not be permitted to refuse."

"I would not force thee—"

"It is not force," Kit said. "For I am begging thee."

"Dost thou?"

"So we do," Kit answered, and realized only after the words had left his mouth that he had spoken for himself, and for Mehiel, too. "Bind my hands. And my legs. It will reinforce the sorcery in any case; cut the bonds when thou'rt done with me. If we steal those other Prometheans' symbols to undo their black work, 'tis no more than they deserve."

Murchaud regarded him thoughtfully, and then nodded. "As thou wishest."

Kit closed his eyes as Murchaud left the curtained confines of the bed. The straw tick dimpled under Murchaud when the Elf-knight returned. Kit turned to watch him fasten a yard-long length of silk scavenged from a drapery about Kit's wrist and draw it outward, to one of the massive bedposts. Kit's heart beat faster as Murchaud repeated the process on the opposite side, exquisitely gentle and completely without pity.

Every inch the Elf-knight again.

"Do you have the knife?"

"Aye." Murchaud covered Kit's eyes with a blindfold and carefully tugged it down over his cheeks. "I'll not stop thy mouth," he said. " 'Tis thy poetry I need of thee, and all thy power."

Safer in the darkness, Kit nodded, and Murchaud bound his feet apart as well.

The room was warm, and yet Kit shivered at every brush of the air on his sweat-drenched skin. If he were a horse, he thought, he would be lathered white with fear. Terror, which crystallized into something else entirely when Murchaud, without otherwise touching him, laid the ice-cold blade of the dagger against the brand on the inside of his thigh and—cut. And moved the blade to the other thigh and cut again. And once more. And again, defacing each sigil in reverse of how they had been layered on Kit's skin.

Kit strangled the whimper that rose in his throat, not out of pride—he was beyond pride—but out of fear for how it would sound to Murchaud. Instead he pulled against the twisted cloth that bound him, grunting like a birthing woman dragging at a knotted rope. The pain of

the knife was still better than the touch of Murchaud's
hand.

Murchaud kissed his mouth again, quickly, guiltily,
before Kit could jerk away. And then, the Elf-knight
straddled Kit's belly, with the heat of flesh on flesh, his
weight like stones. *Peine forte et dure.* This time, Kit could
not silence the sound that rose in his throat. Murchaud
swallowed it, kissed it away. He settled over Kit's hips,
toes dug under Kit's thighs, and must have laid the knife
aside, because the next touch was the flat of both hands
upon Kit's breast. The brands on Kit's sides burned so
hot Kit thought they must blister, knife slashes trickling
blood across Kit's ribs to soak into the coverlet.

"For Christ's sake," Kit snarled, "get it *over* with."

He felt a small, cruel joy when Murchaud flinched
hard enough to shake the bed, but then the Elf-knight
drew himself back and said, "As you wish it," and that
was a small kind of victory. Until Murchaud wrapped
a rough, calloused hand around Kit's prick and began,
with abrupt motions, to manipulate it.

Every touch was irritation, and the longer it continued the more Kit's rage grew. It started in his belly, a
small uncomfortable coal, and grew swiftly to a venom
that would not be contained; he cursed and whimpered
and heaped abuse. He used the name of God like a whip,
and felt the Fae Prince shudder under it and continue,
while Mehiel struggled in Kit's breast like a fox in a
snare's sharp jaws.

Kit visualized the tumble of crimson fur rolling, tail
flagging like a banner against the snow. *Not much longer, sweet Mehiel. Soon we part company. Soon you go
home.*

And as for Kit? He supposed he had a destination,
too.

Kit thought they would tear him apart between them,
the angel and the Faerie Prince. He was grateful for the

bindings, which let him thrash however he would and yet held him secure. He was grateful for Murchaud's hands that held him likewise, and with a strength and negligence that carried no remembrance of Baines' sick mock-gentleness. And he was grateful for his unstopped mouth, for the freedom to blaspheme and beg even when he knew the efforts would be ignored.

He thought it would grow easier to bear, the Prince's touch, that in the darkness it would be all he had to focus on and he would learn to withstand it, as he had Baines' damned iron bridle. But he grew instead angrier and fiercer, an unstopped wrath that would not be silenced again. Murchaud, meanwhile, was thorough and remorseless, and Kit wept when his body at last surrendered, arching himself to the touch, scrabbling against the bonds.

Murchaud tarried for a moment, ducked to kiss the bloody scar on Kit's thigh with a mouth that was wet and hot, and then kissed each of the other three ruined brands in turn. It was a farewell, and that was all it was. And Kit, to his shame, fought and wailed like an orphaned child. It was well he was bound, or he should have used his fists against Murchaud.

When the Prince at last placed pillows beneath Kit and knelt between his thighs, placing the dagger upon his breast, Kit's gratefulness swelled. The straw tick crunched under the Elf-knight's knees; his flanks were warm against the insides of Kit's thighs as Kit bent his legs, taking the slack from the bonds. "I have thy freedom in my hand."

Kit wasn't sure how he found his voice, but find it he did and made it firm to support his lover's hand. "Finish it."

"So mote it be," Murchaud said, and pressed the dagger to the center of the brand upon Kit's breast. "The Fae should know better than to love mortal men."

He leaned into the dagger as he rose into Kit.

The dagger slid through Kit's heart like a serpent's tongue, slick and easy. He *felt* the force of it, felt the gallant muscle striving to beat, shredding itself on the ice-cold blade. He might have screamed, but all he could manage was a breathless whine that he meant for a sorry sort of joke: *Consummatum est.* And then the darkness was no longer merely the darkness behind the blindfold, but encompassing and deep and edged with penetrating cold.

And thou'lt go to Lucifer after all, but shed of the thing he wished of thee.

Kit's last thought through the pain was that he was glad—so glad—that he could not see Murchaud's face as he died.

Murchaud, who pulled the dagger free and gathered Kit close to his breast, while the sharp heat of blood spread between them and Kit felt warm arms and stickiness and the wetness that might be an elf-Prince weeping all recede on a river of dark, as he remembered something long forgotten—that he had come this way before, not once but twice, in Deptford and at Rheims.

Pure white light enfolded him and he smiled at the lie. It would not be Heaven awaiting beyond that gate, but there was something to be said for the refinement of that deception. Some must come this way, Kit imagined, who did not honestly know what to expect.

Imagine their disillusionment.

And then Mehiel's falcon-cry of a voice that was not a voice, and his eyes like living suns as he bowed down in the space that was not a space and spread his wings before a Kit who was not Kit. Kit who was whole, and who was not in pain. :God is good. I shall not be able to save thee again, poet:

Farewell, Mehiel, Kit answered. *I expected no salvation. I expect we shall not meet in Heaven, Angel of the Lord.*

:Thy life thrice: the angel answered. :Rheims, Deptford, Hy Bréàsil. Be healed one last time, child, and may our paths cross nevermore: Barred black and gold, the bright wings blurred, and Kit stepped back, or dreamed he did.

:Consummatum est!: Mehiel shouted. And rose. And was gone.

"Consummatum est," Kit whispered. He opened his eyes, lashes sticky with his own red blood, and cursed because his hands were bound and he could not bury them in Murchaud's hair.

There was a scar in the center of the scar in the center of his breast and another on his back between the shoulder blades and to the left of his spine, where Murchaud's weight had driven the blade through his body and into the featherbed. Beside the witch's mark, in fact, and just opposite it.

And there was blood: so very much blood, indeed. Blood through the ticking and onto the floor.

Blood, and blood only. That was all.

Epilogue

"I hate" she altered with an end,
That followed it as gentle day
Doth follow night, who like a fiend
From heav'n to hell is flown away
"I hate" from hate away she threw
And saved my life saying, "not you."

—WILLIAM SHAKESPEARE, Sonnet 45

April 22, 1616

Annie helped Will lean back in the pillow-upholstered chair as he finished coughing. He was weak, too weak. He couldn't get air into his lungs and the fever that burned him wasn't even strong enough to grant the surcease of delirium, just the misery of aches and sweat.

He thought it was a natural sickness, at least. *We've seen an end to the Promethean plagues. That's something. And something I've lived this long, with Kit's help and Morgan's.*

And who would have thought 'twould not be the damned palsy after all?

Annie soothed his forehead with a cloth, her grayed brow wrinkled with concern. Will opened his eyes as a second shadow fell across him. Kit, bringing a basin cool from the well.

Will sighed. "Was ever man so unworthy, so well loved?"

"Unworthy?" Kit scoffed. "Who's worthy of love? It makes us worthy by loving, I wot."

Annie said nothing, but Will knew the twisted mouth she gave Kit for approval.

Will coughed again, too weak to raise a rag to his lips. Annie did it, and when she lowered the cloth it was spotted red. Will did not miss the look she traded with Kit, or the way Kit looked down and to the left. "Do you suppose I'll be damned for sorcery, like poor Sir Francis?" Which wasn't quite what Will had planned to say, but talking weakened him too much to retract the question and start over.

"You must not think such things," Annie said. "Tomorrow's thy birthday, husband. Surely thou'lt heal?"

Kit met her eyes again when Will did not manage an answer, and set the basin aside. Annie cleared her throat and turned hastily away. "Sorcery was the least of Sir Francis' sins," Kit said, stroking Will's hair back from his brow.

"I've lost my ring, Kit," Will said. "At Judith's wedding—" His trembling fingers tried to tighten, and Kit took them in a savage grasp.

"You won't need a ring with Annie and I to hold your hand."

Will turned his head to regard the smooth line of Kit's jaw behind the beard. "Thou didst age nary a day, my love."

"The price for dying young." Kit stepped away to

make room for Annie as she came back with a cleaner rag.

"Love," she said. "Thou shouldst rest. Thou shouldst sleep, and thou wilt heal—"

Will closed his eyes. The cold water did help, but his thoughts were startlingly clear for a fevered man, and from what he knew of deathbeds, that was no hopeful sign. "I don't want to go to Hell, as Sir Francis did."

"Thou dost wish not the Promethean Heaven, either. You'd know not a soul." Kit, still joking, but his fine-fingered hands were knotted in the sleeves he had folded them over.

Will forced a wavering chuckle. "Nay.... Oh, there's going to be such poetry, Kit. I am sorry that I will miss it."

Annie cleared her throat. "You're not going to Hell, gentle William," she said, and wet her cloth again. Kit rose when she gestured him away and left the fireside to lean against the wall. Will saw his face, and turned his face away. *Oh, Kit. Were you ever privileged to love where love was not given first elsewhere? Even once?*

"Annie. Kit will tell you—"

"Kit told me," she said, and Kit cleared his throat and looked down at the floor. "Will, the priest is here."

"Priest?"

"A Romish priest," she said firmly. "If after thirty-four years of marriage, you think I'm going to Glory without you, you're a bigger fool than I imagined, Will Shakespeare!"

Kit, leaning against the wall, stood suddenly upright, turned his head, and laughed. "Annie, you're brilliant."

"Hardly," she said, taken aback. She twitched her hair over her shoulder and turned.

Kit's expression practically shone with excitement. "A Romish priest. Whose doctrine is that bodies must be buried in hallowed ground, and that the soul remains with the flesh until the End of Days." He paused, and looked down at the rushed floor, laughing harshly. "Apparently, God can't be arsed to check under the cushions for the souls that slip out his purse."

"Aye," she said. "It'll give you a chance to get what you owe Will sorted out before Judgement Day, and find this kinder God you've been pratting about for the last three days. Lord knows, Kit Marlin, it's likely to take so long, for thee."

Will huddled under his muffling blankets, sick with stubbornness. *Repent of your sins and be forgiven.* No. He would not. He would not repudiate Kit, on his deathbed or for any reason. "Nay. I shall not repent of thee."

"Will—"

"Wife," he said. "Do not ask it." He looked to Kit for support, but Kit, looking as if his heart were squeezed in a bridle, shook his head.

"Do you," Kit commanded, and Will flinched—not at the command, but at the distancing—and saw Annie look away. "Do you repent of me, and you are Heaven bound. Thou didst brave Hell for me one time. 'Twill serve."

Will glared. "And wilt *thou* repent, Kit?"

"I will not."

"I will not leave thee alone in Hell."

"You will. Imprimus, I have no plans to die. Secundus, you married Annie. You *will* honor your loyalty to her."

"The world . . ." Will said, frustrated. And turned his face aside. He would not see Kit weep. Kit would not care to have him do so. The list of what the world would not allow was long for mourning over.

Kit, his face strangely taut, turned to Annie and clapped her on the arm. "Only a woman would think to stall God to her convenience. Well-reasoned, chop logic."

She nearly smiled, and touched Kit on the shoulder lightly. And Will almost imagined he heard, nearby, the flicker and settle of massive wings.

Author's Note

First and foremost, I would like to thank Mr. Tony Toller, trustee of the Rose Theatre Trust, a nonprofit organization dedicated to preserving the remains of Bankside's first theatre, the Rose. It was through the kindness of Mr. Toller that I was able to visit the site of that theatre, and stand—quite literally—where Ned Alleyne, Philip Henslowe, and Christopher Marlowe stood, although the Rose was not then an archaeological site housed in the damp, breathing darkness under a modern skyscraper.

Plans are afoot to preserve the site and continue excavations and research, and as of this writing, fundraising for these projects is under way. If you are interested in learning more about this important historical and archaeological work—or in supporting it—details may be found at www.rosetheatre.org.uk.

This pair of novels has been a labor of years, and over the course of that time a lot of people have offered comment or listened to me whine. I also wish to thank first readers, bent ears, inspirational forces, and others both on and off the Online Writing Workshop (and the denizens of its invaluable writers' chat) and various other online communities: Kit Kindred, Matt Bowes, Lis Riba, Sarah Monette, Kat Allen, Stella

Evans, Chelsea Polk, Dena Landon, Brian and Wendy Froud, Liz Williams, Treize Armistedian, Rhonda Garcia, Leah Bobet, Chris Coen, Ruth Nestvold, Marna Nightingale, Hannah Wolf Bowen, Amanda Downum, Rachele Colantuono, John Tremlett, Gene Spears, Mel Melcer, Larry West, Jaime Voss, Walter Williams, Kelly Morisseau, Andrew Ahn, and Eric Bresin. I would also like to thank Ellen Rawson and Ian Walden, who graciously opened their home in England to me when I visited on a research trip in 2006. I'd also like to thank my editor, Jessica Wade, and my agent, Jennifer Jackson. Most sincere gratitude to my copy editor, Andrew Phillips, who is not only something of an Elizabethan historian in his own right, but also meticulous and intelligent. And I'm sure I've forgotten several people who deserve to be here, but as I've been writing this book since Christmas of 2002, I hope they will forgive me.

The present work would have been impossible to complete without the recent outpouring of popular scholarship concerning the Elizabethan and Jacobean stage, and in particular Mssrs. Shakespeare, Jonson, and Marlowe. In addition, I consulted the work of multifarious authors, dabblers, artists, and historians. I have never met Park Honan, Anthony Burgess, Stephen Booth, Peter Ackroyd, Charles Nicholl, Michael Wood, Liza Picard, Stephen Greenblatt, David Riggs, David Crystal, Constance Brown Kuriyama, Peter Farey, Jennifer Westwood, Antonia Frazier, Alan H. Nelson, C. Northcote Parkinson, Elaine Pagels, Jaroslav Pelikan, Lawrence Stone, Gustav Davidson, Richard Hosley, Alan Bray, Michael B. Young, Peter W. M. Blayney, Katharine M. Briggs, or any of the other wonderfully obsessed individuals whose work I consulted in preparing this glorious disservice to history. However, I owe them all an enormous debt of gratitude, and I spent immeasurable pleasant hours in their company while in the process of writing this book.

A couple of historical and linguistic quirks for the reader's interest: the Elizabethan year began on Lady Day, in late March, rather than January 1. In result, Christofer Marley was, to his contemporaries, born at the end of 1563 and William Shakespeare at the beginning of 1564. To a modern eye, their birthdates would be in February and April, both of 1564.

I have chosen to preserve this quirk of the times, along with a characteristic bit of English in transition: at the time to which the writing refers, the familiar form of the English second-person pronoun (thee) was beginning to drift out of use, but had not yet lost the war, and the plural pronoun (you) had—under French influence—come to be used as a singular pronoun in more formal relationships, but was not exclusive. As a result, conversation between familiar friends showed a good deal of fluidity, even switching forms within a single sentence, depending on the emotion and affection of the moment.

I have not availed myself of such transitional forms of address for nobility as were in use at the time, under the belief that it would cause more confusion than it would be worth; instead, I've tried to limit courtesy titles to one per customer, for clarity. Also, I have discarded the Elizabethan habit of referring to oneself in the formal third person ("Here sitteth—"), with the exception of sparing use in correspondence, etc. As well, during the time period in question, that same older third-person verb conjugation -eth (She desireth, he loveth, she hath, etc.) was being replaced by the modern -s or -es, so that in some cases words were written with the older idiom and pronounced in the modern one. In the interests of transparency—this is a work of fiction, intended to entertain, after all—sincere attempts have been made to preserve the music of Early Modern English while making its vocabulary transparent to the modern eye and ear, but what is rendered in this book is, at best, nature-identical Elizabethan flavoring rather than any near approximation of the genuine animal.

I recommend David Crystal's excellent books *Pronouncing Shakespeare* and *Shakespeare's Words* for an accurate picture of the speech of the times.

I was unable or unwilling to avoid the use of some words that have a well-defined meaning in Modern English, but are slipperier in EME, and to which our own cultural assumptions do not apply. Those who were spoken of as Atheists did not necessarily deny the existence of a God, though they denied God's goodness and agency in intervening in mortal lives, for example. Likewise, the word "sodomy" covered a lot of ground, and it was legally punishable in proportion to witchcraft and treason ... but the practice of male same-sex eroticism seems to have been largely winked at, or at worst satirized. You can explore two conflicting takes on the homoeroticism of the day in Alan Bray's *Homosexuality in Renaissance England* and Michael B. Young's *King James and the History of Homosexuality;* feel free to draw your own conclusions, as I have. At the very least, the modern ideas of homosexuality or heterosexuality as the foundation of one's persona did not have much currency to the Renaissance mindset; however, we can be fairly certain that, the social demands of reproduction aside, the desires of men (and the less-well-documented desires of women) no doubt inhabited the usual sliding scale of preferences.

Of course, even Platonic Elizabethan same-sex friendships could be very intense, passionate in modern terms, and one can find examples in Shakespeare and other chroniclers of the times of the vocabulary of love used casually between friends and nothing thought of it. However, some squeamish criticism to the contrary, it is this reader's opinion that the language of Shakespeare's sonnets is homoerotic rather than homosocial, and I have chosen to run with that reading. It also seems to me that, while those poems were at first only privately circulated, he does not seem to have believed his friends would be too shocked. Of course, this leaves open the question of whether any biographical analysis of those selfsame sonnets can be considered reasonable; they may very well have been an interesting work of fiction.

Much as this.

Back to cultural drift. On the family front, a cousin was not the child of an aunt or uncle, but merely any relative close enough to be considered kin, but not a member of the immediate family—a niece or a third cousin twice removed as easily as what we might consider a "cousin."

Some historical events have herein been consolidated for the sake of narrative clarity, and a few dates altered (notably moving the construction of the Globe back a year to ease narrative clutter, moving the Essex rebellion by a day for purposes of pacing, and removing Master Richard Baines to France some few years *after* his historically documented tenure at Rheims to put him there when Marley might have theoretically been in residence). Several taverns of historical interest have been condensed into the famed Mermaid, which I have made the haunt of poets and playmakers some years before its historical heyday. Certain notable individuals have been dispensed with entirely, or prematurely, or their lives extended somewhat. In addition, Robert Poley's daughter, Miss Anne Poley, has received both a sex and a name change, and Mistress Poley is the recipient of a first name chosen only for unobtrusiveness in the milieu, as her own is lost to history. The relationship of that same Mistress Poley, born "one Watson's daughter," to our old friend Tricky Tom Watson is strictly a matter of conjecture. And that is merely the most glaring alterations listed. . . .

As I was trained as an anthropologist rather than a historian, and as the preceding is a work of fiction, I have chosen to apply the standard that absence of evidence is not the same thing as evidence of absence, and I've chosen to make free with some conjectures frequently presented as absolutes (such as Anne Hathaway's alleged illiteracy) which are not documented but rather a part of the common legendry and educated guesswork. In addition, certain questionable bits of tradition relating to the authorship of various notable works of sixteenth- and seventeenth-century literature (*Edward III*, the *King James Bible*) and the original ownership of certain objects (notably the Stratford churchyard "W.S." signet ring) are treated as fact rather than rawest speculation. And I must admit that my interpretation of intentions behind the post-Lopez revival of *The Jew of Malta* and *The Merchant of Venice* is, at best, bogus—though not quite as bogus as my chronology of Shakespeare's plays.

History is not narrative, alas. And Elizabethan political and theatrical history is less narrative than most. To paraphrase Velvet Brown, the facts are all tangled up together and it's impossible to cut one clean.

This is a work of fiction. While there are any number of *actual facts* enmeshed in the web of its creation, it should not be treated as representative, as a whole, of my opinion on any particular historical theories or opinions. Nor should my suggestions regarding additions to the seemingly endless litany of Christopher Marlowe's suspected lovers be taken seriously. It's vilest calumny, all of it.

Well, except the part about Edward de Vere's proclivity for transporting choirboys across international boundaries for immoral purposes. That's the gospel truth.

The choirboy in question was sixteen at the time of the transportation; his name was Oracio Coquo. "I knew him, Horatio—"

. . . okay, that was uncalled-for.

To sum up, I consider this novel to be a grand disservice to antiquity in the tradition of those innovators whose Fictionalized Histories linger in vogue to the present day, and don't consider it necessary to be any more faithful to Kit and Will than they were to assorted British Sovereigns not of the Tudor persuasion.

Really, considering what they wrought upon various Edwards and Richards and maybe the occasional Henry or so, Kit and Will deserve whatever the Hell they get from me.

It's been a deep and abiding joy telling lies about them, however, and I'm pleased they came into my life. I do, however, hope that they are sharing a fine laugh at the irony of it, wherever they are.

After all, we're each storytellers here.

About the Author

Originally from Vermont and Connecticut, **Elizabeth Bear** spent six years in the Mojave Desert and currently lives in southern New England. She attended the University of Connecticut, where she studied anthropology and literature. She was awarded the 2005 Campbell Award for Best New Writer.

ALSO AVAILABLE

FROM

ELIZABETH BEAR

BLOOD AND IRON
A Novel of the Promethean Age

*For centuries the human Mages of the Prometheus Club
and the otherworldly creatures of Faerie have battled for
control over Earth's destiny with neither side capable of
achieving victory over the other. Their impasse has come
to an end...*

She is known as Seeker. Spellbound by the Faerie Queen, she
has abducted human children for her mistress's pleasure for
what seems like an eternity, unable to free herself from
servitude and reclaim her own humanity.

Seeker's latest prey is a Merlin. Named after the
legendary wizard of Camelot, Merlins are not simply those who
wield magic—they are magic. Now, with the Prometheus
Club's agents and rivals from Faerie both vying for the favor of
this being of limitless magic to tip the balance of power,
Seeker must persuade the Merlin to join her cause—or else risk
losing something even more precious and more important to
her than the fate of human kind.

**Available wherever books are sold or at
penguin.com**

ALSO AVAILABLE

FROM

ELIZABETH BEAR

WHISKEY AND WATER

A Novel of the Promethean Age

Matthew the Magician followed Jane Andraste
into Faerie to rescue her half-human daughter
and destroy the Fae. But when Matthew
discovered Jane's treachery, he betrayed her,
the Promethean armies fell—and he lost his
brother, his mentor, and his power. And he's
about to need it.

**Available wherever books are sold or at
penguin.com**

THE ULTIMATE IN
SCIENCE FICTION AND FANTASY!

From magical tales of distant worlds to stories of
technological advances beyond the grasp of man, Penguin has
everything you need to stretch your imagination to its limits.

penguin.com

ACE
Get the latest information on favorites like
William Gibson, T.A. Barron, Brian Jacques,
Ursula K. Le Guin, Sharon Shinn, Charlaine Harris,
Patricia Briggs, and Marjorie M. Liu,
as well as updates on the best new authors.

ROC
Escape with Jim Butcher, Harry Turtledove, Anne Bishop,
S.M. Stirling, Simon R. Green, E.E. Knight, Kat Richardson,
Rachel Caine, and many others—plus news on the
latest and hottest in science fiction and fantasy.

DAW
Patrick Rothfuss, Mercedes Lackey, Kristen Britain,
Tanya Huff, Tad Williams, C.J. Cherryh, and many more—
DAW has something to satisfy the cravings of any
science fiction and fantasy lover.
Also visit dawbooks.com.

*Get the best of science fiction and fantasy
at your fingertips!*